NO ONE IS COMING
TO SAVE US

NO ONE IS COMING TO SAVE US

A NOVEL

STEPHANIE POWELL WATTS

ecco

An Imprint of HarperCollinsPublishers

NO ONE IS COMING TO SAVE US. Copyright © 2017 by Stephanie Powell Watts. All rights reserved. Printed in the United States of America. No part of this book may be used or reproduced in any manner whatsoever without written permission except in the case of brief quotations embodied in critical articles and reviews. For information, address HarperCollins Publishers, 195 Broadway, New York, NY 10007.

HarperCollins books may be purchased for educational, business, or sales promotional use. For information, please email the Special Markets Department at SPsales@harpercollins.com.

FIRST EDITION

Designed by Suet Yee Chong

Library of Congress Cataloging-in-Publication Data has been applied for.

ISBN 978-0-06-247298-4

17 18 19 20 21 RS/LSC 10 9 8 7 6 5 4 3 2 1

The light seems somehow brighter brought to rest . . .
shimmering at my fingertips, so close
I have to reach for it, the twice-bent gleam that passes in the swirl
my reaching makes.

"The Light at Hinkson Creek" by Bob Watts

For Bob and Auden, forever my green lights.

NO ONE IS COMING
TO SAVE US

1

The house he's building is done mostly. All that's missing now is the prettying, stain on the sprawling deck, final finishing inside. At least that's what they say. This house has been the talk around our small town. Not much happens here but the same, same: a thirteen-year-old girl waiting for the baby her mother's sorry boyfriend gave her; the husband we wanted to believe was one of the good ones found out to be the worst kind of cheater with a whole other family two towns over. The same stupid surprises, the usual sadnesses. But this thing is strange. The boy we all saw grow up came back to us slim and hungry-gaunt like a coal miner. With money. JJ Ferguson made it. The poor child who lived with his grandmother, dead for years now, the ordinary boy we all fed when he wouldn't leave at dinnertime, looking like he was waiting for somebody to ask him to play. We had no idea.

JJ was the newest resident on Brushy Mountain Road. The

car they say is his was parked on the long driveway most mornings until evening while JJ worked alongside the Mexican men he
hired. Every town has a section where the people are rich and their
lives so far from yours you almost expect them to speak another
tongue. Brushy Mountain Road is that place for us. You can't help
but get quiet driving on that road, like even your noisy breathing might disturb the beauty or rupture the holy calm that order
and clean create. When we were young we used to love to see the
houses, all lit up with their curtains and blinds open, glowing
yellow like sails of ships in the black faraway on the ocean. If we
went slow enough we could see the brilliant colors of their decorated rooms, their floor-to-ceiling bookcases and fine furniture,
the floral designs with wallpaper you couldn't get at the regular hardware store festooning the entryways. We might even get
a glimpse of one of them sipping from a mug or snuggled into a
chair staring out into the darkness. Though we knew they lived
among us, bought white bread and radial tires like the rest of us,
we loved the proof of them. *I see him. I see him with my own eyes.* We
breathed in the houses, dreamed about the ones that would have
been ours if our lives had run in different directions, if we'd had
different faces, if we'd made all the right choices.

When they were young Sylvia and her husband, Don, would
drive the road that curled like a potato peel all the way up to the
almost top to experience some of what those people had. Don
pretended he didn't want to do it, *who gives a shit how them people
live,* he'd say, but he was as interested as Sylvia. He was careful
not to be staring if a body stood in the yard or looked out at him
from the window. You can't let people know what you dream—
especially if you can't get it. You knowing that they know opens a
wound in you, an embarrassing naked space that you can't let just

anybody witness. If the rich see a woman looking, fine. A woman can want. But nobody alive could claim to have seen longing on Don's face. You got to be immune, Mr. Antibiotic or else you hurt all the time.

Why they looked at those places, neither of them could exactly say, since when they came down from the mountain to their own dark little house that they'd fought hard to have and harder to keep, their space felt smaller, meeker, and as tear-filled as a broken promise. Habit is one explanation. Sundays, when they were apt to get lazy and the last thing you need is boredom, a slowed mind, the leisure to think about the man you love-hate, the face that won't stop looking tired no matter how much you sleep, that thing you do, whatever it is—the driving, the crying, the sinning—calls to you, begs to you to keep getting it done, keep at it, don't think, keep at it.

But habit is only part of it. The sting of not having or not having enough bores a pain black hole that sucks all the other of life's injuries into one sharp stinging gap that you don't need a scientist to remind you may be bottomless. Returning to their house means returning from those mountain drives to their sagging furniture that was old when they got it twenty years before and to a yard that looked even smaller than they remembered. That beautiful house is just a street away, but as out of reach as the moon. But that house-pain is just one lack, and everybody knows one pain is far better than a hundred. That is the mercy. That is the relief—the ache of one singular pain. It was hard not to believe that we, the black people in town in dog trots and shotgun houses at the bottom of the mountain, houses stuck in the sides of hills scattered like chicken feed, weren't the ugly children. What a relief that in our hearts we knew that no coloreds, no

Negroes, no blacks, were welcome, even if they could afford to buy there. At least we didn't have to believe that we'd done everything wrong and were not the ones that God had chosen.

So much has changed since we were just starting out. The furniture plants that built the town are all but empty. The jobs on the line turning yellow pinewood into the tables and beds for the world are mostly gone. Without the factories there is little work to do. What a difference a few years can make. The jobs that everybody knew as the last resort or the safety net are the jobs nobody can get anymore. Used to be at 3:30 P.M. the roads from Bernhardt, Hammary, Broyhill, and Bassett were hot with cars, bumper to bumper, the convenience stores full of mostly men, but women too with cold ones (Coke or stronger) in one hand, Nabs or Little Debbie cakes in the other for the ride home. These days, go anywhere you please at 3:30 with no trouble. Here's a math problem for you. How many casinos does it take to make a town? Are you calculating? Got it? No, sorry that's a trick question. No number of casinos make a town. But if you want a stopover, a place to throw your balled-up trash out the window as you float by in your car, you just need one good casino. Don't get me wrong, we love a casino and wish for one like the last vial of antidote. We believe despite all experience to the contrary in easy money and our own fortunes changing in an instant like the magician's card from the sleeve. If one quarter came miraculously from behind the ear, we would milk that ear for days for the rent money. We believe. We hope for the town to morph into an all-resort slick tourist trap, looking like no real person had ever lived here. We are full of the fevered hope of the newly come to Jesus. We can reinvent. We can survive. At least some of us think so. What choice do we have?

Still the rich have moved from the center of town and the near hills to other places in the county. Their homes are estates where their windows look onto the rolling acres of kings. The houses, the once mansions in town that they and their kind left behind, belong to the flippers to turn into cramped and oddly configured apartments or raze altogether. The message was clear as day, the richest person doesn't live in our midst anymore and what the rich had now, we couldn't ever see it for ourselves, couldn't even pass by it and let the images settle in our dreams. Even so, even though we know all that, Brushy Mountain Road loomed in our thinking, in our childhood imaginings. You think you forget those dreams? You get old, but the dreams remain, spry and vigorous. Swat them and they come back like gnats, like plague. You can't kill them. They can't die.

The first thing JJ did on that mountain was cut out a whole new road up to his house. Heavy machines of industry, Kubotas and Deeres, used to make the path dotted the hills for weeks, like kids' toys abandoned in the weeds. Men in town speculated about the tons of gravel and the weight of red clay they had to shift from one place to another to level the hills. The women didn't care about the road. They knew from their own yards how difficult it was to make a way to get from there to here. They'd dug their own paths, moved their own dirt and rocks in the stubborn Carolina soil. What excited the women was the river rock foundation, the big beautiful windows, the walls rising up like raptured dead.

Most days, JJ would be up there himself, walking around the site, talking to the Mexican men or working hard himself judging by the reports of his sweat-soaked clothes, his close-cropped hair grayed with sawdust. Living in a small town means knowing the news, the broad strokes as well as the lurid minutiae of your neighbor's life. Your dirty kitchen, cancer treatments, drugged-out child all on the sandwich board of your back, swirled around the body with a stink you could not outrun. JJ was from another small town and did not have nearby family. Few people knew JJ to give out too many details. We are not surprised. We knew too little about him when he lived in Pinewood as a young man. But soon he would show his face. When that house was done, Sylvia knew JJ would be knocking at her door. Years ago that boy had spent too much time in her kitchen, on her back porch and staring at her beautiful child Ava. That JJ had loved Ava was obvious. That Sylvia loved JJ too, like a son, like Devon, her own son, was just as clear. Her son was Devon pronounced like Levon from the Elton John song, though Sylvia was embarrassed to admit that fact to anybody. Devon was her firstborn baby, the baby she wasn't supposed to have. She never had any romance about being a mother and knew that having a baby was easy if your body was willing. Girls, hardly older than the ones Sylvia passed at the school bus stop at the end of the road every morning, became mothers. But Sylvia's body had been unwilling until Devon came. She was almost thirty, old in those days and sure that her baby days were long past. It wasn't that Sylvia loved Devon any more than her daughter, Ava, but Devon was the child that changed her status, the child that made her look at the ordinary world as a big and dangerous paradise. JJ was so like her Devon: both calm boys, funny children with soft voices, with the same warm puddled eyes like they'd been caught crying and they were trying to recover.

Almost a generation had passed, a long time any way you look at it, but Sylvia knew that the feelings were just there under the pancake makeup of the surface. JJ felt them too, how could he not? He had left them, but he was back. That counted. Of course it counted.

They used to say if you love something set it free. Don't you believe it! Love means never letting anything go, never seeing it stride on long confident legs away from you. You think love leaves? You think you are ever free? Then you are a child or a fool. Flee in the dark, spend a lifetime away, never say its name, never say its name, but one day, or if you are very unlucky, every day, it will whisper yours. And, you know you want to hear your name. Say it, love. Please say it.

2

"I've called you," Marcus said.

"What's that noise? Is that the boy yelling?"

"Tay Dula. Getting loud. The fat heads will stop it."

Sylvia had rarely heard any sound in the background when Marcus called. She could almost forget he was in the county lockup.

"I told you about him, Sylvia. He's like that this time of day." The brokenhearted sound of the moaning boy scared Sylvia, gave her a sick feeling like she'd uncovered a snake in her yard. She would be trying to forget the sound for days to come.

"Are you okay?" Sylvia said.

"You've been somewhere. Why didn't you answer? I started to think you were gone."

"Marcus." Sylvia fought to keep the scolding tone from her

voice, but she was way past believing it cute to have a man questioning her comings and goings. "I've been sick."

"What's wrong? Sylvia? You okay?"

"Not sick. I shouldn't have said that. Tired. I'm not sleeping."

"Did Devon get there yet?"

"No not yet. I told you I have a lot to do. I work and I've got bills. I've not even been here." Sylvia searched her mind for what else ate up the hours of her day but nothing materialized. The truth was she had been trying to stay away from her daughter's house and spend some time in her own apartment for a change. "I have a lot of things to do and that's all there is to it. You need to worry about yourself and don't be thinking about Devon." Sylvia sighed. He's just a scared boy. He's just a scared boy, she reminded herself. "I'm here now, honey. I'm not avoiding you. I'm here now."

"I was worried." Marcus attempted a laugh and sounded younger than the twenty-five-year-old man he was, a boy to Sylvia. Marcus had called her from jail. Not jail; Andy Griffith and Barney Fife run a jail; Marcus was in prison, for months now. Sylvia always accepted the phone charges.

"Just tired, Marcus," Sylvia said

"I thought you must be busy with Devon."

"I can come to see you Sunday. I'll bring you something. What can I bring you?

"No, no don't do that," Marcus said. He had always refused her visits, for months now, but Sylvia thought she heard a small hesitation in his voice this time. Please don't say yes, she thought. Please. She hated to admit it, even to herself, but she was glad he'd said no. The truth was that prison scared the hell out of her.

It was her good luck that she'd not been inside a prison for nearly thirty years since she'd gone to see a son of a friend. That was enough to hold her for a lifetime. Many times Sylvia thought that the people sitting around waiting for the zombies to attack ought to visit a jail sometime. That's an apocalypse nobody knew what to do with.

"I'm a good sleeper. I can sleep standing up most of the time," Sylvia snorted. "But these days I've been walking the floor. It'll pass."

"Have a drink before bed. You've got vodka don't you? When I first got here I didn't sleep for weeks. They keep you up. For real. Anything to make you crazy."

Sylvia hadn't meant to talk about her sleeplessness, her daily problems that couldn't sound like anything but petty and small ones in comparison. "Forget about all that. You'll make it," Sylvia said, momentarily unsure if the conversation had led them into a slick-sided hole. All that was left was to struggle back out. "You've got to work on yourself. You hear me? This is the time to improve. Fight the shame, okay? What did I tell you about that? Worse has happened to people. Worse has happened to me," Sylvia said.

"Not to me." Marcus cleared his throat. "This is it."

"Well, it's done now." Sylvia resisted the impulse to sigh. "What are you going to do about it but live through it?"

"You cut to it, don't you?"

"I'll bring you a hamburger on Sunday. I can cook, but probably not this week."

"They rob you here. You have to buy the stuff they've got. Three dollars for cheese crackers."

Sylvia heard loud voices again and what sounded like the muffled-from-the-bottom-of-a-box sound of Marcus's hand over the receiver. She imagined the life going on around going on around Marcus. He stood in a hallway of a dorm, the common phone large and heavy like a dumbbell in his hand. Marcus leaned against the wall as the other young men (they are white with deep parted hair) lined up behind him in their shorts and baggy underwear waiting their turn to talk to folks back home. Sylvia knew better. But in her fantasy, the whole enterprise of the prison industrial complex was no more sinister than a boy's summer camp circa 1968. "I'm just glad I got you. You don't know how glad."

"I'll bring you some books then. What do you read?"

"I thought I lost you, Sylvia. You don't know how glad."

"Pay attention, Marcus. You need to read something. Focus your mind. I can bring you books."

"No books. I can't concentrate for long."

"You can change. Keep your mind sharp. Believe in that, Marcus. Life is sad, but there's some good moments and you have to live for those. That's all we got." Sylvia couldn't remember the last time she waited for a good moment instead of holding on through the bad ones for the next wave of bad to shock her into a different kind of sadness. "You know what, Marcus? I changed my mind. There's nothing wrong with shame. Most people could use more of it. Shame can make you better. Yes, it can." Sylvia wondered at the statement even as she said it. In her experience nobody got better from shame, only more afraid. Fear moved underground is the most dangerous feeling in the world.

"I'm okay. I feel better. I'll get used to being a monkey in a fucking cage," Marcus whispered.

"Don't talk like that."

"I'm sorry, sorry." Marcus's sigh sounded to Sylvia like a shudder. "There's guys in here that sold a little dope, stupid asses like me."

"I'm not trying to hear that, Marcus."

"What would you call it? Crack rocks. You believe that? The drug world has moved on, Sylvia. I couldn't even get arrested right." Every third news story around the area was about meth and now even heroin was making a comeback. Crack. How 1992. There's a guy in there that was just in the same room where it was. I'm not trying to say that was me. I screwed up, man. But some of these guys. Like Tay. He needs to be in the hospital."

"You don't have a choice. Understand that. I tell my son all the time, if you say something enough times it's true. You have to be strong. You hear me, Marcus?"

"How did he get over it?"

"Get over what?"

"Everything. This life, everything," Marcus said.

A memory of Devon at her father's geese pen emerged. He was four, maybe five, a tall boy for his age, as tall as the geese. The birds became very still as the two of them approached. The geese stared at them with their murderous beads of eyes and hissed loudly, all of them in different voices like a pit of snakes. If Sylvia had before or since heard a more hateful sound she could not remember it. Devon stopped short, his boyish movements over. He screamed, too afraid to look back at her for the reassurance she wasn't sure she could give him. She'd wanted to scream too.

"What I'm saying is that he just keeps on trying, just like you have to. There's boys your age and younger fighting overseas in a disgusting desert."

"Sylvia, don't start with the boys overseas."

Sylvia heard the mocking tone in his voice her own children used when she pronounced mature with two oo's or salmon with an L. "Now listen, smart ass. Think about how they feel. Everybody is struggling, Marcus."

"Please don't say anything about the starving children in China, Sylvia."

"Well, there's nothing wrong with your smart mouth." If Marcus joked that was a good sign. For the first time in the conversation Sylvia felt a little relief.

"I've never been strong like that. How pathetic does that sound?"

"There's more to you than you think? Hasn't anybody ever told you that? You've got short time. What is it now?"

"Fourteen months."

"See there! And you're here near at home. You can make it, Marcus," Sylvia said with as much conviction as she could, much more than she felt. If someone told her she had to be locked up for over a year she'd jump in front of a train.

"Short time? Have you been watching *Law and Order*?"

"I know what the kids are saying." Sylvia laughed.

"Sylvia, can you hear me?"

"I can hear you."

"Sylvia?"

"I can hear you, Marcus," Sylvia said louder.

"The phone is about to cut off. I'll call you in a couple of days. Okay?"

"Don't get down on yourself. You have to fight for your life. Believe what I'm saying, Marcus."

"How long can you fight, Sylvia?"

"Get a hold of it before it takes over, Marcus."

"I'm better. I'm better. I'm okay."

"Think about the next fifty years you have to live when you get out."

"I'll try." Marcus's laugh hissed between his teeth.

Sylvia wished she had some encouraging idea to add or a religious verse about Jesus's enduring love.

"Will you be there? I'll call. Sylvia?"

The line cut out before Sylvia could answer.

3

Sylvia tossed the phone onto her daughter Ava's couch. Her daughter bought from IKEA everything she didn't drag out of people's trash. Ava called it Dumpster diving, but Sylvia had other names for it. Turns out there were plenty of good reasons to throw stuff away. Sylvia tried to get the image of Marcus on a chain gang being dragged by bigger prisoners out of her mind. Every visual she had about prison came from shadowy Charles Bronson movies with snarling men in gangs, the lead prisoner either a skinhead or a giant very black man with laughing minions in his wake egging him on. She prayed those scenes were from some pampered white writer's Hollywood ideas and not what Marcus had to endure. What could she do about that? She had no say, no control, nothing at all to say about what happened to Marcus in his locked-up life. Instead of further frustrating her, his calls made her feel strangely useful though she knew she had done practically nothing. She had the same kind of feeling she used to get from working out at the gym. The gym. The word felt foreign and difficult in her mouth, like when she accidentally said porridge. She had forgotten the smug virtue she had felt going. Just telling somebody she was on her way to the gym or that she needed to go to the gym or finally that she missed her visits to the gym had a certain satisfaction. *Virtuous* was the word. Virtue without sweat was still satisfying, do not be misled.

Though she tried to relax, Sylvia couldn't get comfortable on the hard too-little couch. She would not say another word to Marcus about Devon. He had enough on his plate without thinking about a man he'd never even met and besides that too much had happened for Devon to return. The lie she told to Marcus was not easily untold. But nothing was easy about her relationship with Marcus. Not relationship, that wasn't the word. Relationship sounded both too formal and too intimate at the same time. Friendship? Desperate collision of desperate people?

Prisoners at the minimum security prison could make phone calls three times a week. Some of the very sad ones called random numbers to get someone, anyone to accept charges and get a message to a loved one. Marcus had used up his loved ones and improbably Sylvia had become his best and only friend. Why Sylvia answered Marcus's call in the first place was a mystery. Why she accepted the charges that day months ago, she could not really say. All she knew for sure was the ordinary days melted into each other and the spark of the new thing drew her in. Boredom can be an answer. Wasn't it always an answer? But the reason that nagged at her and threatened to take her breath was that growing certainty that she had failed her mother, her children, even her piece of man husband. A voice bubbled up like heartburn and popped softly in her head; you have ruined everything.

Marcus had just turned twenty-five, young, black, and in that first five-minute conversation had told her that he was an ugly duck in a family of pretty ducks. No swans to speak of, none that he'd mentioned anyway, but a lot of pretty ducks. She imagined him chubby with a round schoolboy's face. His hair too short for the current styles, his clothes neat and matching, like his mother picked them out in the mornings. He said that he was a father and hadn't seen his daughter for seven months. He told her about his girlfriend who was disappointed now, but who might love him again. He wanted Sylvia to know that he was a nice man from good people who kept their houses clean, didn't set cars on blocks in their yards, didn't hang their oversize panties and BVDs on the clothesline for just anybody to see. He wanted her to believe that they were the kind of black people that whites saw some good in. They were a better, more acceptable subset of the race that spoke well and presented well, more and better than a cut above the great mass of regular black folks that they (whites and the special blacks) all looked down on, tolerated, and pitied. Get a message to his people, he asked. Come to see him. Write to him. Don't forget him.

If Sylvia were being completely honest she would admit that his need attracted her. So few people needed her exclusively and with so much heat that she was strangely flattered. But the calls had amounted to more than that. She liked Marcus. No matter how her conversations to him started, she now wanted to help him. She needed to help him. She might just show up at that prison on Sunday. Twenty minutes in the car was nothing. The gray squat building built against the wishes of the community was better looking than they expected (but that wasn't the point) and just on the outskirts of the south of town. Sylvia could surprise Marcus with a pie and a couple of magazines. He would be glad to see her once she was there and the decision made. But she shouldn't go, not as long as he asked her not to. Even a man in lockup ought to be able to make some decisions without the imposition of someone else's better knowledge.

Sylvia dragged herself up to the sound of her popping knees. Once in the kitchen she fixed a tray with a pitcher of iced tea and two tall glasses. No limes again like she liked—another thing to put on the grocery list. Until Ava came home she'd sit on the patio in the backyard. Of all the spaces in her home the yard was the only area she worked on and primped like it was a loved child. What she'd inherited was scrabble ground, a few pokeberries, choking weeds, and honeysuckle rooted in among the high weeds, skinny sticks of maple trees sprouted up around the perimeter of a half-acre lot—not much land, she knew that, but enough.

She'd grown up on a dirt road in the woods near the Wilkes County line. In her early years, they'd had no bathroom, no running water at all, and their heat came from a woodstove at the back of the house. Though the shack was surrounded by green rolling hills, a pebbled creek bubbled just out of sight, and the clearing where they burned garbage circled by rows of honey blond broom straw, none of them had thought to consider the place beautiful. Part of that inattention was just a by-product of being young and believing that every day had a possibility of being better than the days before. But mostly what Sylvia remembered about her childhood was the outhouse and the lingering smell of shit. No matter where she went in her life, Sylvia felt she couldn't entirely wash herself clean. Even at her most accomplished she expected to find flecks of it on the soles of her good shoes.

Sylvia's new house (new though she'd lived there for over twenty-five years) was a small brick split-level (what a wonderful name for a house) with a carport on the side. Not a mansion by any stretch, but so perfect for Sylvia that she could not recall many details about the trailer to mind, a trick of memory she appreciated. Except for the occasional feel along the wall for a light switch, except for that nagging moment of muscle memory, that trailer in the woods where she and Don had lived had almost never existed.

The builder set the houses on half-acre lots on Development Drive, slung a handful of grass seed, spit with a go with God, and hoped that it would take root on the red clay hills. The seed promptly got carried by wind or washed down the sides of the yards into ditches. Grassy lawn or not both she and her husband, Don, had thought the place a miracle. Development Drive was a longish stretch of paved street with small houses owned by black families. This was once one of the nicer places for blacks to live in town. Somebody had thought ahead, thought big. A few black people would slowly move up in the world and would want homes without junk cars. A development for them would do the trick and keep them all on their own streets. The developers had not imagined a possible future with blacks and whites in the same neighborhoods. Enterprising builders created separate communities—no block busting necessary. But whatever was in the builder's hearts, the new homes were remarkable steps up from ramshackle old clapboard houses, sagging porches, or old rusted trailers. Black people with a few dollars could get a half-acre plot with 1,000 square feet or in the deluxe model 1,250 feet, fridge, stove, ready to make your life in.

What dreams they all had of progress! Each year the house would get a little better, the white linoleum the thoughtless builders put in the kitchens and baths exchanged for hardwood floors and porcelain tile. In the coming years decks got added to the rear of the houses, small decks sure, but big enough for a grill and a four-top table. They moved from all the poorest crannies of the county where people sat on porches and fanned themselves in the heat of the day and built fires to keep away mosquitoes and no-see-ums that anesthetized when they bit so the itch, the pain came later. They moved from dirt roads and clusters of men on front lawns playing cards, fighting again, playing music *that's my song right there* much too loud. They moved to escape it all. Sylvia told her children about her own poor childhood days. She could see on their faces that her lack had sounded to them like fairy tales, like weaving straw into gold. Her feeling of triumph was like nothing else she had ever known, though her children could not share it. What was more surprising was that her children didn't see her accomplishments as particularly triumphant. Their life was their ordinary life, their working class, regular way of being. That very feeling, freedom from the drag of poverty, was what she wanted for them. No struggle, no strangling scarcity, no wishing to be somewhere, anywhere else. Was it too much to ask that they feel a little pride for what she'd been able to wrest from this stingy world?

Of course there were drawbacks. Douglas, the middle-aged man across the street, revved his motorcycle for his grinning friends. The neighbor Forrest kept a steady stream of down-and-out relatives at his place. Sylvia knew it wasn't her business, but she was unnerved to not know who she might see puffing on a cigarette staring into the horizon from the next yard. But those were small pains. How soothing to have an answer to the young white women at the social services office when they talked about their own places and the hours they spent decorating, repairing, and improving. Before she'd owned the house that kind of talk hurt her, signaled her as an outsider. That little place with the too hot second floor gave Sylvia a way to relate to the women and share a lament about the high cost of this or that, a little taste of the pain at this particular lack, which she felt had scarred over more than less. One less fear in a life ruled by fear.

Sylvia thought many times that she'd spent her whole life tensed and waiting for the worst thing to happen. The list of fears was long: spiders, snakes, and death were all reasonable and easily understood, but like her long-dead mother Mabel—Mabe to friends and family—she was afraid of everything else too. How could that have happened that she ended up like her mother who cringed in fear from the threat of rapists, popping balloons, the shrill horror movie sound of wind chimes. Everything. Mabe spent the precious years of her youth scared and mealymouthed, always too accommodating, especially when it came to men. Maybe her fears came naturally or maybe they were forged from her interactions with Sylvia's father. Fear as a symptom or causation? Whatever. But men and the fear of them took up most of the thinking in her mother's life. She'd been scared into being a good girl, scared into staying with a man she wanted but who didn't want her. Scared to be by herself even when that's what her life had amounted to anyway. She thought she wasn't going to get anybody and she didn't. No damn body. Nobody who was anybody anyway. Who had ever counted on Sylvia's father and had not ended up alone?

Nobody can say her mama hadn't tried everything. They say there are only three reasons to go to South Carolina: to get fireworks, to get married, and to get dentures—or if you are having a good day, all three. They should have added to the list going to see people like Mrs. Janey. Once when Sylvia was just a girl she and her mother had taken a trip to get the potion that would make Sylvia's father, Carl, love her mother once and for all. With ten dollars and the cost of gas, you could banish the darkness in your head, cast out demons, make him love like you needed. The old woman's house smelled of cooked food and the coconut grease she put on her scalp, like most old women's houses Sylvia went to. She had thought that she would be afraid of Mrs. Janey, but the woman was no more frightening than any other old woman she'd ever seen. The three of them sat at the small table in the small kitchen while Mabe told her story. Her mother wrung her hands, was teary eyed and softer than Sylvia remembered her ever being as she talked and avoided looking directly at Mrs. Janey's face. Sylvia had kept completely still and couldn't shake the feeling that she was someplace she did not belong, like she was watching someone on the toilet. Mrs. Janey shrugged her shoulders at Mabe's terrible confessions of loneliness and lack. Mrs. Janey occasionally patted her mother's hand like she was an old dog. No doubt she'd heard every pathetic tale, every permutation on the same sad themes many times. She gave Sylvia's mother a cleaned jelly jar.

"Put one of your little hairs in the jar here," she'd said with her eyebrows raised so there could be no question about which little hairs. "Right after you go to the pot, you hear? Make him drink it. Don't wait too long. Two days at the most." Mabe thanked Mrs. Janey and refused her offer of collard greens, though she and

Sylvia shared a square of corn bread. On the road home, Sylvia held the glass between her legs afraid to touch it with her hands, though it looked no more powerful than watered-down tea.

"Why don't Daddy love you, Mama?" Mabe had not answered for nearly a full minute while Sylvia waited, afraid to speak again. Her mother was silent so long Sylvia began to wonder if she had spoken at all.

"I really don't know," her mother had said, a cloud of wonder on her face like she really considered the question. The genuine interest in Mabe's voice was the first and one of the only times Sylvia ever felt that she and her mother had a real conversation. Mabe had never again mentioned the visit or the little bottle, but if her father had any more love for her mother, he kept it to himself.

Sylvia thought, like we all think, that she'd never be like her mother, but the man she chose for herself was just as sorry, did just as much dirt. Sylvia's man, Don, was now shacked up with a girl much younger than his children. Sylvia was sure she could remember holding Don's new girlfriend in the crook of her own arm when she was a fat toddler crying after her mother.

If she and Don had not had a life, they did have a house. That's something. Don't let anyone tell you that's not something. What you got and can count on your fingers can give you a cushion, a bank account, a security against universal losses. Nobody has to know the hollow spaces you shock yourself by living through. You can survive the shell of nothing that ordinary living produces. Buck up! Organs rearrange, the blood reroutes, and you deal with it. You think you can't but you do. Sylvia thought of the house as her stake, her sacrifice, her due for a life of sacrifice. There are worse things.

What was hers could be given away or at least rented for four hundred dollars a month. Ava and her husband, Henry, moved into the house with the idea that sometime, some year in the near-ish future they'd own it outright. Sylvia was mostly glad that the house was becoming Ava's by degrees. But old habits die hard or better said they don't really die at all just lie low, waiting for the cloud cover to part and desperation to rear back up on its hind legs. Sylvia knew the house was Ava's but she visited almost daily. Sylvia's new home was supposed to be a one-bedroom apartment with builder-white walls and the stink of industrial carpet she couldn't rid the place of even after five years. When she was a young woman she had dreamed of a cute version of that apart-ment. In it were knickknacks from her travels, avant-garde art she liked but didn't understand, but liked that she had to think about it. In her imagination she was *That Black Girl* and her apart-ment told the story of her worldly and sophisticated life. Every-one she knew had wanted to be sophisticated, grown in a world of grown people with their own homes rented or owned, hosts of glittering parties in their form-fitting dresses, their dramatic jewelry jangling and glinting in the light, hair slicked back into a fist-size chignon mail-ordered for the occasion. She planned to have drawings of nudes and Persian rugs, books that lined built-in shelves, weavings made in countries where the brown people were not the usual black folk variety of dirt road North Carolina. It saddened Sylvia to see old women sick to be young, wearing too long hair and short skirts or worst of all wearing saucy words on their sweatpanted behinds.

None of that hoping and believing girl was left in Sylvia now or at least she couldn't be found. The woman she was now didn't yearn for sophistication, and as far as she could tell she'd stopped yearning for much at all. The woman she'd become was fat and weighed down, but not just fat, dumb too, and always in the process of adjusting, like there was two of everything, the real thing and the shimmering copy that her brain had to work with focus and concentration to integrate. Her brain in slow-mo or she felt slow—same difference. The result was the girl she'd been had evaporated from her body like an emancipated soul.

Sylvia loved tea, the sweeter the better, but she'd been diagnosed as prediabetic at her last checkup and that meant she had to take it easy, or she was supposed to. Old people used to call it sugar. As in, cut her a small piece of that pie, she's got sugar. Sylvia would never say that. Ava lived on steamed vegetables and the occasional organic meat that made Sylvia's head hurt to smell cooking. Who wanted all that freshness? The smell of bovine growth hormone could produce nostalgia. Sylvia was proof. All of that good eating to bribe her daughter's body to take on a baby. What surprises this life turned out to have! When Ava was young, Sylvia had done a lot of praying that her baby wouldn't get pregnant in high school, though she'd never known for sure if Ava was doing anything or not. She was afraid to ask her and admit that she didn't know. How it happened that she was afraid of her own child, she had no idea. We pray anyway. Even when we know most of the prayers are a waste of time.

The front door closed softly on the frame. In her mind, Sylvia saw her daughter dropping her leather bag on the floor; tossing her jacket on the arm of the couch.

"Mama?" Ava yelled.

"I'm in the back."

Sylvia imagined Ava coming through the front door, the large picture window at her back. The room that Sylvia slept in now was immediately to Ava's right. Ava would not look in at Sylvia's room and the mounds of clothes all over the bed and floor. Sylvia had never been a good housekeeper and she wasn't about to fix years of bad habits or she wouldn't. Either way it was easier to swing the door of her room closed. Sylvia imagined Ava rushing up the stairs to the room she shared with Henry. On the ottoman at the end of their bed were her home clothes—a tank top and stained sweatpants in a sad little melted-wicked-witch mound. Sylvia had mentioned to her just once that she might want to look a little more put together when her husband got home. Ava had cast what could only be called a murderous glance in Sylvia's direction that had screamed that under no circumstances would she take any advice from Sylvia. How Ava had managed to say nothing out loud was an everyday miracle. Any good advice about men could not come from her. Sylvia had herself worn that same face to her own mother.

Ava would hang her skirt on a silk padded hanger, let her shimmery slip puddle on the floor, grab her hair from behind and wrestle it into a ponytail or pin it to the back of her skull. The whole transformation complete in a couple of minutes.

Ava came to the back patio with her clothes changed, her face washed and clean. At the bank she'd been a senior loan officer for several years with a real office all to herself, a desk job, an office job so she had to look the part. From time to time Sylvia caught a glimpse of Ava in town or going into the bank, her small frame a hanger for the expensive suits and dresses she liked, a confident turn of her head that made her own child unrecognizable for a hair of a second. How she had learned that poise Sylvia could not imagine. Not from her, she thought. At home Ava was young, and even her limbs were more liquid and unassuming. At home she pretzeled herself on the seats of chairs, her legs in configurations that hurt Sylvia to imagine on her own body. Her daughter had become a professional woman, a woman with a profession, a member (a new member for sure), but a member of the middle class. Sylvia thought of the young slick skinned black men she'd been raised with in Pinewood, a few of them dead young, some dead for years, but most of them still kicking, had masked themselves, moved like robots in the factories, restaurants, and yards they worked in with no expression on their lizard-dead-eyed faces. A few of them, a very few imagined that one day they would take their places among the secure. But on their own time, they ruled the room, sailed into clubs and parties, like beautiful ships, dressed to the hilt in their high glossed gator shoes.

"Mama, did you remember not to sweeten it?"

"I remembered."

Ava brought with her a stack of her home and self-improvement magazines, poured herself a glass, and positioned her magazines in front of her like they were just more work to be done, like Sylvia wasn't sitting right in front of her. Somehow Sylvia had become as ridiculous and easy to dismiss as her own mother had been to her.

Ava's Victoria's Secret bra peeked out from the narrow straps of her shirt. Sylvia's bras she got from the discount bin at JCPenney. Every mother thinks her child beautiful, at least good mothers, but Sylvia had the advantage of being right. Ava's heart-shaped face and sweet bow mouth took her by surprise. A good face, a little girl's face, innocent as a girl's, not the hard lines and knowing that looked like experience. People dropped their guards, felt protective. No one would ever look at Ava's face and call her an old soul. Or, if they did, it would be so far in the future that Sylvia wouldn't live to see it. Sylvia tried to tell her it was a blessing to look innocent. But Ava was always annoyed by people's assumptions that she was younger (which she didn't mind so much) and dumber and frailer than she knew herself to be.

Sylvia stifled the urge to stroke her daughter's back, tickle her bones with spelled-out letters like they used to, but Ava was a bundle of nerves these days, anything could set her off. Sylvia told her that her baby was coming to her. Any day now, she'd said. Besides, she'd never heard of a black woman having problems having a baby. Ava had called her a racist. Her, a racist! Of course Sylvia knew that anybody's body can disagree with her mind—black or not. She stated a fact, reported what life had demonstrated to her, lessons she'd learned from her own pain. Of course her world was small, of course she didn't know it all, but when had she gone from knowing enough to knowing nothing at all good enough to repeat?

"I'm not telling Henry this time, Ma." Ava pursed her lips, stared at Sylvia hard. "So don't say anything, okay?"

Sylvia slowed her breathing to stop the tug of anger building in her chest. "I won't mention it, Ava," Sylvia said.

"Sorry." Ava swirled her tea and tried not to ignore the tension on her mother's face. They were both too jumpy these days and too quick to be annoyed. "Did you bring the agave?"

Sylvia shook her head and watched her daughter move to the kitchen. Sylvia was not a superstitious woman, not really, but she felt sickening guilt about her daughter's infertility. She'd hoped from the beginning of Ava's marriage that she would leave Henry before she had any of his babies. Henry wasn't a bad man, but even after almost fourteen years married and almost twenty in a relationship, his presence had not felt permanent to her. Any day it seemed he might be up and gone from them, and finally she and Ava could continue the life she thought they'd have from the moment Ava was born. A life together. A fool's dream, entirely selfish, a mother's dream, but it persisted. If no one knew it, did she still have to be ashamed?

"Are you ready for all of this again, Ava?" Sylvia attempted to keep her tone casual, but she was afraid. "It's just been a couple of months."

"It's been five months, Mama. I've got to be ready." Ava shrugged, she would never be ready.

"I'm worried about your body. I don't know everything about all these processes and procedures, but I do know that you can put too much on your body. It needs a rest."

"At my age you mean?"

"No, honey, that's not what I mean." Sylvia sighed. "You know Mama was up there when she had me and Lana." That the weird angst between Sylvia and Ava skipped Ava's teenage years and was waiting for middle age to bloom was an infuriating surprise. She and Ava had not experienced the usual run-ins that teenage mothers and daughters famously have. Now whatever Sylvia did she was always wrong. Nothing she could say came out right either. Ava had come to Sylvia's room a few weeks pregnant the last time in just her bra and gym shorts. "Look, Mama," she's said holding her completely flat belly. "Don't you see the bump? I think there's one there for real now." Sylvia had rubbed her daughter's smooth skin no bump to the touch, none visible to the eye. Her daughter had watched her mother's face for confirmation. Sylvia's own stomach had been stretched hard and early from both of her pregnancies, but she'd had much more of a belly to start with. More than forty years after her pregnancies and she had the extravagant stretch marks on her belly as proof. She willed herself to feel the baby, feel anything underneath her daughter's skin. Nothing. "What a beauty you are," she'd said. Ava frowned and sucked her teeth. "So you don't feel anything then," Ava said and left the room.

Sylvia's mother had gotten pregnant six times, the first when she was sixteen and the last time when she was thirty-seven and each and every time was to her a miserable surprise. Sylvia and Lana, her last two, the only two now left alive were especially infuriating to her and she never got over that feeling. Mabe had resented Sylvia's physical body, any happiness in her voice, the sight of her broad smiling face. Sylvia had become quiet in her presence, but looking for any opportunity for her mother's attentions. Sylvia had never felt that embarrassing jealousy with Ava. Hardly ever. And she had never tried to lock her daughter out of her affections. At least she hadn't thought so. What had gone wrong at this late date was beyond Sylvia's comprehension. Sylvia liked her daughter and liked spending time with her or she had. Even when Ava was a teenager Sylvia had liked her. Ava had not brought home airheads and name-brand-obsessed silly girls, who would include her in their groups just for the joy of later locking her out and telling her secrets to anyone who found that kind of cruelty particularly amusing. Ava had not been drawn to the heartless or mean but to the sadly broken, the missing, and the ones left behind.

"I wish you'd give it some time. I don't know anything. Don't roll your eyes. I saw you." Sylvia wanted to stop talking but she couldn't help herself. "I know nothing about nothing." Sylvia crossed her arms over her chest. She knew she looked like a brat but she couldn't stop. "But I wish you'd take a break." When Ava was very young she'd played house with another little girl from down the dirt road. Instead of playing dolls and motherhood the ways Sylvia and her own sister had done, Ava had played a game of their own invention called Girl. *Girl, I'm so tired,* the children would say. *Girl, work is about to kill me. Girl, let's go shopping.* Not a baby bed, no dinner making for a man, not even a man present in the make-believe. Sylvia had wanted to play herself.

Ava attempted her kindest look. "I know you didn't mean anything. I'm just nervous. Running out of time, Mama."

"You know I understand that," Sylvia said.

"I know. Can we change the subject? I'm getting a headache."

"What you think now you won't think forever. I'm telling you, Ava." Sylvia couldn't figure out a way to explain to Ava that her current feelings were not exactly untrustworthy, but too short-lived to rule the trajectory of her life. In a few years Ava would see her worries as not exactly trivial but from a different angle and more comprehensible, compared to the hurt that was coming. Everyone acknowledges the angst of adolescence, the hormone stew that can rule the body and mind. Why had no one told Sylvia that the changes do not end? Sylvia had always imagined that there is a fixed adult state that a woman sails into until her golden years. The pain of the loss, the true loss of youth, the change of life, THE CHANGE, the terrible sure feeling of being shunted out of the everyday progress of living, the move from a player on the stage to a member of the audience—until finally, the fear that crept and inched into your mind, then your soul, that your life had amounted to too little. Like some version of that joke, life was terrible and in such small portions. And finally, the realization that you hadn't performed enough or well enough and now everyone you loved would suffer. Why hadn't anyone said something? Of course older women had said in their way. By way of warning and encouragement, they had told Sylvia not to get old. "Don't get old!" they'd said. Like anyone ever in the history of time had had any intention of that.

Sylvia could see that Ava was trying to smooth things over and get through the bump in the conversation. Stop talking, stop talking, she thought. She said, "All I'm saying is you don't have to worry as much as you do."

"Did you like it when people told you that, Mama? Did it make you feel better?"

Ava's sharp tone hurt Sylvia to hear, but she pretended otherwise. She wasn't sure when it happened that Ava started talking to her any way she pleased. She started to protest, but the truth was Ava knew much more about this subject than Sylvia ever could. Sylvia had not dreamed of babies when she was a girl. She didn't think of herself with children at all and looked with confusion and a little bit of envy at other women who saw the world of children and were neither slack jawed nor afraid. She had dreamed of grown children, talking to them. Having her son did not take away the fear but made her realize that the body adjusts quicker than the mind, and whatever she had thought those other women possessed the secret knowledge that unraveled the trick of mothering was mostly in the doing. She figured it out. She had done a good job when Devon was a tiny baby. Once he started to move around on his own, pull himself up on a kitchen chair, his back to her, fat legs wobbling as he focused on a sound in another room, she knew she started to lose him. Lose him isn't quite right. Misplace is better. Like those lost keys that might show up right under your nose in a place you've looked a dozen times. But what is lost or misplaced can be found, can't it? Stuck between the cushions of the world. All she needed was a lucky strike, a glad day, and she'd reach down into a crumb-filled cranny and he'd be back—a baby who craved the sound of her heartbeat as he rested on her chest. What Sylvia knew was she had no real idea what Ava felt. Sylvia had been an old mother for a poor woman, but her daughter seemed to feel that her own inability to get pregnant was a moral mistake and not just the body doing what it does. Sylvia had never felt the weight of judgment for not getting pregnant early. She had not felt like she'd done anything wrong. Of course who knew what she might have felt if she'd never gotten pregnant at all.

Ava sighed big and rolled her eyes. Her mother would think her condescending, and maybe she was. Her mother had been nearly thirty when Devon was born, not over thirty-five, the magic number and certainly not in whispering distance of the forty, that Ava was. Ava was technically thirty eight and a half, though the doctor always added a year to her age, the age she would be closer to when her baby arrived. Either way, she was now what they called geriatric maternal age. What she wouldn't give to be twenty-nine and three-quarters.

Ava sipped from her tea. She felt corked. She was bloated and full like a shaken champagne bottle. A queasy feeling but strangely hopeful at the same time. Maybe this time. Her mother would probably see something on her face, a hurried look, a tightness in her grin that suggested a lie or evasion. She usually did. She had tried for years now to get used to the taste of food without the cloying satisfaction of sugar. Everything you read said that Americans were too fat, too slow, at risk for the most serious ailments and all those ills pointed in sugar's direction. At first who cared if the sugar was gone. Food had its own subtle realness. A taste! That was a surprise. But tastes took a palate, some discernment to differentiate and appreciate. Very soon, she despised the realness of the foods and ached for the sweet, just sweet. She even liked the strange, exotic sounding word, *sugar, sugar*. She'd almost given up eating at all. Ava drank the tea and held the glass to her face to disguise her wince. "Lana called."

"Lana called me or you?"

"She called me to talk about you."

People loved Lana. When they found out Sylvia and Lana were sisters they expected Sylvia to have Lana's brightness, her humor, her unmuddied outlook of the world. They were always disappointed.

"What'd she call you for?"

"She wants me to talk you into going on a cruise with her this fall. Why don't you go?"

"I hate boats." Sylvia crossed her arms over her chest.

"It's not just a boat. They have a casino and shopping and dancing. All kinds of things."

"Don't you think I know all about that? People get stranded out there. No bathrooms, no food. Don't you watch the news? Who wants to be floating on a stinking toilet for days?"

"You forgot about icebergs." Ava laughed. "Come on, Mama, those are excuses. You'll have a good time. When is the last time you had fun?"

"I'm having fun now." Sylvia twirled her finger in the air. "See? I can't afford it anyway."

"You can afford it. You can pay by the month, Mama."

Sylvia shrugged her shoulders. She didn't want to pay by the month. Shelling out that money to a travel agent would multiply her feelings of dread with every payment reinforcing the idea that she was making a bad, bad decision. "I don't want to go and I'm not going to."

"You sound like a little kid."

"I feel like it too," Sylvia said.

"Like I could make you do anything anyway." Ava stared at Sylvia, intent on making her laugh. Her mother's face was not sweet but kind, a pleasant face that missed the mark of beautiful by so little, the hard jaw, her forehead in wrinkled annoyance or despair. She did wish for her mother's happiness.

Sylvia wasn't going to laugh and nobody was going to make her until she got ready. She rolled her eyes at Ava's stares and concentrated on the lawn. She had considered going with Lana just to satisfy Ava. She knew that kids want the security of their parents' happiness, and she had tried to reassure Ava to let her know her life might be diminished but it was not destroyed. Sylvia had wanted her children to think that she had lived an existence that brimmed with possibility. But smart kids know and know better. She wanted more for her children, for Ava, than struggling with a difficult man or working too hard just to keep the lights on. But it might not be possible to pass on something you don't really know yourself. "You should get more out of life than just a ham sandwich," Mabe had said. But what? Her mother should have told her what more she should be expecting. Two ham sandwiches? How could she expect to get what she didn't know she needed?

"What are you doing?" Sylvia watched Ava pick up her phone and punch in a number, though she knew who she had to be calling.

"I'm calling Lana. Talk to her." Ava held her phone finger in the air like she was testing the wind direction or signaling she was about to be talking.

"I'm not talking to nobody," Sylvia said.

"Hey. Mama's right here. Okay, okay. Here, Mama." Sylvia rolled her eyes at Ava and considered refusing to speak.

"Hello," Sylvia said.

"Don't hello me. What do y'all want now?" Lana asked. "Don't get me involved in y'all's mess. I told Ava that Noah couldn't get you on a boat and I wasn't about to try to talk to you as crazy as you are."

"Who is this?" Sylvia laughed.

"You better stop and come on this trip with me."

"Get Gus to go. What's he got to do?" Sylvia asked. Gus, the old man Lana married, was about as exciting as a paperweight and almost as useful. Sylvia didn't exactly dislike him. Who can dislike a rock? But two people were never more poorly suited to each other. Or, at least it seemed like it from the viewpoint of the outsider.

"Unless they're shutting television down, Gus is busy. Come on and go. Just me and you. We've never done that. Don't get old on me."

"Too late," Sylvia said, but she was interested she had to admit. The spark of the idea of reinvention, becoming different, even for a few days stirred her. "I'll think about it."

"Don't think too long. It will be too late soon. Too late."

"Don't be overdramatic," Sylvia said.

"Quoth the raven, 'too late,'" Lana said.

"Take your gun." Somebody said they saw a gun in Lana's handbag that was actually a black hair dryer.

"I might." Lana laughed. "Watch me. I might dry somebody to death. You don't know what I might do."

"Well whatever you do stop calling me."

"I didn't call you," Lana said.

"Well, stop talking to me."

"See you tomorrow, hateful." Lana laughed.

"Bye." Sylvia handed the phone to Ava. "How long have y'all been planning that? Y'all ain't a bit slick," Sylvia said.

"Will you even try to have fun? I know it's been a long time, but try to remember what it felt like."

"I might. I'll think about it, Ava. You're the one should go." Only the idea of travel appealed to Sylvia, but she could see the reality too acutely. That was one of her problems. She could see the sordid underbelly of a thing and often little else. She was too serious. If she'd had a dime for every time somebody had told her to cheer up, lighten up, stop thinking so much, stop being a downer. She used to love smoking pot for that feeling of letting go, just laughing to hear herself laugh. Those had been nice days, but it had been years, decades since she smoked any. Other people saw a boatload of people dancing, eating from the large and plentiful buffets, watching the roiling waves in the moonlight. Sylvia saw only the desperation, the straining of these same people to have fun, to not go back home exhausted and sad. You shouldn't have to try that hard for fun. She knew these were mostly excuses. If she left what would Marcus do? He could hardly make it a few days without hearing her voice. How could she help him if she was on an ocean trying not to be miserable? Of course he would be okay.

"Lana needs to mind her own business."

Ava squeezed more agave into her glass. "She's your sister. You are her business." Ava looked around for a spoon and ended up swirling the tea with her finger. "That's nasty, I know."

"I didn't say anything," Sylvia said, but Ava must have seen it on her face. "I talked to Marcus today."

"The prisoner? Is that why you won't go with Lana? Mama you've got to stop talking to him. I know you feel bad for him, but you can't help him."

"I know you feel more for people than that," Sylvia said.

"I'm not trying to be mean. I'm thinking more about you than him."

"How he remembers my number I don't know. How many phone numbers do you know? I know yours at work, your cell phone, my work number," Sylvia said.

"Mama don't change the subject. You need to stop with that prisoner."

"You don't get many collect calls anymore."

"He's calling you collect! You're paying to talk to him?"

"Nothing is long-distance anymore. It's fine." If Ava knew how expensive it was to talk to Marcus she would have a fit. Thank goodness the phone bill still came in her name. If there is a way to make a buck from even the saddest, poorest people in the world, you better believe some company has been created to do just that. "I'm tired. I should just go on to bed and call it a day."

"Mama?" Ava searched her mother's face for something she hadn't seen or had ignored, some sign she was in pain. "What does he say?"

"Who? Marcus?"

"The prisoner."

"Stop calling him that. He has a name."

"You don't know anything about him but his name. He could be dangerous, Mama."

"Over the phone." Sylvia laughed.

"You know what I mean. How do you know you're not talking to a killer? How, Mama?"

"They don't let the killers stay in county." Sylvia sighed. "He wants me to get a message to his girlfriend and daughter."

"What message? You're not going to do it are you?" Ava hadn't realized that her mother had been that lonely but she hadn't asked.

"That woman might be crazy," Sylvia hissed through her teeth. She hoped it sounded like a laugh, like seeing Marcus's girlfriend was the last thing she planned to do in the world. "You have to be careful with people these days."

"Mama, are you okay?"

"What are you talking about?" Sylvia reached for one of Ava's magazines. She didn't bother to flip it open. "JJ's house is looking good."

"Mama!"

"I'm just talking to a sad boy, Ava." Sylvia raised her voice, she hoped she hadn't shouted. She couldn't tell sometimes. She started to think that late middle-aged women lose their hearing and they shout to hear themselves. Loss of hearing felt better to believe than the thought that she was disappearing from view, shouting for help before the last of her vanished into thin air. "He doesn't have anybody," she said. "I'd want somebody to help my son."

Ava had never experienced real jealousy for Devon, at least not strong jealousy. They were separated by two and a half years, he a boy; she a girl. They never got labeled the athletic one, the pretty one, or the smart one, the way some people speak of siblings close in age. Still she couldn't help but imagine that her mother must know a closeness with Devon she could never feel for her, the number two child. Oprah grinned up at Ava from under the brim of a wide hat announcing the arrival of spring and a new body, a new turn of mind. Of course her mother helping Marcus was about Devon. So much of their lives eventually shifted in her brother's direction. Her mother had her eyes closed, though Ava knew she was not relaxed. She was done with the Marcus subject. "Mama, get some sleep. You're not listening to a word I say."

"I heard you, Ava." Sylvia crossed her legs at the ankles and sloughed off her beat-up shoes. Her daughter's shoes were lined up in military rows on the upstairs landing, beautiful high heels, boots standing upright and at attention like a small regiment, expensive wooden shapers poking from their tops like in a show-room. She would get better shoes, she promised to remember. She had been a stylish young person, hadn't she? She could almost remember looking nice. But who can remember? The mind plays tricks, or better said even reasonable people forgot the honest particulars of their pasts. Her feet were alligator feet without the charm. When did it come to all this? There had to be a start to this decline. If she could pinpoint the moment of decay maybe she could reverse it. That was the logic in the sci-fi movie. Get to the source.

"What are you smiling about?" Ava asked.

"I'm not smiling."

"I saw you."

"You wouldn't believe what goes on in my head these days. I've got too much going on in there. Right here," Sylvia said and tapped her temple.

"That's for sure not it." Ava smiled at her mother. "Hard to believe so much time has gone by. I hope he hasn't moved on."

"Who moved on?"

"JJ, Mama. You're the one that changed the subject to him." Ava tried at a lightheartedness she did not feel. JJ could have moved past them. He'd been away and seen different people and situations and it could be that they were part of a past he needed to lose. He hadn't bothered to contact them for years and years, a fact that Ava could not have predicted and could not quite believe. When they were young Ava and JJ had wasted so much time together, in front of the television, riding around the downtown and on the bumpy dirt roads near the county line. All the harmless time wasters that most poor young people do in one-horse towns. All except for screwing the life out of each other. That they didn't do. At least not until they left town. Ava had known even then that the stories that get told about you can spin wildly out of control without the buffer and framework of a known family history. The new kid drifting alone could be anyone and anything, while the town sniffed out clues, prosecuted the case of his life by his every stray comment, by his simple reactions to everyday events.

They had been nearly inseparable shortly after he arrived in town. All that time Ava pretended to be oblivious to JJ's infatuation for her while he pretended that his feelings were simply lustful and incidental, easily contained, easily disposed like a used carton of Chinese food. Often in these infatuations, the pretty girl uses the boy as a playmate, like another girlfriend but one who reflects back to her proof of her beauty and desirableness. His gaze proprietary but not competitive, his inclination was to do whatever the girl wanted. A teenage girl lives for that power, so often the only taste of it she gets. In that situation, the boy waits patiently for any opening in her amorous attention, any suggestion that his being the confidant and best friend might lead to her love. Not just sex, but of course the boy wanted sex, but these sorts of boys are romantics, the ones that hear the same call to love that so many of the girls hear. Theirs, Ava's and JJ's, was not that story. They had been friends. She had made an important friend in a life that had not produced many.

Sylvia tried to sound confident but she worried he might not show up too. "He'll be here. He so reminded me of Devon. Always did." Sylvia couldn't wait to see JJ. She thought how a face, his face, a body slicing through the air in a room, can crack the shell of your memory and erupt into your present. When that happens the past is not just ephemera or even pictures darting in and arresting your train of thought, but real in ways it can never be otherwise. The body makes the proof that you lived other than the moment of your last breath. JJ would materialize for them and it would be like they were all young and together again. The logic of it clear as day to Sylvia.

"I never thought he looked like Devon, Mama. I know you did."

Sylvia tried to keep her face a stone. She knew Ava was tired of hearing about her problems with Devon. Everybody was. Some days she'd resort to chatting about him in the car or to a wheelbarrow full of topsoil, a dirty coffee cup or a drawer of sensible stretched-out panties.

Maybe Sylvia would go back to her own apartment to sleep and let the television be the only noise in the room. "We'll be seeing JJ before too long. I hope he doesn't need a job. He'll be barking up the wrong tree around here." Sylvia was glad for JJ that he could come rolling into town like Big Daddy Rich, money like a superpower at his fingertips. Vanity wasn't vain if it wasn't about you. Of course Sylvia realized JJ's triumphant return had to be about her too. Someone like her, someone black, someone once poor, could come back to town and smash it underfoot. No, not smash it. That was wrong. He could be in control now and not tossed in any direction the wind blew. The cool of the ground, even the rocky places on the patio, felt good on Sylvia's bare feet. She bent to pull some small weeds from between the pavers. She had never wanted Ava to have to hold her up or become her helper.

Ava stared intently at her mother's face.

"What are you looking at?" Sylvia asked.

When a parent has trouble it can be very hard, maybe impossible not to make it into the child's sadness. The child becomes a helper, a new creation. Not quite a spouse but no longer young enough. Some of that was inevitable of course, part of the unfairness life doles out.

"Don't start talking to me about a pedicure again," Sylvia said.

Ava tried to laugh, but she couldn't get the sound out and into the air. Of course JJ's absence had hurt her mother too. "You're right, Mama. He'll be here when the house is done."

Sylvia hesitated. A look, a panic had flashed on Ava's face and was just as quickly gone. She would mind her own business. When Ava wanted to tell her she would. No need to pry.

"Now, let's talk about what's wrong with you," Sylvia said.

4

The body knows the day. Monday lies in your bones different from Thursday, different from the urgency of Friday. But Sunday's drag is the strongest no doubt, pulling like it means it, like it is working for its life. Sunday has to be the biggest day for suicides. If Henry was ever going to take his own life, he was sure it would be on a Sunday. The terrible struggle done. The struggle used to be all about work. Henry used to feel like he'd tried to swallow a pill that would not go down, that threatened to choke the breath out of him as he worked at his station at the furniture plant. He felt less of that now. Inside the red tape on the concrete floor that marked the territory of the machine, he was the owner and proprietor. If you are not Henry Bailey, do not cross the tape. Henry could get beamed up from that space and if the mother ship ever came they would know for sure where to concentrate the light. Henry took solace in the security of his routine, the work burnishing the stubby places off his life. He might not have long to work there anyway. The weeks before saw a new round of layoffs with more to come. Henry worried that his would be the next job cut, but everybody worried. The older guys who did the work of three were kept on, absorbed into other furniture factories, at least so far. Nobody worried too much about the kids, the twenty-year-olds, at least not when the first closings began. They needed to move around a little bit anyway. A twenty-year-old can take on a little adversity, they had time to recover.

One closing felt like lightning and not the first domino in the sequence. Most days Henry considered quitting just to stop the suspense, but there was nothing else a man like him could do but hang in there and hope the inevitable would pass him by. Years ago the first furniture plant had closed and moved to Vietnam. These things happen and nothing that an ordinary man can do about it. If anyone saw that closing as the end of an industry he kept it to himself. There were no signs. Business was good. Productivity was high. Probably even the line bosses didn't know that the end was coming—ten years at most.

When Henry started on the line a couple of years before he got married he thought he wouldn't be able to stand it. The first week he found any excuse to go to the toilet, sit in the stall, and stare at the pitted metal door. Never before had he been tempted to write a note on the walls of a bathroom, but the urge to speak almost overcame him. Almost. Every man on the line would know he was the author, and they already thought he was either lazy or had an abusive, bullying bowel. Henry had not known before the kind of misery he felt on that factory line. The smell of sawdust and furniture stain seeped into him, aging him twenty-five years with his head of silver hair. God almighty did he hate it. Under his fingernails a dirty dust line remained like the vein in shrimp. But that was nothing, nothing compared to the assaultive sound, the constant, crazy-making whirring from the saws that churned into his chest as they cut the tumbling wooden legs and tabletops another man loaded onto the conveyor belt. When the quitting bell rang, Henry sprinted like he was on fire, the first one to the time clock, oblivious to the shaking heads from the older men as he spun his car out of the gravel lot.

The only real choice for him was to work at one of the stinking chicken plants a couple of towns over. Eight dollars an hour was the starting rate back then—a good amount for the time and place. Everyone started in the blood and guts room, stood in a plastic apron all day while the yellow guts of chickens ran through their fingers. Many quit after a few days. A very few made it weeks. Some sturdy ones lasted a lifetime. But nobody who worked there ate chicken for months. Henry knew he would never survive the smell of the dead meat or the slick bloody floor and chicken viscera on his smock. But he tried. He clocked in a one and one-half hours. Plant Four by comparison was mostly dry, the particulates of wood as fine as snowflakes landing layer on layer in his lungs like the sludge in a drain a delicate violent process.

Henry had come home one night and told his mother he didn't think he could stand it on the line another day. "Mama, it's loud," he said, sounding like the child he was. His mother had listened, hadn't interrupted. Henry may not have known exactly what she'd say, but if he was being honest, he probably knew what she'd mean. "Don't do it then," she'd said, shrugging her shoulders. "You don't have to eat." His mother's unsympathetic but sure grasp of the ways of the world had been just the thing Henry needed to hear. He hadn't meant to think about her today.

But the body adapts, the mind adapts. Henry had seen it for himself with the guys on the line. Henry wasn't one of the oldest guys in the group. Some of the men had spent decades at the machines. Randy Hightower, Alvin Lodermilk, Donny Goodman all had at least thirty years already and they showed no signs of leaving. Henry wasn't a kid, but it made him feel better not to be part of the old guard. After nineteen years, he had a hard time convincing himself that the job was temporary.

Linda and Shelley, the white women in the main office, greeted him as they did as he took the side entrance into the building. Linda, the younger of the women, had been the subject of talk when she was first hired years ago. Her big chest highlighted in sweaters, her tiny little waist, thin blond hair dark at the roots that she fed into her mouth when she was nervous had all been noticed and discussed. If she liked the attention from the men, she gave no indication. She said nothing to even the boldest of them but smiled at them in a detached indulging way, like you might a child who had stepped on your toe. Henry never flirted with her. Shelley probably just seemed older than Linda. She'd come to the plant many years before Henry, looking like someone's wife's idea—a settled woman in elastic waist pants and sensible shoes.

A small maze of cubicles where the salesmen and low-level executives kept desks was one wall away from the machine room floor. Every day Henry passed by pictures of kids in baseball uniforms, ballerinas, and fat babies that looked like old men. Several of the men had plastic toys and fast food toys and dolls from comic books that Henry could not understand why grown men collected. The men on the line were supposed to come in the other entrance, but neither Linda nor Shelley minded him coming in the mid-management door. Henry needed that soft light moment before he entered the room and the grind of the machines.

For months now the plant opened only four days a week, which meant Henry had Fridays to himself. Not that it mattered much. As much as they try to get you to think so, there is no such thing as free time. Without money the days stretched like taffy, measured in judge shows and *Family Feuds*. At first that open Friday meant sleeping in, lazy mornings of pleasurable dozing, followed by a midmorning nap that felt like a necessity. Lunch meant a handful of sugary cereal, bologna he rolled into cylinders and dipped into the fancy jar of mustard Ava liked, or leftover anything, sometimes all of the above. For a short time Henry had loved that leisure. He'd worked for an actual paycheck since he was sixteen and for cash before that. The open day had made him feel lucky, like the rich must feel. Now a day off alone was worse than work. Ain't that some shit?

If the teenage Henry could have known about the sad feel of time and days, the enormous weight of them, stacking up with nothing making them matter. The awful truth was that he had nothing, nothing to do with his hands or his mind if the work disappeared. He'd be like the old dudes sacking groceries or dragging socks over the electronic eye at Walmart. The economy was very bad. He suspected that he was suited for repetitive work that used to be the domain of teenaged kids, but now more and more often was done by grown-ass people, his age and older. He was like those adding machines or busted typewriters you see at the thrift store, out-of-date, picked for parts and made into terrible jewelry or sad coffee table art. Small town economic theory said if white people worked at those jobs the town economy is bad. If those white workers are over thirty, the economy is very, very bad.

People were supposed to feel some of that dispossessed feeling when they retire after a lifetime of work. There had to be days of wondering what to do with yourself, the phantom pains of getting yourself up, rushing before the sun rose with the taste of quickly made coffee and toothpaste in your mouth—none of that leaves you overnight. You don't work every day and then turn it off like a light. Henry expected to feel the loss, but not at thirty-eight years old.

5

Henry had tried to run. After he graduated from school he and his brother Sean had driven straight through and all night to New Orleans. They'd missed Mardi Gras by months, but they figured the town always had a party so why not. Henry and Sean found Bourbon Street easily and walked side by side past bars, restaurants, tattoo and dance parlors. A topless overweight white girl watched them from the patio of a nightclub. "Look at that," Sean said and jerked his head at the girl. Henry had nothing against naked women, even not so beautiful ones, but the sight of her smallish breasts and large pink nipples pointing in slightly different directions made him uneasy. "Let's go, man." He grabbed Sean's arm. He was eager to get to St. James square to have his fortune told. In some parts of North Carolina so-called psychics put up signs with painted red hands at the ends of the yards. Five dollars a pop for the secrets of your future as told by a little old lady con artist. He'd pass on that. Years before at the grocery store Henry's mother had pointed out to him a small mousy-looking woman wearing hospital shoes. "There's your great fortune-teller," she'd said. Henry had watched the woman walk slowly with her grocery basket down the chip aisle, pick up orange cheese doodles, and toss them into her cart. Doodles! He'd never go to a North Carolina psychic. Mostly he didn't believe in the dark powers at all, but he needed a hint, any hint about where his life was headed. He and Sean were determined to do and be more than they'd seen, but they had no clue where to start.

The day was already hot, but the forecast said oppressive heat, heat too ridiculous for late spring, heat that almost made you forget all your home training and act foolish. Not many buskers and performers had set up yet this early in the day, but a boy of maybe eight or nine and two older men who looked to be family were sitting on a large piece of cardboard just ahead of Henry and Sean. The brown boy of eight or nine jumped up at their approach and tap-danced in a jerky, untrained way on the cardboard. The boy locked eyes with Henry. "Hey, mister," he yelled. "Mister!" The boy must have learned to never let a prospective customer look away, no matter how artless and embarrassing the performance, don't let them look away. Henry shrugged his shoulders at the boy and considered pulling out his pockets like the broke Monopoly man. He doubted that would stop the dancing boy. Henry and Sean had maybe forty dollars between them to get back home. The dead-eyed boy tapped more vigorously as Henry struggled not to look back at him.

"I'm going back to the car," Sean said. "I've got to sleep."

"I'll meet you later. If you move the car come right back here to find me. Okay?" This was the days before cell phones were extensions of the hand and people did not know every waking second what everyone else did every waking second. Henry thought that if he got lost in the city walking street after street that looked alike that it might take him days to find his brother and get back home. That wasn't going to happen. He was young; he was beautiful. Nothing was going to happen.

Henry would stop at the first table that called to him. He walked some distance from the bored-looking black woman with a head rag, old black woman with a head rag, bored-looking white woman with a head rag, long-haired white woman with witchy gray hair under a head rag. None of them looked promising to Henry. Some of them ignored him altogether, but most glanced up briefly as he passed. There were no young fortune-tellers and no men. Henry would never go to a young psychic or a man for that matter. A man has no patience for anyone else's future, even Henry knew that. What he didn't understand yet was that young people didn't even know enough to know that they wouldn't always be young.

"What are you looking for, honey?" At the third-to-last table in the row, a white woman called to him. "I've watched you. You want to stop. I know you do."

Henry scanned the woman's card table, which was covered in a dark blue tablecloth festooned with yellow stars and slivers of moons, the whole thing more appropriate on a preschooler's bed. Behind her table the woman had maybe a half dozen bags and totes full of what looked like hastily stuffed clothes and household goods. The telltale triangle of a clothes iron nosed out of the top of one of them. Henry's mother used to say you could always tell trashy people because they'd have a pile of junk in the corners of their rooms. By all appearances this woman had no room at all.

"You just get to town, honey?"

"Everybody just got here." Henry smiled at the woman, not sure if he was being clever or obnoxious.

The woman did not say anything, but smiled indulgently at him.

"We've been here, me and my brother, about three hours," Henry said. He and Sean had stopped at Rite Aid and gotten a jumbo bag of chips and some sodas after they peed in the mostly clean toilet, then come immediately to the middle of town.

The woman looked amused at him and motioned for Henry to sit in the open chair. She was younger than he initially thought. Forties, maybe.

"I don't want a fortune," Henry said as he sat down.

"You want to sit, so stay," the woman said.

Henry crossed his hands, not entirely sure what he was waiting for. "Are you from here?"

The woman shrugged. "Might as well be. I've been here for twenty-some years." The woman reached for his hand and turned it over in her own long fingered hands. Her nails were painted a deep plum color and nicely manicured, her obvious pride. The woman traced the dark lines on his palm with her index finger.

"What are you doing?" Henry asked.

"Your hand, honey." As she traced the lines she whispered. The most Henry could make out was life, heart. She looked like she retraced her lines and looked for mistakes. "Let's do the cards."

"Why?"

"I don't like how your lifeline looks. See?" The woman whispered this to him, her forehead near his own. "This line is dark and full, but hardly there. See this? If the lines coming off of it were pointing up then I wouldn't think a thing about it. You see how this one points down?" She put her finger on a jagged line near his thumb. "I want to see something else." The woman frowned and reached into her bag for the cards. She pulled them out without ceremony and cut the deck. The first card she turned over had a smiling skeleton against a dark background, curlicues swirling in the air around the bones like turbulent wind.

"That's death isn't it?"

"It's hard to say. Death isn't always death. You know that, don't you?"

"It looks like death to me," Henry said, but he was not afraid.

"Change, honey. Don't hold on to things that can't work for you. What's your name?"

"Henry."

"Henry?" The woman looked him over as she considered his name. "I don't like Henry. It doesn't fit."

"I was named for my grandfather. Everybody loved him."

"Doesn't matter. Henry doesn't fit you. Change it," the woman said. "What about Hank?"

Henry laughed out loud. "I'm not a Hank. No way."

"Maybe not." The woman looked him over and conceded. "But change everything else."

"I can't change everything," Henry said. He thought he'd feel something scary, some eeriness that meant dark forces had been summoned. What he felt was the same feeling of annoyance at an old woman telling him what to do.

The woman hesitated. "Listen to me. You have to make some hard decisions. Big change and transformation is coming for you. Do not ride in a white car. Ever. Stay out of parking garages. You won't die there but there's no good that will come from it. Go home as soon as you can. Don't stay here. This is a sad place. It might not look like it, but there's a lot of pain here under all this whatever. All this here. But whatever you do, don't stay still, you'll get stuck. That will unravel you. Don't forget what you've heard here. Don't ignore good advice."

"Don't ignore good advice?" Henry laughed. "You sound like my mama."

The woman pursed her lips in an expression Henry couldn't read. "Well"—the woman stared hard at Henry—"you also need to let the girl go. You'll never be happy until you do. But I don't see you doing that."

Henry smiled slowly at the woman. She had his attention and for the first time since he saw her, a tickle of belief wormed its way into his head. Ava had been flitting through his thoughts all day. She was going to college three hours away (three hours!) in just a few months. Though she declared that she would not forget him and their relationship would be stronger than ever. She promised that being apart for a little bit would just make them happier to reunite. They would make it, she promised. Henry knew better. She would find somebody better, somebody smart, maybe even someone rich who would give her a life that he would one day watch from the sidelines like a child at a parade. He was sure that a good life was in Ava's future. If he wasn't a scared, selfish kid he would let it happen for her, be glad for her.

"I'm not going to let her go."

The woman smiled and shrugged. "It's up to you. People never listen. I don't know why they bother asking. I'm just telling you what I know. It won't be easy."

"What else is new?"

The woman looked meaningfully at Henry. "You want to meet later? At four?"

Henry placed ten dollars in the woman's hand. She held on to him too long with her beautifully manicured fingers. He was accustomed to women trying to get closer to him, flirting with him, but her interest took him by surprise. Like all attractive people, Henry knew he was beautiful, what he didn't know was the expressions he wore and how his face registered his reactions to the world.

"I didn't mean to shock you. If I don't see you again, you need to remember what I said." The woman smiled at him like she was memorizing his face. "Have a good life, honey."

But Henry did come back. Right at four and directly to the spot. The woman brightened at his approach like she'd had the first good surprise of a very long time.

"My brother has the car." Henry didn't tell her that the car was where he and his brother slept.

"Here, help me with these," she said as she handed him some of her bags. Henry grabbed most of them and followed the woman to an alley. The woman's old car had the windows already down in the front. "No air," she explained. "And yours won't go back up." The back of the car was stuffed with other bags of her belongings.

Henry stuffed the bags into the backseat. "Ready?" For a fleeting moment he thought about Ava and her dissolving face, her incredulity if she saw him with this woman. If he lingered on the thought it would pain him, he might even ask the woman to let him out and he would find his way back to Sean. He did not let the thought linger. This sex was less than nothing to him. Nothing at all. In a few short years his memory of this day would fade into a blur and he would not even recall enough about the woman to form a picture of her in his mind.

They drove through neighborhoods miles from Bourbon

Street. The breeze thick like opening a hot oven bathed their faces. The woman's thin pale hair flew up around her, and for a moment Henry imagined that they were breathing under water like another species. Very quickly the landscape changed from the Victorian balconies to small homes in rows of close-together shotgun houses that were mostly white, but some with unusual vibrant teals and pinks, the occasional deep purple one in the row. They stopped behind one of the houses. "This is where my dog is," the woman said and pointed to a light blue house surrounded by a white split rail fence. "Black people don't like dogs, I know. But I'm going to get her back."

"Maybe black people don't like your dog," Henry said.

"Maybe." The woman glanced at him quickly to gauge his annoyance. "I used to live right there."

"Why don't you now?" Henry asked.

"Somebody else lives there. I'm not welcome anymore."

Henry nodded not sure how he was supposed to respond to her. For a second he feared a jealous man with a shotgun running out of the house with a gun trained on his face.

"Nobody's coming, honey," the woman said. "Don't worry. Nobody but you gives a damn about me. But you don't know anything about that. Lost love." The woman smiled at him as she moved to his side of the car. She pulled her flowing skirt up to her waist and straddled him in the passenger seat. "You like me, don't you?" Her body was light, like her bones were hollow, her face pretty and delicate in front of him, her skin an intricate map of tiny little lines. "Is this okay, Hank?"

Henry was in the passenger seat of a piece-of-shit car with a woman old enough to be his mother. He did not know her name. "Light as a feather, baby," Henry said.

6

Henry remembered to take his shoes off at the door, but he would never change and shower first thing like Ava wanted. She didn't want the shavings and sawdust he shed from his clothes and hair through the house. Once upon a time she liked the taste of sawdust on his skin. They'd meet at lunchtime in whatever darkness they could find. Back then she couldn't get enough of the smell of him and she kept some part of her body touching some part of his. He thought many times she kept him grounded with her damp palm and short little fingers. Now if Ava touched him it was by accident or during their joyless baby-making days.

"Ava, I'm here. Where you at?"

Henry passed through a maze of thrift store finds to the back of the house. Ava watched too many home improvement television shows and took too many of the ideas to heart. He'd made the mistake of calling her a hoarder one day and she'd cried like he'd hit her, though anybody who knew him would tell you he would never hit a woman. After that he let it go, stopped mentioning any new thing she brought in the house.

Sylvia's car was outside for what seemed like the thousandth day in a row. He warned Ava of the hazards of buying from family—nothing good can come from it—but whether that was actual wisdom or reality judge show wisdom Henry couldn't be entirely sure. He should have insisted that they find their own place, even if it had to be a rented house or an apartment or a basement somewhere. He had been opposed to that house on Development Drive from the get-go. Not that what he felt mattered. Both Ava and Sylvia had their minds set.

"Hey Henry," Sylvia said as she caught his eye. The sight of her pretty-faced son-in-law often startled her. She never remembered him that pretty. He was lean without looking drug-addicted or starved. He was brown and smooth, like leather, not milk chocolate or caramel. Food descriptions for black people made her crazy. Black people were not delicious. Henry had a vacant look like he was seeing everything for the first time. He was dumb, that's all there was to it. Pretty didn't keep him from being a dumb ass.

Henry took off his hat and scratched his head. Like Don he probably had a handful of sawdust in the kinky coils of his close fro. He better not let Ava see him scratching.

"You doing all right, Sylvia?" Henry had never had any inclination to call his mother-in-law, Mother. His wife was not his sister. When he and Ava told Sylvia they were getting married, she'd told him to call her by her name. She'd had enough children.

"Tired. I'm okay. You?" Henry thought Sylvia looked disappointed. Her mouth in a sad turn or worse she looked at him sideways like she couldn't stand to see his whole face.

"Are you cooking, Ava?" Henry asked the question, but he knew what the answer had to be. When Ava was trying to get pregnant she ate very little and cooked even less. What was worse than the sex by the clock or Ava's pretend seductions was the lack of hot food. "I'm going to get fish, if you're not cooking."

"Go ahead. Just get me hush puppies."

Henry nodded but he knew he'd see those greasy hush puppies later in the trash. "I'm going on then." Henry turned to go back into the house but swiveled back around to Ava. "I saw your boyfriend in town," Henry said.

Ava looked up at Henry to see the expression on his face. "Funny," Ava said, though he saw a spark on her face. "Where'd you see him?"

"Standing at the car wash beside Food Lion. He looked like hell. I almost stopped to say something to him."

"Why didn't you?" Ava asked.

What would Henry look like, slapping JJ's back, like they were friends, like they had ever been friends?

"You been up there yet?" Henry directed his question to Sylvia but he hoped Ava would answer.

"No, but I expect to." Sylvia glanced in Henry's direction in time to see the softness of his expression, the vulnerability that she usually interpreted as weakness. She felt sorry for him for a fleeting moment.

"I'm outta here. You want something, Sylvia?"

"No, I won't be here when you get back. I've got to get ready for work. Tomorrow's my last day this week."

"I've only got thirty years to retirement. How many days is that?" Ava laughed.

Sylvia brought her fingers to her lips. For years she'd kept a coat of clear polish on the tiny little nails, the slick feel of the polish gross on her tongue probably slowly poisoning her to death. When she was a child, she had sucked her thumb unless her mother was anywhere around. Her mother tried everything from hot pepper to castor oil to get her to stop. And she did stop in public, but at night she'd pop her thumb in her mouth. After all those years the urge had changed but had not left.

"Don't rush it. It'll come soon enough," Sylvia said.

Henry hesitated between the two women and as usual he was not sure what else there was to say. "Be right back."

7

Henry knew Pinewood like the back of his hand. Most of it anyway. He had spent too many teenage nights drinking in cars, riding with other boys until the cars moved on gas fumes or didn't run at all because they'd flipped them into ditches. Many of them lived to stand around the overturned cars, trying not to look like drowned rats. Ava had been in Raleigh at school, a day trip easy, but that distance had given her other scenes in her head, other stories that Henry had listened to with eagerness, with jealousy like she was talking about walking on the moon.

A big old-fashioned sign shaped like a fifties atomic triangle announced your arrival to the center of town. The big red letters, missing the final S but everybody knew what you meant, the place was an institution. Simmy's burgers and fries, home of the big burger, had been in business since just after the Second World War. The mess of a cheeseburger with a bun as big as a baby's head came (for the past sixty years) in a paper checkered basket. Simmy's was a place that did not change. Going there was an event.

When Henry's father was young if he ate at Simmy's he ordered his food from a sliding door in the back of the restaurant. There was no colored entrance or sign that marked a separate space, but the blacks in town knew they would not be welcome at the front door. To this day some blacks preferred the pickup window to going in the restaurant. Others loved the idea that the times had changed enough, the wounds healed enough that they could walk proudly through the front door on their own terms. But not Henry's father. Once the place was integrated he still wouldn't go in. It was Henry's Uncle Buddy's favorite place. He would bring in king burgers or barbecue for them in bags so damp and heavy, he'd had to keep his meaty hand underneath the bag to keep the sloppy food from falling out the bottom. Uncle Buddy would cut a burger in half for Henry and his brother Sean, and though they protested about who got the larger piece, neither of them ever finished their share.

The town was bisected by a main street and divided into four sections. All four corners had changed only slightly in Henry's lifetime. A KFC had replaced a family restaurant on one corner and a McDonald's opened in the early eighties. Back then his family swung their boats of cars into the parking lot running out their little bit of gas as they waited for a parking space. Gone were his elementary school teachers' names, the address of his grandmother's house, his first day of school, when he was told his mother almost lost her job at the cafeteria because she sat in their station wagon in the school's parking lot until noon. All of that gone, but the Big Mac jingle he learned from the commercial abideth.

Henry turned right on Main Street away from the center of town. He'd wanted fish but he found himself behind Simmy's in the back parking lot. A few years before, a woman had gotten killed by her boyfriend in a struggle for the night's receipts. He took the money she was supposed to deposit and paid his light bill, his water bill, put gas in his car. What a relief he must have felt to have those bills paid, no more creditors on his back, free for one quick minute. Dear God why are we such fools?

Since then none of the employees was allowed to go out alone, even to take out the garbage, even to smoke. But the years had softened them all, dulled them to the unpredictable possibilities of mean in the world. Instead of worry, if they thought about it at all, they reasoned that there was little harm in ten short minutes in the evening air.

Henry turned off the ignition. As usual, the car was a mess. He flipped the visor in front of him as dust floated into the air and he reached to pick up the solitary dime in among the litter of napkins and dried clay on the soiled carpets. He used to care about a car and was at the Crossroads Carwash and Laundry every Sunday morning, coaxing crinkled dollars into the change machine. There were times he even got there before the Jehovah's Witnesses who were replacing or adding to the *Watchtowers* on the tables, a blur in long skirts and sensible shoes. He meant to take one of the magazines, but he was afraid of what they would mean to him. That he was a man so easily bought by images of wholesome children and the promise of good love in paradise. In those days he kept a bucket in his trunk with Turtle Wax, chamois, and dishwashing liquid (preferably lemon fresh Joy, nothing made better lather than that), a stiff bristle brush for scrubbing the tires. The cars he owned were never special, but the sparkle of his, all his, even on the roof where nobody would look, gave him a satisfaction that to the untrained eye looked like happiness.

In the visor in a stretchy band was the cracked plastic window of a yellowed bill. He had forgotten the light bill again. Ava would scream when she saw it, or worse, cry, like some real tragedy had struck. People get folded up in the creases of their lives.

Carrie was thick through the middle, her face rounded out, but she was a beautiful girl. The pouch below her belly button, the apron some women get who've had babies, was never concealed by the long shirts she wore. Nobody cared about her flabby belly. Carrie opened the passenger door and leaned in to Henry as he kissed her lightly on the lips. "I'm glad to see you, baby," he said. He held her shoulders afraid of the long blondish brown strands of her hair that might find their way to his clothes. Ava had pulled a strand of it from him one day, pinched it between her fingers, and dropped it in the trash. She'd said nothing, but Henry knew her well enough to know she had stored the information for later.

"What are you doing here? Jerri told me she saw your car or I'd have missed you." Carrie slipped the apron over her head and positioned herself in the passenger seat to face Henry.

Carrie and Henry had met in high school, though Carrie didn't know him then. She knew few of the black people at the school and was friends with none of them. A lot had happened to the world in twenty years. Back then no black kids dated white kids, not in public. Nobody Henry or Carrie knew was interested in making that public stand. What would be the point? And at that age there had to be a point. The mission of high school was to come from money and have great hair, but blend in and be invisible and envied by everyone.

"I can't stay. I just got off from work."

"Look at you? You've got sawdust in your hair." Carrie brushed Henry's hair with her hand. Henry stopped her and rested his face in her palm. "Baby are you okay?"

"I'm fine, just listening to the radio."

"You depressed?"

"No I don't get depressed. Just bored." Henry took Carrie's hand and placed it on her lap. "Don't make everything so serious."

Carrie searched Henry's face for deceit. Not that she needed proof, he was obviously sad. "I miss you, Henry. We don't get to see you anymore. When are you coming to the house? Zeke asks about you all the time."

"I don't know." Henry rubbed the back of his head. "Maybe Thursday. Are you working? I'll be off. I'll bring him something." Henry wished he could be more like Zeke with no need to name and define his life, no time for a one-eyed squint at the world trying to really see it. He just took things as they came. Five-year-olds have it made. "Ava's going to be with Sylvia. I'll know more tomorrow."

"Are you coming in?"

"I'll just do the drive-through."

"Come on in a few minutes. If you sit in my station we can talk as long as we want to."

Henry was shaking his head no.

"She's not going to notice you gone for a few minutes," Carrie snapped.

"Look, don't get mad. I'm tired. I came straight from the shop." Henry reached for his wallet in his back pocket, the tight fit of his jeans and his position behind the wheel making him squirm to reach it. He lifted his hips to get a better hold. He knew he looked ridiculous but he couldn't quit.

"Stop struggling, Henry. Just get out of the car." Carrie knew as soon as she said for Henry to do the most obvious logical thing there was no way he would do it.

"Maybe I don't want to get out the car. I don't have to." He gripped the wallet pinched it with his two fingers until he squeezed it out of the tight pocket. "Dammit!" he said and tried again.

Carrie tried not to watch Henry wrestle with his pants. He would get that wallet his own way or die. He lifted two tens and handed them to Carrie. He didn't want her to see that there were only three or four ones still left in the leather folds. "Give this to Zeke and tell him I'll come on Thursday okay? We're only working three days this week."

"You give it to him. Come here and give it to him."

"Why can't you just do it," Henry said, but he was aware he sounded whiny. "I'm not asking for much."

"If I take this," Carrie began, she hated making him promise like they were children themselves. "You promise you'll come. You promise?"

"Why don't you let Zeke stay home? How much can they do in kindergarten? I'll take him to the park. We'll spend the whole day."

"He needs to go to school. Just get in a few hours with him before we start talking about the whole day." Carrie sighed hard and rolled her apron between her hands. "I'm tired too. Bethany had a birthday party for Sam, and Zeke didn't get invited."

"She's a bitch."

"Don't call her that."

"You know it." Henry held his mouth with his hand until the terrible sensation to cry washed over him. Maybe Carrie didn't see. He couldn't stand it if she saw that. "Do you want me to come?"

"I shouldn't have told you." Carrie sighed and reached for the door handle; the smooth handle cool in her hand, a different temperature and texture than she had expected. She faced Henry. "Why can't you understand this?" She hadn't wanted to scream, but as soon as she pulled up her anger it dissolved. Their time together was so short that she didn't want to waste it. It occurred to Carrie that Henry probably never made that kind of emotional adjustment for her, he wouldn't even think of it. Carrie tried to calm herself, but she could feel the emotion rising in her chest. She would not cry. "She's my sister, Henry. Do you understand any of that? She's not a stranger or some girl I work with. She's the only family I've got speaking to me." Carries stifled the urge to shake Henry's shoulders. "She the best one out of all of them. You know that."

"You see how good she is, don't you?" Henry asked, but Carrie could see the doubt on his face.

"Why do you make this harder for me?"

"I can't help it your people are racists."

Carrie shook her head. "I could throw up. You know that? That's how sick I am."

"Ah shit, Carrie. Why are we going to do this now?"

"You aren't being for real. I know you understand."

"All they know is who they think I am."

"She said she couldn't have Mama and me in the same place. She always used to invite us to everything. Where does that leave me, Henry? You know what it feels like not to have any family?"

Henry shook his head. He did know. His father was as good as dead. His brother locked up. The mother who loved him, the one person he could say that about with full confidence, was long dead. He couldn't make himself think about Ava right now. Yes, he understood being alone. He knew very well. Henry stopped before he held his head in his hands the way he craved. "Does Zeke know?"

"Know what?"

"About the party? Any of it."

"I don't think so, but kids see things. They put it together. You know that." Carrie was embarrassed not to have considered that her son might know about the situation. He had not asked her anything, but kids know things.

"I will beat the shit out of other kids," Henry said.

"You make me sick." Carrie laughed. "You suck." Carrie punched Henry lightly in his arm.

"I can beat just about any five-year-old in the world."

"Probably so."

"Probably! That's cold. You don't think I could beat a toddler? I'm not much of a man am I?" Henry laughed. Carrie hesitated but let a laugh escape too. Henry could tell the air in the car had grown stale again and one wrong word would ruin the calm moment they'd just found.

"I'll bring something. I'll be here right after school," Henry said and held Carrie's two hands between his.

"Okay, Henry. He'll be so excited."

"Don't make me feel bad. I told you I'd be there."

"I'm not trying to make you feel bad." Carrie sighed.

Henry looked out the window at the restaurant, not sure what to say but not wanting to say the wrong things again. "Did you ever think we'd be living like this?" Carrie said.

Henry looked into Carrie's light brown eyes, at her romantic face, with its turned-down mouth. "We aren't going to start this. Let's don't start. Please. Okay?"

"You have ideas about your life. This is it?" Carrie snorted.

"I can't do this today." Henry made coffee in the morning on his break. He poured coffee into the Styrofoam cup, tore three packets of sugar, and let the particles swirl into the mix. It could have been any one of a hundred days. A thousand days dissolving in front of his eyes. "Did I ever tell you about my Uncle Buddy? Big guy. He used to love this place."

"Why are you talking about him? Is that why you're sad?"

"Don't make everything mean something. I just got reminded of him. He was funny. If it wasn't about you, he was funny." Uncle Buddy made fun of everyone. Don't have stuck-out ears or fat or a turned-out toe in front of Buddy. But he'd never found anything to say about Henry. With him he was gentle, like he sensed the soft center of Henry. "He fed us. He'd bring us barbecue from here long time ago."

"What made you think of him?"

"I don't know. He was a good old dude."

"I was going to say maybe you need to see him. Maybe that would make you feel better?"

"I'm fine, Carrie."

"I try not to worry about you, Henry." Carrie hesitated and then let out a long dramatic sigh. "That's the truth." Carrie opened the door and put her apron back on. "I better get back." Carrie blew a kiss to Henry. "I'll see you later. Come before dark, okay? I'll be there by four."

Henry went through the drive-through and ate his fries, his greasy fingers marking up the steering wheel. After all these years the memory of Buddy was so strong. Buddy funked up his room when he spent the night with clothes he carried in a pillowcase that didn't get washed very often. Years before, Buddy had picked up eleven-year-old Henry from school. "Let's go for a ride," he said. Buddy's fingernails were just long enough to be unusual and were painted with clear polish. How had Henry never noticed his nails? Buddy tapped the steering wheel to every tune coming on from the white light rock station, *baby, baby don't get hooked on me, I remember when rock was young, take it to the limit one more time*, he sang. Henry didn't worry in the twenty minutes it took to get to Statesville or even the sixty or so miles they drove to Charlotte. "Welcome to the B side," Uncle Buddy said and parked the car at a Denny's just as they reached the city. Only when Buddy had gone inside leaving Henry in the car alone did Henry consider being afraid. Henry counted the few coins in his pocket and added it to the change in the car and called his mother from the phone booth in the parking lot.

"Did you call your mama?" Uncle Buddy asked when he returned.

"Yeah." Henry nodded and admitted the act, but for some reason he felt ashamed.

"I would have done the same thing. I sure would have. You know," Uncle Buddy began with his freckled face up close to Henry's, "I never would have hurt you. You know that, don't you?" Until that moment Henry had not considered himself in any danger. Henry wanted to ask Uncle Buddy so many things, but even as a child he knew the answers didn't matter. The only question that meant anything was one Buddy probably couldn't answer. Did you feel it when your mind slipped like a backbone, like a bad knee?

8

That night Ava had the dream again. The three of them are in their dirty kitchen. Ava is stacking dishes to make room in the sink and runs water into the breakfast pot. Their son is crying softly in the next room because he can't understand that he can't *go pay, go pay* at the park. But they must start the day. The man stirs the bubbling oatmeal as she pours the milk thick as cream into the fancy bottle proven to reduce gas bubbles in little bellies. A fortune in bottles and nipples, her husband says, her brother says, a man she does not recognize says, depending on the night. But she doesn't need money, not at all. The baby drinks and the cat the baby wants is thankfully still imaginary with imaginary winding around and through their legs, begging in that sullen privileged way cats do.

"Can you please take out the trash please," she says to him. But there is no please in her voice. Whining, whining, an unbroken record or do what you are supposed to in her tone. Not like he hears or has heard for a long time. He is turned from her. Her brother, her husband, the man she does not know hides his face. She thinks about the days they would dance on this very floor barefoot and light as children. There were times when the food was greasy and fried and they ate with their fingers and wiped them on already soiled jeans. But life is not compromised just because it is tiring, and a small body reaches out for them, calls out to them from other rooms. She will wake from this dream with a feeling like floating, a lightness she will wear for the rest of the day.

9

"I'm drawing you now," Marcus said.

"You don't know what I look like. Just don't draw me ugly."

"I won't." Marcus chuckled. "Do you draw? I know you said Devon does."

"My hobbies are working and sleeping," Sylvia said. She poked her tongue in the space where her right molar used to be. Did messing with her teeth count as a hobby? Her dentist said that eventually her teeth would shift away from each other, trying to make up for the hole in their ranks. That was too much for just the dumb movement of the body. If there is space something moves to fill it with no intention to it at all.

"You ever see one of those movies with painters lined up in Paris? They're all outside and people are strolling by. Do you remember?"

"I think I do. I've probably seen one or two"

"I'm going to be one of them."

"You going to wear a beret?" Sylvia chuckled.

"Everybody looks stupid in them, why not me," Marcus said.

"Why not you?" Sylvia said. She sometimes thought that Marcus was in another country. When Sylvia was a girl, if a relative moved a state away you might not see them but once a year. If they moved across the country, you might not see them for years or you might never see them again. Your relationship with your people reduced to a few phone calls, *hurry up, long-distance*! Young people Ava's age and younger wouldn't stand for that. What Sylvia and her generation had accepted as obvious was ridiculous to them. Just get on a plane, get in the car, believe in all kinds of possibilities. But who could believe? Before long too many things weighed you down and left you hoping in nothing farther away than the reach of your hand. Sylvia didn't want that kind of settling for Marcus. He was far too young to have all the doors shut and latched right in front of him.

"I never told anybody that," Marcus said. "You know I've never been anywhere but one time to South Carolina in my life. I've never even been on an airplane."

"You'll get there. People like us go places every day," Sylvia said.

"You start thinking about going. Going anywhere. Tay won't shut up about it. Every single day. I wake up to him begging. I go to sleep to it. Everybody's thinking the same thing.

"He's the one to say it so you know he's messed up." Marcus laughed.

"Can you talk to him?"

"Nobody can," Marcus said.

"You'll be going before you know it. Flying, driving, whatever you want to do."

"Where do you want to go, Sylvia?"

"I don't want to go anywhere. As soon as I got there I'd just want to be home."

"Don't give up, Sylvia. Did you hear that? Did you hear me? Sylvia? Sylvia?"

10

Sylvia opened the back door of her house and the man stood with his back to her in the yard. Some people change dramatically with age. Pictures from their youth look like pictures of another person altogether. Though he was no longer a skinny boy, he looked exactly the same. Sylvia would know him instantly and anywhere. "Look at you."

JJ was startled, like he wasn't sure what was happening, but his face recovered quickly. "Mrs. Sylvia," he said and rushed to her on the patio.

Sylvia held JJ in a loose embrace, patted his back like an acquaintance. "My good god, JJ. You look like you've been gone fifteen minutes, not fifteen years," Sylva said, but as she looked closely at his face she knew he was a grown man. Somehow we can tell the young from old, even if they are slim and stylish not-young. People change as they move into their age. How that happened Sylvia was not sure, but the difference is real, a heaviness, not fat but weight and gravity less visible than girth or flab but no less perceptible. JJ's back was warm, no doubt from standing in the sun. How many days had she imagined him standing in her yard with his back to her ready to turn around like in a melodramatic movie, the span of time blowing away between them, numbers flying off the calendar like leaves in a storm. The thing you want is never the way you think. Sylvia kept her arms open her hands on his shoulders. She did not envelop him or squeeze. She had no muscle memory of holding JJ, or resting her face on the side of his. No memory of touching him at all. She wondered what he thought, what he really thought of her aging face. She must look like an old, old woman to him. She let him go.

"It's all me. Just more of me." He laughed, holding on to his slight belly.

When Ava brought this boy to her house, she thought JJ was Devon sitting on the floor with her daughter. "Mama, this is JJ," Ava had said. JJ had looked up at her, nervous, goofy, and smiling, looking not so very different from how he did at this moment.

"Look at you," Sylvia said, careful not to rest her gaze at his thinning though not yet balding head to his expensive shoes, which had a resemblance to sneakers that had gotten above their raisings.

"Look at me." JJ grinned. "You look good, Mrs. Sylvia."

"I guess I do," Sylvia said and they both laughed. "What are you doing here? Trespassing is what it looks like."

"I didn't mean to be. Can you believe I remembered just how to get here after all this time?"

That wasn't what she wanted to ask JJ, not at all, but they could start there. "What are you doing here?"

"I had to see the house. I had to. Besides I didn't think anybody was home." JJ laughed.

"Does it look the same?"

"Not really. Yeah. Maybe some things." JJ pointed to the edge of her yard. "There's your birdbath." Her homemade crooked little birdbath made from the rocks she collected from the lawn and a bag of quick mix concrete adorned the back corner; the nubby texture had broken only a little and had not fallen apart in hunks as they had all predicted.

"You remember that thing?"

"A thing of beauty is a joy forever."

"I don't know about that. I was crafty back then. I got old. Sit down, sit down."

JJ moved to the table and took a seat. His frame made the chair look small. He sat the way men do, with his legs spread apart, his arms on the rests of the chair, as large in the space as possible. "Last time I sat here, I was still in my twenties. I wasn't even twenty-one yet, I don't think."

"Long time ago, honey," Sylvia said.

JJ was so close Sylvia could smell his strong scented soap. He must have showered just before he came to the house.

"You don't look much different, Mrs. Sylvia, you really don't."

"Well I am. Don't you know anything about how to talk to a woman?"

JJ laughed behind his hand. "You look just the same. That's what I meant to say."

"Did you walk all the way down here?"

"My car is around the corner. I didn't want to block the drive."

Sylvia knew he didn't want to be seen. If she hadn't shown up he probably would never have admitted he was even there.

"Well, since you caught me"—JJ grinned—"I want to invite you to my place." JJ pointed up, like his place hovered in the sky.

"Your big fancy place. What took you so long?"

"I know, I know." JJ looked down like he was embarrassed. "I'm slow. But I wanted you to see it all done first."

"I couldn't get rid of you a long time ago." Sylvia spread her hands across the surface of the glass table, and yellow dandruff of pollen floated around them and away. "You know I'm joking, don't you?"

"I know."

"You heard that Mrs. Graham died?"

"I heard." JJ's face took on the intensity she remembered, his eyebrows crinkled in a concentration and seriousness that worried her years ago but finally fit on the face of this older man. Her son's seriousness scared her too. Barely out of diapers, he'd put his head on her knee, "I'm a bad boy, a bad boy." He'd say it until she'd coo and hold him to stillness. Sylvia had often heard mothers of teenagers long for the early years of their children's lives when their babies' hurts were slight and frivolous, easily forgotten. Devon had never had those days.

"I go by Jay now. I haven't heard JJ in years."

"I hope you know I'll never call you anything but JJ. You know that, don't you?"

JJ laughed. "You don't change do you?"

Sylvia knew that Mrs. Graham wasn't none of his grandmother, that he had only pretended she was. Would they all ever be old enough to speak the truth? It used to be the custom to lie about every unpleasantness. They'd all done it at some point for somebody. The most common one was a generation ago some mother tried to pawn off the new addition in the house as her change-of-life baby. We all saw the fourteen-year-old daughter swelling up like a balloon, but we pretended anyway. JJ had been a foster child whose father had shot his mother to death. The story came out in drips. They say his father was still in the yard, found crying when the police arrived, they say he shot her at such close range she could not be recognized. The girl was sent to live with a great-aunt, so precious little was known about her, but about the quiet boy, there was rampant speculation about what he had seen and heard. We do not know what the children saw. Sylvia had never asked JJ and he never volunteered any information. The most he'd ever said was that his mother was dead. He never mentioned his father to her at all. Before JJ had been in town a year, everybody knew some version of the terrible details.

"That woman never did like me. You know what, Mrs. Sylvia? I'm been trying to forget her for years." JJ smiled at Sylvia. "I'm laughing but I'm not joking."

JJ didn't need to explain. Sylvia never liked Alice Graham one bit. Alice had been a woman drifting alone, little family, few connections to the town. She looked through you when you saw her and wouldn't even pretend to be interested in your life. Civilization runs on people pretending to be interested in your life. What a shock when she popped up one day with a grandson. She had to be the last person in the county you would expect to be taking care of children. A grandson my eye, a grandson my black ass, Sylvia thought. All JJ ever was to the woman was a five-hundred-dollar-a-month check.

"I couldn't get back for her funeral. I thought about it. I really did. I know I owe her something. But I was in the middle of a house flip." JJ hesitated, like he wasn't sure of the story himself. "In California."

"A flip huh? Is that what they call it?"

JJ raised his eyebrows unsure how to respond to Sylvia, the boy coming out in him all over his smooth broad face. "A flip is when you buy a house to sell and fix it up and wish you never started the damn thing in the first place."

"I know what a house flip is. Believe it or not, we have television here." Sylvia hesitated, to see if she'd hurt him, she might need to balm her words to keep them from stinging. She was once the kind of person people told their secrets to. She had a trusting face, she was told. Sylvia thought it was probably because she stayed still enough to listen. JJ was still smiling at her. She smiled back at him. "This is what you've been doing with yourself then?"

"Yeah, mostly."

"Are you working now? Because you won't find anything around here."

"I've got a workshop set up at my house. I make parts for the military and businesses sometimes. When the old machines break, they call me."

"So you're a machinist?" Sylvia pictured JJ as the traveling man in a western, MR. FIX-IT or something like it on a handmade sign hanging from the wagon, soldering pots and pans, farm and kitchen tools, or taking the unsalvageable for scrap, his cart swaying like an elephant's rear, jingling from the metal hitting together as he traveled.

"There's money in that?"

"If you can get contracts there is. I'm doing okay."

"A lot of machinists here are out of work," Sylvia said. "Whole factories of them. You must have noticed all the empty parking lots at the plants on the bypass?"

"I noticed. What are people doing?"

"Being poor, I guess," Sylvia said.

"From what I remember people were always poor."

"Being destitute then. That's all I know," Sylvia said, but she wanted to tell him about the grown men she'd seen in Dooley-town hugging the streets, smoking and hanging, trying to swag-ger their way out of no job, no money, no prospects.

"Are you doing okay, Sylvia? You working?"

"Same place for the past hundred years, but I am this far from retired." Sylvia compassed her fingers in front of her face. "This much from the finish line," Sylvia said. For nearly thirty years Syl-via had been an intake clerk at county social services office. She was the first face the elderly, but mostly young women registering for food stamps or rental assistance or help with the heating bills, saw. Somebody must have decided that a black face would set the right tone for the office. The girls that came in now looked just a few years older than the babies they wheeled in with strollers.

Sylvia nodded like she was accepting everything JJ said. "You've got a big place started up there."

JJ looked up, like he might be able to see the house.

"What are you looking at? You can't see it from here, can you?"

"I thought I just might be able to. I can see this house from my deck. The roof anyway."

"I wouldn't have thought that. This house? For sure?"

JJ nodded, but Sylvia could tell he was not entirely sure. "You know what, Mrs. Sylvia, turns out you don't get over being poor."

"I wouldn't know anything about that," Sylvia said.

"You know what I'm really excited to see? The ice maker. I'm getting an ice maker." JJ rubbed his hands together like a cartoon bank robber.

She loved his face. Something was breaking up, unmooring

in her chest, cracking and moving around like glacial ice. Being useful would settle the movement or at least keep her mind busy. "Let's get something to eat. Ava ought to have something around here. What do you want?" Sylvia knew that Ava wouldn't have much, but she had to let her hands act, keep her brain in gear. On the miserable last day of Uncle Monroe's life he couldn't wait to clean out the drawer in his bathroom. If you had fewer than twenty-four hours to live, would you waste time tossing slivers of soap, rubber bands his dead sister Lula used to trap her gray shoulder-length braids? Would you smooth with the wedge of your hand your kinky hair all of it into the plastic grocery bag you use for a trash liner? If you were dead in twenty-four hours would you clean out a drawer? Why not? Keep those hands moving, keep going. Sylvia understood.

"Nothing for me, Mrs. Sylvia."

"You don't have to call me Mrs. anymore. It makes me feel old." Sylvia opened the cabinet over the dishwasher. There had to be some crackers or something lurking in there. She would bring some tuna and peanut butter tomorrow at least. "I had to tell my friend that I would hang up on him if he called me anything but my name." Only after about a month of phone calls did Marcus start calling her Sylvia. She had secretly liked that he was a nice boy with some home training.

"Did you say your friend?" JJ asked, a sly grin on his face.

"Yes, I did. Can't I have a friend?

"Are you and Mr. Don split up?"

"Split up? That's funny. When do you remember us together?" Sylvia asked. "What are you asking me? Do you mean Marcus?"

"No, ma'am, I was just wondering. You were talking about your new friend. I should just mind my own business. You don't have to say."

"Oh no, honey, he's twenty-five years old."

"Twenty-five! I was wrong, you have changed."

"Lord, don't even say that out loud. He's just a boy I've been talking to on the phone. Nothing like that. He's like a son to me, a friend." Sylvia considered what she'd said. It had been a long time since she'd made a friend. She wasn't sure about the boundaries of it anymore. "Are you crazy? I've got drawers older than him."

JJ put his hands up like he was being arrested. "I don't judge." JJ nodded like he was giving serious advice.

"You better stop." Sylvia laughed. "About time you came down here to see us. We've been waiting for you. Why'd you tease us like that?"

"I wanted to get the house done. I want you to see it."

"Well welcome back anyway. I'm sure there's some good news in this town, but I don't know it." Sylvia laughed. "This isn't my house anymore. This is Ava's house now. Ava and Henry, I should say."

JJ blinked, not sure of what heard. "But I've seen your car." JJ paused, like he'd revealed something he hadn't meant to say.

"I'm here all the time. Too much of the time."

"I never would have come if I'd known. I thought you lived here. Tasha told me you lived here."

"Tasha Jenkins? Where did you see her? At the grocery store? She probably meant I still own it. People always think they know your business. Small town living. You remember all about that don't you?"

"I could have got into trouble," JJ said, but he seemed excited, not afraid of that prospect.

"Come into the kitchen with me, okay? I'm hungry."

"I'm fine. Y'all got any government cheese?" JJ laughed. "You remember that? Some of it was always in Alice Graham's refrigerator. I'd have died without that cheese."

Sylvia shook her head. "I'm not eating that nasty mess."

"Why did they send it in four-by-four blocks? Blast from the past." JJ chuckled. "Just like me. I'm government cheese."

"Yes you are. That's exactly what you are." Sylvia knew JJ was joking of course, but she didn't like the comparison he made with the cheese. He was not unwanted, or just good enough for the hungry poor. She was not the hungry poor. What did the kids say? "Get over yourself." She was trying. Not everything had to hurt.

"I know there's some crackers in here," she said as she searched the cabinets for any snack. She could eat. In fact, she found that she could eat any time. The craziest part was she even liked the weight. The only time she really liked her body in her life was when she was big-pregnant when she knew she looked like she was supposed to and was not unacceptable by mistake. She would never again be as fat as she'd been when she was young, but a few pounds comforted her, made her feel like herself.

"You know I'm going to ask you. You know that right?" Sylvia turned to stare at JJ.

JJ shrugged, like he couldn't imagine what she was about to say.

"You think I don't know why you came back?"

"I came to see you and Ava."

"I know what you came to do. You got grown and you got your little nerve up. Ava's married, JJ."

"I heard. I know Henry. I knew Sean better."

"Sean's in prison. That beautiful boy. All those Bailey boys were beautiful. Nothing good has happened to a one of them, except Henry." Sylvia paused, careful with Jay's feelings. "He should be out or close to out by now."

"How long?"

"Six years."

"Damn. Sorry. What did he do?"

"What do they all do? Drugs. I've said it for years. Whatever you see going on with the very poor is just a few years away for every-body else. People think they outrun it in their little suburbs. You don't outrun nothing for long." Sylvia had moved to Development Drive running from a poor, dirty past. Even then she was grown enough to know she was only buying them all a few years' time.

"Was it crack? Might be meth. There's a lot of that out here in the woods." JJ nodded. Back then in the least valuable neighbor-hoods in town, Jay remembered a line of young men and old boys on Sugar Hill, on the creek and West End, stationed every few yards, waited for you to slow down with your folded bill, no con-versation necessary, a drive-through service for what you needed and in the background, run-down houses with poor people, poor families and old people in dark ugly rooms like the one he'd grown up in. Sean right there hustling with those boys, even then.

"What do you know about prison?"

JJ looked surprised but he wouldn't look directly at Sylvia. "I just know that's a long time to be locked up."

"You get yourself caught up with the police, in the system any-thing can happen to you. You know that don't you?"

"I know."

"I'm telling you right now, you need to not worry about Ava. She's got her mind on other things."

"Is she okay?"

"She's fine, honey." Sylvia put her back to JJ and opened the cabinet behind her, scanned jars of ingredients like edible food or some junk food (please Lord) might suddenly appear. "She's okay, JJ. I don't know what you expect, but she's fine. She's been working at Wells Fargo now. It used to be Wachovia, if you remember that. Anyway, she'd been there since she got out of school. They told her to come see them when she graduated and she did. She's one of the chief loan officers. Can you believe that?" Sylvia had gone into that very same building years before in her best dress, with her pay stubs in her pocketbook, asking for a five-hundred-dollar loan that she didn't get. It felt like a hundred years ago. "She's okay. Nobody has everything they want," Sylvia said.

"She always was smart."

"She is still. At least she thinks so." Sylvia smiled. "You can't tell her nothing, but that's not new."

"Good to know some things are the same then," JJ said.

"You should go by the bank and surprise her. She was just talking about you. We both were. She would be tickled."

"I want to." JJ paused. Sylvia could feel him trying to gather his thoughts. None of this was going to be easy for any of them. "I will soon."

"You should see her when she's working. You wouldn't even know who she is. She's mine and I take a double take when I see her in town. Well, wait until you see her. I can't believe she came from me."

"Is she happy?"

Sylvia wasn't sure what to say. Whatever JJ wanted from her, from the town, from the house he spent the past few months building, was tied up with her child. What he needed from her and what her child needed probably did not connect. It would be a miracle if they did after all this time. Sylvia had not known if she'd ever met a black man who was a romantic. The ones she knew had too much harsh life, too much reality drilled into them from early on. But this man in front of her thought he could star in his own adventure, be the hero in his own story. Sylvia smiled at him, this strange creation.

"What?" JJ said looking around. "What is it?"

Sylvia shook her head. If Sylvia were being honest she wasn't entirely sure she knew the whole truth of how Ava was. She didn't know that much about herself, much less about her child. "She's as happy as anybody."

"How are you, Sylvia, really?"

Sylvia thought she'd never again know happiness. The dead spaces in her now, the ones inured to feeling couldn't connect her to that emotion. Of course she loved, a few people, some days, but never again could she access happy—a diamond ring down the drain she'd had to dismantle the whole works to get at. "I'm all right."

JJ stared into her face with his naked face, his eyes scared to death. "I'm going to be happy, Mrs. Sylvia."

"Honey." Sylvia resisted cupping his face in her hands.

"She has feelings for me."

"There is no way on this earth you can know that. Have you talked to her? You don't even know her anymore."

"I know it was way back." JJ shrugged his shoulders. "Some feelings don't go away. Maybe they aren't supposed to."

"She wants a baby, JJ. She's on to another part of her life. That's all she can handle right now."

JJ nodded like he understood. "I'm not trying to make things difficult. I swear about that."

"I need a drink of something." Sylvia opened the vegetable drawer in the fridge. One lone shriveled lemon rolled in the fruit compartment. She picked up the dry fruit and smelled it.

"Am I driving you that crazy?" JJ said.

"Not that kind of drink. Tea. But I thought of it. Don't think I didn't."

"I'm not just thinking about me, Mrs. Sylvia."

Sylvia rolled the hard wrinkled lemon under her palm. She could already tell the meat would be juiceless and rigid inside.

"How's Mr. Don?"

"Why do you keep asking about him? I don't know. He still looks pretty much the same, which had never been all that good. He's living with a child younger than you. Much younger," Sylvia said. "You know me and Don used to go up Brushy Mountain just driving and looking around. A long time ago. You see I've got one good memory of him. I don't see him much, which is fine with both of us."

Sylvia had not thought about the driving trips in a long time. Don had said that the trips up the mountain made Sylvia sad and when she was sad she got angry, usually with him. She wasn't angry at him; that was too easy. She hated him. The fact that Don didn't understand that most fundamental fact of their relationship was just enough reason for her to lash out and remind him.

"I see you looking at all of Ava's junk," Sylvia said. She imagined the house as JJ must. What was better or worse, fixed or still lacking from the last time he saw it.

"This house feels the same. It really does," JJ said, taking in the wall art and figurines of the small rooms. "You have a lot more decorations than I remember. Who loves owls?"

"You know I've never liked an animal," Sylvia said. She wondered what JJ had expected from the house, bowls of stuck-together candy, a closed-in stale smell of old people and used shoes. "I did try one time to put up some velvet flocked wallpaper. I always did love the way that looked. Ava said it was for old ladies or whorehouses." Sylvia had gone so far as to order a roll of red fleur-de-lis pattern special order from Lowe's. That roll was probably somewhere in the attic in the bottom of a box. "You think you'll work on your house every waking minute. You'll see. Up there is your first house?"

JJ nodded yes.

"Well get as much done now as you can. If you don't get your work done in the first couple of years, it is not going to happen. Believe me on that. I always meant to put a screened porch off the back."

"What happened?"

"What did I just say? Everything starts to look fine to you. Your raggedy old couches and your mess look perfectly reasonable until one day something shakes you up and it doesn't anymore. Nothing looks fine. You see all the nasty paint and scraped-up floors and all the ugly dark little rooms and you walk in the door and say, how the hell was I living like this?" Sylvia laughed. "That's when the renovations start. You've got to make everything new. Before long you wonder why you ever started down that road either."

"I'd never do a renovation. After this build, I'm done," JJ said.

"I thought you flipped houses?"

"Oh, that's different. I've flipped a few houses, but I wouldn't live in them."

"Anyway, my screened porch money went for groceries and lights." Sylvia laughed. "Sometimes you can't talk money into doing what you want."

"Money won't act right for long, that's for sure." JJ looked around the kitchen, like he was waiting to find something he recognized. "I don't see any Barack plates on the wall."

"You know I've got one. I might even have two. In one of them he's smiling and the other one he's looking off in the distance."

"You know where he was looking don't you? The future."

"I know it," Sylvia laughed. "I've got a little apartment near the community college and I don't have a single picture or bric-a-brac or anything up yet. I keep thinking I'll get around to it."

"You're going to get your black woman card revoked if you don't get Barack on the wall."

"You mean my *old* black woman card, don't you?" In the refrigerator tofu in the meat storage looked more disgusting in its gray soup bath than usual. She wouldn't offer that mess to somebody she liked. Other than condiments there was precious little else around. Sylvia found the natural sweetener and held up the bottle. "I can make you some tea with this mess. I've got crackers too. Want some?" She gestured to JJ with the sleeve of saltines.

"No, thanks. But you go ahead."

Sylvia opened the crackers, put one of the stale crumbling squares in her mouth. "I didn't know these went bad. Did you?" She said and kept on chewing.

"He came out of nowhere, didn't he?" JJ said.

"Who? Barack? That's a funny thing for you to say with your disappearing act." Sylvia paused, wiped her mouth of crumbs. "I'm thinking about those plates, do you remember when all the barbershops used to have Kennedy and Martin Luther King Jr. pictures up? Is Barak up there with them now? He should be, I'd figure."

"Some have him up."

"I guess they do. Of course I haven't been in a barbershop since Devon was a little boy. Oscar Michaux probably cut your hair when you were here, didn't he? I think he's still in business. He still has a shop anyway."

"I mostly cut my own. I didn't have the money. That seems to be the punchline of most of life. No money and for my next trick no money. Devon had clippers and I borrowed them a couple of times. He cut it for me one night."

"I don't remember that."

"Well, let's just say it wasn't his best. That what I get for getting my hair cut in the dark. It was pretty late and we came out here so we wouldn't wake you up."

"I can't believe all that was going on with me right here. Do you remember when?"

"No, ma'am. It was pretty late. It might have been summer. I was over here like I always was. We wanted to go into town to get a hamburger but nothing was open and we were afraid we'd run out of gas. I don't think we had two dollars between us. We sat out here for a long time at that picnic table you used to have. There wasn't a floodlight out here back then. I needed my hair cut so Devon did it."

"I didn't even know that and I thought I knew everything that went on here." Sylvia looked at JJ's face to gauge his reaction.

"I'm sure you knew about everything important," JJ said unable to keep the grin off his face.

"What are you grinning about?"

"Nothing, nothing, I just laugh when I get nervous. Though I've got no secrets," JJ said with his hands up.

"Like I believe that." Sylvia poured tea from a glass pitcher and drank it without sweetener. She winced.

"Not good, huh?"

"I keep on forgetting that there's no sugar in anything around here. Don't even think about a Sweet'n Low." Sylvia chuckled to herself. "When I was having my babies you didn't even know you were pregnant until about the baby had cooked for two or three months. The doctor wouldn't even see you until then. Half the women I knew smoked, drank, did what they wanted. Did I ever tell you I smoked?"

"You? I can't even see that."

"I did. When I learned the babies were coming I quit, but I smoked like a choo choo for a few years. Now they tell you no nothing, no sugar, no flour, no plastics. Of course most people I knew had babies at seventeen or eighteen. That makes a difference I'm sure." Sylvia paused. JJ should know that Ava had moved on, had a life with jagged edges, but she had not meant to be the one who told him. "Don't tell Ava I told you that. I don't talk about that to anybody."

"I won't mention it."

"I know you won't, but she will. She'll tell you herself, I feel certain. I really don't tell Ava's business. Not usually." Sylvia laughed.

"Life goes on. I know it has to. But that other life that we already went through, it might come back. Remember that old jam 'Second time around. Do it one more time.'"

"What are you talking about?" Sylvia laughed.

"I don't know myself. All I'm saying is we only know about the past. Why not redo it?" JJ looked about as young as he sounded.

Sylvia laughed. "How did you get optimistic? You're going to redo the past, are you? You went away from here and lost your mind," Sylvia said, but the fact that JJ believed or even pretended to believe in the power of reinvention (in the redo, the most childish of all rules in any game), made her momentarily buoyant. "Well if it happens I want you to let me know." Sylvia said.

"I will. Just wait." JJ grinned at her.

"Where are your babies? You have any?" JJ's life hadn't paused in nearly seventeen years since she'd seen him. He might have nearly grown children, of course he might, big boys and girls looking him dead in the eye when they talked to him. "That's not my business. You don't have to tell me, JJ."

"No kids. I've never been married and no kids. Lucky or unlucky, I guess. Just been me all these years." JJ started to say something but seemed to change his mind.

"No kids. Are you sure?" Sylvia asked.

"I'm sure, Mrs. Sylvia."

"I know you've had plenty of girlfriends. If you're not crazy there's a line of women for any man these days. Even if you are crazy there's a line, tell the truth." Sylvia laughed.

"I don't mean I haven't had friends. But you know what, most of them older than twenty-five."

"You stop that. What if somebody heard you saying some mess like that?" Sylvia pursed her lips, attempted her best disapproving face. She fooled no one. "There's time if that's what you want. You're still young. You know that don't you?"

"Not that young. But that's okay. There's so much time. I believe it," JJ sat up straighter, excited about what he was thinking. "I was nervous time was running out, at least my time, but since I got back here I feel okay. You know what I mean? I feel like I can reboot. Start again, you know?" JJ asked.

Sylvia smiled. She missed this sweet, silly boy. She never believed that a move could shift everything into clear and brilliant focus. But she saw every day poor women that did. In they'd come to Social Services needing help to move town or sometimes even a couple of streets away, searching for that place that fit. Of course they would infect their children with their wanderlust, always looking for the perfect houses, apartments, the town that once and for all ticked all the boxes. She waited for JJ to continue describing his life on the giddy lip of midlife hysteria. Stay on that funny edge as long as you can, she thought.

"I started to think too much has happened in my life. I started to feel it." JJ touched his chest like what he felt was there and he might get it out if he just knew how. "I thought maybe I couldn't get past it. But you know, Mrs. Sylvia, I can."

"Well, you're doing the right thing. Build you a house. Make yourself as happy as you can. Get some things you want. This is it. You realize that, don't you? One go-around. Listen to me, trying to tell you something and my fun for the week is a couple of trips to Food Lion. Don't pay any attention to me."

"You're right, you're right. I'm trying."

"Anyway as soon as I can I'm getting my Barack plate up. Remember they used to say Clinton was the black president? You remember that or are you too young?"

"I remember. I was a kid, but I remember."

"You know, I think the black people around here were more excited when Clinton was in."

"People are going to think you voted for Mitt." JJ grinned, waited for her reaction.

"What would I look like?" Sylvia laughed.

"Romney thought it was about being rich. Nobody cared if he was rich. Hell, we all want money. We love rich people. He just wasn't for real. You know what I mean? Authentic, that's the word."

Sylvia nodded, but she wasn't sure what being an authentic

human being meant or if she'd ever been one. "That's harder than it looks, honey."

"Remember when he was talking to those kids and started saying who let the dogs out? He's never heard that song in his life. You know it. I know it. He's an old rich white man. Just be that. Nothing wrong with it. Unless you don't want to rule the world."

"Look at you. You're still young. Old people don't get excited about nothing. Not one thing. You hear me? You need to trust me on that."

JJ shook his head. "Like what I think matters. He's still a millionaire. I'm still not."

"You must have something. That big house up there didn't just make itself." It had been an unusually dry spring. A house that should have taken several months, as long as a year with contractors' rain delays and juggling job delays, was moving right along, ahead of schedule. A forest became a clearing that became a recognizable structure in no time, like it had been raised up then supported from the back like a picture frame—the house no more substantial than a prop in an old west movie, but there it was.

JJ shrugged. "I've got one house money. One." JJ grinned. "Did you watch the election results?"

"Both times, honey."

"I was in the car when I heard about the first election. I thought about you."

Sylvia swirled the remaining tea in the tall glass.

"I thought about how Barack must be wanting his mother."

Sylvia drained the glass, hoped she hid her face, her emotions too complicated to have to try to explain. "Probably was."

"I wanted my mother and they weren't making me the president." JJ laughed.

"My phone number has been the same." Sylvia tried to sound harsh or at least firm, she sounded sad.

"Not until I could show you something."

A word can bring the heart back to life sputtering and spitting like an almost-drowned man, gasping at life. JJ had thought about her. He had wanted her when he felt proud. Sylvia had not become a known person in her town though she had lived there all her life. She was not connected in the ways so many people she knew found anchors to a town and a community. She had very few family members living. She was not a churchgoer or activist, or interested in local government. She would never receive a key to the town or a commendation for service. When she left her job, the few people who had been there more than a couple of years would get her a cake and gift certificate and never again call or see her on purpose. At times she felt unknown in the world, like she sleepwalked unconnected and alone. To know that she had been important to someone moved her in ways she could not have predicted. Wasn't she easy? Sylvia thought. "I guess we'll see it now."

"I've been a lot of places. More places than I ever thought I'd go. I've lived all over the country for one reason or another, some job or just needing a change."

"I used to want to travel," Sylvia said.

"You did? I wouldn't have thought that Mrs. Sylvia."

"Just because I'm old now doesn't mean I always was," Sylvia said.

"Where did you want to go? Paris? Everybody wants to go to Paris."

Sylvia thought of Marcus with an easel set up at the Seine, a painter's pallete in one hand, his silly beret covering one side of his forehead. "What would I do in France? I really wanted to go to Las Vegas."

"You're kidding?"

"I'm not kidding even a little bit. I don't know why." Sylvia counted her reasons, "Number one, I'm too cheap to gamble. Two, I hate crowds. Three I don't like nasty buffets or sick, crying drunks. I just wanted to see all those lights and those hotels right there in the middle of the desert. Wouldn't that be something? But I let it go."

"You can get there for pretty cheap. They've got all kinds of deals you can get online."

Sylvia smiled. She would never look up any deal online or anywhere else. Her dream to go out there was just a fantasy, and fantasies should stay tucked away in your heart, easy to access for a cheap mental thrill or some put-up-your-feet thoughts, but forever out of reach. JJ was still young.

"I don't blame you if you don't go. It's all the same, Sylvia."

"What's all the same?"

"Everywhere. Some flat, some hills. Big towns, small ones. All the same. But being here matters to me. It's hard to explain. It's about time. I'm just starting out. Most people my age are thinking about how to wind down."

"You might be surprised at what people are doing, JJ. Any kind of pain or crazy I guarantee you there's somebody in this town that is going through the same thing. We figure out a lot of ways to be unhappy. Trust me on that."

"I'm going to stay here and settle down," JJ said.

"This is your home, honey. That means something," Sylvia said.

"Like it or not." JJ laughed.

"Take it by day," Sylvia said softly. "I don't want you to suffer." JJ was feeling more and more deeply about the town than the town deserved in her estimation. "The place is different from the way you left it," Sylvia said.

"You can't go home again, right?" JJ said. "I know, I know."

"Have you seen your sister yet?"

"She's in Columbus, Ohio."

"Have you seen her?"

"Nah," JJ said, and shifted his eyes away from Sylvia. Even without the obvious evasion, Sylvia knew he was lying.

"You going to see her now?"

"I'll talk to her eventually. I remind her of too many bad things."

"That doesn't even make any sense. What do you mean too many bad things? That's ridiculous. You're her brother, her only one."

JJ shrugged. Sylvia knew as sure as she was sitting in her cluttered little kitchen that JJ had seen his sister and had been hurt by her. It would take some doing to get him back there.

Sylvia wanted to ask him what he knew about his sister's life, her children, any of the small group of family that had looked the other way when he lived with an unkind stranger over twenty years ago. She knew as well as anybody not to open that manhole cover. Drop in that hole and you might not find your way out.

"You don't worry. You hear me? You don't let it get to you. We used to say keep on keeping on. That's what you've got to do. She'll come around. She will. One day she'll realize." Sylvia hoped she sounded convincing, but she was not convinced. Some people figured out life much too late to do anyone including themselves any good.

"Now I need a drink," JJ said.

"Listen to me. I have to say this. I know you're here because you think this is home. But you can't go home because there is none. It's just you trying to make it in a place that holds some memory for you. That's not the same as home. People can be like home sometimes and that's if you are very, very lucky. Are you hearing me?"

JJ's face looked like he was concentrating, like he listened to what she said.

JJ smiled, sadly Sylvia thought, like every cold fact of wisdom she'd told him he'd already considered, calculated as true, but decided to ignore, put the whole bet on the ridiculous long shot.

"Don't tell Ava I came by here? Would you do that for me?"

"I'll let you tell her. Tell her yourself."

"I didn't mean for you to know, but you caught me." JJ pointed his finger at her.

"Listen, JJ, all that mess you went through when you were coming up, and, me too, I'm not leaving myself out." Sylvia shook her head, trying to coax out the right words. "You try to forget, but you don't. You never do. This place might be paradise for some people, but it never was for me and it never was for you. Maybe it can be. I hope so. But, honey"—Sylvia leaned in closer to JJ, she wanted him to see her, to really see whatever it was that registered as serious and meaningful on a face—"I don't want you to count on it. Make sure you aren't counting on it."

"I've seen a lot out there. I'm not a kid anymore," JJ said.

"I know. I know you're a grown man. But you have to know that every child in the world is trying to get away from a dead-end town. Just like this one. Where are they all going to, baby? When they've had enough they go back to the town they left. That's not the same as coming home."

"I know." JJ smiled though there was no happiness on his face. "But I've got nowhere else. This is it, Mrs. Sylvia." JJ shrugged his shoulders, opened his hands.

Sylvia understood all about the last stop on the line, the inevitability that only appeared to be a choice. She nodded. "When do we see the house, honey?"

11

Mommies2B.com

Hello. I'm Ava, I'm new to this site. It's nice to know you are out there. I won't go through all the details of the journey. A lot of it is familiar to you I can tell by your posts. I'm so glad to find you all. I have never posted anything (not even a review of a dress LOL). I don't know where else to go. I can't tell anybody else. I feel like I'm talking to myself or talking to God. Do you feel like that? Okay, here we go. The newest thing: I am well past my two week wait—2 WW. It has been almost four weeks since ovulation, no period! But I'm scared to death to find out. I ovulate on day 17 through 20 (I know! Way late!) and now I'm waiting. Again!

I haven't been on birth control for about nine years. But my first pregnancy was only about six years ago. Followed in three weeks by my first miscarriage. My second miscarriage was eight months ago, the last one was almost five months ago. I have never had a successful pregnancy. NO BABIES. I'm scared. I have had Intrauternine inseminations (IUI) several times, way too many drugs. The doctors don't know what the deal is. He's been checked out too, by the way. I had IVF once, but I can't really afford it again. I will have to get another mortgage on my house and I don't have enough equity. That's all the ready money I've got. I think this is my last shot. It feels funny to even write that. Wish me luck. Who would have thought after years of trying not to get "knocked up," I'd be worrying like this. LOL

Anyway, I don't have any major symptoms. Did anybody else get a BFP—BIG FAT POSITIVE (don't you love this language? ☺) without symptoms? My natural pregnancies came on like tsunamis. I guess this is natural too. Assisted is the word, right? I did have one little moment three days after the hormone injection. Six sharp pains in my ovary or at least in that direction. Six of them like little chicken pecks. But nothing since then. PRAY FOR ME. Any information you have will be appreciated. I will pray for you all. Ava2WW

Ava picked up the laptop and moved it from the counter to her kitchen table. She never thought she'd post to one of those sites, telling her business to a bunch of sad strangers. She could talk to Jenny, the youngish white woman at work who had made several overtures of friendship to her. They had gone out for coffee a few times and walked together through town at lunch in their dresses and tennis shoes. They had even gone out to dinner and once to a movie. But Jenny was gossipy and needy, too eager to latch onto someone, anyone, and it didn't seem to matter who. A couple of times Ava gave in and decided that they would be friends. Why not? Both of them could hold the other as a place-holder until the real friend came along. Wasn't that better than nothing? Apparently not. Ava just couldn't stand her. Did people, grown people spend time with folks they couldn't stand? Sylvia never had, but Sylvia was mostly alone. Not on purpose (but who ever does it on purpose?), Ava had ended up with a life like her mother's. But she could change, couldn't she? Just writing the one web message had made Ava feel oddly hopeful, like she waited for the arrival of a friend. Ava could change.

Jenny recommended a Chinese herbalist in Raleigh who had helped Jenny's hairdresser's daughter with acupuncture and herbs. The daughter had gotten pregnant right away. Ava couldn't count how many stories she had heard just like that one. Some woman was struggling with infertility and click, the right switch got turned on from an unlikely source. Ava knew it was pathetic to believe every story. But you get in too deep, you start to fig-ure what the hell? Why not? What could it hurt? You start to see logic in every dumb idea you heard. One weekend Ava pretended she had a work retreat and drove to Raleigh to visit the herbalist. Turned out the man worked out of an inside booth at the flea market.at the State Fairgrounds. The herbalist watched her walk in, sized her up, looked over her body with not a shred of sexual interest, and then asked her age. When she told him, he'd stared at her like she was crazy, sighed audibly with scornful resignation. "You too old," he'd said and shook his head. Ava had been so frustrated she felt like crying. The man reached behind his counter and gave her some tea leaves in a mesh sack that she was supposed to brew and drink every morning before she ate. Ava boiled water for the tea one morning, but didn't drink it. Whatever was in the mix might work against the drugs she already took. She'd later flushed the sack down the toilet.

She backspaced over the PRAY FOR ME. That sounded wrong. She'd never asked anybody to pray for her in her life. She then backspaced over the *I will pray for you*. She reread the post and retyped *I will pray for you*. She would pray. In her way she prayed all the time. Ava pushed send and closed the laptop. The women on the site would answer. That she was sure of, since she'd spent entire evenings reading their posts. So many stories just like hers. Some worse. Ava was glad she could reveal herself without shame online. If you had a secret in the old days, your family held your story in the vaults of their hearts until you died or until they did. The weight of the shame, the sorrow, the terror stuck and dragged down a body in the world. But you could survive, if the particulars did not emerge or emerge completely, if the family could be discreet. Ava had never heard of a discreet family.

Ava's great-aunt Lula, dead for at least thirty years, had not married or had children and had lived in her mother's house and then her sister's house until she died. Whatever had made her stay out of the commerce of ordinary life was a mystery that Ava did not know and had never attempted to find out. Maybe she was content or maybe they all wanted to avoid the inconvenience of her pain. What would Aunt Lula have written online to her secret best friends?

Ava closed the computer and put some clothes in to wash in the basement. In the morning she would have to remember to put them in the dryer or she'd come back (not for the first time) to them half dry and mildewed, her attempt at industry having backfired and giving her more work to do. When they'd first moved into the house she was a kid and afraid to go to the basement alone. She still didn't love this dimly lit, dirty part of the house, with so many hidden nooks, but it interested her. No wonder they made horror movies about damp basements where the disgraced items of everyday life moldered, not in the bowels, though she could see that metaphor easily, but in the ovaries waiting to reemerge damp and changed. Would anyone but an infertile woman think that? She laughed out loud. She could still laugh about it. Now that had to be progress, right?

She came back up the stairs to the kitchen and clicked back onto the site.

Dear Ava2WW, My first and second IUI didn't work either, but hang in there. My third gave me little Jon, I've attached his picture. He's three now. It can happen! Don't give up. Some of us need a little help. Hang in there! Baby Luv Jon

---

Hello Ava2WW. I've been where you are. My angels came close together, four of them. I know what you feel, even if I can't put it in words. Sucky club, right? You didn't say how old you are. I'm 43 and have been TTC (that's trying to conceive) for about eleven years give or take. If you have to stay with us, you will learn the lingo, that's for sure. I've been TTC for a good part of my adult life. SUUUUUCCCCKKKKSSSSS! I've tried it all: injectables, Clomid, progesterone, IVF (five times!—they won't do it anymore for me) IUI too many times to count. You name it, I know it. Sorry, I don't mean to be a wet blanket. Maybe God will give you your bundle of love. He's stingy with them though. Just kidding. Don't mean to rain on your parade. MOM 2 B

Thanks for the encouragement everyone. I know how you feel MOM 2 B, believe me. I AM SO TIRED OF HEARING PEOPLE'S SUCCESS STORIES! LOL. They don't help me. I'm a terrible person. I feel like one. Somebody at work actually said to me that I should be glad I can at least get pregnant. Can you believe that? Like getting pregnant is the goal. She has two kids and thinks infertility is all in your head. I am trying hard not to hate those people. If somebody else tells me to relax I'm going to start screaming. That will prove I'm relaxed, right! Has it ever helped anybody in any situation to hear that! Enough ranting. LOL! My ears won't pop. Is that crazy? I've been to the bathroom a hundred times today. The gas. Impressive, but EMBARRASSING. Is this in my head? ☺ Hormones? I made the appointment for a blood test. If I can wait that long. I have a whole bathroom vanity full of pregnancy tests. I cannot even tell you how many freakin pregnancy tests I've bought! Gotta laugh so I won't cry ☺ I do have a practical question. I was on Gonal-f with the trigger shot and progesterone after. I hate it! I am thick-headed and stupid and so fat. Thank god I'm usually trim or I'd be completely round. My face is even fat. I stopped counting the chins! Does anyone have any good experience with this combo? AVA2WW

My third pregnancy was on GF and the works. I got pregnant but my little one wasn't in me long enough to feel her move. I always thought she was a girl, though it was all over too early to really know. Your fate might be better than mine, Ava! Look at what you ate Ava2WW. That's what's causing the gas. YOU CANNOT HAVE SYMPTOMS THIS EARLY. I don't mean to be mean, but any weird thing you are feeling is just because you are in tune with your body and noticing everything. Please don't go off the deep end. We are all enabling each other in our crazy. I want this as much as anyone, but it is not good to fool ourselves, is it? Can anyone hear me? Am I talking to myself? MOM 2 B

Dear MOM 2 B, Please try to be positive. This site is for us to encourage each other. We are all hurting. Can you understand that? I'm trying to conceive another bundle. Any tips would be appreciated. BellasMOM

After 8 months of drugs I now have one, count them one mature follicle and a late one at that, that doesn't get around to producing until day 19 of my cycle. My husband is tired. "We are enough" he says, but I see the way he looks at me. I can read his face. I've known him fifteen years. Worse than that I see the way he looks at other families, a sick little turn on his mouth like he just learned he got a raw deal. He's probably the problem. I've wondered a hundred times if my body just doesn't like his body. You know? What if we had different partners? He said the last time he had to go to the clinic, "I'm bringing my own porn next time. No more German dominatrix." Maybe I'll get him Jugs for Christmas. HA HA.

My estrogen is good. I should be thankful for small things. But everyone, including BellasMOM, just because I'm for real doesn't mean I'm not positive. MOM 2 B

Ava2WW, Good luck. I don't have experience on Gonal-f, but I did other drugs. It took me over five years to get pregnant. I lost the first one, but I did get pregnant a year later. It can work. I know how you feel. I just kept thinking that the whole thing was kind of a combination lock and I just had to have the right numbers. That sweet baby you wish for might just be nine months away. This might be just the combination you need. Baby dust to you. Baby Luv Jon

---

Everyone, When did we all just become somebody's mom? I'm as guilty as anyone. I might be the worst, but this is a legitimate question. When did we just become mommy? Didn't we fight a revolution to have names? Baby dust!! Are you people for real? MOM 2 B

Everyone, PLEASE IGNORE MOM 2 B!!!!!!! They should do a better job of getting people like her off this site. BellasMOM

I was just frustrated. I forgot to say good luck. I forgot to wish baby dust. I forgot to tell you all that God loves you and is making your baby right now. Face it, kids, you are your Barrenesses. This is your kingdom. All those symptoms are a joke, Ava 2WW. Did you eat Mexican last night? Bingo, you have your answer. You are not having any symptoms yet. Your maybe-baby is the size of a pin dot. You can't have symptoms for God's sake. You want to hug a sweet baby with warm milky breath on your neck? Get a cocker spaniel, they're a sure thing. MOM 2 B

MOM 2 B, GET OFF THIS SITE. PEOPLE LIKE YOU MAKE EVERYTHING HARDER. BellasMOM

MOM 2 B, SEE A SHRINK, LADY. YOU NEED HELP! Baby Luv Jon

I'm sorry, sorry, sorry. Everyone, I've been in a state lately. I need your forgiveness. I need to belong to this community. Twelve-year-old girls with no future, or forty-six-year-old menopause women wind up with babies in their arms. They don't even try. They win and they don't even try. I can't stand it. Will someone explain that to me? MOM 2 B

Dear Ava2WW, Try to stay positive. You have a big day coming. BellasMOM

Ava2WW, Here's hoping for that BFP. Fingers and toes crossed. Baby Luv Jon

---

Is anyone listening? Can anyone hear me? Don't drive yourself crazy. You will go insane looking at every little thing, wishing for a sign. Please listen. MOM 2 B

Women have symptoms all the time. Medical science doesn't know everything. Stay strong Ava2WW!!!!!! BellasMOM

Ava closed the laptop. She wouldn't read any more tonight but wanted a diversion that wasn't reality TV or game shows from thirty years ago, which depressed and demoralized her. The house was quiet with Henry gone and her mother in her own apartment. Henry said he would be at his father's, but Ava wasn't sure how much she believed him. She believed in her father-in-law's need and in the chaos of his house, the filthy rooms he maneuvered poorly in with his pitiful walker, his pill bottles lined up on the television table like an audience. He and Henry were the only ones left from their immediate family, except for Sean, and he was in jail. What Ava doubted was that Henry spent more than a few minutes in the cave of that depressing house with a man he hardly knew. He was escaping from her plain and simple.

A sensation, an ache bubbled up in Ava's stomach and into her chest to finally pop in her mouth. Henry had another woman. Flashes of him close to her, his hand on her hip, the liquid movements of his torso inching toward the woman's chest. Ava could see it plain. The woman she did not know. Henry had little game, but he didn't need any. So many women saw him and figured they'd make up whatever lack he had, get back with the Lord later, or not. How many of them had made this calculation, Ava couldn't be sure. Henry wouldn't give her the number. Ava suspected that he wasn't sure himself. There are secrets in a relationship that probably should remain secret. Little lies of omission, artful (or not) evasions that reminded you that you woke up with a stranger, even if you think you know him down to the bone. Every once in a while you get reminded how truly impossible it is to know another person, even if you love that person, even if you live with him for years, for decades. The paradox of love was how you manage to feel it with so little information. But you negotiate in this life for the best deal you can get. When Ava and Henry first married Ava had convinced herself that she was happy. Henry's remoteness, his moods were in stark relief when only the two of them maneuvered together in their first apartment. Ava said nothing to anyone, though her mother and her aunt were not fooled. She thought for years she could deal. That's the key to marriage. Learn to deal. Play the game right and you might even end up reasonably happy. And, good news, if you can manage the machinations and intrigue of a functional marriage you have all the tools you need to rule the world.

Ava willed the thoughts of Henry with another woman away as she had become accustomed to doing in the past few years. She didn't have time to think about what Henry did. The past few years had been hard on both of them. That alone should have produced some compassion in Ava for Henry, for his hurt and frustration about what had happened to them. The fact that she felt nothing for Henry's pain surprised and shamed her.

She would try to sleep. She turned off the light at the bedside table and closed her eyes. Sleep, sleep. Go to sleep, she hummed to herself. But she wouldn't be sleeping anytime soon. When she was a child she loved listening to the women her mother knew, relatives or women from one of the churches her mother tried. Most of them were very young like her mother, in their twenties and thirties, black women who had had enough hard life already and said another baby meant a tether to the meanness of too little. The women talked in kitchens, shabby living rooms, public parks and backyards, and plotted about how to avoid the pregnancy, how to end it (with a potion or an accident that was sure-fire), and if all else failed finally how to endure it. This talk was not about their children—they were another issue altogether.

The idea of their children was divorced in their minds from the pregnancies. Maybe you have to be there, to live there, to struggle there to understand it. But most of them loved their children or at least tried to. Ava remembered them speaking in code to keep their intentions from the kids playing in their midst. Ava was convinced that children were a burden, a worry, the last nail in the coffin. Like her grandmother Mabe said enough times, "Children ruin your life."

She reached for the laptop in the dark.

I AM GOING CRAZY, everyone. When I was in high school and college just about everybody I knew had a pregnancy scare. I felt so smart and superior because I never had to go through all of that. I didn't have sex in high school and only a few times in my college. I thought I had it all figured out. Did you all have pregnancy scares back in the day? I never did. Not even one time. Not ever. Not even when I got married and not as careful as I could have been. I thought because I was a good girl or just careful or lucky, but now I think I might have been INFERTILE. I haven't even been able to think like this until lately. Maybe what I thought was luck back then was a curse I'm feeling now. Has anyone else felt like that? Ava2WW

I had a scare or two, but that doesn't matter. You didn't really have a sex life just a few experiences and you were just careful back then. That's all! We are all learning that this whole baby making thing is a lot harder than we thought it was going to be. So many things have to go right. Who knew? I used to think that I could get pregnant anytime. This is embarrassing, but I didn't really know about ovulation. I really didn't. I soon found out that a lot of women don't know. I told my mother I missed my ovulation window when I was trying the first time and she said try again in a few days. In a few days! She didn't know about ovulation and she has four girls. I don't know how anyone ever gets pregnant with so little information. LOL! Now that we know better, we just have to adjust. You are going to get pregnant and have your baby. YOU HAVE TO BELIEVE THAT. You have to be strong. Your little one needs you to be strong. Don't give up, honey. I know you hurt. BellasMom

---

Oh, Ava I cried when I read your post. We have all been there. Try not to worry. Babies come when they get ready. I don't mean to sound magical, but I think our bodies have to be ready. There's so much we don't really understand. Don't keep your feelings to yourself. Keep writing us. We will help. We are the only ones who really know how you feel. Baby Luv Jon

12

Sylvia picked up the phone and put it back down again on the kitchen table. He would want to know about JJ. He would want to talk about that.

"Devon," she said, but the line was quiet on the other side.

"Can you hear me, Devon? Are you there?" Sylvia put the phone back on her chest. He was not going to speak.

"Mama."

Sylvia fumbled the phone, getting it to her ear. "Devon, Devon. Thank God. Can you talk right now? Can you talk to me?"

"I need to go, Mama."

"I hear your voice all the time. In my dreams. Everywhere I go. I saw a boy who looked like you in the office the other day. He was with his girlfriend and baby. He was so tall and straight-standing, so handsome. I told him I was sorry to stare but he looked so much like you. That's what I told a stranger."

The line ticked on the other end. Sylvia couldn't even hear him breathe.

"Don't call me, Mama."

"I know, I know. But I knew you'd want to know that JJ is here. Back in town. I know you remember JJ. Ava's friend? He told me you cut his hair. I didn't know that. You don't want to hear this, I know. I'm getting off the phone. But he's back. After all this time. Can you believe it?"

The line was quiet, but if he would let her, she could listen as long as she could to the steady rhythm of his breathing. "I know you can't forgive me. I don't deserve your forgiveness. I'm sorry. I tried not to call you, but I thought you'd want to hear it. I know you have to go. I know, but Devon, don't go. One minute. You don't have to say anything. Please one more minute."

13

A year ago maybe more, Don started going to a neighborhood restaurant called Sisters, a man's place—spare and dirty—run by Mae and Jonnie Norwood. The name sounded good, but Mae and Jonnie were actually mother and daughter, separated by fifteen years. Sisters wasn't a fine dining place, just somebody's converted living room of an old house on Damascus Church Road, with three lightweight dirty tables and chairs bought for a couple of dollars from the recently closed up Chinese place called House of Chow. Mae and Jonnie covered the uncleanable table-tops with plastic cloths, set salt and pepper shakers and hot sauce in the middle of each like a bouquet. At first Mae kept napkins on the tables, but customers would use them like they were the last paper products on earth. Take five when the corner of one would have done fine. Use them to wipe fingers, noses, the tips of shoes, eyes, clean underarms, and save for panty liners. When they were sitting out like that, who wouldn't assume that there was always more? Sisters wasn't decorated except for a yard sale clock, but neither woman cared too much for fussing over things, creating some kind of room with the books just so, the pillows fluffed, no shoes or spilled toys to spoil the scene, neither cared for the fantasy decorating encouraged. Besides, Sisters was not the establishment to go to if you were looking for scenery, garnishes, or flourishes to please the eye, food piled in artful stacks, or for watching fancy people. The mission at Sisters is to get all you want to eat and go home full. That's enough entertainment for anybody.

Mae was good-looking for a woman her age. That's what people always added, a woman her age. She was skinny but carried herself like a big woman with her arms out to her sides like parenthesis, always straightening her top over her hips like she had something to hide, smoothing her clothes from the creases her imaginary rolls of fat made, habits probably picked up from years of watching her large mother negotiate the world. Mae would have been pretty except for her black-rimmed lips, which she tried to hide except when a big laugh made her forget. When she was a little younger the rumor was she'd open her legs for anybody, though like most things, it wasn't all the way true. She'd been fooled a few times, standing and lying down, small and lonesome because somebody said on Saturday night that he'd be around on Monday, but who hasn't felt some of that?

Don thought if he had been looking for a woman at all his first glance would have lighted on Mae. He wasn't looking. He was never really looking, but somehow he had no trouble finding women. To analyze the way of a cheater is a losing game. They just do. They just will. Only death or the smell of it will stop them.

Many people aren't loved enough, have lousy parents, have too much responsibility, blah, blah. But most of those unfortunate people aren't whores who will take anybody they please to bed. Don was not most people. The generous way to think about it was that beauty moved Don, spoke to him, coerced him to set aside what he might believe was good sense, right actions, the proper way. That beautiful face or body or (Lord have mercy) both reasoned to him that this time his body next to her body didn't really count. Like candy bars in the middle of the night, like sex in prison. If nobody sees and if you don't care, how can it count?

Mae was the one close to his age, and besides that he'd known her all his life. At one time that familiarity would have repelled him, but the unknown and exotic had just about lost its appeal. Don even liked the weave that stretched Mae's neat little Afro to silky black hair beyond Mae's shoulders. Hair everybody in town knew had recently belonged to some Korean woman. Hair that everyone knew stood in for the hair Mae pulled out herself the second she discovered her beloved mother would never wake up from her last dream. At the funeral Mae didn't even bother to hide the bald patch but let the world see on her own body a piece of what had happened to her heart. At the end of the service, as she tried to pass by the coffin the pallbearers set up at the door, Mae saw her lying like she had all the time in the world, patiently, like she never was in her real life, and Mae couldn't stop screaming, for minutes that seemed like hours that had everyone teary in the middle of their own private losses. Reverend Johnson, Mae's own daughter, her longtime boyfriend, everybody tried to console her, but she knew that the luster had flaked away from her life, like leaded paint. People felt sorry, but they talked: *she didn't need to do all that* and *she should have got hold of herself, for the children,* but Don admired her for it. When else do you get to rail and plead with God, beg him for a last chance, another day? When his time came, Don used to want none of that uncivilized mess, but the idea that somebody, anybody would say NO! made him less afraid.

Though Don wasn't searching for a woman, one found him. "What you need, Mr. Don?" Jonnie said to him. "You had all you want, Mr. Don?" Just like that every time he stepped foot in the tiny restaurant, until she finally dropped the mister altogether. Don knew what Jonnie was doing, feeling out her power, seeing if she could make an old man light up just because she wanted him to.

Friday was fried fish day, good croakers with crisp cornmeal overcoats on their itty-bitty bodies and black rubbery skin. Mae and Jonnie sold sandwiches every Friday, and the line ran out the door and into the yard. Men and women, but mostly men, crunching and spitting little bones all up and down the pitted road. Don was eating at Sisters like usual, standing in the yard when the Martin sisters, real sisters, less than a year apart, started to sing two-part harmony, "His eye is on the sparrow, I know he watches me." Generations of Martins sang in churches, soul bands, and then back to churches, but how unusual for them to break into song just like that. Don loved the combination of their high rich voices, their almost identical faces, and their sweet bow-lipped mouths opening at the same time. He had nothing against the Martins. Not really. James had spent too much time with Sylvia. Don was almost grateful to James for being Sylvia's friend, for loving her in ways Don didn't know how to. He pretended he knew nothing about Sylvia and James's relationship, if you want to call it that. He wouldn't give Sylvia the gift of revenge. He wasn't a saint.

Don listened while he ate the hot sauce-soaked white bread with the greasy fishy taste of the fresh catch. Jonnie told him later how she watched his face that day. How sad and unloved he seemed, she said. If Don's face looked sad, he couldn't help it. Don wanted to tell her that people take the insides of themselves, put it on someone else's face, but it wouldn't do any good to tell her that. There are things you learn from words and gestures, the sad human mistakes of others, and there are things you can only get through the bitter taste on your own smooth tongue. "What were you thinking," she asked him later. "Nothing," he said, which was true, but she believed that she and Don had shared their first secret moment.

Later that same day, Don took Jonnie to his home, a tiny rented trailer in the back of Sammie Park's yard. They were both shy. Don had been with girls since he was fourteen and women not long after that. He knew sex wasn't what you think. Women are all afraid they'll look bad, have people laughing and shaking their heads because they put themselves on the line, body and all, to believe in something. The idea that they might get ill-used made them crazy. Even a mild woman will break every dish in the house if she whiffs betrayal. Don had seen it too many times. But Jonnie didn't want to know any better than to believe.

Jonnie sat cross-legged on Don's ancient couch. Don thought she looked like a spider with all those spindly arms and legs, in her tiny T-shirt, shorts creeping up her high tail. He felt dirty looking at her slight body and tried to watch her mouth, concentrate on what she was saying. But Don couldn't shake that Jonnie looked like a child. He'd never hurt a child, a fact even his wife, who mostly hated him, wouldn't deny. Did people see him with Jonnie and think he was leeching the life out of her? He was just another old man hooked up with a young woman foolish enough or low enough to say yes?

"How old are you?" Don said with as much tenderness as he could, but he realized he sounded harsh.

Jonnie laughed, but she sensed that inside this innocuous question was a test she couldn't pass. "Old enough." She said, trying to sound playful, but ending up sounding like a pouty child.

Don wasn't sure what he wanted to hear or what age would stop the magic, fix the image so they had to stop exactly where they were. There was nothing wrong with sitting with a young woman, even a beautiful one, even one he desired. Nothing in the world had happened that couldn't be backed down from, explained away as a moment of silly weakness. "No, baby, how old?"

Jonnie hesitated, played at cleaning her fingernails. "Twenty-four if you need to know."

Don thought of Devon and what a nice match this girl would have been for him. He imagined Devon bringing her home. He imagined himself jealous and maybe proud of that beautiful body his son would roll over to every night. Devon and Jonnie in this very room, Devon's hand on her warm brown belly. Jonnie smiling at him with all her teeth. Good God this girl was too young for his son. The thought almost made Don shudder. "Go on home."

Jonnie laughed but looked scared. Don was a grown man with grown children and she had the power to frighten him. Love is tenacious, the crabgrass of emotions, it will grow anywhere, hold on in the smallest crack of desire. Even Jonnie knew that, but she wanted Don to be full up with her, consume his thinking, his desires, so much so that he couldn't remember to be wary and sad.

Jonnie rolled the T-shirt up and over her head, slowly tried not to think about a striptease, tried to forget about her body being nearly flat everywhere except for an inexplicable roll of fat below her bra. She stood to wriggle out of her tiny shorts, tried not to notice that Don had modestly turned his head. Jonnie wanted to show Don that she was confident, not somebody's piss-ass child at all, but she wished she had hips to show him, big legs and a full backside, a body that would make him sure about anything.

"Want to see my birthmark?" Jonnie turned her leg, her inner thigh pointed in Don's direction, to a dark amoeba-shaped mark the size of a silver dollar that looked like a splat of used chewing tobacco or spilled acid on her otherwise slick amber skin.

"Ugly, ain't it?" Don said.

Jonnie looked around for her shoes. Don laughed, but he wasn't sure what to do. He never meant to hurt her feelings. Young women often don't know when a thing is hurtful or just laughably true, nothing to be done about it.

"It is ugly but you're not supposed to say that." Jonnie smiled. She slid her feet into run-over sneakers and turned the corner to the kitchen.

Jonnie's behind eased out of her high-leg underwear as she walked. She pulled the elastic leg hole from one of her cheeks, like she and Don had known each other all their lives. "You want a drink," she calls, her head hanging out of the refrigerator.

"No, baby," he said. The common domestic gesture, Jonnie's eager face questioning, eased his mind some. "Yeah, bring me one."

She seemed to be staying.

But like most things, Jonnie didn't just change Don's everything all at once. She came into his life and his trailer not in a whirlwind but by degrees. Every day bringing clothes, a lamp, shabby cotton curtains to replace the blue velvet dust catchers in the living room and other small items and knickknacks to mark the place as hers. Don was embarrassed that he didn't have any of the trappings of a real home, that all of his furniture in the trailer put together wasn't worth the effort to throw it out. Jonnie didn't seem to notice, or if she did, she didn't care a great deal. Don knew he was being unkind, but he thought worse of Jonnie for that acceptance, for being so young and not wanting more.

After a few days, she brought her little girl to visit, Sasha, a sweet little thing with curly hair the color of sand. Don had seen Sasha before at the restaurant, but she always stayed close to her grandmother and never let Mae get more than an arm's reach from her sight. If Jonnie came to stay for good, Don wasn't sure where Sasha would end up. You'd have to kill Mae to get that little girl away from her, and Don had no desire to fight. Jonnie might. You never knew what a mother would do to keep her child. Don didn't want to think about how Jonnie would react if it came to all that. If Don were being honest, he'd tell Jonnie that he didn't want the girl. His babies were all grown and it had been a long time since he'd had to talk to children, entertain them, or pretend to be interested in their tiny triumphs. Now he wasn't sure how much he could fake.

But that wasn't it. Don knew he shouldn't blame Sasha but couldn't quite get over that her daddy was a white man from the Love Valley Church Jonnie belonged to for a short time. The child couldn't help who her daddy was, Don knew that. She had no say at all over who brought her into the world. But every time he looked at her soft hazel eyes he felt something close to betrayal, a sickly uneasiness that went with anything associated with white people.

It didn't help that Jonnie met the man at an Eternal Enlighted

Masters meeting. That's what they called themselves. Don, of course, called them other things. A whole group of them lived together not in one house, but by spells. Two of them, then three, then switch up. Every week they'd met in the leader's basement and talked and shared food. Jonnie missed the talking with people who seemed to be interested in her life problems and her daily struggles to be good. Religion shouldn't smell musty, Don told her again and again about her basement church. But she missed it. Especially the dancing. Everyone in the flock was taught to waltz. Dancing is what brought Sasha's father into Jonnie's arms, and his smooth flowing rhythm, his careful way of finessing her into turns, his small, dainty little dips. The day he found out that Jonnie was pregnant, he waltzed out of that basement, out of the county, and by the time Jonnie heard tell of him, she couldn't really remember anything but the dancing that she liked about him. Turns out there's not that much enlightenment in the world. But even that love gone wrong wasn't enough to totally sour Jonnie on the Eternal Masters. She loved the idea of good country people, black and white, mostly white, in their bare feet, spinning on someone's old shag carpet like members of the royal family.

Jonnie even taught Don to waltz. He didn't want to at first and briefly considered letting that be the first time that he told Jonnie no, but he finally decided to wait until he had something more important to protest. As it turned out, he liked it. He thought about loving it but wouldn't commit to loving a new thing, not at this late date, but he couldn't deny that the oompah-pah music, the swishing across the floor, holding a woman lightly but with precision like holding a tool, took him out of his head like nothing he'd done in a long time.

Don had to get up early to get Jonnie to the restaurant. Mae and Jonnie had hours of preparation work to do to get the lunches and dinners carryout ready.

"You coming by for dinner?"

"I'll be by to pick you up, but I'm not sure about dinner."

"Be here by seven, okay? I'll miss you."

Don gripped the steering wheel tighter, hoping Jonnie wouldn't notice. "I'll be here, baby." Jonnie got out of the car, wiggle-walked for Don's benefit on the concrete path to the restaurant. She turned to make sure that he saw her performance. Don hadn't moved but watched Jonnie play her game. Framed by the picnic tables on one side, the thick yellow grass on the other, and on both sides low-reaching poplar branches' spring green leaves highlighting Jonnie in the center, her chin just over her bare shoulder, her face expectant and bright. "I'm a lucky man," Don yelled. But even as he said it, he realized that this was the first time he was telling Jonnie what he knew she wanted to hear.

After work Don waited just as Jay had the day before on Sylvia's patio. She might stay in that apartment to get her clothes and to sleep, but Don knew if she could, she'd be messing around in her own yard. He wouldn't have to wait long. Don took a seat at the table and closed his eyes. He didn't want to see any more of Sylvia's industry, her flowerbeds cleaned and neat, already prepared for summer growth. Sylvia never kept a neat house, but her yard was another story altogether.

Used to be when Sylvia and Don lived together at the trailer in Millers Creek, she'd had little pots, terra-cotta, plastic ones, pots all over the place that she'd bought at garage sales and thrift stores, all full of tiny little seedlings bursting out of the red clay soil she'd scraped up from the yard. This tacky mess grown on a few dimes would in the summer become Sylvia's lush garden with great masses of old-fashioned color in a jungle all over: bleeding heart, sweet peas, purple coneflower, coreopsis, even some showy annuals as long as she could grow them from seed. When they were very poor and not just ordinary poor, years ago, Sylvia would find birdseed and plant giant sunflowers around their trailer. Don loved their great brown faces and, though he never told her, thought Sylvia a little magical for willing them into being. Don searched the pots for the Magic Marker shorthand only Sylvia understood. He liked her simple printing, a man's way of writing, bold and unadorned.

A few years ago Sylvia wouldn't speak to him at all. She peeled potatoes at the sink. Water steaming hot as she stroked a brush across the speckled potato bodies. The water sang into the silver sink, making Don content to be with her. Sylvia looked to have forgotten he was there and concentrated on the sweet-looking potatoes, not soft or mealy-looking, but plump just the size to fit nicely in a fist. Don arranged the junk in his pockets, gum, receipts, a cigarette stub he'd fished out of Sylvia's garden.

"You gonna wash them all day," he said not particularly hateful, but he could tell that he took Sylvia's moment and ruined it. Before she had time to really think about it, Sylvia threw the knife into Don's leg, propped on the chair in front of him.

"Sylvia!" Don watched the blood rush through his white sock onto his fingers. It was a good shot, but hardly fatal, a little more than a scratch really, anyone could see that. Still Sylvia wanted to feel something, rush to Don with genuine concern. All she could manage to do was pull another knife out of the drawer and continue washing the potatoes.

But they were beyond all that now. They'd had all their arguments many times. Now there was little else left to be said.

Sylvia rolled her car into the driveway, parked, and waited just a minute, trying to pretend she didn't see Don's car. She grabbed the canvas tote bag she was using for a purse and considered looking at herself in the rearview mirror, get some idea what Don was about to see. No reason, she thought. Might as well get it over with.

Don appeared in the backyard. "Don, what are you doing here?" Sylvia opened the car's back hatch, grabbed a grocery bag, motioned for Don to pick up the other one.

"Nothing. Just come to talk to you."

"Well, you better talk quick, I'm getting ready to go to sleep." Sylvia hoisted the bag to her hip fiddled for her keys.

"You're not asleep now," Don said.

Don was always saying something stupid, Sylvia thought, always tried to get her off her guard. If he said something dumb enough it was like a smack in the middle of the forehead, stunning you into silence, and he could keep on doing what he wanted. You don't spend nearly forty years messing around with a man and not learn at least a few of his tricks.

"Come on then. Put the food in the refrigerator."

Don put the damp packages of fruit and vegetables from the plastic bags and stacked them in the refrigerator. He would have liked a little more to do, keep his hands busy and moving, let Sylvia see him working. She always liked him in motion, doing a chore, sweating, proving he had a plan. His luck, he was in the middle of a break when she decided to check on him, either leaning on a hoe, resting his eyes, or in a just-took-off-my-shoe-to-remove-a-stone position, the exhibit A to her belief that he was of little use and couldn't be trusted.

Don eased into the tweedy den chair and felt into the dark sides for a remote control.

Sylvia fished from the mound of towels in a plastic laundry basket at her feet. She folded the pile of towels in a mound at the end of the couch. She popped the cotton, smoothed each with the side of her hand. Don watched her pop and fold a few while the lint flew in the already stiff air around them. Don tried to latch onto one piece of lint and follow it to the ground, but the mote kept disappearing before his eyes.

"If you're just going to sit there, you could fold some. How long you staying anyway?" Sylvia threw a pile of towels to Don on the recliner. He tried to imitate Sylvia's actions, but he was slow; Sylvia folded three towels to his one.

"What are you doing here?"

"That's not very polite," Don said pretending to be hurt. Sylvia laughed through her teeth, the sudden air sounding like a hiss in the room. "I just come to see how you are, that's all."

"You see me all the time, Don. You know how I am."

"I know."

"Have you been talking to Ava?"

"What about Ava?"

Sylvia stared Don down, debated about whether to get into it with him. "What I do with my time is my business."

"Who said it wasn't."

"Well, just mind your business."

Don held up his hands in surrender. "Whatever you want. Call me Bennet 'cause I ain't in it."

Sylvia glared at Don. How she got hooked up to this idiot she could not say. "You should call Ava sometime. Do you know how to use a phone? Apparently not, you're here."

"What's wrong?"

"What do you mean with what? Call her and find out." Sylvia took the stack of dish towels to the kitchen drawer. She considered walking out the door and leaving Don where he sat.

"How's that little girl you've shacked up with?" she yelled.

Don was surprised, though he shouldn't have been. Of course Sylvia would know about Jonnie. There are secrets in a small town but only if you blind yourself and refuse to know them. Once enough people suspect the abuse, the other woman, the drugs you take, there is a tipping point and the information spills over and out to everyone. Don had learned that the hard way.

"She's all right. All right. A little girl."

Sylvia came back into the room and sat opposite Don on the couch. She laughed at him. He clearly didn't think she knew about Jonnie, but she had seen them together months before. The two of them standing innocently enough at the Laundromat. Don stared with intention into Jonnie's face like he was interested in her conversation. Don interested in somebody's ideas! Sylvia had smelled a rat right then.

For a few months when Sylvia was eighteen and worked at the cotton mill sewing elastic bands on women's underwear, she had taken an older man up on his clumsy advances and shared her body with him a few times. The men at the mill congratulated the man with nods and sly grins. The women were haughty and mostly silent. Sylvia didn't care. After work and a few times when he told his dull stupid wife he was somewhere else they'd gone together to the reservoir and parked at one of the secluded exits. Both of them had been nervous at first, but that thrill of deceit, the power that came from so much at stake made them both feel bigger and more important than either thought they had a right to be. Sylvia had not felt sorry for the plump, tired wife. It was hard for Sylvia to understand how she'd felt then, how she'd had no pity for the woman at all. If she thought of her at all, she imagined her ugly at waking, her hair a wicked spiked halo, the skin of her heels flaking. Sylvia was sure the wife was common and too comfortable, belching at the table, wearing unflattering hand-me-downs from her grown children. But most confusing to Sylvia now, was how she hated the wife. How dare she have the gall to feel safe in her own skin? That was reason enough to destroy her. By the time Sylvia told her sister about it, the affair was over anyway. Lana wouldn't judge her, like she wanted her to, like she needed her to, but offered sad forgiveness. Sylvia had not wanted to be forgiven, at least not then.

Sylvia returned to the living room, not sure what to do with herself, not sure what to do with Don.

Don kneeled in front of the chair she'd sat in and put his head on the fleshy part of her thigh. He didn't want Sylvia to see his face.

"You ever going to let me come back here?" Don said into the soiled denim of Sylvia's lap.

"Why should I? I see you more now than I ever did. Besides that, I don't live here anymore. Did you forget that too?" Sylvia asked. What she wanted to feel for Don was underneath the meanness, a smooth emotion like a river pebble, cool words, without venom that declared that she didn't care anymore.

Don raised his head and looked up into Sylvia's face.

"You got a drink?"

"Get some water."

Don grunted his way up, his skinny legs like pipe cleaners in his blue jeans. Sylvia wondered what he might have looked like if he'd fattened up a little. She'd figured he would the way most people do. Most men don't stay rail thin but spread in the middle, and their faces broaden in a way she thought manly. Not Don. He was strong though, stronger than he looked. Sylvia thought his hair especially unruly today, spiky like the goldenrod bushes she liked, uncut, not careful shrubs, but radiant and irreverent. She knew that wildness was nothing to admire. Anything out of control was beautiful only to the distant looker, the woman passing by swiftly in the moving car.

Don searched the fridge, sliced a small section of butter into his hand. Butter greases the insides, his mother used to say. Every morning if they had it his mother gave all three of them still living at home a pat to eat before they separated to school and work. Don held (just for a moment) the slippery fat between his fingers before he popped it in his mouth. Of course the bad stuff would slip out of his body riding out like on a greased slide. His sister would do a quick chew then swallow hers to get it over with. But his baby brother, Nate, struggled and whined making the whole process a much bigger production than it had to be. Don hadn't thought about eating butter for a long time, but now the moment seemed a kind of communion with the three of them standing and waiting for the fat to melt on their tongues. He hadn't meant to think about that right now, but there in his wife's kitchen, his sister's narrow back rushing out the door, the way he was accustomed to thinking about her, always leaving, always gone. Dead now. And a clear picture of Nate, just as he was back then, a skinny kid, his face squeezed from worry, standing beside him, waiting for the world to let him down. Don had not meant to think about any of that. You are way the hell too old when butter can bring down a whole world of experience to you.

Don brought a bloody-looking drink made from carrots and beets to Sylvia. He took a long drink. "What is this red mess?"

"Don't drink Ava's stuff. Find something else."

"Good god." Don shuddered. "What the holy hell!" Don said and wiped his mouth, shook his head in disbelief.

"I told you not to drink it." Sylvia shrugged. "She didn't make that for you. She's got enough on her without you taking her special food."

Don took another swig just to make sure.

"What did you take another drink for?" Sylvia laughed. "I swear to God you are an idiot."

"That's some nasty mess."

Sylvia laughed. He could always make her laugh, even if she also despised him at the same time.

Don replaced the container in fridge and wiped his mouth. Several familiar pictures stared back at him from Ava's fridge. Ava and Henry at the beach in lounge chairs. Ava standing with the tellers at the bank, a flickering cake on her desk. Her happy face reminded him momentarily of Jonnie. He hadn't forgotten about Jonnie at all. But anybody paying attention knew they weren't a forever couple. That was easy math. Sylvia would always be in the picture, it was as simple as that.

The kitchen was his favorite part of the house. Each instrument, pan, and object had a reason to be, a function you could name. There had been days when he let himself in the house just to look around and touch the hard things with purpose, the oversize spoons, turners and graters, pots and chopping boards, all there, all seeming more necessary that he was.

Sylvia was still folding the towels, creasing the stained washcloths, stacking them for the closet. Her semiretirement has meant that she had time for things like folding laundry in her child's house. The joy. She would admit that she did like the idea that Ava would come home and see her chores already done.

"That juice hit the spot." He sighed.

"Do you know anything you haven't heard before?" Sylvia rolled her eyes at Don's willing face.

"Let's sit here." Don pointed to the space in front of the couch.

"I'm not getting on the floor with you."

"It's clean. Come on."

"I do the cleaning around here and I know it ain't. Forget it. I need to take a nap anyway."

"Do you still love me, baby?" Don hadn't meant to say that. It wasn't a trick or some line to get Sylvia's attention, but an honest question, one he wanted to know the answer to.

"Why do you want to start all that mess?" Sylvia yelled flecks of angry spit in his direction. The quick meanness of it startled him.

"I don't know," he said as he reached up to her, coaxed her shoulders forward, guided her to the floor. She rested her head on his shoulder, though that's not what she was set on doing at all. She looked twisted and uncomfortable leaning into him like that, and Don worried over the contortions Sylvia had to do to be close. Don smoothed her hair, wanting Sylvia to be soothed, if just for a minute, like she was finally okay, finally awake from a bad dream. He loved the way Sylvia could open herself up for him, as easily and quickly as a child, her ire and disappointment forgiven or at least held in abeyance as her body slackened and fear rippled through and then escaped her face like an ousted demon. Just as quickly as she leaned into him she sat upright.

"JJ Ferguson came by here yesterday."

"About time."

"You know how many years it's been? You understand that don't you?"

"What did he want?"

"Why don't you understand anything, Don? What makes you such an ignorant ass?"

"I'm not ignorant."

"I'm happy to see him. Do you understand that?" Sylvia knew Don couldn't understand. He had never really wanted anybody, not really, not more than a few minutes. Not in the ways she'd wanted. Nobody but his mother anyway. Any longing that went beyond his own gut, his own selfish pleasure, was beyond his comprehension.

"You don't know, Don. Why I waste my damn time, I'll never know."

"I know you're not happy to see me."

Sylvia laughed. "I haven't been happy to see you in about twenty years."

"How did he look?

"JJ? He looked like you'd expect. Older. Good."

"Did he say anything? What did he have to say for himself after all this time?"

"What could he say? I'm just glad he came."

"He's up there on the Brushy Mountains. I bet he's got a view. Hard to believe. I'd have liked to have built up there, but it wasn't in the cards for me." Don clapped his hands hard, like the idea was finished in his mind.

Sylvia searched Don's face for the joke. She wasn't sure he'd ever really wanted anything except the next gullible woman. Maybe sex was what he thought he actually had access to in this world, the best thing he had a chance in hell of getting. This was the problem with Don. He'd screwed her over all their lives, with women, with general trifling ways, and now she was feeling sorry for him. If the world was even a little bit fair, she would have never met this man. Sylvia closed her eyes and stretched her legs out in front of her, swung her arms overhead, tried to make herself as long as she could. If it were a good day when she opened her eyes, Don would be gone.

"You should have fixed the house you had," she said.

Don laughed and pulled up Sylvia from the couch and led her into the guest room that had become her room. The bed was heaped with clothes, clean and dirty, some free weights Sylvia always planned to use with her exercise tape, and her large rolling suitcase.

"You going somewhere?" Don asked, a flutter of nerves worming its way into his stomach.

"Where am I gonna go?" Sylvia snapped. "Lana wanted it."

Sylvia had a collection of postcards that Lana had sent her over the years from Europe, from Kenya, from several tropical ports of call. People sent postcards to bring their loved one into the strange place with them, and Sylvia was grateful to be remembered. Even if she did feel that the postcards were designed to inspire envy. Still Sylvia kept them all. In her whole life she'd never received any other mail from her sister. No cards or notes in Lana's tight controlled handwriting had come with baby or birthday gifts. Besides, the postcards were so much better than suffering through the albums of pictures with Lana and her husband, Gus, smiling in front of monuments and statues all over the world, groups of middle-aged white people clustered all around them.

Don ignored her tone, tried not to let Sylvia see his exhale of relief. "Lana's always wanting something," he said.

"Don, let her alone, she don't need to be in this."

But she was there. Sylvia had always loved Lana but she'd always envied her too. Lana was the beautiful girl with the no-nonsense attitude and the long ponytail that swung from the back of her head. Hair Sylvia used to dream of sneaking up behind her and cutting off with pruning shears and lofting the hair in the air over her head like a prize. When Devon was born she finally got over the pettiness. She didn't have time for it. All the issues that had separated the sisters, Sylvia just didn't care about them anymore. Devon helped them be the sisters they were meant to be. Lana had no children. She was married to a man more than twenty years older who had counted himself lucky that he'd made it out of his first marriage childless. Too bad, too bad. Lana would have been a wonderful mother, much better than Sylvia. Everyone, including every child, always liked Lana better.

Don took off his shirt, then his jeans. "What's wrong?"

"I'm thinking about my sister, do you mind?"

"She ain't welcome as far as I'm concerned." Don reached down to take off his socks.

Jonnie had soaked all of Don's athletic socks in a bucket with bleach to get them white again. She'd been so proud of herself and presented his clean socks to him like a gift. Like white socks would ever be anything that mattered to him. "Are you going with her?"

"What did I tell you about my business, Don?"

"Okay. I'm just thinking about you. I know you don't like happy people congregated in one place."

Sylvia laughed. Don was a shit, always had been, but his concern softened her. He still had that power over her. Sylvia stood in front of the bed waiting for directions. Nothing about Sylvia was shy, but her relationship with Don, this marriage that wasn't a marriage, confused her, angered her and finally defeated her. She was not in uncharted land with Don, but he disoriented her and gave her the feeling that everything familiar was gone, suddenly oddly shaped like it was covered in drifts of snow.

"Come here, Syl," Don whispered and pulled Sylvia into him, swayed with her, hummed in her ear.

Sylvia grinned though she hadn't meant to. Nobody in the world but Don would think about dancing in the middle of the mess they were in.

Sylvia looked so young when she really smiled and Don felt a surge of warmth for her, for the fun young girl who drank beer as well as he ever did, let the foam dribble on her chin, if she wanted. The girl who from the day he saw her naked liked for him to take in her whole long body, her legs thick and strong as tree trunks, the pooch of her belly, her big heavy breasts, nipples dark as plums. She convinced him that she was the way a woman should look and anything else was a compromise. At first he was afraid to tell her how good she was and lived in terror that she would realize the whole truth and walk away. A young man won't believe that holding back the truth won't keep a woman close.

When Sylvia laughed it was the only time she was truly a beautiful woman. Her grandmother's tiny freckles weren't pinched into a seagull shape on her cheeks, her mother's disappointed mouth finally twisted into happiness. "JJ Ferguson. Can you believe it?"

"Here, look at my face, but follow my feet." Don pulled her into his body. Sylvia stiffened, unsure. "What's wrong? Are you worried about that boy? Does he want something from you?" Don knew that one event doesn't make another, but many elements converge and mix together like the ingredients of a cake, to set the events that rupture the membranes of our everyday lives. By the time you see the thing and recognize it for the danger it presents, it is, of course, too late.

Sylvia thought quickly about Marcus but realized Don must mean JJ. He wants everything from me, Sylvia thought, but she didn't know how to say it right.

"I knew he'd come back sometime." Sylvia had never felt that sad and wonderful last time feeling with Don. She had wanted to lock the door of her feelings on Don, let him live the life he wanted with whomever he chose, but not with her. Sylvia found hating Don easy, but the prospect of never seeing him again never quite settled into finality in her mind.

Don let it go. He wouldn't pressure Sylvia. She so seldom seemed happy he would back down and let her enjoy the moment. Sylvia tried not to look at Don's face. He was ugly close up, as were most men. In his embrace, Sylvia knew Don was following a script he'd learned from another woman. Sylvia knew that men need direction from the woman they choose. It makes them feel cared for and safe. She leaned into Don's naked chest and tried to pretend that was all there was to it. She was the most stable part of Don's world. Always had been. He would stray, but didn't he always come back? Didn't he end up wanting her? But feeling his body move from the care he'd taken from that child hurt her more than she'd anticipated. Sylvia remembered when Jonnie was born, a fat, bald-headed baby with the mystery father.

Don's leg caressed Sylvia's thigh, half expecting to see a spot like a tobacco stain, but quickly took in the whole of the woman he was next to. Bodies are often the same, often interchangeable. Don had seen many women's thighs and underarms, drooping behinds, secret crevices and folds—and though some were longer or fatter or darker or younger, all blurred into one body, one body he'd spent the last forty years screwing in the dark spaces all over town.

Don shifted Sylvia's weight to the other foot, moved her, however awkwardly into a tiny square in the space between her disheveled bed and the wall. Sylvia was not going to cry. What was there to cry about? She should have never stopped crying years ago, if she was going to cry. As quickly as the feeling came, she felt an old hardness building, the dike that kept Don away from the best part of herself, a part she held for him, a gift really, but he would never have it, not all of it.

Don realized he'd made a mistake though he wasn't quite sure what it was. He felt the stiffness return to Sylvia, the closed-off place he hated in her that would one day brick up against him.

"Come on baby," he said. "We don't have to mess around with that. I just want to be here with you."

Sylvia swiped the clothes from the bed, leaned to the footboard, and untangled the complicated sheets. She should divorce this man. The same reasons she told him again and again to leave and don't come back were the reasons she should make it legal, go ahead and sign the papers. But not today. Today she pumped gas across from the now closed movie theater where white people had lined up around the block to see *Coal Miner's Daughter* in 1980. She and Don had passed by them in their car twice. Neither of them had ever seen people lined up for a movie, and out of all of the people in line not a single one of them was black. She remembered how sick she'd felt to be driving by, not included in the celebration once again.

Besides no one had noticed her today. Not the girl at the Bi-Lo supermarket, who didn't pause as she looked around her to the next customer, not the teenage boys, all baseball caps and over-sized shirts loud-talking outside of Lana's hair salon, not the old man at the gas station on the other side of the pump, watching the numbers roll on the display like he was hoping against all hope that seven would not follow six, just this once, and none of the passing people in the mountain town, not another soul, besides this man, had thought to remember that Sylvia Ross was even alive.

"How long are you staying, Don?"

Don reached his fingers to the clasp of her bra, popped it open like a combination lock. "How long you need me?"

14

Ava secreted the expensive digital pregnancy test into her
purse and walked the few steps into the bathroom at the
bank. She couldn't imagine how many tests she'd bought over the
years from drugstores and from the depressing dollar stores that
had popped up all over the county. *Good news! you can still shop,
poor, poor people.* But a dollar times a hundred, a thousand (who
knew at this point?) was a staggering number. There might be a
section of floating trash in the ocean with mounds and mounds,
millions of used pregnancy tests. One day in the far future, they
might coalesce, fuse together (the tectonics of it unknown to the
lay observer) into a pee-smelling island. Ava thought not for the
first time that she was losing her mind. She held the pee stick to
her side and waited. How much of her life had she dolloped out
in three-minute intervals she couldn't say. Maybe in heaven you
get back all the time you lost hoping, the gift for not giving into

great despair. Ava willed herself not to look at the pregnancy test. She looked.

On the walk back to her office Ava glanced up at Jenny, who smiled back at her. Ava nodded. People meant well. She would say something nice to Jenny today. Ava entered her office and sat down at her computer, she glanced back again to her purse and at the nasty pregnancy test she'd hastily put inside.

Everyone, BFP! BFP! Big Fat POSITIVE, POSITIVE. I just took another look at the glorious smiley face on the readout to make sure I wasn't imagining it! I couldn't even wait the three minutes, but I didn't have to. I'm going to call the doctor as soon as I finish writing all of you. Now if we make it past the 7-week mark you will hear my screams. My first two were gone early. People call it losing a pregnancy, but it felt like they were taken from me. I wasn't expecting to feel ripped out. I know you know what I'm talking about. I told myself every time that I was done. But here I am! And you know what? I am going to enjoy it this time. Maybe life is about these small moments maybe that's all some of us get. But I'm going to be hopeful. Hope with me! Is that dumb? It's probably dumb. At 7 weeks the books say the baby will probably survive. A good heartbeat at 7 weeks—I need it! Pray. Pray. Ava2WW

15

Ava parked her car near the Goodwill truck at the back of the lot at Walmart after work the next day. Her plan was exercise, but the walk to the door of the big-box store would be the totality of her day's exertion. She wasn't rabid about exercise, far from it, but she had heard about weight all her life from her mother, how it crept up, how it stuck, how the menace of it changed a body from a young and vital one to a bulbous old one, a beautiful face embedded in the fatty rolls of a large head. She vowed to avoid having more of her than what she wanted. She'd planned to go to the Y and walk for half an hour on the elliptical, but her car with its own stubborn mind wouldn't make the turn to the gym. She tried. Instead Ava put on her workout clothes after her last meeting, cut out early, and headed to get a few groceries, mostly for her mother. The town hadn't had a Super-Walmart for that long, but Ava still tried to avoid it. The store was too big, not a store at all, but a big-box store, like entering a charmless small town. She hated the epic trek from apples to Preparation H, the awful cool-blue light that made the rows of Tide, ice pops, the plastic toxic-green gleam of Mountain Dew look like they belonged on an autopsy table. This was not experience-shopping, but necessity shopping.

The trailer truck door was open and a large white woman sat in a folding chair in front of the opening. Her job seemed to consist of waiting long intervals for someone to drop off plastic bags full of the junk they couldn't give away at their yard sales. Ava clicked her car locked, positioned her purse under her arm. The woman looked up at her but did not speak. Ava nodded in the woman's direction. How in the world did she pass the time with no book, no radio, just the blacktop vista of the dullest parking lot on the planet? On the back of the Goodwill truck over the woman's head were two large signs: NO DUMPING and PLEASE DO NOT TAKE DONATED ITEMS. Nothing in this scene would have been remarkable to Ava, except she noticed a child's bicycle with a pink banana seat in the small pile of trash bags full of clothes, garish toys made of indestructible plastic and too many housewares straining for escape against the flexible sides.

"Look at that bicycle," Ava said. "You know I had one like that."

"Mine was purple," the woman replied.

"No tassels. That's a shame." Ava walked over to the donation heap, held the handlebars of the small bicycle, and examined the scratched-up blue and white frame. "Can I buy it?"

"You have to go to the store. We're not allowed to sell anything out here."

"I'm going to have a baby."

The woman looked Ava over. Ava imagined that the woman

saw Ava's flat stomach, low percentage of body fat, no telltale spread of her nose and face. "Good for you," the woman said. "You know they've got plenty of tricycles in Walmart."

Ava laughed and let the bicycle fall back onto the plastic bags. "You are the first person I've told. I don't think I've said it out loud until now."

"We aren't even that close." The woman managed a half-smile. "Come on to the store in the next couple of days. We'll have put this stuff out by then."

"I guess it can wait," Ava said and rubbed along her belly, as she had seen so many other expectant moms do. "She won't ride the thing for years. I probably have some time."

"I'll see you," Ava said and lifted her hand in almost a salute. Ava had no idea what she'd do with that beat-up old bike. She was just being spontaneous. Nothing wrong with that. Though it was just about three-thirty, the parking lot was three-quarters full. The parking lot was always at least three-quarters full. Ava wished for the hundredth time in her life that she'd had a twin. With a twin she could share everything, tell all her secrets, her fears. She would know how she looked. How she really looked, without the filter of her own happiness or depression. For the hundredth time she scolded herself for having the most narcissistic wish in the world. Who wishes for another self, another body just to see your own fool face?

She hated coming to Walmart at all and mostly avoided it, but it was too much effort to find a mom-and-pop store or make the forty-minute trek all the way to Hickory for a better selection or a quainter setting. Ava, like most other people in town, found her stubborn car turning into the Walmart parking lot nine times out of every ten, her resolve to shop local gone again. Walmart had become for most people in town the only shopping for miles. That song that was driving her crazy kept running through her head. *All that glitters is gold, all that glitters is gold. Only shooting stars break the mold.* But no way could she make out most of the lyrics. She reminded herself to look up the song so she could at least sing a verse. Is that what old people do? Probably. New music was as foreign to her now as it had been to her mother when she was a teenager. Back then she'd wondered how anyone avoided music, how the newest raps, the inevitable boy bands, how in the world did old people fail to notice?

She would not go to the office supplies. For once she would stay out of that aisle. Last year during the back-to-school sale she had bought a hundred notebooks at ten cents each. The clerk had asked her if she were a schoolteacher. She had nodded in a noncommittal way in case anyone who knew her overheard the conversation.

Ava would tell Henry about the pregnancy in a week, two at the most. He would not share her excitement, only her worry. Ava didn't honestly know exactly what he'd think. Even after seventeen years with him, she still felt love, she felt loyalty, but she couldn't claim to really know what the hell he wanted.

In the parking lot, almost to the door, a white woman and a small brown boy were about to enter the store. They were holding hands. The boy skipped, tugging on his mother's arm, his happiness a contagion that made Ava smile along with his mother. She recognized the woman. A number of customers from the bank knew her even when she didn't know them, but Ava knew the woman was not a customer.

The boy struggled to get a shopping cart from the corral at the store's entrance. His father had to have been black or maybe one of the Mexican men that were now a significant part of the population. When Ava was the boy's age, the children of one Hispanic family went to her school. One. The Hispanic kids now nearly outnumbered the black kids. That's a lot of change for a generation. The boy was part of a growing number of interracial children in town. White mother, brown child equals a brown father somewhere in the picture. That was an easy equation. The boy turned to face his mother, the cart wrestled from the rest of the pack. Ava did not know the woman personally, the mother, but more than once Henry had mentioned her. He saw her at the store, he'd said, in passing. Did Ava remember her from school, he'd said. Even as he said the woman's name, or even just mentioned her, Ava could see the mistake on his face. Ava had hoped he was just infatuated with her. Men get that. It passes. Maybe everybody felt some of that heat from a forbidden person, but Ava wasn't sure. What she knew was she had no attraction for any man anymore. They were too much trouble, even for sex the trouble just wasn't worth it. In fact the whole enterprise of romantic love was just too hard to be worth it. Her grandmother had told her more than once that the thing about men was once you learn them you won't want them. Though there were minutes, never much longer, that Ava wanted to be wrapped up and consumed, the best part of sex hands down, it was only minutes of that longing, no more. These days when she got a glimpse of a beautiful man, she sized him up like a jeweler. Good cut, good sparkle, nice setting, but not something she herself could afford.

The boy's face was all teeth as he pushed the cart toward his mother. What a beauty he was. Ava smiled at him the way people smile at beautiful children, her eyes puddled, her face soft. "Mama, I got it," he yelled.

"Shh, you're not in the woods, Z," his mother said, but she wasn't really bothered.

Maybe it was the slide of the automatic door, and the rush of the pretty woman suffering with the heavy load of her baby carrier on her way to the shopping carts. Or, maybe the boy sensed Ava's eyes on him and in the way of small vulnerable things felt danger in her concentrated interest. Whatever it was the boy looked past his mother and directly at her, their eyes locked on each other.

"Come on, baby," his mother said, motioning him forward. The two of them began their shopping. Ava turned to leave, but not before she dropped her bag and keys. She kneeled to pick them up. The sensation to lie down and stay on the floor at the dirty entrance, let one after another of the shoppers stomp her body into the ground, grind her until she was unconnected dust, was almost irresistible. The boy had Henry's face. His complexion was lighter for sure. His hair was finer with less kink. But his face was unmistakably Henry's. Ava stood up straight, turned to the place the boy and his mother had been. She watched the boy go to his mother with strawberries. Though she couldn't hear them, the mother, what was her name? The mother instructed the son to get bananas. The blood rushed into her head. Is this how it felt to faint? The boy's head had straight dark hair cut close, like Henry's. She had known it. Of course she had. The days Henry had mentioned the woman, she saw his embarrassment, and if she'd allowed herself, she would have felt the secret. He had been trying to tell her, people do that. People need to tell the shames of their lives. Good God! He had wanted her to know. The third or fourth time he mentioned that woman's name, *her name is Carrie, that's it,* she had almost asked Henry, how long has it been? But she hadn't wanted to hear it. She had realized it all, but what a difference between knowing and seeing with your own eyes.

The mother and child roamed through the produce. The boy pulled lines of plastic bags from the little stands for apples. The woman let him pick out his own pears. Ava turned to leave, the automatic door dutifully opened for her though she was leaving through the entrance. No, she shook her head like a toddler. No. She would stay. She would not be run off like she had done something wrong. Ava grabbed a shopping cart to steady herself and have something to do with her hands. She followed the woman and Henry's child to the dairy section.

"Hello," she said. The woman had her back to the organic milk and turned to the sound of Ava's voice. Her face dropped, a cartoon face. But what a doll's face the woman had, wide pink lips, thick longish hair she clearly didn't appreciate. Hair that men would think looked bed tossed. She was a thick girl. She was beautiful.

"Hello," the woman said, but she looked stricken. She held her son's hand tighter. "Hello," she said again.

"You don't know me," Ava began, not sure she could continue for her pounding heart. "I saw you when I came in. I just saw your boy. He's beautiful."

The woman gripped the boy's hand tighter, positioned herself a little in front of him as slyly as she could without being insulting. The boy sensed a problem. Ava could see it on his face. He must spend a great deal of time with his mother, reading her reactions, sensing her moods. He looked at Ava and back to his mother.

"Thank you. He is a good boy too," Carrie said, her mouth twitched. She was nervous but tried her best to look composed.

Ava was the one who looked like she might cry. The woman in front of her was not a trashy woman. Trash would look defiantly at her, look smug or smirk at her. Trash would goad her, hint at what she'd taken from her, at all she'd won. This woman was not trash.

Ava bent to get closer to the boy's face. "You are a beauty. Do you know that?" Ava said to the boy. "How old are you?" She saw the woman flinch from the proximity. Ava raised herself to her full height. She would not scare him.

"He's five."

"What a face. Are you good to your mother?" Ava's voice broke, but she would not cry.

The boy looked at his mother not sure what to say.

"He's perfect. He's my heart."

"You're lucky for that," Ava said to the woman. "You are Carrie, aren't you?" Ava tried not to sound cold, but she was sure she did.

The woman nodded, like she was not sure what she was admitting to.

"You be good to your mother, okay?" Ava said to the boy. She wanted to say more, and searched her thinking for a more lasting idea, one that might seem wise to a little boy. For a long second she considered saying something cruel that would ring for years, maybe forever in the boy's ears, about his mother, about his status as a boy without a father's name in the world. She would not do it. She was not trash either. Ava steered her cart away from the dairy section all the way to the other side of the store as far away from them as she could.

"Thank you," she heard Carrie call after her.

Ava moved quickly to the health and beauty aids, pushed the cart as quickly as the weak front wheel would allow. She stopped her empty buggy in the safety of the shampoo aisle. She had moved fast. There was no way they could see her hard ragged breathing, her body's impulse to curl on itself, to make herself as small as she could manage. Whatever the items she'd come for were long forgotten, recalled later, and for years to come they'd be associated with this moment. What was she going to do? What could she do after what she had just seen? When she was very young she would have cried herself thoughtless, blinded with the crying, sick with it until she could do nothing else but sleep. She was used to covering herself, guarding her emotions, her every action. Because she did not wail or gulp breaths until she hyperventilated with the pain did not mean she didn't feel it.

"You okay, ma'am?" A young man in his early twenties put his phone to his chest, looked quizzically in her eyes.

Ava nodded afraid of her voice.

"You sure?" the man mouthed.

Ava turned to the shampoos tried to focus on the many bottles.

The man put the phone back to his ear. "And I'm like why is this girl talking to me. And I'm like whatever okay and she's like seriously calling me and the next day I text her and she says, 'let's meet next Monday' and it's like crazy dude there's like lightning bolts flying all over the air and she's like sitting real close to me. And she's really sweet and we spend the entire day together and then like two mornings. For the most part we've been hanging out for a week. No, she's normal. She's like one hundred percent normal. She doesn't bullshit around. Like me. She's dealing with some stupid stuff but she's like, dude, you know how people say you look familiar, you look familiar, you know? She's familiar. She's like the most familiar. I swear it seems like we hung out years ago, like when we were kids. I couldn't wait to tell you, dude. I know. I know."

The young man picked out a cheap shampoo and its matching conditioner and gave Ava a last lingering look.

"I'm okay," she said. The man nodded at her, gave her a thumbs-up, and continued his phone conversation.

Ava left the cart in the aisle. It wasn't even quitting time from work. So very early. God what a beautiful day. Ava and her baby would walk out of Walmart into the sunshine. She had everything she needed.

16

The motel room was spare and unadorned. Ava rested on the bed on top of the sheets. She thought for the hundredth time that she should have gone home. She didn't deserve to be running and she sure as hell didn't deserve to be spending any time in this shabby jail. The Rowen motel had to come up a few notches in the world to be as stylish as a jail. Jails are midcentury cinder block, not the funky, seedy look of a seventies basement. Ava had put her purse and keys on the bedside table. She had pulled off the nasty bedspread immediately; they never wash those things, even in nice places. The remote was huge and black like a giant roach—that thought alone meant that Ava wouldn't touch it. Without cable there were no choices anyway. Ava had heard about the Rowen motel for most of her life, but she never thought she'd end up there in this hole-in-the-wall for people in between homes, the poor newcomer, the faithless middle-aged.

Ava would not go home. Her mother would hurt right along with her at least as much as Ava hurt herself. As long as her mother was alive she'd feel Ava's hurt more than Ava did. You have to protect a person who loved you like that. There was no way Ava could avoid telling her mother what she had seen. But not right now. Thank God for Henry's child. Without that little boy in the world, Ava thought she might get a gun, put the nose in Henry's worthless stomach, and happily pull the trigger. She'd never pulled the trigger of a gun before, but plenty of idiots had, and she could be one of them. Once she'd seen her father with what she thought was a cap gun, a toy. "Don't you ever let me see you with it," he yelled at her, angry because he was afraid, though Ava didn't understand the reason at the time.

The room had a sweet funky smell, like the skin under a roll of fat. Ava closed her eyes and put her hand over her mouth like a kidnapper. She clinched her fists to gain control, but the effort was giving her a headache. What was that smell? She wasn't sure she could stand it all night, but she'd already paid. Not that it was so much money, she could afford it and better than Rowen, but she didn't have it in her to go out again, greet some indifferent face at the hotel counter, shell out money all over again. She almost made the turn to the other side of town to her Aunt Lana's, but she would ask too many questions, need too much assurance that Ava was going to be okay. Ava was not in the mood to take care of anyone else's needs, even a kind well-meaning person. She needed silence and solitude and anonymous space to think. Anonymous not stank.

She must have dreamed because when she opened her eyes instead of the unfamiliar room, dark except for the fading light through the plastic shower curtain window treatment, she fully expected to see the ugly, crumbling face of the boy who had a crush on her in high school. Her admission to him that she liked someone else was supposed to stop his advances, but she almost declared that she liked him after all. She had not forgotten his disintegrating face. Ava got up to close the curtain but decided to walk outside. She still wore her shoes, but she grabbed the little jacket she'd tossed on the floor. Her car was parked in front of her door. She leaned on the back of it and looked around. So many times she'd wondered who rented a room from the Rowen. The motel had been the subject of a hundred stories and even more rumors in town. One of Ava's white school friends told her the story of going to the Rowen with her mother when she was a child. Her friend had witnessed her mother beat her father with her fists the moment he opened the motel room door. The father had tried to explain, to convince her mother that the woman hastily putting on her jeans was not who she imagined she was. Even then Ava had thought the story ridiculous in a hundred ways, but the most disturbing part was the inclusion of her friend, the child, in all that stupid.

Even then Ava had known that her own father was a little scandalous, too taken with his power with women. Don had probably been to the Rowen more than once himself. But her mother hated Don's guts at home, behind closed doors like a good mother is supposed to. You don't take your child to a motel to witness all that impotent emotion. That story had been one of Ava's clear proofs that white people do at best the same kind of dirt as anybody else.

The motel was surrounded on three sides by tall pine trees that made the place look more like Vermont than North Carolina. Behind the trees on one side just a couple of streets over was the Plant 4 where her father worked for forty years. No other building was visible from the parking lot, but the Simmy's sign glowed. For about fifteen years, maybe more, the new sign was the brightest light in the evening sky in town. An outsider might imagine a new restaurant, but the sign was where the renovations to Simmy's ended. Inside the place was still segregation-era chic, all browns and fake wood, linoleum tables and chairs one step up from the folding ones. But that depressed neglect matched the dull wash on the town. Pinewood was not a tourist mecca, since visitors are not usually interested in a downtown full of closed factories and businesses. At least the Simmy's sign had the virtue of looking prosperous and alive.

Ava had been to Simmy's, not often, maybe as much as once a month with some of her coworkers, but she always felt guilty about eating there. All the stories the older people told couldn't be erased with a fancy new sign or repaved parking lot. Ava knew that none of the stories involved her directly and the restaurant could never be for her what it had been for her mother and what it might have been for her baby. Her father had gone inside with a couple of his friends right after the place integrated. The young men had sat at a table, ordered coffee from a waitress who had not and did not say a word to them. Once they got the coffee they stirred in sugar and milk, took a couple of sips and left the restaurant. All they'd wanted was to go inside, show everybody in the room that they could come in. The men had not wanted it this way. They didn't want to take things, force the hand, pry the fingers open one by one. They wanted to be invited like friends, like men. But no invitation ever came. Though Don had not said, she knew he must have felt like a conqueror that day. A feeling that can sustain a body, keep it light and agile, ready to bob and weave for years to come.

If the baby was hungry she was not saying. Of course the baby was about the size of the head of a pin. Ava decided to wait it out. She could find food in the morning. Who knew who might wait for her in the terrible little room? This uncertainty kept her fixed to the spot. Other than her car and an old Saturn there were no other cars in the lot. Where was everybody? Fornication doesn't go out of style, Ava thought. The silliness made her laugh. People had higher standards these days or maybe just a few dollars of open credit on the Visa. That's all it was. Or could it be possible that grown people were reverting to their teenage pasts and making out in cars? Whatever the reason for their absence, Ava wished a few more cars would show up. She would have liked to see more people unpacking or milling around. It had been a long time since she'd been afraid, at least that kind of afraid of who might be watching her. There was a movie about a young woman alone at a deserted old motel, and though Ava was afraid to watch it all the way through she knew it did not end well for the woman. Nobody had ever been killed at Rowen's, at least not that Ava had ever heard, but it was just the kind of place where you'd expect passionate crime, murderful and ugly, poor in every aspect, from the pimply pebbles instead of grass in front of the windows, to the garish purple doors. Every little thing about it screamed cheap, cheap, cheap and worse than that—desperate. And what's more desperate than killing some other warm body?

The calmness of the night, the vomit taste at the back of her throat that meant fear, reminded her of the evening she and her friend Kim walked through the woods. They were chatting like friends do about nothing and everything. In her memory, they are young, younger than Ava can remembering being. What started it, Ava cannot say, but the realization that they might die became real. Not someday, but that day. A boy or a man with thick fingers might grab one of them while the other held fast or ran to find another man (anyone to care, anyone strong) while the other is dragged through the delicateness of ferns at the edge of the trail. Though it is a worn path for walkers and hikers, there was no one around. They couldn't see the car they drove, the pebble-sided water fountain was a mile back, maybe more. Even the imaginary safety of the cinder block bathroom was in the distance. "Let's run," Ava said. The last one to the gleaming car, too hot from the high sun, the last one there is the dead girl. Last one to the car can't tell the story. Last one to the car is the story.

The neon light for the Rowen sign was not yet on. The days were already long and balmy. Ava got in her car, locked the door, and turned on the radio so quietly it almost seemed like music from another time or from her dreams. She could sleep there until discomfort forced her back inside.

But she wouldn't. Ava drove the few miles from the center of town to her Aunt Lana's. Lana's house was a small brick ranch with a long driveway. Her place was always neat and clean-looking with two impressive pots of some flower—now impatiens already in riotous bloom—flanking the door. Lana had the brick on the home painted a creamy white to help her forget that Gus's ex-wife had once lived there. Even after thirty-odd years of marriage Lana still remembered.

Lana came to the driveway as Ava closed the car door. "What are you doing here?" Lana put her hands on her hips but seemed to think better of the attitude, "Syl okay?"

"She's okay."

"I can see, Ava. It's something. What's wrong?"

"Nothing."

"Come on in. I guess you'll say when you get ready. I've got eleven *Judge Judy* shows taped if you want to join me."

"Okay," Ava said and followed Lana into the house.

"Oh lord, I know something's wrong now. Come in here."

Lana had painted her oak cabinets white and the walls were a pale yellow, her kitchen a cheerful little room with copper pots hanging like moose heads on the soffit above the sink. Ava sat at the small table in the center of the room.

"What do you have to drink, Lana?"

"I take it you don't mean Kool-Aid," Lana said as she reached into the upper cabinet and poured two fingers worth of liquor for Ava and a splash for herself. "Don't tell your mama."

"I'm not twelve, Lana."

"She doesn't know that. And it won't do any good to remind her."

Ava sloshed the liquor around but did not drink. Lana watched her play with the whiskey. "Give me that," she said and drank the liquor herself in one large gulp. "Tell me what happened."

"Henry has a child."

Lana nodded her head like she'd just heard the most obvious news in the world. "That skinny-ass weasel. Is he leaving you?"

"Leaving me? I'm leaving him."

"Well good." Lana put more liquor in her own glass. "Now I can tell you what I really think about him. I've been waiting for years. You know I'm not patient." Lana tried to remember the comments, any comments she'd heard about Henry at her salon. Were there knowing looks she should have recognized? Maybe once, a very pretty young girl had mentioned Henry, she wouldn't mind some of that, or some other fool talk she'd said, and the salon had gone quiet. The girl had not remembered or maybe she didn't know Lana's connection to Henry. The women in the salon had not looked directly at Lana but they all waited for her response. Lana should have realized what that silence could have meant. The silence allowed the space for a secret.

"One day I want to hear every word of it," Ava said as she got water from the sink. Lana had a sleeve of Dixie cups in a holder beside the faucet. The sight of it almost made her laugh out loud. The last Dixie cups on earth. Ava used to pretend she was a giant with the Dixie cup in her hand, the bottom soon soggy with liquid, bulged out threatening to break. She remembered the one-handed sensation of crushing the paper cup with her powerful and decisive grip while the waxy outside of the cup crumbled and flaked like icing on a doughnut. "I saw him in Walmart."

"The baby?"

"The child. He's five."

"Shit." Lana reached out and held Ava's hand. "Is he pretty?"

"Who? The boy?"

"The boy."

Ava nodded. The frightened moon face of that black-haired boy took up all the space in her memory.

"That's even worse. Be good if he was a little troll."

Ava half-smiled at Lana who always managed to say the unexpected thing. "I would prefer it," Ava said.

Lana picked up the glass and drained it quickly without a wince. She thought, for not the first time, that she really should drink more. "Listen to me, Ava. I know you're hurting right now. But I want you to see this as a chance."

"Why would you say something like that? That's not what you

say to somebody whose marriage is over." At the first good opening Ava would get out this house.

"Don't get mad. Don't get mad. To tell you the truth that's
exactly what you should say to somebody leaving a sorry marriage." Lana rubbed her finger along her glass and stared at the
ring of irretrievable brown liquor caught in the bottom. She knew
Ava watched her but pretended to be absorbed in the intricate pattern on her glass.

"Maybe you know this and maybe you don't, but I got myself
in a situation." Lana gestured to her room, her home. "Sometimes
by yourself, without some pain, I mean, you can't think of a good
enough reason to do what you need to. Women are sometimes like
that. A man will pack his longings in a minute. If a man gets tired
of us, he takes the first train out. But us." Lana sighed. "We always
have a hundred good reasons why we can't make the change. You
understand me?"

Ava listened but did not speak.

"But if you get a little luck. I know it doesn't seem like luck,"
Lana said as she held up her hand to stop Ava from speaking. "If
you get lucky, a way out can present itself. You hear me? You have
the push you need."

"I loved him." Why Ava felt like she needed to say it she wasn't
sure.

"You still love him. Who said anything about that? This has
nothing in the world to do with love. He never was and he'll never
be what you want. You know and I know that you'd have never left
him otherwise."

"That's not true, Lana. It's not. When we were young it was
different."

"I guess it was. At least you thought it had a chance to be different." Lana nodded the bottle in Ava's direction. Ava covered her glass with her hand.

"He's pretty but he ain't shit. You know it. Something's wrong with him. You know it's true. And another thing, I better not hear you defend him again."

Lana's hair was pulled back in a severe bun with a couple of short tendrils stuck out from the top of it. On Lana the imperfection looked intentional. She wore no makeup but her skin was slick and dewy like a girl's skin with only the slightest hint of jowl and a weariness around her eyes that made them look like they weren't fully open. Those small telltale signs announced her as an older woman. Ava had thought that women in her mother's generation were so far removed from her that they might not be the same species. It took great pain for her to realize she was a woman in the world of grown women.

"I hear you, Lana. I hear you." Ava wiped her eyes and drank the last of her water. "Lana," Ava began. She wanted to ask how she could have missed that Lana was a woman, how she could have known her aunt all of her life and not know a damn thing about her. Ava couldn't think how to say any of it.

"This is a chance, my girl. See it. Can you?"

17

Carrie waited for Henry like she always did. He was late of course, like he always was. "Why do you put up with that?" her sister asked her a hundred times.

"It's not that big of a deal," she'd said, and it wasn't. When you love somebody you decide what you can take and what will kill you and work backward from what will kill you. It's as simple as that. At least this is what she told herself. You have to have a good story that binds the whole mess together. Most people construct the story to explain the life later, but people living the crazy make up the story as they go. Right there in the moment. She wasn't a mistress, she was a girlfriend waiting for her man to get his affairs together to move out. She wasn't a fool, she was a mother not giving up on a man because life with him was hard. Hadn't she been chosen? The thing about being chosen that her sister never understood is the exhilaration, the knowing that he wants you. Women do anything for that. Carrie knew she wasn't thinking about the situation like a feminist. But from what Carrie had seen everybody called herself a feminist until a man gets involved. Then it's to the chosen go the spoils.

Carrie had always been a girl men looked at, but it had been a long time since men had locked eyes with her, half smiles on their lips, pretending to listen to their wives while they tried to get her attention. But she wasn't that lovely kid anymore. Those days had faded, *was it a fade or an acute stop?* and she couldn't remember exactly when. Becoming invisible was just as strange a process as being visible. So much so soon. She had more than her beautiful face to carry her in this life. Carrie had gone to the community college for two years and she had been a very good student, eager to please and more intelligent than people expected. She talked little in class and could see the faces of the professors change as they regarded her with renewed appreciation and a little amusement for the smarts they hadn't considered that she possessed.

Henry had told her she was too beautiful to be serving platters of food. At the time it hadn't sounded slick or like a practiced line, but she make the mistake of telling her sister, who had rolled her eyes, like she'd fallen for the oldest trick in the book. Carrie had to look around to see if he was talking to her. He was a handsome man, a respectable man, not a bum or a user-fool like most of the other men who hit on her at the restaurant. There was nothing nasty about the way he admired. He seemed to have been thinking out loud. He remembered her from high school he said, from class he said, but he couldn't remember the class. She had not remembered him. Most of the black people, even the ones in her own graduating class, had been a mystery. She had not been friends with any of them.

"You don't remember me, do you?" he'd asked.

"I probably do," she'd said.

"I sat in the seat with your name carved in it. Some lovesick boy carved it."

"Kids." She laughed though she'd been flattered at the memory.

"Okay let me know if you need anything," she'd said, but she was sure something had just started with the two of them.

HENRY WOULD SHOW. He always came eventually.

Her sister was afraid to believe. People are afraid to believe in their own hearts, Carrie thought. She couldn't blame her for doubt. The fear, the judgment from those who always have the answers, those whose cynicism makes them fear faith in the sunrise, how much less will they believe in the power of transformation in the lives they were living. Carrie knew she was a little ridiculous, but she loved Henry. Was it so impossible that their situation might end well? That her faith in that love could be rewarded and everything turn out okay? She wasn't gambling. Gamblers lose. They know they will lose and wait for things to come crashing in on them. She wasn't gambling.

Of course the start of a day can be very different from the end. Carrie had started the day feeling all that hopefulness. She had seen Henry sad, she knew he was hurting. It couldn't be long before their real lives could begin. After fourteen unanswered texts and the after the clock struck 9:00 P.M., then ten and now five past eleven, and, she couldn't keep believing, her love, her hope which is love in action, had bled away from her body.

Henry's key turned in the trailer door. He opened it slowly like he feared he might be too noisy. "Carrie, baby you awake?"

Carrie watched the television as if she had been struck deaf and hadn't heard Henry enter.

"How are you?"

"Did you bring anything?" she said still staring at the television screen.

"What?"

"When you used to fuck up at least you'd bring a gift."

"I'm here. I said I'd be here. What are you watching?"

"Television." Carrie had seen that episode of the *Twilight Zone* many times. The newlyweds have car trouble and end up in a town where they find a machine that tells the future. Quickly the newlyweds became obsessed with the vague predictions from the toy in the diner. People looked for signs everywhere.

Henry sat at the edge of the couch and made sure that a full cushion separated him from Carrie. He had not wanted to hurt her or his baby. She knew that. She had to know it. He wasn't sure how not to hurt them. Henry almost got up to look in on Zeke. The door to his room had a wooden sign with his name in different color letters. Carrie would go crazy if he woke up their son.

If you squinted and didn't look up, you'd think you were in a condo. Once inside you wouldn't know you weren't living in a nice-looking apartment. and not a trailer at all. The only trailers Henry had ever seen before this one had been flimsy things with walls that looked and felt like corrugated cardboard and if a big man fell the whole works might tumble down after him. Not Carrie's trailer. It was a nice one, a double-wide, nobody's cheap. You might hear the word *trailer* and think extreme poverty, tin can living, and there is a reality to that, no question, but some of them are nice, built well, and only in some moments with some turn of thought do you remember the world under your feet could be hooked up to a truck or hoisted on a flat bed and taken anywhere. Carrie's trailer felt permanent and open with good height ceilings. The walls solid, real-feeling, not like living in a gas station bathroom like Henry had assumed. Carrie's parents had bought the whole thing for her, almost brand-new, gave to her the three acres of land that the house sat on. From her porch there was a beautiful view of a copse of trees and just beyond them, the surprise sparkle of a faraway neighbor's pond. Nice if you liked that kind of thing or if you hadn't spent the best part of your life trying to escape it. Carrie's father and uncle had cleared the land for her and leveled the road to her door. They didn't say it, but these kindnesses were their last acts to her, a generous good-bye that meant they wouldn't have to feel guilty for never speaking to her again. She was invisible or worse, she never existed. They were the answer to the question, What kind of people buy off their own child? All Henry could think about were the underbrush, the small animals, the ticks that lived in those woods unheard and unseen except for the nasty discovery of them stuck to you eating you alive from the inside out.

On no day did Henry ever conceive of himself living in that trailer. Henry had never loved Carrie, though he liked her. He tried to love her, but it wouldn't take. Years ago he had almost walked out on her and the relationship. They saw each other so little and nothing had happened that he couldn't just walk from yet. He'd never planned on a relationship, but a casual thing, nothing serious, just a nothing to get him over the hump. She had not wanted more than that either. But she'd gotten pregnant. How does that even happen anymore? They were grown people with grown people's choices. The fact that they were in this predicament was terrifying and ridiculous. But there was nothing to do. Henry tried to believe that he wanted a permanent life with Carrie, and there were moments over the years that he almost convinced himself that his future would include her. But that feeling never stuck for long.

"I didn't know if you would let me in."

"I didn't asshole. You have a key."

Henry didn't push it. There had been days Carrie had put the chain on the door and he'd looked like Jack Nicholson from that horror movie. All work and no play, all work and no play.

"What are you doing here now?"

"I told you I was coming today."

"You said you'd be here to see Zeke. It's eleven o'clock. He's been asleep for hours. I didn't even believe you so I don't know why I'm mad."

Henry moved over on the couch to get closer to Carrie.

"Don't move over here. I'm not kidding with you."

The couch was a good one, with down back pillows, probably a hand-me-down from her parents. "I couldn't get away." Henry thought about what he had done with his day, an early breakfast at McDonald's, followed by general wandering around town, a quick trip to the thrift store to paw through their DVDs, and finally two episodes of *Murder, She Wrote* to round out the afternoon.

"You didn't work today. I'm not stupid."

"I'm sorry, Carrie," Henry said, and he meant it. He'd had every intention of seeing his son, he wanted to, but he couldn't help but disappoint. He considered that maybe he liked feeling like a failure, but that didn't seem to be it. He feared he'd feel like a loser whatever he did. "I'm here now, baby," He said.

"Why did you ignore my calls?" Carrie asked and looked directly into Henry's eyes. Henry was smart enough to know there was no answer that would suffice for this question.

"I told you to call me. I told you it was an emergency. Didn't you worry or care? Didn't you even wonder?"

Henry had finally turned his phone off to avoid talking to Carrie. He couldn't stand to hear her disappointment. "I'm sorry, baby," Henry said, and he felt it. If she kept drilling at him he would cave and tell her how sad he was, how his life left him turned inside out, nothing satiated him for long, but any good feeling ran with ferocity out the sieve of his heart, how he couldn't imagine how he would make it from this year to the next year until he finally didn't have to worry about it anymore, how the best he could do, or make, or believe gave him so little. Worst of all, he was a grown man, almost a middle aged man and he still didn't understand what the hell he wanted.

"There is really something wrong with you. I'm so sorry I didn't see it sooner." Carrie looked back at the television screen. The actor that would later play Captain Kirk was frantically reading his fortunes from the penny machine. No matter how insignificant every one of them sounded like prophecy.

"I saw your wife," Carrie said.

"Where?" Henry asked.

Lights flooded the trailer windows. You didn't venture out there in the sticks, not out as far as Carrie lived, unless you are very lost or on a mission. Henry got up to see and turned on the floodlights outside. "Where did you see her, Carrie?"

"So now you're interested in talking to me?"

"Did you go to my house?" Henry turned to look at Carrie. His organs were melting, his inner self dissolving into a slime puddle that would eventually ooze out his ears and onto the carpet.

"You expecting somebody Henry? Don't you dare bring anybody to this house."

Henry opened the curtains. "Why would I do that? What happened, Carrie! Stop messing with me."

"I saw her at Walmart." Carrie stood beside Henry at the window. A car passed by the trailer and was in the process of turning around. "Do not let anybody in this house? Do you hear what I'm saying?" Carrie hated her breaking voice. "What ass comes to somebody's house at eleven o'clock anyway, besides you?"

"Did you talk to her? Why won't you just tell me?"

"I tried to tell you. You didn't care. Who is it?"

Henry studied the car, a new one with good wheels, a flash of metal not plastic rims.

"Is it Ava?" Carrie asked.

"I don't know," Henry said irritated. He had not until that moment considered that it might just be Ava. "Looks like just one person."

The car stopped in the middle of the dirt road. The driver turned his lights off, thought better of it, and turned the headlights back on.

"What's he doing?" Carrie glanced at the door to her son's room. If there was danger she could take him out the back to the old people that lived down the road, past the pond. They might not like her, but in an emergency they would take her in.

"Let him wait," Henry said.

"Who are you talking about?"

Henry stepped out onto the porch with his hands on his hips, tried to look brave. The door opened to the car and the man approached the trailer. "You stay in here," Henry said to Carrie. "Stay in the house, okay?"

"JJ," Henry said to the man who just stepped into the floodlight. He hoped he didn't sound surprised or intimidated. "You better move your car from the road."

Jay walked back to his car and parked it beside Henry's in front of the trailer. He stopped on the bottom step of the trailer and looked up at Henry and then Carrie standing on the small porch.

"It's Jay. You doing okay?" Jay had seen Henry with the curtains open staring out at him. He'd almost lost his nerve and gone back home, but when Henry came onto the porch he couldn't just leave.

Henry waited just long enough that he hoped Jay would be annoyed.

"It's late man," Henry said with as little warmth as he could. Jay hesitated on the bottom stair, unsure if he should come up on the porch. "What you need?" Henry said but he didn't look over his shoulder at Carrie. She was almost certainly pissed off by now and he wanted to maintain the upper hand with somebody.

"I saw your car," Jay said.

"Gimme a minute." Henry turned around and stepped back into the trailer, grabbed his bottle, and walked out onto the small trailer porch.

Jay waited for him on the bottom step.

"How are you?" Jay said to Carrie. She stood in the doorway and stared at him. "Didn't I see you the other day in Simmy's?"

Carrie nodded as she crossed her arms over her chest. In the crush of people during the lunch rush, she did remember this quiet man all by himself. He might not have said two words his whole meal.

"I'm Jay Ferguson." Jay raised his hand in greeting. Carrie did not wave but kept her hand limp and noncommittal.

"He just got here anyway," she said and tilted her head in Henry's direction. "Are you the one building the house up the road?"

"Yeah, that's mine."

"My parents live near you on High Top. They can probably see your house."

"I could see over the whole valley." Jay smiled to Carrie. "That's what I liked about it from the beginning."

"Look, man. Visiting hours are over." Henry tried to make his voice sound easy, but he was annoyed at Carrie and Jay's conversation.

"Keep your voice down. Zeke doesn't need to know you finally showed up," Carrie said. She wanted Jay to know that despite what was happening to them at that moment she had a respectable house where people worked, sat at the table to eat, didn't allow strange men in at all hours. Carrie imagined that this man in his nice car and expensive shoes might just think she was Henry's trash—cheap and disposable. Why else would he come to her house, get out of his car in the middle of the night? You don't do that with people you respect. She could see in his face he was now ashamed of that.

"I'm sorry. I didn't know you had a child here," he offered to Carrie. "I shouldn't have bothered you," Jay said. He'd expected to find out about Henry's secret life, a woman probably, maybe drinking or drugs, gambling away his money in somebody's basement. He had not considered a child.

"Let's go man," Henry said.

Jay nodded at Carrie, who looked over her shoulder at the television screen. The young Captain Kirk and his new wife were in their car, riding away and into an uncertain future they could not predict. That's what people did, right? Face their uncertain lives together? The *Twilight Zone* ending almost made her cry. The men had once again noticed each other and she was invisible in her own house.

"Don't bother coming back," Carrie said.

"Leave me alone right now, Carrie," Henry said.

"I mean it this time." Carrie closed the door behind them.

Outside the air smelled like gravel dust. The only sound out there in the woods was Jay's cooling car still ticking in its many joints, an old man making the slow descent down to a low-riding couch. Jay loved the sky up here, inky black so many stars that even the most cynical started to believe in other worlds.

Henry slid up the bottle he took from the kitchen out of the paper bag. He slid the neck of it up and out like a trombone.

Jay shook his head no.

"It's good. Made in Ireland," Henry read from the label. "You know those fuckers know how to drink." Henry took a dainty drink and readjusted his face from the peaty smell. "She's a good girl." Henry nodded his head toward the trailer. "She's just tired." Henry drank a sip of the whiskey between his clenched teeth. "Tired of me mostly."

"That's on you, man. I don't know anything about it," Jay said.

"I know." Henry felt his face go hot. "I told you so you would know." Henry held the bottle on his knee while both men watched the golden liquor settle, the hurricane inside slowing to a stop. "Been a long time."

"What does that mean, Henry?"

"Hell, I don't know. You look good to a lot of people around here. You know that? That must feel good, right? You must feel like somebody."

"All the people in the world that care about me are in this town. That's all I know."

"You think I've got fans all over the country? That's all you get, man. Wait, wait," Henry said, though Jay had said nothing.

Jay reached for his pocket for his cigarettes, an old habit he couldn't shake after six years quit.

"What do you want, Jay? Its spooky as shit out here." Henry took a quick drink of the whiskey that burned at the back of his throat.

There are two hundred billion stars in the galaxy, and from where they stood he could see them all. Jay wasn't afraid. "I don't mean you any harm, Henry."

"You don't mean me any harm, that's the funniest thing I've heard all night. I know what you're doing here. You're not fooling nobody, man. You want me to tell you everything is all okay? Is that it? When did we get to be friends?" Henry spat out. "This is how people lose their goddamn lives, JJ. Running up on people in the dark. Nobody would ever come looking for you out here. You know that?" Henry's hand started to shake. He could hear everything in that moment, the creaking of the trailer, his son's turning in his bed, Carrie's rushed, angry breaths. Everything had fallen and broke into pieces. Somebody had to pay for that. Henry didn't mind if that person was JJ.

"You'd have to kill me first," Jay said quietly. "Can you do that, Henry?"

Henry gripped the bottle tighter. He had never been a violent man, and beating a man to death, even one he'd been comparing himself to for most of his adult life, wasn't a part of who he'd ever been. Years and years ago, Ava had told him that JJ had been in Raleigh for days with Ava in her room. He had suspected JJ was somewhere in the picture, but she told him herself. He should have found and killed JJ then.

Jay reached for his keys, jingled them in his pocket. "This was a bad idea, Henry. I swear to God, I'm not here for craziness. I swear to God."

It was almost midnight and the air was still warm, still pleasant enough for a walk. So much violence lay dormant under the surface of the world, waited for the slightest provocation to explode into being. How easy it was to find chaos. These woods that should have consumed them all years ago from foolishness, drunken car rides, hateful men and boys, women too, predators with evil intent, waiting in the shadows for the vulnerable and the left behind. Let those beasts stay hidden.

Henry let the bottle drop to the ground. The last dregs of liquor spilled on his shoe. Henry paused and willed the wildness in his chest to settle.

CARRIE LOOKED OUT THE WINDOW at the men in her yard, standing in the shallow light from the trailer porch, their expressions unreadable, passing a bottle between them. She sure as hell knew how to pick them. But how could it be her fault when all of them, every last one, was an ass? Carrie let the curtain fall back closed. They hadn't noticed her watching. They didn't care. She thought about crying and she almost did, but she didn't come from people

who respected crying even in children. Crying was at best embarrassing and at worse a sign of unforgiveable weakness. She would
not cry. She opened the front door. "Y'all go now."

"Go where. Come on, Carrie." She looked first at Jay's face
and then Henry's. Was it that hard to understand that she didn't
want two men at her house talking about another woman? She
wasn't about to *come on*. Men tried to make you believe in your
own crazy. If you are hysterical they don't have to see you as an
equal, look you in the eye like a person they have to respect. It
suited them to make you think that all the shit they pulled, all
the lies they told, were in your head. The only crazy part was that
most women did believe their men or chose to pretend. Most kept
on believing right up to the point the men walked out the door
or killed them.

"You can sit and be an idiot anywhere, Henry. Get away from
my house." Carrie spoke in the calmest voice she could manage.
She wouldn't have her son awakened to a scene. "I told you for the
last time." Carrie almost closed the door, thought better of it, and
opened it wide again. "And you better believe that she knows. I
saw her and she knows everything."

"What did you tell her?" Henry yelled.

"Keep your voice down. I didn't have to tell her anything."

"What did you say to her?" Henry said, his voice wavering with
emotion.

"I said hello. I didn't say anything."

"What did you tell her then, goddammit?" Henry yelled.

This whole night, this whole twisted episode of their lives, and
Henry reserved his real feeling, his true emotion for what his wife
felt. "She came up to me and said how beautiful Zeke is. But I'm
telling you she knows. I can tell. And you better hear me," Carrie

said, her voice strong though she never in her life felt more like sobbing. "I'm glad she knows."

"She might not know. Right?" Henry directed his question to Jay.

"You were supposed to be here," Carrie hissed. "He wanted to see you. He always wants to see YOU. He asks all the time about when you're coming. I didn't even tell him this time. I knew you wouldn't come. I knew it. He is always counting on you and you let him down over and over. Now we don't have to count on your sorry ass."

"Sorry, sorry, Carrie," Jay said as he walked down the steps to his car.

"Don't try to come here and act like you know anything," Henry yelled.

"I'm leaving. I shouldn't have come here," Jay said and opened his car door.

"You don't know what you're doing. That's all. You don't know." Henry kept his eyes on Jay.

"You don't know me," Jay said.

"Five more minutes and I'm calling the police."

Henry opened the door to his own car. "Don't judge me by this," Henry said.

Jay got in his car, turned the ignition, and the engine hummed on, the radio pulsed a slow jam from a generation ago. Henry went down the steps to his own car.

"I should get drunk for real," Henry said.

Jay shook his head, not sure what to say. Listening to Henry, seeing his crumbled face, knowing the mess that spread out around him in sad concentric circles, a lonely child, betrayed and disappointed women, made him so defeated and exhausted, he could barely speak. Maybe that's why he'd come. He'd wanted to get angry, hate Henry, so when he exploded Henry's life the way he dreamed of doing, he wouldn't blink an eye at the carnage. He had not counted on being sad. The thought had not occurred to Jay, at least with such clarity until that moment.

"Get it together, man."

"What do you think showing up here?" Henry sounded like he was asking a genuine question. "You don't know. You better believe that. And another thing, Ava is never going to be with you. She can't do it man. She's messed up. I love her, but she's messed up. I'm telling you."

"Henry, your secrets are out, you better figure out some way to get behind that."

"Is that what I need to do, JJ? You know everything about my life now? Is that it?" Henry stood up straight and walked to the passenger door of Jay's car. "You know, huh?"

Carrie bolted and chain locked the door. Both Jay and Henry looked up at the sound of the locks connecting.

Jay backed out the driveway just as the light in the trailer went out, but Jay could just make out Henry's outstretched body on his hood of his own car.

"Get off the car, Henry," Jay yelled out of his passenger window.

"I'm not a bad man," Henry said.

"Who thinks he is?" Jay said.

Henry opened the door to his own car, but Jay didn't wait to hear the engine start.

18

Ava went home early the next morning from the motel. Lana asked her then told her that she was staying the night, and Ava did stay almost. She wanted nothing more than to sink down into Lana's couch under a blanket and let Lana bring her popcorn as they watched episode after episode of trash television. But a heaviness was settling in her like sand swirling then settling in water that made her feel like moving, keep moving or she might plant to the spot and never move again. She went back to the motel but got up before the sun rose to get back to her own house. She hoped that Henry was home. She dreaded the idea that Henry was at home. She craved seeing Henry at home. Henry wasn't there, which made Ava alternately sad and angry and relieved and sad again.

Once in her bedroom, her first act was to take a long, hot shower. Henry hadn't been home. He probably hadn't come home all night. After the twentieth time he'd called her, texted her, left messages, she'd finally had to turn the phone's sound off. After the first call or two she silenced her phone, let it vibrate in her pocket. Let him think about her. Let him wonder. Let him ride around town trying to find her. The bed had not been made from the day before and Ava attempted to straighten the covers but it looked a baggy mess like an old man's neck. She had not decided what she would do if Henry been there but she had worked out three or four scenarios in her head for confronting then hurting Henry: she would catch him in a lie; she would pretend to know nothing and see how he reacted to her seeing his son; she would beat the hell out of him the second she saw him. All of the options had their merits.

Ava had texted Sylvia early in the evening with a lie her mother would not believe, that she was out with friends until late, she might stay over with a friend, she'd said. Ava had plenty of acquaintances she'd go to lunch with from time to time, like Tommy the skinny white teller at the bank who told her that his other coworkers "oppressed his identity." He really said that. Ava wasn't sure how she managed to plump his identity back to normal, but whatever made him happy. Ava had a few more casual acquaintances and no friend she would trust with the dirty secrets of her marriage. The only friend Ava was likely to stay over with was her mother. Her mother knew that too.

Ava had called in to work but she had almost decided to get dressed and go in. The sheets felt good though. She folded her thin pillow into a sandwich and propped her head on the top of it. She had not been able to believe her luck when she found the four-poster bed at a yard sale. The couple selling it even brought it to the house, refused the twenty dollars she'd offered as a delivery charge. More than once Ava had thought the couple had passed on a curse of an unhappy, unfruitful bedroom. Sometimes she thought she remembered clearly that there had been no large plastic kids' toys in the yard, no outgrown baby clothes for sale. Though now she wasn't sure if that was a true memory or just a sad attempt at an explanation. No matter what happened to her in the rest of her life, she would get rid of that bed.

Had that woman been in her bed? Impossible? Thank god for her mother. Even Henry wouldn't risk running into her mother at the house. Though she couldn't help but torture herself with the image of their little one who had probably crept between them in the early morning, snuggled warm against his chest. That was supposed to have been her life. Ava folded her arms over her chest, closed her eyes. That's it, she thought, keep hating him, cauterize the wound as quickly as possible.

Ava entered Devon's old room beside her own on the second floor. She'd moved the few wire hangers of sloop-shouldered button-down shirts, the picture of sartorial disappointment, that their mother had bought for him to wear to church during one of her many tries at religion. A couple pairs of shiny polyester dress pants lurked with the shirts in a box somewhere. Devon was a private boy and a private man, and all of them had given him his space. She had understood that he was a boy with collections, for the art he found and claimed, for strangely shaped rocks, bent pieces of metal, including an iridescent sliver of silver plate he kept on his dresser. Nothing else would wiggle back into her thinking. Ava sat down on Devon's bed. If she closed her eyes she was sure that she could picture what the walls had looked like back then, but no image appeared. But the disco glitter ceiling looked the same. Devon had wanted to paint over the dirty

cloud places where water had leaked and stained. A teacher had
told him that Michelangelo had taken years to finish the Sistine
Chapel. "You got to be joking if you think you'll be under my roof
wasting time painting," their mother had joked. But she hadn't
meant it.

The room now said little about the boy who had lived there. An
old painting of a clipper ship Devon drew when he was in eighth
grade, a WORLD'S GREATEST GRANDPA mug he'd loved was still somewhere. Years ago she'd found several of his notebooks under the
bed, full of drawings of cars, airplanes, caricatures of people they
all knew in the opening pages. She'd leafed into the notebook and
had come upon drawings of young women, topless with strange
expressions, like they weren't aware of their naked selves but were
instead doing ordinary things like picking apples or watching
television, topless girls as wholesome as the farmer's daughter.
And every girl was the same girl, the sad little white girl he worked
with, the puny little thing he brought around the house a few
times. Devon was a loner but hadn't seemed lonely. She'd had no
idea he had longed for her. Joy, that was her name! Never had a
child looked less like a Joy. Of course he had loved her. Ava said
the first prayer she'd uttered in a long time, maybe since she was a
child beside her grandmother on her knees. *Please let her have loved
him back.*

Ava took the drawing of the ship off of the wall, a good one for
a boy his age, *what had he been, about twelve, thirteen?* to straighten
the frame. On the back of it Devon (who else?) had drawn a cartoon sheep with a thought bubble above the sheep's head. The
caption said, IT AIN'T SO BAAAD. Ava laughed. "It ain't so baaad,"
Ava said aloud. She would get on with it. She was going to work.

19

"Ava Bailey, how may I help you?"

"Is this Ava?"

Ava drew in her breath. She knew he would call, it was just a matter of time, but hearing his voice startled her anyway. Her office had glass walls, a glass-topped door. She could be seen by the tellers in the front of the bank, by the customers in line if they decided to look around for anything of interest as they waited to make their deposits and withdrawals. Ava shifted in her chair and rested her head in her hand. She glanced up quickly and sat up straight. For the thousandth time since she started the job she wondered what the tellers or the customers had seen. She quickly adjusted, and erased the expression from her face.

"Ava? Are you there?"

Ava knew the voice from the first word, even after all this time.

She had slept with two men in her life, her husband and the man on the phone. "This is Ava," she said.

"Ava?"

Ava cleared her voice to try to keep it steady. JJ Ferguson had finally called.

"This is Jay Ferguson. How are you?"

"I know who you are, JJ," Ava said and held the phone, not sure what to say next.

"Are you still there? Can you talk now?"

"It's about damn time, JJ." Ava paused on the line. She felt a glad rush like her body was taking in light except it was a stinging like she'd just released a long-held breath. This was nothing like her feelings for asinine Henry. For him, for Henry, she was overwhelmed, like walking in the ordinary world and suddenly and inexplicably falling in a hole. She'd wanted Henry, her body reacted to him, with an aggressive hum that surprised even her. She ached for Henry, but not like hunger—hunger is unpleasant, not hunger at all more like the tingle of bicycle bells bright and insistent and impossible to unhear. Her feeling for JJ was pleasure, the warmth of real pleasure. A feeling that bounced back to her through the detritus of almost twenty years. She had chosen Henry all those years ago and JJ had disappeared from her life. She had not known that she would lose JJ entirely. How could she have known that? "How are you?"

"I'm going to be your neighbor," JJ said.

"Everybody in town knows that, JJ."

"I forgot about the grapevine around here."

"Did you?" Ava asked, but she was sure the grapevine was the last thing JJ forgot.

"You're right. I was hoping you'd know." JJ laughed. "You sound the same."

"Ha! I'm not even close. You wouldn't believe what's happened even if I told you," Ava said. Ava and JJ paused on the line.

"Can we meet? Can I see you?" JJ said.

"Why not? This is my week for crazy. Why not?" JJ hesitated unsure what Ava might know about what had happened with Henry.

"Okay then, that sounds like close to yes." He laughed. "I'll take yes any way I can get it. How about today? We can eat somewhere, get a drink maybe."

"Not in this town we can't. Still dry."

"I heard that. Unbelievable. You know we don't have to stay in Pinewood. I can take you anywhere you want, girl."

"Your rap is still weak, JJ."

"I'm the king of weak raps."

Ava laughed and imagined the grown man on the other end of the telephone line. He was not fat and he had hair and teeth from all reports, but he couldn't look exactly the same. No one ventures into middle age the same as he started. She was different too in ways that she felt more than saw with her own eyes. Though she was sure other people could tell. A woman, sixty years old at least, had asked her if they'd gone to high school together. That moment had ruined a few days in a row for Ava. "I'll get some lemonade with you, but I'll be here until late. Besides, I'm pregnant, JJ."

"Well, I'll come by the bank."

"Did you hear me?"

"I heard you."

"You're only the second person I've told. You and the Goodwill woman."

"What, Ava?"

"I'm pregnant. Knocked up. I'll see you later."

"What else did you say?"

"It doesn't matter, JJ. I'm just talking."

"I'll pick you up there."

Ava wished she'd dressed better, with her highest heels. It was probably better that she looked like she normally did. People would notice differences in her appearance and get suspicious. For sure somebody would see her get in Jay's car and whisper to the others and by the next workday everyone in the bank would have heard that she was with a man they did not recognize, a black man yes, but not her husband. "Come by at six. I'll try to be done by then. If you aren't here at six, I'll be on my way home," Ava said.

"I've been waiting a long time. I'll be there. I'll be early."

"Don't be early. You'll just be waiting. I won't be done until six today. Okay, JJ?"

"I'll be there."

20

"I can take you to a nice place, Ava. Let's go to Hickory." Jay kept his hands on the steering wheel, determined to drive away from the Simmy's parking lot.

"This is fine. I just want a greasy burger. Just don't tell Mama, JJ. I mean, Jay. I'll get used to calling you that," she said. She had not drunk the whiskey she'd asked Lana for, so she thought she deserved the greasy food. If she was lucky someone would tell Henry and he would know that she hadn't wasted a second before she'd forgotten completely about him. "You probably don't remember how she is about this place."

"I'm not telling." Jay doubted Mrs. Sylvia cared anything about Simmy's anymore. What more damage could happen that hadn't already been done anyway? Everybody was keeping the wrong secrets. Jay looked around the restaurant as they walked in. Don't let Carrie be working, please, please, he thought. Ava waited for him at a booth in the corner. "One second," he said to Ava as he walked to the front counter and got the attention of the fifty-ish white woman behind the cash register. "Y'all can sit anywhere you want," she told him.

"Is Carrie working?" Jay whispered.

The woman looked hard at him, like she wasn't sure if she recognized him or not. "She's not coming in tonight."

Jay nodded and joined Ava at the table. He had no idea what he would have done if Carrie had been there. Gotten Ava the hell out of there was all he knew.

"What's going on?" Ava said.

Jay shrugged and sat down across from Ava.

"I hardly ever come here, but some of them from work bring takeout every week or so," Ava said. The same waitress followed him to the table and took their order. The waitress's lipstick was old and creased in the lines of her lips, her eyes lined too heavily with a dark brown pencil. She was pretty but not as young as she hoped you thought. "Your order might take a couple of minutes. We have so many call-ins tonight. Everybody has to have a king burger one last time, you know."

"Thank you." Ava watched the woman walk away from them. Her Bermuda shorts, the kind older women preferred that covered wrinkled knees, hung straight up and down like a young boy's might, with none of that middle-aged spread. Poor women, Ava thought. Always worrying about what some man might think. "Men suck, you know that?"

"Yep, I do." Jay laughed.

"That's the best answer," Ava said and sipped from her water. "Tell me where you've been. I've wondered where in the world you might be."

"I'm boring." Jay chuckled. "There's not much to tell."

"Well you can't be more boring than me," Ava said.

"I've thought about you a hundred times. More than that. I usually think about you in your house. That's where I imagine you most," Jay said.

"That's where I've been for the past hundred years. Tell me what's been going on with you," Ava said.

Jay told her a story about his life in the army, about the months that turned to years when he meant to write or call her or e-mail her, but couldn't imagine what he would say. He told her about traveling and spending so much time alone he talked aloud just to hear another voice in the room. He'd lived in Texas for two years, but he couldn't get used to the heat. "Nothing prepares you for it," he said. A certain kind of dry air still made him gulp oxygen like a starved man. For years he had lived in an apartment complex where he didn't know the names of any other tenants. He told her about his time in a small town in Pennsylvania and the crows that darkened the sky every evening at dusk on their way to Crow Hill. Jay laughed at the memory. "You wouldn't believe them. I heard an old man say one time they were around when he was a child. They tried everything to get rid of them. They cut down trees, played music, made all kinds of noise," Jay said. "But they couldn't get rid of them." He laughed again. Jay told her about seeing his sister and her saying her life was full without him. That's just what she'd said, that her life was full. He told her about being alone and feeling like the last of his kind.

"Why didn't you come back here?" Ava asked. "You could have come back home."

"I'm here. I did."

"Took you long enough." Ava tried to count up her years and

distill them for Jay. Nothing felt important enough to recount. She had lived and worked and the years had piled on like cordwood virtually indistinguishable from each other. She wished he'd reached out to her.

"I looked you up on Facebook. There are more JJ Fergusons than you think." Ava had searched through the list of JJ Fergusons and found teenagers, white girls, JJ's of all ages and descriptions. She wasn't sure what she would have done if she'd found him, probably sent him a note and tried to sound light and breezy like he was never important to her, something like "Hey stranger!"

"I looked for you too."

"You knew where I was, Jay. I've just been here. Have you seen Alice's yet?"

"A couple of weeks ago. The place is run-down. Same as ever. The barrel where she had me burn trash out back was still there." Every few days before trash burning day, Jay had had to jump in that barrel, tamp down the trash that accumulated. Nothing else he had to do in that house made him feel more forlorn, like the boy in the novel begging for gruel.

"What's going to happen to the house? Does her daughter want it?"

"I doubt it. I don't think she spoke to Alice for years. I don't care. I really don't, Ava. I wouldn't care if it burned to the ground. Don't worry about me. I just went there to see the end. If I saw the house, then that part of my life happened. I hope it makes sense to you, because it doesn't to me," Jay laughed. "I just started thinking that I could put it behind me. How many times do you get to see the end of anything?"

"You're looking for closure? Is that it?" Ava asked.

"Maybe."

"Did you get it?" Ava asked.

"Not so you'd notice," Jay smiled at her.

"Maybe it'll come. If it does tell me what it feels like."

The waitress brought the burgers to the table in red plastic baskets, mounds of shoestring fries spilling over the side. "Pure fat and salt. I'm going to miss these," Ava said, holding a fry. "I'm not worried about you." Ava smiled.

Jay picked up the burger, the bun glistened with grease. He took a huge bite and wiped his face.

"Are you married, Jay?"

Jay wasn't sure how much he wanted to tell Ava about another woman. He took another bite of the burger to consider what to say. The waitress watched him from behind the fifties-style counter. He couldn't tell if she watched him because he was a suspect or a patron. It could be both. "I spent about five years with a woman. Not married. It should have been two years."

"What was her name?"

"I shouldn't tell you. That was a long time ago," Jay said, but it had only been three years.

"I'm not sure why that matters, but it does. What happened?"

"*Bea* said I was unreachable."

Ava nodded sagely like she was intimately acquainted with a world of unreachable men. "Did you try to get her back?"

"It had played out. With some people it plays out like that." By the end, Jay had imagined himself on an ice floe and Bea on another. At first they pretended not to notice the drift. Once the distance became unavoidable, they'd just kept going. Jay had loved Bea's kids. The three of them had been little when he and Bea started together, and he had not wanted to leave them behind. He had told this to her, to stay together, let the children have the best of both of them. She'd looked at him like he had lost his mind. It pained him to think that someday in the not so distant future those children would not even remember his name.

"I'm sorry it didn't work out," Ava said. They looked at each other and laughed. "We all get disappointed."

"Maybe." Jay shrugged. "We want what's missing. Everybody wants what's missing. That's it, Ava."

Ava pushed her food away and wiped her mouth. "Henry's got a child. I just saw him."

Jay nodded.

"He is beautiful. God, Jay. I couldn't take my eyes off of him. I hated him. That's the first thing I felt about that beautiful child. Isn't that terrible? I felt almost nothing for his mother. You know that doesn't make sense."

"You didn't hate anybody. I know you. You were sad, baby," Jay whispered.

"I would never have done anything to him. I don't know what I felt."

"Hey you know what? People think crazy shit all the time, and you get to think crazy shit. That's all allowed." Jay looked around the restaurant to see who heard him. He hadn't mean to get loud. "You get to think anything you want to. Okay? Listen to me, Ava. Don't worry about it," he whispered.

Ava stared at Jay an uncomfortable amount of time.

"What? What is it?" Jay asked.

"You don't know me, Jay. Maybe you used to know me, but I'm not the same."

"People don't change, Ava. I wish they did. You can hide but you can't change. I've tried everything to improve." Jay laughed.

"That can't be true. We have to be able to do better. Right?" Ava felt her lip begin to tremble. She was not going to cry in goddamn Simmy's.

"Y'all need anything else?" The waitress mercifully addressed the question to Jay. If she saw Ava crying she did not let on.

"Maybe in a minute," Jay nodded.

"Let's talk about something else. You caught me at a strange time, but maybe every time is strange. I miss being young. Not my twenties, they sucked," Ava laughed. "But you here makes me remember being a kid. I've wondered so many times what it would feel like to see you again."

"Take a look. It must be good. To see me, I mean," Jay said.

Ava smiled at him. His teeth were slightly bucked, his lips large with a tendency to chap. His face fuller now than the skinny boy she'd known. He had a thoughtful more than handsome face, a kind face. Had she never noticed his very curly lashes? She couldn't remember.

Jay tried not to return her stare. Who knew what registered on his face? He probably looked like he wanted her to say that he was in her thoughts; that he had never left her, that their time together however relatively short had meant as much to her as it had to him. He wanted her to say that there were days, many of them, that on the job, in the grocery store, in the car on the way to anywhere that she found herself breathless and disconsolate at the loss of him.

"Don't think I'm going to say something nice, Jay," Ava said.

Jay reached for her hand.

21

Night crept on them as they drove the curvy road to Jay's house. Ava closed her eyes for most of the trip. No need to see the fine details of the landscape that blurred by. The first time she flew she imagined a giant movie reel outside of the plane, the landscape playing like a film, the plane unmoving. When they finally landed, she would not have been entirely surprised if the pilot announced they were in just the place they started. The landscape on the mountain was unchanging, tree after tree, curve after curve playing on the window screens.

Ava followed Jay to his front door. The yard was still hard-packed red clay, but the possibilities were enormous. Her mother would love to see all these big open spaces ready for planting.

"I'm glad we got here before dark." Ava turned her back to the door. The house sat in the middle of a flat expanse at the top of a rise. Behind the house were large trees, the tangled woods and weeds that did not invite hikers or walkers. The front yard sloped to another flat-ish space of land that one day could be a tennis court, a camping space, a massive garden, anything your heart and pocketbook could imagine.

"Watch this," Jay said as he punched numbers into the keypad. Four quick beeps and the locks clicked open. "Keyless."

"Check out James Bond," Ava said.

Jay turned on the light and let Ava look into the rooms and the staircase from the foyer.

"God," Ava said. She turned to look at Jay as he stood in the entrance watching her. "You live in a mansion. What the hell?" Ava had pictured Jay many times over the years usually in an apartment or a run-down rental home, chain-link fences holding back vicious unhappy dogs in patchy yards. Jay all by himself making his own simple meals from cans, walking around in dingy underwear. She almost laughed aloud at the thought, the movie image of the lonely bachelor. Why she had not assumed that Jay could do at least as well as she had felt like vanity and embarrassed her, but she had never once pictured him successful or happy in a clean bright room.

"I didn't think anything was possible," Jay said and took Ava's hand and looked around at what Ava saw. The house Jay grew up in was a rented one with jaundice-colored walls and an ugly dog bed of a sofa slammed against the wall. Jay remembered his mother's slight back at the sink, the circle movement of her arms as she washed dishes while she stared out the window. In the evenings after dinner, he'd rest his head on her skinny hip, the smell of her dish soap and grease in his nose, the television the only light.

Jay reached for Ava's hand. "Have we ever held hands?"

Ava laughed at him with an "are you kidding?" expression on her face.

"I know, I know, but I don't ever remember us holding hands."

Jay led Ava to his bedroom. A new mattress and box spring were on the floor dressed like spring in cheap floral sheets. Ava sat on the bed and ran her hand along the buttercups.

"Nothing has to happen here. I just don't have any chairs." Jay smiled at her.

"You are so full of shit."

Jay laughed and sat by her. "I'm serious. Nothing has to happen that you don't want. I just want to be here with you."

Ava nodded and looked around the bedroom in the fading light. "This is a big room."

Jay leaned back on the bed and searched the ceiling for something to count. He closed his eyes. The two of them danced at a party in a dingy basement apartment in Raleigh twenty years before. The well-worn furniture had been moved out to the yard, the music so loud it rumbled through their chests and their hips while a couple dozen of them, young, young people moved together like a throbbing living thing. She had wanted to go outside from the smothering heat and into the backyard. A few people smoked, others whispered and laughed together, but one couple talked quietly, she seated on a picnic table and he facing her between her legs. Ava and JJ couldn't stop watching them. Their conversation too low to make out any but a few words in between their groping and devouring each other in the relative public of the backyard. The sight of the couple, their desire for just that feeling. Consumption—that was the feeling. More than anything else that had happened to them before that night that had made them go to Ava's dorm room to attempt that same passion for themselves.

Jay rolled over to his side. "I don't have television. I'll get one if you want it."

Ava stood up and unzipped the back of her dress and let it puddle on the floor. She stepped out of its ring. She felt slightly erotic, slightly disgusted like she stuck her finger in the muddy soil of a potted plant. She had never cheated on Henry, not once. Ava would have told Jay that fact, but she didn't want to ruin the moment by saying Henry's name.

Jay reached for Ava's hand. "Don't worry. Please. Let's talk."

"Talk dirty?"

"No." Jay laughed. "That's not what I meant."

"No, I don't think so," Ava said. "You talk. I want to hear you."

Jay hesitated not sure what to say. "I hate sleeping by myself. Did I ever tell you that? All this time by myself and I've never got used to it. Is that not manly? I shouldn't tell you that, right?" Jay chuckled. "You're supposed to say no, no, Jay you're very manly."

Ava smiled at him but said nothing.

Jay unbuckled his belt and took off his pants with his back to Ava. When he turned he hoped her eyes were closed. "Are you okay?" Jay asked. He hoped he looked less afraid than he felt. "Baby, no," he said when Ava started to cry.

Ava let the wash of guilt and sadness flood over her. Lying in this bed, mostly naked on a sheet about as flexible as a piece of cardboard, she knew without question her marriage was over. She was not sad for the fact, but for the knowledge of the fact. She leaned back to look into Jay's eyes. She wanted to tell him something important but she wasn't sure what it could be. Jay's bed was much bigger than the dorm room bed they had squeezed into so many years before. The first time they slept together she willed the ancient condom he had carried in his wallet to break as he unrolled it, but it hadn't. She'd wanted a life, her life, but she'd had a small but palpable, unreasonable hope that she would get pregnant and the hard work of planning and focusing would be taken from her, out of her hands, and bound up in a baby with this sad sweet boy.

Jay put his hand on her thigh. She wrestled her bra off her body and tossed it on the floor.

"Turn off the light, Jay."

"I don't want to move from here," Jay said, but he got up and turned off the light. He put his arms around Ava and let her rest her face on his shoulder.

"This is my first affair." Ava said. Jay held her tighter.

"Nothing has to happen right now. Okay, baby. Everything I want is here right now."

Ava reached to the end of the bed and pulled the cheap new sheet up between them and wiped her face on the scratchy material. She rested her chin on Jay's shoulder. "In a little bit, okay?

Jay held her tightly like she might fall off the side of the bed, his arms around her back, his fingers pressed into the hollow curves of her sides, the only sounds in the room their exhalations escaping their bodies, rising to the ceiling, winding around the thumping blades of the ceiling fan.

22

Sylvia waited in the driveway outside of Lana's house. She tooted the horn for the second time in five minutes. Lana stuck her head out the door. "Stop blowing the horn, fool. This ain't the getaway car."

"Hurry up," Sylvia yelled. "I've got things to do today." Sylvia leaned the back of her head against the headrest. She would have to remember to smooth down her hair so she wouldn't have a dent before she went anywhere in public. Black women are always thinking about their hair. She closed her eyes. Maybe Lana wouldn't come out and she could sleep in the sun like an old dog.

"Okay," Lana said as she plopped in her seat, buckled her belt. "Let's go, you're in such a hurry."

Lana had coordinated her outfit, a black and white flowing top and black Capri pants. Her toes were done. Her toes! She had managed to look chic as usual. Not that Sylvia didn't care about how she looked. Some women would go to town looking any old way, pink sponge rollers in their hair, housecoats and slippers in the grocery store. Not Sylvia. She would never do that. Never. Sylvia would see somebody she knew, some neighbor, some friend of a friend who couldn't wait to talk to her. Sylvia believed in propriety, in time and place for things, in an orderly world with rules. Times had changed. The town had changed. Nowadays she could go anywhere most of the time in her hometown and not speak to a soul. That didn't mean she wanted to go out looking like she just got out of bed. Despite her many efforts, she had still managed to look disheveled, unlike the women who wore linen, had manicures and beautiful haircuts, hair and makeup that stayed in place, shoes without scuffs. They were the very girly, feminine women that if she was being honest, she realized that she had always envied even as she mocked them. Women with ruffled shower curtains and dressing tables in their bed-rooms, powdered and perfumed as loved babies. Women who never looked down at their hands at the dinner table and saw arcs of ashy skin in the space between thumb and forefinger or dirty, bitten nails. She hadn't felt so unkempt until she saw Alma Parks at the gas station. Her husband had just left her, and her two grown girls were states away. None of that seemed to have fazed her, since she looked maybe just that side of forty-five, a few wrinkles on her forehead, but no waddles or marionette mouth that distracted. She could be a model for some menopause cream or adult diapers. If she was suffering Alma Parks would never let it show.

Sylvia had long ago understood that she would never be one of those pulled together women.

"Where are we going?"

"I want to find that girlfriend of Marcus's."

"What! That woman might be blind, crippled, or crazy. No wonder you didn't tell me. I'm not going. I thought you were going to Hickory."

"Come on and go with me. I need some help."

"For what? To get cussed out? I don't need a stranger cussing me. I've got you for that."

"Marcus says she's a nice girl."

"What's he going to say?" Lana said. "This is not a good idea. That is an understatement. Do you understand what *understatement* means?"

Sylvia hadn't talked to Marcus for a few days, but she would find his girlfriend. Maybe the girl could be convinced to send Marcus a letter or maybe even go see him. Her visit was bound to take some pressure off Marcus and give him enough energy to do his time out. It was worth trying to find out.

"We won't be a minute. She's just on Main Street in one of those houses you like. Don't you want to see what one of them looks like inside?" Charlotte and their daughter, Dena, lived just off Main Street. Those old houses were now mostly rentals, a few of them had been turned into apartments. All of them showed their age. Still the luster of long ago money was there in the high ceilings, fireplaces (not functioning anymore, but still lovely to see), hardwood floors, and charming features that made a body feel rich, like pocket doors and leaded glass windows. Nothing that would keep you warm or safe, but there was more to life than warmth.

"What if she won't let us in? Then what do I get?"

"How many times have I helped you? Do you always have to get something?"

"Yes, I always do," Lana said. "Otherwise this is all just ridiculous. What are you talking me into? Drive then."

Charlotte's house was a small Colonial, a charmer in its heyday. Pink azaleas were at the end of their flower in the curved beds on either side of the door. The houses in the neighborhood had been some of the best in the town—the homes of factory bosses and line managers. These were places that people had cared about that wouldn't take too much to set right again. Sylvia passed by slowly in her car.

"Is that it?" Lana said.

"I think so, but I don't see any toys or anything"

"Well, she could be neat. You've heard of that, haven't you?"

"Maybe this should be a silent trip," Sylvia said.

There was a car in the driveway, but she didn't know what kind of car Charlotte drove. Sylvia passed by the house fully intending to turn around and go back. Instead she pointed the car back to Church Street.

"What are you doing?"

"I don't know," Sylvia said. "I'm not sure."

"Well you better get back to the house. I didn't come out for nothing."

Sylvia turned the car onto Highway 18, speeding in the opposite direction of the street.

"Are you turning around?"

"Yes," Sylvia said, but she continued down the road.

"Stop up there at Teague's Meats," Lana said. Past the light was the butcher they all went to for special occasions. "I need some ham," Lana said. "Gus loves their ham and I live to make him happy as you well know."

Sylvia pulled into the parking lot. "There's a lot of things I well know, but that's not one of them."

"You coming in?" Lana asked.

"You go ahead." Teague's Meats was at the south end of town. About this time of year every year she used to go there to get her ten-gallon bucket of chitterlings. The kids would complain at the cooking and hold their noses like they were being gassed, roll on the floor in agony, especially Devon. He was the worst. And no matter how many times it happened, Sylvia thought it was hilarious, though she pretended to be offended. "You all don't know what good eating is," she'd say, but neither one of the children would touch the finished product, the grayish mush like scrambled breakfast eggs on the plate. "Try just a bite," she'd offer. "You can't even smell anything," she'd say. "The secret is to cook them with a potato," she'd offer to Ava, like her child was taking notes about how to feed her future family. The smell of pig intestines cooking for hours on a stove meant celebration to Sylvia. It meant everybody was home. For many years she had passed by Teague's Meats and never stopped. She didn't care how good the ham was.

Lana came back swinging her plastic bag from her wrist. "Nothing happier to a black woman than a bag full of ham," she said.

Sylvia pulled onto the road past Teague's. She cracked her window for a little breeze. The stores became much more spread apart, the parking lots turned to fields with crooked old houses peeling toxic paint set up right next to the road. One of the houses had become a thrift store Sylvia always meant to visit, though she couldn't image what she would do with a butter churn, dangerous-looking wooden chairs, or a rusted wheelbarrow with a flower pot sitting in the middle. Save them for her own yard sale probably. She should turn around and go buy a knickknack to make her apartment feel like someone lived there rather than like someone forgot a few things on her hasty move out. But Sylvia couldn't stop and let the town be still around her, her thoughts darting like gnats.

She had gotten up in a bad state of mind. Something was wrong with Ava. Something was happening and she didn't know why. Sylvia had checked her e-mail and wandered the Web. She could enlarge her penis, meet for a discreet affair, get to know some horny Russian girls who were already hot for her. All this technology and that's the best people could come up with was passing dirty notes to each other. She knew she shouldn't but she began to search the Web to read about the families of the children killed at the school up north. She navigated through pages and pages of links, memorials, the parents' memories, the notes of surviving children. She couldn't stop the flood of thoughts of her son: Devon found a story in his schoolbook *I Heard the Owl Call My Name* and said the title fifty times if he said it once, an incantation they both found strangely soothing. In the mornings, Devon always a large boy, hovered over her in the kitchen, his cereal bowl close up to his lips, the shadow of his bulk on the table. *Can't you sit down? Stop hovering.* A flash of giant shoes in the hall. Legs hung over the shabby couch, slow swinging as the blue flicker of the television lit his face. Ordinary things. Days and years of the everyday, ordinary thing. Every passing day was more empty of the living proof of him, the sounds of his voice and movement, the sweaty funky boy smell of him.

Sylvia turned the car around at the Run In convenience store. "You want a snack?"

"No, I want to do what we set out to do." Lana pulled out her phone.

"Who are you calling?"

"Harriet Tubman. I am being kidnapped ain't I? Who you think? Ava," Lana said into the receiver, "your mama has finally gone off the deep end."

"I'm fine, I'm fine. Tell her I'm fine," Sylvia said.

"I'm just saying hey. Are you okay, honey? Talk to your mama, hear? Okay, don't let me interrupt high finance. Okay. See you."

"What did you call her for?" Sylvia asked.

"You need to talk to her."

"What do you know, Lana? I'm not playing with you."

"I know you need to talk to her. Don't put me in the middle. You need to talk to her. Right now or sooner," Lana said.

Sylvia turned the car to home. Charlotte. All these young people with old-timey names. Sylvia would not go see that woman like she was some kind of fixer, like she'd ever solved a single problem in her own life. That woman was not her business.

23

Ava was twelve when James Martin came into their lives. Some people are constants like the soil, always with you, never an arrival date or a beginning to recount. But with James she knew the second he became part of them. In the parking lot of the Winn-Dixie grocery store, Sylvia pushed a rusted cart, Ava trailed behind her mother, her attention shifted from the quaking wheel on the buggy and her mother's swaying hips in her polyester maxi. James materialized from the thick, humid air.

"Ree Ree," they heard behind them, her mother's nickname. Nobody but family and people Sylvia knew when she was a child knew to call her Renee, and only a very few had any idea that once upon a time she had been called Ree Ree—a nickname, a name from Sylvia's girlhood—a country name Sylvia resented for being what it was.

Sylvia jerked her head up, recognition on her face. "James

Martin?" A question, though she was sure her mother knew the sound.

Her mother was lonely. Even she could see that. But she wore alone poorly, always hoped that the buffer of people would save her from having to navigate the world with just her own counsel.

"Little Ree. Is that you?"

"Yeah, every bit of it." Sylvia smoothed the front of her top to hide the bulges her fat belly made, hoping to look a little slimmer, but only emphasizing her bulk.

"You look good, girl. Real good. Let me see you," James said, pulling her mother's body into his. I can't believe I just run into you like this."

Sylvia grinned. Ava could tell she wanted to believe James. Believe that she looked real good, even if she knew it had to be a lie. Her mother thought her days of looking good were over and she'd entered into the phase that women fear, of sinking into the background, becoming the silent feature while the young women and girls took center stage, had their babies, wore their high heels, laughed too loud because men liked to hear them. Ava thought her mother was a pretty woman. She was also fat. Ava wasn't blind.

"You been in town long?" Her mother said softly like she was shy. Sylvia Ross was nobody's shy. Nobody who knew her would ever think so.

"I just got out. Two days. And here you are."

Her mother giggled, sounded younger than Ava liked. Ava got in the car and didn't hear the rest of their conversation, but she was sure that her mother was pleased. If she'd had the keys she would've turned on the radio. If she'd had a notebook, she would have written something witty or drawn high-heeled shoes, her newest drawing project. But there she was by herself and unprepared.

Sylvia and James put the groceries in the trunk.

"I'm gonna call you, girl," James said as he opened the car door for Sylvia.

Sylvia positioned herself into the plush seat, arranged herself behind the wheel.

"Good to see you. Don't be a stranger."

James waved to her mother from the other side of the glass. Ava waved back to him from the backseat until he finally looked in her direction.

"Don't mention Jamie to your daddy, hear?"

"Who is Jamie?"

"You know what I'm talking about," her mother said as she pulled the car out of the parking lot. "Just keep this to ourselves."

Ava nodded. She had no intention of saying anything to her daddy and it wasn't until that very minute that she thought she had anything to tell.

Ava's grandmother's house was too small for a Sunday dinner with everybody, children of her own, and their many children, so everyone showed up throughout the day, in shifts with one group coming just as the last left. Usually Ava and her father came together, but today Don stayed in bed.

"Come in here, Ava," Don had yelled to her from his bed.

Ava stopped at the doorway. She could not remember when her father had ever been in bed in the middle of the day. He was never a sick man, never a layabout. It made her nervous to see him red-eyed and wrapped up in the sheets. "Go get me some water, baby, with plenty of ice," Don said from his bed.

Ava cracked open a rack of ice cubes from a metal pan and

brought Don a glass of water and a glass of ice, like he liked. Her father's eyes were red, puffy, and he had slept in his clothes. "Just set it down on the table," Don had said and rolled over to face the wall.

"Get up from there, Don, and stop scaring Ava," Sylvia said as she brought a snack for herself to watch television. "Don't let him bother you, Ava," she said.

"Is Daddy sick?" Ava whispered to her mother.

"Oh he's sick, but there's no help for him," Sylvia yelled loudly enough for Don to hear. "Don't worry. He's just a fool. There's no cure for that. He'll get his sorry tail up by evening," Sylvia had said.

Ava had nodded, strangely comforted.

"Avery, wash up those few dishes before everybody gets here," her grandmother yelled.

Ava knew that her grandmother knew her name was not Avery. Calling her Avery was her idea of protest against her daughter-in-law, Sylvia.

"I've already started, ma'am," she yelled from the kitchen. Her grandmother hated anybody to yell in her house, unless it was her.

"Come in here if you have anything to say to me."

In the fifteen or so steps it took to get to the den where her grandmother watched her movie Ava got her mind right and her face cheerful.

"I'm already doing the dishes, Mama Lora."

"What are you standing around for?" Mama Lora had not looked up from the television screen. "You need to see this woman play. This is a good movie."

Ava hated the movies her grandmother watched. Always black-

and-white, the people too grand and too dramatic for her taste. Why she wanted to see a screen full of hysterical white people was beyond her understanding.

"I'm going back to the kitchen."

"You should already been done with the dishes."

The greasy water in the sink had grown slimy and cold. She would have to start again. There had been a time, she vaguely remembered it, when she thought washing dishes would be fun and begged to stand on a chair beside her grandmother to watch her work. "One of these days you'll be begging me to get away from these dishes," her grandmother had said.

"I can't wait to wash," Ava'd said.

"Remember you said that."

That was back when she and Mama Lora had spent a lot of time together. Ava's mother had left the house with her and Devon and stayed with their Grandma Mabe. Sylvia had fled to her mother's house thinking that maybe life had passed her by on the bus, though it would not wave. What looked so much like life had hidden behind her, crept in the house and yard for years, persistent as a shadow, but she couldn't whirl around quick enough to see it. Her mother had never planned to actually leave Don, but she hadn't told Don that. Ava had not even remembered the week and would know nothing about it if Mama Lora hadn't mentioned it. Don had not been worried about Sylvia's absence and it took five days for him to call. Sylvia was in the middle of making dinner, chopping onions for the salmon patties, the fishy smell of the canned meat all over the kitchen. Whatever it was Don said was not inspired. Sylvia saw the chipped plate her mother used as a cutting board as she watched herself chopping at the same counter. The fact that she hadn't moved, not one inch of progress in all those years, made her sad. It was time to go back home.

Maybe they had looked pitiful and dispirited and Mama Lora had felt sorry for them then. Whatever came over her then was past tense now and she was just as direct with Ava and Devon as any other of the grandkids. Mama Lora never forgave Sylvia.

Even during the comparatively sweet time with her grandmother, Mama Lora was natured nothing like her son Don. She was not fun, not easily amused. She could never see the good side of a situation. She didn't believe a situation could have a good side. Don was always a good time. Even when Ava had not wanted to love her father, she couldn't help it.

Ava hardly had time to fill the chipped plastic bowl her grandmother made the older kids wash the dishes in before her daddy's brother Skip and his two little girls showed up. Skip's wife Gina came to visit exactly twice a year—Easter and Christmas, both times in honor of a past when loving Jesus had been a part of her life. She was like a comet that way. Skip was not his real name, but he hated the awkward depression of the name Earl and renamed himself in high school. Too bad there was never a name that fit a body better than Earl fit her sad uncle Skip.

"Y'all doing all right?" Skip lowered himself into the chair like he was in his eighties instead of the forty-six-year-old man he was.

"You want to eat. There's supper in the oven. If you get here earlier it might not be cold as a rock," Mama Lora said as she took plates out of the cabinets for Skip and his girls. The two little girls watched from either side of their daddy. They were cute and dressed alike as usual, though they were not twins.

"You hungry girls?" Mama Lora said.

The girls looked afraid to commit. "Yes ma'am," Jessica said.

"Just give the girls something. I'm too sick to eat today," Uncle Skip said as he rubbed his round little stomach. Her grandmother spooned sweet potatoes and chicken casserole, collard greens and a square of corn bread.

Mama Lora handed each girl a plate.

"Avery, give them some milk in plastic cups."

The girls glanced at their plates and then at their father. "Go on and eat all you can. Go on," Skip said.

The girls took small bites that might register under a microscope. It was clear to anyone who had ever been a child that they hated everything on their plates. Uncle Skip and Mama Lora were apparently too far away from those wonder years to remember. Don, Ava's daddy, was the opposite of Mama Lora, but Skip she spit out identical to her and slapped a big porn star-approved mustache on. Never have you seen two separate people more alike. Both happiness killers. If they came close to a flicker, a spark of happiness, they'd stamp it out quick before it spread.

"Here, baby, put me a little of that chicken on a plate, a few of them greens too. I might be able to keep a little of it down." Ava started with a spoonful for Uncle Skip's plate but he kept nodding for her to add more. She handed Uncle Skip his full plate. He pulled his eyebrows up, leaned his face close to hers.

"I seen your mama at the grocery store with James Martin," he whispered. "She needs to stay away from him, from any Martins. I ain't never liked none of them. You know he just got out of county."

"I know."

"Well if you know, tell her. People see you. You better know," Skip said as he stuffed a forkful of casserole into his mouth.

"All she was doing was standing in the parking lot."

"You keep thinking that."

Ava finished up the dishes while Skip ate and his girls leaned their heads on their hands as they wished for rapture or death outright. "You want some more potatoes, girls?" Ava asked as she reached for Jessica's plate, revealing to anyone with eyes the clearest picture of profoundest despair. Ava scraped off most of the turnip greens into the trash and all but a bite of her casserole. She did the same for Joslyn. Ava couldn't have been more loved if she had saved them from a burning building. Now to save herself. She rushed as fast as she could through the remaining dishes.

"I'm going out on the porch to wait for Mama," Ava said to nobody and everybody.

"The dishes done?" Mama Lora yelled.

"Yes, ma'am," Ava called as she rushed past the table. It would be years, decades later when Ava was wallowing in middle age herself before she thought to wonder if Mama Lora ever wanted to run like hell out of her living room, crank up her rattling car, and never look back on the dark little rooms.

The girls looked up at her from their places at the table, longed for her, the pardoning governor for their ruined Sunday. "Bye, girls," she said not without some shame. She had done all she could, the last bites of food they would have to negotiate on their own. Ava had lived through her own shameful days of five-fingering food from her plate. There were many a scoop of palmed green peas, slivers of crispy ends of fried eggs thrown into closets, stuffed into socks, slimy okra thrust into pockets. But every child must find her own path. It is the way of their people. "I won't be far," Ava said, but what she meant was you might see her body on the porch, poised to run as fast as her mama's car could get there, but her mind would be gone, gone, gone.

Behind the house was Ava's great-aunt Teen's trailer. Sad little wormy apples in a tiny grove blocked the trailer from view, but Ava thought if she could get down to the trailer and back before anybody noticed she was gone she might survive having forgotten her book. She was *the bookworm, always your nose in a book* type. Everyone says that reading is a good thing, but Ava had started to wonder. People look at you with suspicion if they see you reading, like the reading itself shames or indicts them, like it is a plot against them. But worse than that, Ava was starting to believe that books were ruining her for real life. Life was duller and less interesting than what she read. The girls in her books were doers, who always knew the right way. Seldom had she gotten that role in life. All she seemed to manage was the good, quiet girl who caused few problems. She wouldn't even rate as a sidekick in most of her books. The characters she read would look at her as inevitable and dull as a fire hydrant, her life unfit somehow to be on the page.

Ava started down the hill. From the back of her grandmother's house, she could see a long stretch of the valley, small houses of people she knew or her family knew in every direction. In a few years, many of these houses would be gone—too old, too old-fashioned for young people, too damaged to renovate, at least that's what the kids think. By the time Ava is grown and home, graduated from college, the kids in her generation will be scattered. Some will be dead, some in jail, many others miles and miles away from this valley and this starting point. The anchors that kept them in the community, grandmothers like Mama Lora, family land, or remaining family were gone too. Back then nobody had ever heard of Chinese places like Dalingshan or Guangdong province. Back then jobs that were never glamourous were at least plentiful. Some of the stronger and more industrious among them had two. This happens everywhere. Of course it does. But more so in places that people are more than eager to put behind them. Having too little in life, being the underdog, is only good as backstory, not the constant every day of your breathing. Ava was years from knowing any of that. Ava followed the trail down the hill to her aunt's trailer to kill some time. Teen got picked up every Sunday morning by one of the deacons at the church. She wouldn't be back home until nearly dark.

Before she got to the apple trees behind Teen's Ava saw her mother's car parked on the gravel driveway, but close to the trailer, impossible to see from the road. Sylvia sat in the passenger's seat while James Martin opened the driver's side door with a large Styrofoam cup in his hand as he sipped from a bendy straw. James rushed around the front of the car and opened the car door for Sylvia like he was her butler. Sylvia got out, laughed like she was in a commercial, like she was getting paid to laugh and waited like an obedient child as James kissed the top of Sylvia's head. She was a precious thing, a flower, a tiny animal you fear frightening in your palm. Ava didn't dare move. The inside and secret places of another person's life are never palatable, especially your mother's life.

James walked away from the car and down the rutted driveway to the blacktop. Ava couldn't see her mother or what she was doing behind the wheel, but she didn't start the car right away, the radio buzzed, the car idled. Both she and her mother waited.

Ava wasn't sure what to do. She wanted to run down the hill to the car and reveal herself to her mother. She wanted to say, I know what you did. I know who you are. But she didn't dare. Besides, she knew so little, her knowledge of either of her parents tangential and elliptical. All she knew for sure was that her mother wore a shroud of mournfulness that she tried to accessorize but was obvious if anyone cared to see. If nobody cared about your pain, like that fallen forest tree, did it matter if you felt it? Ava sat on the ground on the path out of her mother's sight. She waited as her mother started the car and nosed it onto the road. In no time her mother would be in Mama Lora's driveway, looking for her, waiting in the car so she could scoop Ava up and take her home. Her mother's face would be so bright and glad for a few seconds when Ava appeared, but just as quickly would tighten again with sadness that no sight in the world could remove for more than a few seconds. Ava would walk the difficult steps back up the hill, to her grandmother's porch, and with any luck see her mother for the first time.

24

Burkson Municipal Park wasn't exactly on the way to the house, but Don was in the mood to see it. When he was a kid none of the town parks had been open to black people except for Mondays—one day a week—but they all made the most of that day. You wouldn't dare be sick on a Monday, the only day to swing, or run in the large expanse of grass, play on the monkey bars, or catch snippets of the women's conversations about each other, their husbands, or the sheer folly that they all experienced in having children in the first place. A generation would come before fathers would be at the park alone with children. For Don, being at the park meant having the sure gravity of his mother somewhere in sight. He had tried to sneak away from her many times, but she was on him in a second. One of the tricks of time is that your own ordinary life took on a sweetness in the retelling. Like all kids, they didn't experience joy then, just the immediacy of the life they were living. Only time made it rich.

The park looked much the same as it had back then. The swing sets and monkey bars had been replaced a couple of times since Don's time, but the layout was just the same. Don had been many times as an adult with a woman or two foolish enough to think it romantic to have sex out in the open in the grass. But there was nobody at the park yet. Don walked to the swings and he considered for a second or two sitting down on the rubber seat. The thought quickly evaporated. He wasn't about to be caught swinging alone in a park, an indignity he would not contemplate. Nothing new to see. He had nowhere to go but home.

Don hadn't meant to go to his trailer but found himself on the Antioch Church road anyway, pulling into his drive. He knew there was a chance, maybe even a big chance, that Jonnie would be there, but somewhere on the road he had decided to take it. Jonnie would be tired after spending most of the morning at the restaurant, but she was never so tired that she couldn't keep going and doing. Energy the gift to the young. Jonnie was a tough girl. When her time was up she would make it fine. She wasn't a summer woman, like some men he knew had. Women they tricked into thinking they'd be around forever. Let her nest. Let her spend her little money on a house, decorations on a man they wouldn't be speaking to six months in the future. Don tried to be as straight up as he could. Besides that, Jonnie had a good mother, a big asset in the world. Something to bank on. Jonnie told the story about her mother going to their basement and seeing wires hanging from the ceiling. Something told her not to touch those wires but go back up the stairs and get the broom to stuff them back into place. As soon as the broom bristles pushed the wires together, sparks flew in every direction. Sure enough it was a trap set by her husband. "Weren't you afraid, Mama?" Jonnie had asked her mother, trying not to picture the wires' quick combustion and those inevitable sparkles on her mother's slick skin. "Naw, honey, your daddy's too stupid to do the job right and too sorry to kill me his own self." Jonnie had laughed with her mother, tried to get Don to find the funny in the long-ago incident. Don couldn't get it. But Jonnie laughed, feeling sure that if her mother believed it, there was nothing to fear.

Don hadn't gotten out of the car before Jonnie opened the trailer door.

"I missed you today," she said as she held the door open for Don.

"I'm fine," Don said, only vaguely aware that he was responding to the wrong question. He crossed the threshold to the little trailer. "The place looks good," he said as he tried to avoid Jonnie's eyes. She had cleaned, picked up their litter and discarded clothes. They lived like teenagers.

"How long have you been here?"

"A couple of hours."

"It looks nice in here," Don said, appraising the tiny rooms.

"I was hoping we might make something good for dinner. I can go to the grocery store."

"Been a lot going on, Jonnie. I don't want to think about that. I just want to rest."

"Am I bothering you, Don?" Jonnie sounded hurt, though she tried to keep her face unworried.

"My eyes are tired, that's all. You go on doing what you was doing. I'm just going to sit awhile."

Don lifted his eyebrows and the side of his mouth, hoped he

looked lighthearted, but he couldn't make his eyes interested. "Thank you for cleaning up."

"You already said that."

"I'm old."

"Why are you thanking me anyway?"

"Let me rest my eyes a minute, Jonnie."

Jonnie pulled at Don's arm tried to coax him off the couch. "You don't have to say anything. You can keep your eyes closed."

Don pulled her beside him on the couch. The odor of cooking grease from her work was still on her skin. He stroked her hair, soft as cotton on his fingers, ran his coarse thumb along the silky skin on the back of her neck. She was a pretty thing. He felt nothing for her at all. "When I was coming up we all worked for some white people. Did your mama tell you that? This lady I worked for used to fry chicken and give me the wings. 'I love the wings the best, but I can't eat a wing.' You believe she said that to me? 'I can't eat a wing.'"

"What did you say to her?"

"I ate the wings. What do you think? Worked all day for a dollar or two." Don remembered once the woman's grown daughter had come home. "Why do you cook for them?" she'd asked. Like he was a horde instead of one narrow-tailed young boy. "I don't know why that came to my mind. Just let me rest here right now."

"I know you went to see her. You think I don't know." Jonnie sat up and looked at his face, her expression unreadable to Don. Jonnie waited for Don to speak, but he didn't. Instead he closed his eyes and put back his head, like he might sleep. She wanted to scream at him, but instead she studied his old face in the full light of day. He had thick lines in his forehead and beside his nose like war paint. Instead of being a uniform brown his skin was a dozen colors of brown merged together like the thousand dots in a painting. He was still pretty to her though he could easily be someone's grandfather. She had thought that the age difference didn't matter, but she'd been wrong. She would always be superior to him. She would see a world (because she would outlive him by decades) that he would never see.

What she hadn't counted on was that she would always be a few steps behind him, never knowledgeable enough about the good music, a stranger to the lean and hungry times that sounded like an all-night party in the retelling. That past life she had access to only through the tales from her mother. Girls far less beautiful than she was had much more. Jonnie knew this. She understood the unfairness of it all in every direction. To have to rely on a nice face was one burden. Worse still was to be constantly disappointed by it. But she had found a little bit, not much, but a little bit of a life that felt like it could be a regular one, with regular cares—dinner and dirty clothes, a schedule, the annoying routines of living with a man. The idea that someone could take this little bit from her was suffocating. Before Jonnie had come home to live, before the baby, she had worked in a restaurant in Charlotte—an upscale place—where groups of young people her age would order drinks and finger food, spend what amounted to her grocery money for a week, for a meal that wasn't even a meal, but bits of a meal. She served them, smiled at them. The men glanced at her, watched her walk from the table, but she was to them as important as the basket of pita bread.

Don opened his eyes like he was a little surprised to find Jonnie still staring at him. He recovered quickly, but she saw the guilt in his face. She had been guessing that Don had gone to see Sylvia, but his reaction confirmed to her that she was right.

"I've had a lot of life before you, Jonnie. It doesn't just go away."

"And you'll have a lot after me too, is that it?" Jonnie got up from the couch to the bedroom, clicked the door behind her.

Don was tempted to follow her to start a train of lies Jonnie would believe because she wanted to, but he didn't have the heart for it. He was tired. Had it finally happened that women had worried the hell out of him? He picked up his keys and went out the door. His relationship with Jonnie would not end this easily. These things never do. But both of them were on notice that their days together were short.

25

Mommies2B.com

Hey everybody! I am in my fifth week of pregnancy. At the doctor's office today I had my blood taken and just checked my weight for the heck of it. I weigh the same, but it will come, I hope. Who would have thought I'd ever be waiting for the scale to go up! Life, right?

This is not my first time as I told you. Maybe it's the hormones or maybe I'm just an idiot—that is a distinct possibility—but I'm feeling good about it. My marriage is falling apart. Actually that's a lie, it cracked open a long time ago, but we are finally at the point where we can tell each other how much we hate the other. I'm kind of looking forward to that. LOL. I feel relief like I just crawled out from under something heavy! Don't get me wrong, I'm hurt. It is all too dramatic to tell you about here, but I know I'll make it. Does that make sense? I feel lighter. Anyway, I know this isn't a divorce site!

Let me tell you about my doctor's visit. I sat beside a girl in the waiting room, she had to be twenty, twenty-two at the most. She was practically naked with these tiny little shorts, flip-flops, and a halter. In May for God's sake. She looked like she couldn't wait to get her clothes off. You know it's not that damn hot LOL! Of course if I had her body I might take any excuse to go around naked too. She was perfect, everybody. She looked like those pregnant women you see on television—a size two except for the baby, perfect glossy hair that she had in a doughnut on top of her head, and I'm talking young. I was sitting to the right of her and I couldn't help but feel like the after shot. You know what I mean? I'm not that old in ordinary life, pretty young, but not at the OBGYN's office. This girl was at least fifteen years younger than me. But who knows. When you get in your thirties you can't tell how old anybody is anymore. Women look eighteen or thirty-one. I just can't tell unless it is really obvious. You know what I mean? Anyway, this girl was all by herself like I was, but no mother with her, no ring, no boyfriend. I hope she'll be okay. I felt for her. You know? I hope she's not going through all this alone. But man, if I was a baby, I'm much rather ride around in that package. Ha, ha! Do you know my chart says elderly and geriatric maternal age? Elderly! Can you believe that? Despite the fact that all my sentences end in exclamations! Would an elderly person do that? If you met me, you would have no idea I was the same person as on this site. Keep your fingers crossed! Ava2WW

Right on! Ava2WW! Baby dust! Baby Luv Jon

So happy for you! Katie'sMom

Sorry about your husband. I've had one of those, but I cut that ZERO and traded up! Don't worry about it. I'm so excited for you! Just concentrate on the baby. Great news! BellasMOM

Ava 2WW, so happy to hear things are going well. I am trying again, but nothing yet. I've got a little girl, but I want a boy too. I know what you mean about being the AFTER! I'm 36 and I already feel like I'm late to the party. I have a niece who is nineteen and expecting. I look like a grandma compared to her. LOL! I've been trying for many years too. I know I should be grateful for my baby and I am, believe me. But the first time I was pregnant with my Phoebe (eleven years old in two months) I got pregnant the first time I tried. You get cocky when that happens. Let me tell you. I told that story so many times when I was expecting. I never thought about how hurtful it might have been to women trying and trying for years. Like ME! Live and learn or live and don't learn. Either way. I'm hoping for the learning. LOL. Good luck, good luck. Keep us posted. And I'll let you know the absolute second Baby 2 decides to show up☺ WISHING4TWO

I hope you all get what you want. Mom 2 B

Hey, WISHING4TWO. You were so lucky with your first one. I'm sorry about the second. Don't give up. Don't give up. You and others on this site keep me hopeful and encouraged. I would be so alone without you. They gave me progesterone suppositories to try to keep the pregnancy, but things look good. Anybody use those? My HCG numbers are increasing (they didn't last time) even doubling every day. Things look great. I have no symptoms, no morning sickness. I've read too much not to be worried about that, but the doctor says everything is fine. Fine! Have other people had no morning sickness and a healthy pregnancy and a healthy baby? Anybody? I would love to hear your stories. If I can give you hope, that's what I want to do! AVA2WW

26

Ava and Sylvia held on to each other as they walked from the car to JJ's house. Puddles of standing water from the early morning rain dotted the red clay yard.

"Step on the pieces of board, Mama," Ava said as she steered her mother away from the slick mud.

"Look at this swamp. Somebody could break their neck out here," Sylvia said.

Jay waited for them at the unstained open door. "Sorry. It rained before I could get the stepping-stones in."

Sylvia entered the house behind Ava. The ride up the mountain she prepared herself to see what Jay had created. A fist tightened in her chest at the prospect of his beautiful house rising in front of her, a dream conjured from the ground itself. What she would not admit even to herself was that she was jealous. Jay Ferguson and his house advanced the cause, credited the race, as they used to say. Why then was the gnawing, the hollowness eating her from the inside out?

Sylvia stood in the empty foyer big enough for a reception table. Sparkling clean windows along the front of the house still had their maker's stickers on their faces. What in the world, Sylvia thought as she walked to the staircase and silently took it all in.

"Come in the living room," Jay said.

Jay waited by the slate fireplace as Sylvia removed her shoes.

"What do you think, Mama?" Ava asked.

"It's nice. A nice house," Sylvia said.

Ava glanced at Sylvia, a quizzical expression on her face.

"I'm so glad you're here." Jay smiled at her, a boy wanting her approval.

Ava cut her eyes to Jay, and they grinned at each other. Sylvia saw them hold each other's glances, schoolchildren keeping a secret. They had connected before. That much was clear to Sylvia now. She settled into a folding chair.

"I've been living like a turtle, Sylvia. Can you believe a grown man and I don't own a real chair?"

The three of them looked around the room, imagining the space. Oh the television shows and magazines that tried to convince us that our rooms, lamps, and throw pillows are all windows into our truest inner selves. What a crock! If nothing else Jay's rooms proved to Sylvia that anything looked beautiful—even folding chairs—surrounded by enough money. The fact was a chapter of a life story Sylvia knew by heart.

"Take your time, JJ. Get just what you want," Sylvia said.

Jay smiled at Sylvia, then at Ava. He had waited for this very moment and it had happened. Sylvia couldn't help but feel some of his joy. Not many people get a taste of that feeling—getting just what you want just when you need it.

"Want to see your house?" Jay pointed to the deck.

"I do," Ava said.

Sylvia shook her head and motioned for the two of them to go on. The folding chair groaned at her weight. Folding chairs were designed to be portable pain, and this one did not disappoint. Sylvia gave up and eased herself up from the seat, cradled her purse on her belly like the old ladies she had made fun of back in the day. Those old ladies with their boxy pocketbooks shoved under their iron grips secured themselves from the snatchers of the world. Sylvia shifted to get another view of the room. When she moved into her own house she had felt such pride. She had not had to scrub and clean or paint or make do with nasty and old rooms that would never be more than nasty and old until the transformative power of money took hold. What she would have done with all this house she could not begin to imagine.

Ava and Jay stood together in the middle of the unfinished deck. Sylvia stood up to watch them. Jay circled his arm on Ava's shoulder and drew her closer. Ava did not hug him back, did not rest her head on his arm, but Sylvia saw her body give for him and ease into the hollow place of his so that they stood as one unit, no daylight between them and not two people at all. Sylvia couldn't hear if they spoke to each other.

"Ava," Sylvia said as she opened the door to the deck. "I need to go. Come on."

"What's wrong, Mama?" Ava said.

"I'm just ready," Sylvia said as she stared from Jay to Ava and then back to Jay. "I have no business here. Let me get home."

"At least look around. That's why you came," Ava said.

Sylva looked out over the valley. She could see for what seemed like miles into the town, though none of the houses was recognizable. What the lights must look like at night from this height.

"Come here, look right there." Jay pointed. "There's your roof, the greenish-gray one. See?" Jay pointed to a clump of trees.

If Sylvia used the full capacity of her imagination, she thought she might see the smallest sliver of a roof. "I'll take your word for it," Sylvia said.

"You know what?" Ava began. "You should get Mama to help you pick out plants."

"That's right, Sylvia." Jay turned to face her. "I could use your help out there."

"I doubt that," Sylvia said. She was embarrassed that they were trying to include her, like she was a child. "Don't put me in this," Sylvia said. Jay glanced at Ava, a little panic on his face. *Good,* Sylvia thought. *They should be scared out of their damn minds.*

Ava was sharing a bed with Jay. Here it was all out in the open. In Sylvia's youth even the men you desired, hell, even the men you married, you kept at the edge of your feeling. Ensnare them with the prospect of an abundant sexual life, sure, but frustrate them with only glimpses of it. Do this and (better said) be the first to do this to your man and you can control him for the next thirty years. But under no circumstances do you believe your desire, your stupid fallible body. Every good girl and even the pretty-good girls knew this. Follow the code, keep your legs closed, and in return you might keep him or at the very least you might not have to live under the burning gaze of shame.

"Let me show you the downstairs. Five minutes, okay?" Jay said.

"Okay, be quick," Sylvia said, not sure why she didn't run as fast as she could.

"On the other side is the dining room." Jay pointed it out as they walked—the docent in his personal museum. "The family room is down here."

"Jay, do you mind if I lie down on your bed? I've got a little headache," Ava said.

"Are you okay?"

"I'm fine. Go ahead with Mama."

Sylvia followed Jay down the stairs in the back of the house. A large space almost the size of her entire house opened up in front of her.

Jay flipped a switch and the gas fireplace and flame burst into life like a magic trick. Sylvia jumped.

"What are you doing?"

"Oh sorry, I wanted to show you the fireplace."

"Does the one upstairs do that too?"

Jay nodded to her a little sadly she thought.

Sylvia ran her fingers along the cool slate of the fireplace. In the house she'd known as a child they'd had a woodstove in the back where the children slept. The different weathers of the house— arctic kitchen at the front of the house to dry smothering desert of the big open room at the back—were like different geographic zones of the globe. So much can happen in just a few short years.

"What are you and Ava doing? I can see. I'm not stupid, JJ."

"I don't know exactly," Jay said unable to keep the smile off his face. "We have to talk it all out."

"Have you been seeing her since you got here?"

"No, no. Nothing like that."

"I told you to go slow. I told you she's not in any shape to be making changes." Sylvia sighed. "You understand what I'm saying. I know you do."

"You don't have to whisper, Sylvia. She can't hear us." Jay spoke in a calm way that infuriated Sylvia. She tried to be reasonable but it was all she could do not to rush to Jay and yank his arms off his hips.

"Listen," Sylvia said not sure what she wanted to say. Ava had always been lonely and sensitive, always taking in stray people, deciding that she could fill up their lack with her lack. Henry and JJ, and now JJ again. Maybe even Sylvia should count herself in the list, but she brushed off that thought—a problem for another day. "There's a right way and a wrong way to do things. She's got a husband. He may not be shit, but he's hers."

"I've been thinking, Mrs. Sylvia. Why do the good people have to do the right thing?" Jay said. "The assholes don't care and they get what they want."

"Who will be the good people then, JJ?"

"I'm sorry. It looks fast, but it's not for me, Sylvia."

"Is she pregnant?"

"I shouldn't say. She needs you."

"You think I need you to tell me that? You think you're special because you want something? What happened to you young people? Hell not young, middle-aged brats. You want everything and you think you can get it because you want it." Sylvia turned from Jay. She needed to get to her own home, put her feet up on her own ancient couch, and watch her own television. People Sylvia's age didn't expect so much. They understood limitations. They accepted no, they adjusted to no damn way, even when it hurt, even when it meant nothing else mattered. They made their lives and didn't worry all the time about what else they could have made if the universe got shook out and emptied and reset. How had all the forty-year-old fools misunderstood?

"Are you telling me life is hard? I think I know that by now."

"Do you? Don't listen to me, JJ. I'm just the Negro that sits by the door."

"What?"

"Pay me no attention. I don't even exist." Sylvia raised her hands above her head—a surrender. "I'm going home."

Jay rushed to her, grabbed her hand awkwardly, an action that surprised them both.

"JJ," Sylvia began, "this is truly something, honey. You did it." Tears stung Sylvia's eyes. She was not a crier. She shook her head no to will the tears away.

"Sylvia, I want you to be happy for me and for Ava."

Sylvia took a deep breath. She would not be a crier now either. "Y'all have lost your damn minds," Sylvia said and started back up the stairs. "Ava! Come on," Sylvia called. She was breathless, much too tired to have just climbed the eight short steps.

Ava slumped in the hall, her shoes and socks off, her hair in a fuzzy halo like a half-sleep child. "Mama, what's wrong? Are you crying?" Ava looked to Jay for an explanation. He would not return her stare.

"I'm fine. You all need help. Let's go."

Ava did not move from the spot. "I'm going to stay here, Mama. Jay will bring me home."

Sylvia hesitated, not quite sure what to say that would make a difference. "Ava, come home with me. This is not where you want to be right now."

"I'll come down with Jay, Mama. I'll be there soon."

Sylvia wasn't sure what a good mother did now. "You want dinner?"

"Mama, I'm fine."

Sylvia turned to go. She wasn't sure if she should listen to her daughter or to every warning voice in her head.

"Everything's okay, Mama," Ava said.

Sylvia slipped on her beat-up shoes as Ava and Jay watched. She would not return their stares. "Mama, stay for a while," Ava began. Sylvia turned away from them and opened the massive wooden door. They were still young enough to believe in happy endings. That final thought as she turned from them was the most painful yet. She closed the door behind her.

27

Ava's head was sweaty and hot on Jay's chest. He shifted her gently onto the pillow beside him, the bottoms of their legs still touching. He had thought he might make himself a peanut butter sandwich, but he didn't feel like moving. From the first words out of Ava's mouth, Jay knew that she would sleep with him. Ava had a scraped-out inside that her voice betrayed—he would know it anywhere over any number of years. Sex was not the only goal, but it was a start, a first step. They could pretend they had the power to fix their lives. The trick was making themselves believe it. That's what joy is, isn't it? Belief for a little while that you have the power to mend everything?

Jay closed his eyes and tried to keep still. The house still smelled of fresh paint, chemical and new. He had never lived in a new house or even a new apartment before, always in borrowed rooms, somebody else's dust to clear away. The rooms echoed his movement, talked to him as he shifted. People thought houses were haunted, but Jay knew better. The ghosts live with the people, slough off little by little into new spaces, reassemble in a quick minute, returned immediately to you if you tried to leave them behind. Let them rest.

There were not many times he could remember feeling content, safe in his bones, with Ava, sure, with his mother, but only a few other times. When Jay was very young he'd felt that warm stillness too with his father. He'd loved the days his father decided to stay with them. Too few of them, too many day of ins and outs, starts and stops of his living with them., but how good they felt. Jay would be surprised and thrilled if his father stayed with them three full days in a row. But he liked the comings and goings too—his father's reappearances full of the strangeness of a comet. His father a celebrity and not the trifling bum his mother said he was.

A few times Frank had taken JJ with him to his all-night poker games. The men sat at cafés and sheds in the woods, played cards into the morning hours, the smell of rotted wood in their noses—a smell that would call up his father in an instant. At those games the men lost small fortunes, at least to them, a few hundred dollars the difference between a good month and thirty whole days of an angry woman's sideways glances, her hissed mutterings under her breath at the spells she'd have to work those last lean days before the next check. Frank had been the only one to bring a child, but nobody minded, JJ was no trouble. If he wasn't sleeping he was sitting quietly in the corner or he was out in the car pretending to drive. JJ ate the food the men ate, pickled eggs, pig's feet, chips, soda right from the bottle and not just a taste of it poured into a cup like his mother would give him. Sometimes the lovely sister of one of the men came with sandwiches to sell. JJ felt the air around the room thicken with her presence. Some of the men teased her, *pretty thing, this your sister? She's too pretty to be your sister.* These men she shooed off like eager pups, but Frank was quiet. He liked her. It was clear that she liked him. Her attention to his father made JJ inexplicably proud.

"WHAT ARE YOU THINKING ABOUT, Jay?"

"Did I wake you up?" Jay sat up and leaned over her. "I'm sorry. I was trying not to move."

"I sleep in fits these days. How are you feeling?" Ava rolled closer to Jay on the bed and pressed her body against him.

"I feel good. Your mother wanted to cuss me out, but I feel okay."

Neither of them had wanted to talk about Sylvia's leaving, but her departure hung on the air. Jay had fully expected Ava to leave with her mother. When she'd walked out of the bank earlier in the day (had it really been just one day?) she'd scanned the parking lot, searched for him though she couldn't know his car. He couldn't help but wonder if another possibility presented itself: Would she walk quickly and decidedly away?

"She'll be fine," Ava said, though she worried too. "I should go on home."

"She knows where you are. Why don't you bring your stuff later? I'll help you."

"Maybe in a few days, okay?" Ava asked.

Jay wrapped his arm around Ava's back, his face a couple of inches from hers. Ava closed her eyes. She had a few tiny gray hairs at her temple that he could see even in the dull morning light.

Otherwise she looked the same as he had always remembered. "What are you thinking, Jay?"

"Nothing."

"Are you worried about Mama?"

Jay stretched and got up from the bed. "She'll be fine. She's just worried."

"Where are you going?"

"I'm getting a drink."

"Jay, stay here."

Jay stretched his arms above his head. "Be right back. Right back," Jay said but he didn't look in Ava's direction.

ONCE FRANK WON A BIG HAND, a hand he wasn't expecting. "JJ," he said and motioned his son to the table. He pressed a twenty-dollar bill into JJ's pants pocket. "You remember your daddy gave you your first twenty-dollar bill." Frank dropped JJ off at home early the next morning. "Tell your mama, I'll see her tomorrow," Frank had said and drove away. JJ wasn't sure he hadn't dreamed his father, the poker game, but the twenty was real.

Frank had not come back home the next day. Jay's birthday passed, the whole summer too, and Frank did not return. Jay kept the twenty in his pocket, money he never told another soul he had. He fingered the once crisp bill to cure boredom, for luck, whenever a stray thought about his father came to him, when he was at loose ends about what to do with his hands. Until one day, even after the hundredth search of his pocket, his room, his house, his pocket again, he had to admit the twenty-dollar bill was long and forever gone.

28

Ava walked into her house to the sound of the television in the other room. "Mama? Where are you?" she yelled.

Sylvia was stretched out across the sofa. She had not bothered to get dressed. For good money she couldn't have told you the last time she was still in pajamas at eleven o'clock in the morning. "Hey Mama nothing. What in the hell do you think you're doing?" Sylvia rolled her eyes at Ava.

"I don't want to talk about it, Mama. I just want to sleep."

"Oh, you don't? Well, that's too damn bad. Where's Henry? Are you pregnant? Are you laying up with another man while you're pregnant? Is that the best you know?" Sylvia glanced at Ava's stomach, flat as ever. "You're supposed to be smart. This is trashy."

"Mama, calm down."

"Don't tell me," Sylvia said. "Don't tell me. I tell you."

"Look, Mama, I don't know and I don't care about Henry." Ava pressed her temples. The headache would be coming on any minute. "I was at Jay's. I'm not laying up with anybody. Don't make it sound disgusting."

"Is that all you have to say to me?"

"Mama don't do this."

"No, I'm serious. That man doesn't love you. You don't love him. Can I say it plainer?" Sylvia fought the impulse to pull her own hair. "He's another sad sack you can't help. Listen to me, Ava, the hardest thing you'll do is keep moving forward. Don't keep looking back. What did that get you the first time? You think there's nothing out there, but I guarantee you there's nothing in the rearview."

Ava fought the urge to remind her mother about Don's sporadic presence in their lives. Not today. "Mama, I'm not going to let you bother me. You know what? I'm happy. I haven't felt good in a long time. I feel okay. I almost forgot how that feels. I don't want you to think about me anymore."

"What the hell are you talking about? So you don't need me, is that right?"

"No, Mama, don't get your feelings hurt. I'm sorry, you did a good job and I'm okay. I release you," Ava said, throwing her arms in the air like she was blowing a kiss.

"You release me? Am I supposed to go back to the wilderness now?"

"I don't know." Ava closed her eyes.

"You been sick, Ava?"

"I'm fine, Mama."

"Sickness or not?"

"I haven't been sick. I'm going to sleep and then I'm going to Jay's."

"So you don't work anymore?"

"I'm taking a couple of days. I really do know how to handle my business." Ava tried not to sound as irritated as she felt. Her mother meant well. She wanted to help. Ava wanted her mother to know the happiness she deserved. But god knows if happiness wasn't in her mother's reach at least Ava's own happiness could be a comfort. Maybe her mother would see that the same darkness that seemed to swallow the unlucky and follows you no matter where you are or what you do (different place, same sorrow) was not inevitable. At least not all the time. Though Sylvia was right about so much, this time she could be wrong, and life could hum on a different frequency and in a different speed. Finally, finally and once and for all, Sylvia could witness the miracle, the common magic you know is out there, but you have to see for yourself to believe.

29

Lana called the shop Hair-Apy, like therapy for hair, but the name was too strange and confusing, didn't roll off the tongue. Lana hadn't wanted the small town country twang of *Lana's* as her business name, but nobody ended up calling the place anything but. The salon was in the middle of Pinewood's nearly deserted main street beside what used to be a five and dime though no new stores, no twee boutiques or coffee houses had moved in. The only remaining businesses were a thrift store full of leftover garage sale junk on the sagging shelves, a vacuum cleaner repair shop that doubled as the owner's home, and a few storefronts with blacked out windows, empty except at election time. In the coming years, the town hoped to lure tourists into staying a few hours, maybe even overnight on their way to the high country towns of Boone or Blowing Rock. There were plans for festivals, concerts and a whole slate of good feeling days that would distract from the empty parking lots at the furniture mills. Look a band! A parade! Move along folks, nothing to see over there.

Lana was a good hairdresser, and she had a steady flow of clients—most of them older, since she refused to learn to crochet braid or any new weave technique. Let them go to Charlotte or Raleigh for all that, she said. It wasn't that she didn't care. She cared about her business and her customers and she'd done what she could to Oprahize, as in be like Oprah, to entice her clients into coming back. In the eighties she bought black lacquer mirrors and painted the salon walls a royal-looking purple with black trim. On every wall she'd hung posters she had framed of white women with flipping wings of hairdos, fuzzy feather duster head shots she was sure made the place look modern. The uptown feel would not be complete without soft music, a cart with crystal-seeming glasses and tea or wine (perhaps) and while you wait, might you be interested in a homemade mix tape? Doug E. Fresh, Michael Jackson, Frankie Beverly and Gladys Knight side by side at last, all for the bargain price of three dollars apiece. She'd even hired a palm reader, but some church people objected. Spiritism they said. The same people who looked for signs and portents in the flight of birds and put red pepper in their shoes before any long trip had the nerve to call her out. Lana didn't care about church. She was done with that long ago, but she did care about money. In the nineties she'd amassed a lending library of black-authored books. She charged only a dollar per loan, but pretty soon her stock was low and she couldn't fine, scold, or harass her customers for the missing books that she had bought second-hand herself. In recent years, she considered for a quick minute selling the Indian and Korean hair so many women used for their weaves and extensions. But she couldn't and wouldn't. The sight of those see-through plastic bags of hair, 100% human, the sticker boasted, sewn into a weft with the occasional gray hair in the black or brown track, reminded her that a real woman not yet old enough to gray more than a few fine strands had sold the hair off her head. The whole business, the whole idea of the business depressed the hell out of her. But like one of her customers told her, she had hair, she could afford to be depressed.

Lana had not wanted the salon to be like the utilitarian, ugly places that looked more like a back of the grocery store more than a spa. She had had enough of spare, dark rooms that screamed ugly poverty and frugality from her childhood. She was done with absolute necessity and no beauty just to delight the eye. Her mother never had the time or energy to think about how their space looked. The poor must make do, that was to be expected, but Lana wanted the calm of spending time somewhere with aspirations, somewhere that wanted to be better. That meant no yelling, no cursing and no cheap food in her establishment. In some salons the women know the McDonald's menu by heart and order their breakfasts and lunches by memory *get me a number eight with no mustard.* If Lana got her own Wendy's or McDonald's she ate it when the shop was empty and in the back office in a room no bigger than a broom closet.

You might think that a place, a room, a house can't save you, but don't believe it. When people tell you that, they either don't know better or don't want you to know. In your own space that you arrange and brand with the yellow comb and brush set you set out for show, the soft off-white curtains you love to see billow out into the room, a spirit entering, the bathroom paint you spend a weekend deciding on (Crescent Moon or Churned Butter?). These are not just things, of course not, but totems, a reckoning, a low level mathematical equation a young child could do that proved what you've amounted to, the sum of everything.

The shop was closed on Mondays, but Lana spent the day cleaning and paying bills. But not tonight. All she had been able to manage that evening was staring into space into the dark void of Main Street. Lana heard a scraping and then a turning lock in the front door. She'd been so fixed on the void, she hadn't even seen Sylvia approach. Lana heard Sylvia's heavy steps coming down the hall and she almost called out to her. She could count on one hand how many times Sylvia had used the key she'd given her years ago.

"You look so pretty sitting there in the window," Sylvia said.

"You need some sleep. My pretty days are gone. Sit down." Lana pointed to the couch.

Lana was not young and not young-looking, but she was changed, not in a twinkling though it felt that way at times. Some older women would not accept looking like the middle-aged and old women they were. Not Lana. She was not brave, but she had no idea how not to look old. Under no circumstances would she stiffen her face with surgery, and she sure as hell wasn't doing the clowning of makeup some of her peers chose. It was no bargain to trade looking old for looking plastic like some ventriloquist's dummy.

Sylvia dropped into the sagging couch and put her feet on the glass-top table. A stack of hair magazines slid to the floor while both women watched.

"What are you still doing here? You did the Perkins today?" Lana had started doing the hair for the old lady cousins a couple of years ago on her day off.

"I'm gonna quit seeing them," Lana said.

"You've been saying that for years."

"I probably have, but it doesn't take an hour to do both of them they've got that much hair," Lana snapped her fingers, "and what they've got is like cotton candy. That's going to be us in a few years."

"In a few years," Sylvia smirked.

"Let me have my delusions," Lana said. "What brings you out at nighttime? Witchcraft?"

"What kind of mind do you have?" Sylvia pursed her lips but she was amused. "I'm wasting time like usual."

"Bobby Womack died. Did you know that?"

"That's been awhile. I told you that when it happened. Where have you been?"

"You might have told somebody but it wasn't me. He was seventy. About your age. Many, many years older than me." Lana nudged Sylvia on her shin, hoped to get a reaction out of her with the old joke. "A lot of black people are dying young. Famous ones, I mean." Lana started counting on her fingers. "Michael Jackson, Donna Summer, Bernie Mac, Greg Hines."

"That hurt me. I loved Greg Hines," Sylvia said.

"Who didn't? Rick James, Lou Rawls, Whitney Houston and her daughter, I forget her name. What was the little boy's name? What you talking about Willis?"

"I know who you mean."

"I don't think he was much over forty."

"He was sick, Lana. He wasn't supposed to live that long."

"He's still dead ain't he?"

Sylvia sighed and rolled her eyes. She was glad she stopped to see Lana. She'd driven to Hickory to shop, not shop really just to look at a bunch of merchandise useless to her but calming for its order and sameness. Once she got to the mall, parked in a faraway place, watched a few people trek inside like into an ant colony, she'd lost the heart to go in herself. What the hell for?

"You remember that boy the kids said died from break dancing?"

Sylvia nodded. "I saw him on a show. *Dancing with the Stars* maybe. I guess he's not dead."

"Not entirely," Lana said. "Is Danny Glover dead?"

"Why are you talking about this?"

"I'm feeling cheerful today." Lana picked up a bunch of dirty towels and tossed the heap into a hamper near the bathroom door. "I was really trying to find myself a pet on the Internet and saw one of BB King's kids."

"Stay off the Internet, Lana. There's nothing for us on it."

"Maybe not for you, but I'm living in the twenty-first century."

"I better not hear about you using that Twitter," Sylvia said.

"Look here." Lana fumbled in her purse and held her phone out for Sylvia to see. "Puppies for You. So many cute ones."

"You and a pet? Don't do that to a little creature."

"Ha. You know animals love me. I'm going to Hickory tomorrow and get me a dog to carry around."

"Say you're joking."

"Who's joking? Won't I be cute?"

"When did you start liking dogs?"

"I never said I like them. I need something to keep me company at the shop."

"Well if anyone can get away with having one of those mutts, you can. But don't bring him to my house. I hate those yappy things."

"I'm not getting a yappy dog. I want a German shepherd I can carry on my back."

Sylvia's laughter came in a burst that even she didn't expect. "I don't know why I try to have a conversation with you." Sylvia sighed, her first moment of real relaxation in days. She reached to the floor for a magazine. "Is this Beyoncé?" The woman on the cover was all but naked with her lips parted in a way men must find sexy, like they were about to say something but decided to keep it to themselves after all. She looked like a dummy mouth breather to Sylvia.

"You know they're not all Beyoncé don't you?" Lana shook her head like Sylvia was beyond help.

"She looks like her. What does that giant Afro mean? Is that supposed to be funny?"

"They're all doing it. I was in Walmart and some teenager says to me, 'team natural.' Team natural! I always have natural hair." Lana laughed. "Kids think they invent everything. You know how much time and grease-relief it takes to get a natural hairdo." Lana twisted her lips. "You can go on the Internet and find, I don't know how many videos about the hundred steps you do to get your natural look. Well *you* can't find it, but most people can."

Sylvia stood in front of one of the two shampoo bowls and raked through her hair with her fingers. "God I got old. Look at me." Sylvia didn't imagine herself a teenager or even fifty but she didn't think of herself as an old lady usually. She wanted to ask some stranger how old she looked. As tempted as she was to find out she thought she wouldn't survive the answer.

"I'm not looking at you," Lana said.

"Why not? Am I that bad?"

"No more than usual. But you get mad too quick. Here, make yourself useful, help me pack up this stuff up so we can get out of here."

Sylvia adjusted her chin-length bob back into a ponytail. She sucked her cheeks. "Everybody else says I look good."

"They don't say young, do they?"

Sylvia cut her eyes at Lana. "JJ thought Marcus was my boyfriend."

"Hmm." Lana laughed. "I should just keep my mouth closed."

"I've got too much on my mind today. I feel like I've wasted my life." Sylvia glanced up a Lana to gauge her reaction. She had not meant to say the exact thing she was thinking.

"Well stand outside. The last think I need is bad juju."

"I can't tell you nothing can I?" Sylvia snorted. "The Simmy's light was still on when I rode through town. You going before they close?"

"I haven't been in that nasty place for fifteen years and I see no reason to end the streak." Lana peered out the window. She had to crane her neck to see the lit sign. Years ago when Lana was young, she stood with her mother at the Simmy's pick-up window. Even from their vantage point outside the building they could see the white diners inside, the cheap Formica-topped tables, the glint of silver napkin holders and ketchup bottles visible through the commerce in the kitchen. "Did somebody die, do you know?" Lana asked.

"Who knows what the real story is. The kids don't want to do it. Too much work. I don't go in there anyway." Sylvia couldn't remember the last time she wanted to go into Simmy's.

"What do you care then?"

"I don't. I'm just making conversation. I don't care," Sylvia said, but she couldn't put into words that she was glad to have outlasted the place. Not managing to die had become a triumph.

"I sure as hell don't. It looked like a fifties whore in there as worn and tacky." Lana said.

"A fifties whore? Do you even hear yourself?"

"You know what I mean. Places today can't look nasty, but back then we just made do. Reused everything. Somebody would hand you a chipped plate in a minute. Can you imagine if you went to a restaurant today and got a chipped anything?"

"How did I get this started?"

"You know I'm right," Lana said. "But you know what? They don't want me and I don't want them. I know it was a long time ago, but I don't go where I'm not wanted."

Sylvia laughed, "That doesn't leave you many places does it?"

"You know I'm right," Lana chuckled.

"I have to agree or die so I agree."

"Don't be right, heifer. That's up to you," Lana said.

"End of an era. But you know what they say? You can love a crippled mule if it stays around long enough."

"Nobody says that but you, Sylvia."

The past had started erasing behind Sylvia like in a cartoon. Her life as a girl; the lives of her parents; her son; all disappearing as if they had never been. Giving up the pain and exclusion and meant also losing years of her life. The trick was cutting out the bad like a tumor, hoping the nasty had not spread into the rest of your thinking. Cutting it out, but somehow managing to survive. Isn't that always the trick? "Mama used to love Simmy's. You remember that. She wanted one of those big burgers when she was dying, but I don't think she took more than a bite or two. I'm the one had to go get it." In a small town your dead mother haunts nearly every corner, turning up in a thousand places you don't expect. At first she scared you, her face, her smell, a memory of her at the laundromat, at the post office. But soon you delighted in her presence. You remembered her kind moments and her happiness. But in time, as the years progressed you recalled her in the meat of her life, in her ordinary days, the ways she normally existed. You remembered her anger, every-ready, that she gripped like a lifeline. You remembered her ability to ignore you, her pleading child, ignore you and your pain completely.

"Nobody ever said she was easy," Lana said.

"I'd hate to meet that liar. I'm going to the bathroom." Sylvia closed the door to the bathroom that doubled as a storeroom. Lana had a knack for decorating, but you wouldn't know it from this one area of the shop. Stacks of toilet paper, paper towels, and white drying towels for hair and beauty supplies lined the walls. A big gap of flowery wallpaper curled and buckled open in the seam eye level from the toilet seat. Sylvia thought for the hundredth time that Lana should fix the loose toilet that wobbled when a body, even a child's body, sat on it. She would quickly forget or decide she didn't care enough to mention when she came back out.

Lana stood by the window with the broom. The last thing she did at night was to sweep hair (always more than it looked like) from the old linoleum floor. Old people used to say to never let anyone have your hair or you could be controlled, cursed with a single stolen strand and the right combination of words.

"You ought to do something about that bathroom," Sylvia said.

"What for? You need a view?"

Sylvia sucked her teeth, the state of the toilet already evaporated from her mind.

"What do you think Mama ever saw in Daddy, Lana?"

"Don't start talking about them. I mean it. He was available, had a job, was breathing, hadn't been to jail, and his people didn't screw each other or at least didn't advertise it." Lana stopped sweeping. "When you get like this you always start talking about Mama and Daddy. They did what they did. That's all there is to it."

"Daddy wasn't that bad. I'd have killed him but he wasn't that bad," Sylvia said. Their father had a thick country accent, a slow smile, a stillness their mother must have found mysterious at first, but infuriating once she learned him and realized he wasn't a puzzle to figure out, since there was nothing more to him at all.

"Oh, you don't think so? You remember that time I wrecked the car? Remember that? I told Daddy there was something wrong with the brakes, but he sent me out anyway. I hit a tree. Remember? Broke my arm, cut my face. When I got back home from the hospital, you know what he said to me? 'You disgust me,' he said. I don't even know what that means! Let me tell you right now, we did good, honey. We did good just to be here."

"I never heard that story."

"Yes you have. You said that the last time I told it," Lana said.

"Well I don't remember it," Sylvia insisted but something about the story did seem familiar. "I can't keep all the old stuff straight."

"You need to talk to Ava, Syl. I'm being serious with you."

"What do you know?"

"Did you talk to her? You've got to talk to her," Lana said.

"She's up there with JJ Ferguson. How am I supposed to talk to her?"

"What do you mean, up there?"

"Just what I said. She's with JJ. I wish he'd stayed back wherever he was."

"No you don't, you missed him."

"I didn't want this." Sylvia stood up to see out into the street. "I thought Ava would set him straight. I never saw this coming." The storefronts across from Lana's were completely dark. The only shallow light of the evening came from the blue glow of the streetlamp in the square. A memorial to the Confederate dead jutted phallically from the town center. In all the years she'd lived in Pinewood she'd never walked around downtown or stopped to read the plaque at the monument or spent any time on the street. What had she done all that time?

"JJ is a man. He can do what he wants with his life. You should see that house. It hurt me to see it. I'm ashamed to say."

"You ought to be ashamed. A black man gets something and even his people can't leave him alone," Lana said.

"Don't start with me."

"I'm just joking. That place hurts me and I wasn't even there." Lana laughed. "What do you hear from Henry?"

"Tell me what's going on, Lana. You keep asking questions and saying nothing."

"You have to talk to Ava. She's hurting."

"I know she's hurting. Don't you think I know that? Tell me what you know, Lana."

"Henry has another woman." Lana whispered. "That's all I'm going to say. I shouldn't have even said that."

Sylvia stared at Lana hoped she'd misunderstood what she'd just heard. Lana's face verified that there had been no mistake.

"Who told you that?"

"Ava found out, Syl."

"I should have known." Sylvia held together her shaking hands. She should have seen something. Why didn't she see it? A hollow place formed in her chest, a yawning gap that would overtake her. She wanted to scream. "Even the weak ones find somebody weaker. Who is it?"

"Sit down, Syl, catch your breath. It doesn't matter who. At least right now it doesn't."

"I'd want to know. Wouldn't you?" Sylvia tried to think of the signs she should have recognized. She missed the obvious somehow. "Why didn't she tell me, Lana?"

"She's having a hard time. Don't get caught up in that. Be easy with her."

"When am I not easy? I didn't drag her out of JJ's. I thought about it."

"You should have taken me with you."

"I didn't know you wanted to go."

"Why would I want to go anywhere?" Lana snorted. "If we'd both been there, we'd have talked some sense into her," Lana said.

"I did talk to her. What could I say? Do your homework? I wish I'd left here years ago when I was still young enough to start over. My children would have had a better chance." Sylvia and Lana's parents had been country people, dirt roaders who wanted a better version of the life their own parents had led. A bigger house with indoor bathrooms, a desk job, a freezer full of good meat. They hadn't and had not wanted to move farther than a strong man could throw them from their original home place. Had she wanted that life for herself? Had she had a choice?

"Let's go up there, Syl? Let's just talk to her."

"What are we going to tell her? What did I ever do right with a man?" Sylvia had meant to encourage her daughter. Mothers tell their girls that they are too temperamental, unkind, not easy like boys. They remind them that someone must choose them and they are lucky to be chosen. Sylvia had tried not to say any of that to Ava. Had she failed in that too?

"You did good, Syl. She came to me because she didn't want you to hurt."

"I have done too much wrong. I can't fix it."

"Well I see right now you're just going to feel sorry for yourself tonight. Why don't you wish you'd been born the princess of England while you're at it?"

Sylvia's laugh sounded like a hiss. "There's nothing funny. Don't do that." Sylvia closed her eyes. For her final trick, when she opened them back up she would have disappeared. She stood up to leave.

"Don't go. Stay here a minute."

Sylvia walked over to the roller cart and separated the mass of rollers into neat stacks: small green ones with green, purple medium ones and jumbo pink with pink. Lana watched Sylvia a moment but then turned her back to her sister and washed out the shampoo bowl. For a couple of minutes neither of the sisters spoke.

"You know what just came to my mind? You remember when I kept Devon for you that time and I took those pictures of him on the table with a bowl of oranges?"

"I remember."

"He was about what, four or five? Where is that picture? That was such a nice one."

"I've got it," Sylvia said. Thank God for Lana who understood when Sylvia felt anything deeply she was reminded of her son. Good Lana. She filled the gaps. "I think he'll come back."

"What are you saying?" Lana said softly.

"I haven't given up."

"Here, put the rollers down and sit. Sit down," Lana said. "You have to stop it. Do you hear me? You don't get to go off the deep end. You don't get to do that. Please don't leave me."

"I'm here. I'm here. I know he's not coming. I'm just tired and keep shooting off my mouth. Let me get up and go to bed like old ladies do."

"Not yet. Calm yourself. Sit with me. Let's just sit. Okay?"

Sylvia hesitated but leaned back into the cushion of the couch. Lana sat beside her. They did not touch or even look at each other but Sylvia could hear the soft pant of her sister's breathing.

"They said somebody in the county has rabies. A young person too. They used to scare us to death about rabies. You remember?" Lana asked.

"I had nightmares about bats," Sylvia said. "Can you believe that? I lived eighteen years with our mother and I spent a second of worry on a goddamn bat." Sylvia glanced over at Lana.

"You better stop," Lana said and nudged Sylvia's arm. She laughed too. "Rabid bats are amateur night compared to what we saw," Lana giggled. "Rabies, my ass."

"All the time I've spent scared of something." Sylvia said.

"We'll be all right, Syl. We are all right. You want to find some kids with crack?"

"What would we look like? Old as we are," Sylvia laughed.

"Don't you want to sometimes?"

"Crack? Have you lost your mind?"

"Not crack. Crack is whack. Haven't you heard? Now a little weed." Lana raised her eyebrows and put her fingers to her lips like she was smoking a joint.

"What are you talking about?" Sylvia said genuinely surprised.

"Who says I don't?" Lana said, her eyebrows raised in question. "Not that much, but I do."

In Lana's basement years and years ago with their husbands, smoking like teenagers instead of the middle-aged fools they were, listening to music, there was always music, time like smoke undulated around them—elastic and easily bent to their will. She had laughed full-throated and loud. Sylvia had not recognized herself.

"Please, Lana. I'd know," Sylvia said, but she wasn't sure. "If I had some right now, I'd smoke it." Sylvia laughed not sure if she teased or not.

"I got it."

"Well what are you waiting around for, get it." Sylvia wasn't sure what to expect. It wouldn't have shocked her a bit if Lana came back in the room yelling gotcha, Sylvia playing the straight man again.

Lana unrolled a small plastic bag, took out a joint already spun into a twist. She searched around a bottom drawer and found a lighter. "You ready?"

"I wouldn't have guessed in a million years this was going to happen today. I should have known if anybody could surprise me it would be you. You know how many years it's been?"

"You've been missing it, honey. Don't rush now. This is different from what you remember."

"It might be twenty years."

"Well the stuff is different now. You might just feel slow for a minute or two. You might feel like you're floating. It's strong. When you get used to it, it feels good. Don't rush."

Sylvia put the joint to her lips and inhaled, like riding a bicycle, she thought. Both women sat in silence and looked out the window. "I feel dizzy, Lana. I don't like it. I don't like it."

"Give it a minute. You're okay."

Poor Marcus, Sylvia thought. Another in a line of people she could not save. He'd been gathered up by the police with six other boys, too green, probably too terrified to remember what they all told him from the first day, at the first sign of trouble throw the drugs from your pocket as you run. Don't get caught holding. "Twenty-one crack rocks," Sylvia said.

"Crack rocks." Lana laughed. "What are you talking about?"

Sylvia started to cry fat tears that dripped down her face. She made no hiccupping or convulsive sounds. For the second time in a few days she was dissolving from the inside.

Lana could feel the air around them change, her sister change. She turned her head to Sylvia's remarkably unlined face. "Syl? Are you okay?"

I want my son, Sylvia thought, but she would not live another minute if she said it out loud.

"Turn off the light, Lana," Sylvia whispered. The streetlight glowed in the clear May night not yet thick with the blanket of humidity of summer that would crinkle the carefully straightened do's most of Lana's customers preferred. If you were there that night you might remark on how navigable the way looked without the fear of fog settling into the valley or the danger of erupting thunder clouds. You might note that no forgotten men hung in groups like on city streets. You might wrongly surmise their absence made the streets less mean. You might pass right by and never notice the two late-middle-aged sisters in their separate griefs in the storefront window. If you did notice them, you would not stop.

Sylvia put the joint back up to her trembling lips. She wanted to tell Lana that for years she'd heard whispers that sounded like her son. She almost confessed that when she found herself alone she spoke into the air until it vibrated with her voice and waited for her son's voice to echo back. She wanted to say that in waiting for her son she had almost surely failed to hear her daughter who clearly needed her, who probably knew better than to ask her for attention. She wanted to tell Lana everything that would identify her as total-lost like a wrecked car and the county people could certify her gone in the ways that they do and finally, finally she could experience the peace, the calm of the diagnosis. So that's it! Everybody needs a diagnosis. Everybody has disease.

"Oh, honey," Lana said and put her hand on Sylvia's, her warmth a comfort that hurt her to feel.

"Please don't say anything, Lana. Please, not right now."

30

Used to be Highway 321 was the best way to get from Pinewood to Winston-Salem, though the old roadway twisted and knotted like a bad back. The fixed asphalt looked like a black velvet ribbon as wide as three of the old roads, undulating through Yadkinville to bigger piedmont towns. The grass looked like a loved bedspread spread across the rolling hills where small farms surrounded by pure white split-rail fencing lined the road. Devon didn't like the new road. A small section still existed where a body could walk on the shoulder and feel the slight distance from the passing cars. If Devon concentrated he could hear above the din of the passing cars and into the weeds themselves. The air full of the noise of crickets, the brittle leaves shaking with the movement of undomesticated animals, though Devon was rarely quick enough to see more than a sharp flash of their wild bodies. Devon could see the actual expressions on the faces of bug-eyed children who turned, not in an unfriendly way usually, but with surprise as they watched him as long as he lasted through the back window.

Devon walked to Morganton and to Hickory and once to Blowing Rock and almost to Boone. On a whim, he'd tried to find Tweetsie Railroad, the amusement park he'd loved as a child. The icon of the park, Fred Kirby, he'd watched on Saturday morning television had to be long dead. But he wanted to see the steam train that took visitors on a trip around the mountain. By the time he'd found the park it was blue with dark and hours closed. But it had been worth it to see the silhouette of the Ferris wheel against the mountain. He remembered the fast ride of the wheel, the stomach-lifting sensation of being at the top of the ride, his breath suspended as he turned, no other thought but the spinning wheel.

Most of his walks were much closer to home. He would walk to a store at the edge of town where the woman behind the counter always talked to him, always reminded him to drink some water when he walked, "Soda will make you feel worser," she'd say. She'd give him a bottle for free if he tried to leave without it. "Stay in the shade."

The first time he walked was by accident. Joy, his friend from the sandwich shop, came in on her day off with an extra ticket for a band Devon had never heard of playing a show in Winston-Salem. He didn't have many friends and no girlfriends, but Joy had latched herself to him like an abandoned float in a pool, figuring they might as well drift along together. Though she never said it. He didn't ask anything of her, but went with her flow. Or maybe he was shy. Devon had never felt like a shy man, but even his family seemed to not be sure what he wanted or needed from them. It was up to the few women interested enough to stay around, determined enough to drag him out of his cave to stand in the light with them or he'd be ignored altogether. That there were other choices in life simply didn't occur to Devon.

Devon had not wanted to go to the show. As usual he was content to be at home in his room or on his porch or patio. Early in his life he recognized that he was best when he was by himself. Though he hated to admit his preference. People were suspect of loners. They looked for weirdness, strange preferences and inclinations, anything to suggest sinister motives. The things that would bore or annoy most people were fine with Devon. He liked to figure out the small machine that made a thing work. His mother thought he was smart but he actually felt like he was slower on the uptake, the last one to get the joke, while other people rushed on to the next idea. His focus was his brain's attempt to understand what everyone else seemed to take for granted. On the table beside his bed, beside the orange cup WORLD'S GREATEST GRANDPA was his stack of spiral notebooks. He loved to sit and draw. Each notebook labeled in his looping big script. He used to draw cars, trucks, any transportation, before he graduated to caricatures of people. He drew women, mostly he drew Joy. She was a slight girl with delicate thin lips, a face that always looked like she was smarting from a slight. He never drew her smiling. He rarely drew her clothed, though he'd never seen her naked. Her lips he penciled in as black as her nipples. One day he would show her what he saw. She'd be embarrassed at the drawings, she might even hit him in that girl way she did. There was so much beautiful about her that he saw that Joy clearly didn't know. If he wasn't drawing he liked to look at his pictures of her, like looking through a photo album.

Devon liked Joy, but he didn't want to go to the show. But Devon's parents had seen James Brown years before he was born and had talked for years of the concert like it was a religious event. James Brown broke down on cue during his shows and his band members would have to guide him off the stage wrapped like a baby in his spangled cape. For years when his father was in a playful mood, he'd mimic the Godfather of Soul and fall to his knees, begging one of his children to rush to his aid. "The soul has overcome me," his father would insist while Devon ran to get a coat or towel, anything to resemble the clothes of royalty. Don would chant in rhythm like James Brown, break down slain in the spirit of funk. Devon loved to play this game and hurried to be first to his father's side, ushering him to normalcy. Often he'd played the role too well and his eyes would be damp with tears that held like a miracle inside his eyelids. Tears that scared but delighted him at the same time. Devon had wanted a story like that to tell his own children someday, to make himself big and unreachable to them, the way the Gods are.

He and Joy didn't make it to the show. Devon had no car anymore and Joy's car was a piece of junk that stranded them early. Devon and Joy waited at first, neither with cell phones, deep in thought about what to do. What to do was obvious. And they walked the quarter mile to a service station and called her brother collect. As soon as her brother said he would come, Joy started to cry. Devon hadn't seen her cry since a couple of the girls from the high school came into the sandwich shop, girls with hair like horse's tails slick and swinging from their heads, and laughed at Joy's black dyed hair and dark rimmed eyes, their talk loud enough for all the workers in the prep line to hear. "Do you smell something?" Devon had said as loud as he could. "I smell wet dog.

You smell it, Joy?" Joy grinned so wide at him, her teeth under the black lipstick looked menacing, like a wolf's teeth.

Joy's brother was goat-eyed and nasty, "He'll not get his black ass in my car," he'd said, and Joy cussed him in ways that Devon had not yet heard from her but was impressed to witness. "Come on, Devon. Pay no attention to him."

"That's okay, I'll walk." Devon wouldn't have gotten in with Joy's brother for anything in the world. In those days anything might wound him, the wide expanse of an escaped white belly peeking from a shirt, the empty open mouth of a mailbox, but especially any unkind word. He would have to walk the twenty or so miles back home, the road open in front of him, one foot then the other for as long as it took to get there.

"Devon, please, get in the car, Devon. Please," she'd said. "Don't listen to him," Joy said to Devon's back. He had already started toward the exit with the gas station. "Wait, wait! I'll walk with you."

"No." Devon shook his head and started walking, but Joy jumped out of the car and walked with him.

"Get in here, goddammit," her brother yelled at Joy. But the two of them walked the half mile to the service station and waited for Sylvia to arrive.

That day Devon was tired, hot, and sweated through. His plan was to make it all the way to Winston-Salem, but it wasn't looking good. He had walked miles. Ten? More? since he'd last stopped for a soda and wondered what he looked like to the people in the passing cars. He knew it wasn't much. Did they see a man down on his luck? Did they look for that man's hissing car on the side of the road? Or did they see a man who walks not for health or fashion but because he had no car to begin with?

At the service station, a slight girl was perched like a bird on the edge of a stool, her sinewy arms, dewy with fine blond hairs, *Cutie* in glitter letters on her chest, her face bright and round as a moon. Devon caught her eye and nodded in greeting. A handsome girl, Devon thought and laughed to himself. There was nothing handsome about her. That was a silly thing to think. Devon's interest in her wasn't exactly about sex. He wanted sex, with her, with any woman, but the thrill of the closeness was better. The knowledge that he could watch a woman sip her coffee in the morning or brush her teeth or walk around in her dingy cotton underwear or watch her fumble with the hooks of her bra as she pulled it on in the morning thrilled him.

For a few months, Devon had had just that kind of relationship. He had helped an old woman his mother knew clean out her basement. Her husband had left town years before, and it was finally time to get rid of the thirty-year-old couches, mattresses, and everyday dishes, the contents of catch-all drawers in boxes from her husband's mother's old house. Stuff they meant to but had never bothered to go through, but things her ex couldn't stand to part with. "Devon will be glad to help you, Linda," his mother had said. "He's strong." Devon had been working at the house for two days when on a break from lifting, Linda put the light bread and mayonnaise on the table, got a tomato from the windowsill for herself, and sat across the kitchen table from him. She was a skinny woman, but not stringy like a plucked chicken, just small. "Do you want to do it with me?" she asked.

Devon had paused at the question, not as surprised as he should have been. "I guess we could."

"Okay, good," she said, but she looked like she was going to finish her sandwich first.

There was nothing sweet about this woman but Devon liked

her. Every day he came by, after he helped her clear her basement and storage building, her garden plot and attic, she asked him if he wanted to take her to bed. Every day he did. Neither of them had any idea when this situation would end, though they both knew it would. Weeks passed before the woman's sister came to check on her in the middle of the day and found Devon at the kitchen table naked and unashamed.

"Where's my sister," she'd said. Devon had pointed to the bedroom.

The woman had started laughing at him, because of him, Devon couldn't tell. "You tell my sister that I said she's an idiot," she said and walked out the door.

DEVON LIKED STORES, shelves of product, all that plenty. A small store with dog food so old, he wouldn't give it to a dog, he thought. The joke made him laugh. A girl in the candy aisle looked up at him and rolled her eyes.

At the counter the moon-faced girl waited to ring up his items. She was beautiful, Devon thought.

"I'm sad," Devon said to her.

The girl looked up from her register to see what the joke being played on her was, but there was only the tired boy.

"Don't be sad," she said so softly Devon almost walked away without it.

The girl was embarrassed by her concern and shrugged her shoulders slightly, opened her hands like she hid nothing. Devon left a dollar on the counter and walked out with his soda can popped open. Those were the only words he could remember saying out loud in hours. People were always so sure other people didn't care. Devon saw that with most people you had to come into their sight, not just be an idea, and then they could show their goodness plain.

"You've got some change here." Devon turned back to the counter to get his eleven cents. When he faced the door again a white man in black jeans and faded gray T-shirt walked into the store. The man's hair was jet-black and greased into a hair helmet. He looked a little like Elvis, if young Elvis had been rough and worn looking. Behind the man was a skinny woman in her thirties, her skin as pale as a bathroom sink made even whiter with the bright red beehive hairdo floating above her head.

Devon watched the two pass a foot in front of him. He tried not to look at their faces, but neither acknowledged him anyway. Devon turned to the girl at the counter.

"Do you see them? You do, don't you?"

THE PLACE WHERE THE ROAD OPENED UP and became a highway, where lanes of traffic merged with many other lanes, scared Devon. The idea that most people would never know this danger and yes this thrill of hearing the cars from ground level, the sound growing underneath them like a living thing, made Devon sorry for them. There was the most danger here on the highway, but that was to be expected. Not only were there cars everywhere, by this time Devon was exhausted and hungry.

In less than an hour, he stopped at a Neighbors, a big gas station with multiple pumps, with a McDonald's attached. At first glance, it would not be the kind of place that Devon liked, but at the main counter, they carried the homemade chocolate-covered oatmeal bars that he loved. Devon even loved the labels with the white grandmother in a bonnet grinning with too large dentures. He kept a stack of the labels in his closet.

Devon was out of money. He'd checked his pockets at least twenty times, but still nothing. He didn't even have the little bit of change from the last soda he bought. He hated the feeling of being completely broke and was embarrassed to go inside the store. He considered asking people for some change, anything, but he didn't want to bother any of the people hurrying past him, so busy in their movements, so sure like the shuddering off of an old machine.

A black man, old to Devon, with a white shell of hair picked straight up parked his truck at the service station. Devon watched him walk into the store and come right back out. Though the man didn't look in Devon's direction, he knew that he had seen him. The man had on jeans got from a discount store or a worker's store, someplace they make jeans for people to work in and not for fashion. The man looked purposeful and put together, his shirt neatly tucked into his pants, boots solid and wide, almost prim in their insistence on duty not style. Devon thought it might not be too bad to look like this man when he got old.

"Where are you going?" the man asked.

"Nowhere," Devon said but he looked like he would cry. "Just here."

"You all right?"

Devon didn't answer but looked as if he didn't understand the question.

"Are you walking?"

"Walking all over the place." Devon grinned like somebody'd said something funny.

The man looked Devon over. He was a good-looking boy, but

there was something a little lost about him that caught your attention, but didn't make you afraid.

"You hungry?"

Devon didn't answer and wasn't sure himself, been walking some time on the hot asphalt for hours and hours and didn't remember. He'd walked on the dirt roads in the too tall grass, liked to see the bugs flutter up and out of the weeds behind him. A white man had veered onto the shoulder of the road just to scare him and prove that he was more powerful than a walking boy. If the man had seen Devon in his rearview, he wouldn't have gotten what he wanted. Instead of Devon's cringing fear, he would have seen Devon laughing like he was in on the joke.

"I've been walking so long, I haven't thought about food. Yeah, I guess I am hungry," Devon nodded. "Yeah I guess I am."

"Stay right here." There was no harm in this. No harm. His own grandboys were young yet, half the age of this one, but if one of them were ever out and alone, he'd want the same for them. Devon followed the man into the restaurant part of the store. He stood in line with the boy at the McDonald's. "I'm Jimmy Patterson," he said and held out his hand. Devon clutched it like a woman would, grabbing Jimmy's fingers instead of touching palm to palm. "Do you know what you want?"

Devon hesitated embarrassed by the question. He clearly didn't have any money.

"I'm buying. You get what you want."

Years ago, Jimmy had taken his own children, all four of them, to one of these burger places. They had been so excited and he didn't mind that they hummed as they ate the dry sandwiches or put their elbows on the table and laughed with their heads reared back like debutantes, chewed food clumped in their mouths.

Jimmy had to stop a minute to wonder when he had started to think of those hard times as the good gone days. He tried not to bring his grandkids to these places, but they cried for it. The grown boy across from him ate his sandwich in a couple of bites like he hadn't eaten for days.

"How long have you been out in this heat?"

"I'm not sure," Devon said his straw straining against the ice packed in the cup.

"You look like the sun found you. It's hot out there. You got anybody to call?" the man asked.

Devon nodded. "I've been gone since early this morning. It wasn't that hot then."

"We need to call somebody if you've got people."

The man followed Devon out to the pay phone in the parking lot. Devon recited his mother's phone number while the man dialed it in. "What's your name, son?"

"Devon."

"Yes, ma'am. I'm sitting here with Devon at the Yadkinville exit on forty. Yes, ma'am. He just ate a McDonald's sandwich. Oh there's no need for that. Yes, ma'am. I'll sit here until you come. No, he's fine," Jimmy said and looked over at Devon. "Sweaty and tired-looking, but nothing serious. You're certainly welcome. No, I don't mind. All right then," Jimmy said and hung up the phone. "They're coming," he said.

Jimmy walked back into the restaurant with Devon. He had nowhere to be.

"I'm glad she's coming," Devon said. "I don't think I could walk any more today. I'm tired." Devon wiped his face with his hands, covering his eyes.

The man had the thought that like a child, Devon didn't know he could be seen with his eyes closed. "Devon, you been walking long?"

"Oh yeah. I've been walking. For years and years."

The man grinned slowly. He wasn't sure if he was being let in on a joke or creating one himself. "What did you say?"

"I appreciate this food." Devon gestured to the empty wrappings in front of him. "I don't have any money," he said patting his empty pockets, "but I'll pay you back as soon as I can."

"When you get a job, you can buy somebody else a sandwich."

"I can do that." Devon grinned.

"Your mama will be here before you know it. Here," Jimmy said and handed a napkin to Devon. "Wipe your mouth." Jimmy looked away while Devon rubbed the napkin across his face, wiping sweat with it on his face and his neck. "Your mama sounded worried. You should tell her when you set out for a walk."

"I know it. She's a good woman."

"Well, you think about your mama when you're running around." Jimmy rubbed his head a little embarrassed to be scolding this stranger.

"I'm almost twenty-three." Devon laughed.

Jimmy laughed with him. "One day you'll think you couldn't have been twenty-anything, it's so young. You'll look at people, *kids*," Jimmy said, looking around the restaurant for someone Devon's age to make his point. "You'll see people that same age and you'll wonder how you ever thought you were grown. I said to myself 'why did anybody let me out of the house.'" Jimmy chuckled. "I didn't have my head on straight, that's for sure."

Devon nodded wisely. "I know what you mean. I don't feel all that good sometimes. I let my car roll down the hill. I forgot the brake."

"That's a shame."

"It didn't hit anybody, but it was rolling down the road backward until it ended up in the woods."

"Well, don't take it too hard. You can get another one."

"I don't. I like to walk. I hear the road, the outside, and the animals. I don't have to think so much."

"What do you mean?"

"In my mind."

"What do you hear?"

Devon looked at Jimmy Patterson but didn't answer. He liked this man, but there was no telling what he might think of the truth. "It's nothing. Just headaches."

"Whatever it is, Devon, you have to let it go. Keep on trying to get a job. Get a girl. That'll take your mind off of things. Work is the main thing."

Devon shook his head so slightly, Jimmy could barely tell.

"Church is on Sunday. I need to stop preaching." The man took a package of cigarettes and tapped them in his palm. "You smoke?"

"That's not good for you."

The man laughed. "You're right about that." The man put his ashy hands on the table. He needed lotion, but he always forgot or better said he always let it go. He hated the effeminate feel of rubbing his hands together, beautifying. A man didn't take care like that.

"Do it in the bathroom," his wife said. "Nobody will think you're gay in your own bathroom." She laughed.

"I'll be right outside. You hear?" It occurred to Jimmy that Devon wouldn't be there when he came back. "I'll be right outside that door. Okay? Come on out with me and keep me company."

Devon nodded and balled up his trash. "I've got to go to the bathroom." Devon motioned his head to the store. "Gotta go." Devon did not look at Jimmy's face.

"You coming right back? I'll just wait here for you."

Devon didn't answer. "I appreciate the sandwich, sir. Not many people will help you out."

"You're grown, Devon." Devon looked over Jimmy's head. "Devon, listen, your mama's coming all the way out here to get you, Devon. You want her to find you, don't you?"

"She'll find me."

"Be back here, son." Jimmy knew he shouldn't, but he let the boy out of his sight. He thought about going to the bathroom with him and waiting for him outside the door. Jimmy quickly smoked his cigarette with his eye on the door. Devon did not come past him. That he was sure of. He waited at their table for five minutes, maybe less, before he entered the two-stall bathroom. "Devon," he called. "Are you in here?" Though he knew it was no use. Jimmy hurried outside, hoping to catch a glimpse of the young man on the road. He had no choice but to call the boy's mother. For hours, maybe more, long after the dark would consume a solitary figure on the shoulder, Jimmy searched for Devon on the highways.

Devon almost made it.

Two miles from his house. A young man, still a boy, walking the road, watching the red hills melt one into the other. Apple trees sprung in rows. Did they dance when no one was looking? He never saw the car. When Devon was a boy he would lie down in the middle of the dirt road outside his trailer. He didn't mind the rocks and the sharp pressure poking through to his back. From miles away, he could hear a car coming down the road. Feel the car as the warm earth began to rumble, his pelvis bouncing with the rotation of the faraway wheels. He smelled the rising dust kicking up around him as the car got closer. In this secret game, he'd lie there longer and longer never really close to being hit. A secret game, since every other time, long before the driver ever saw him, he would be safely on his way home.

31

The nights were quiet unless you knew where to look. In the country (the real country, not the tourist-rural) there was precious little to lure a grown person off the couch in the middle of the night. Ava loved being up when the world was asleep. Pinewood lacked detail, like the time before Ava got her glasses and the objects and the people she saw were misted, blurred, all their pocked skin and yellowed teeth fixed in her poor eyesight. Ava's glasses had made the landscape much too ugly. The night improved Pinewood, and it was no longer gray and beaten down but sleeping with striking silhouettes. "Go to bed. You're not missing nothing!" her mother had told her a thousand times. But the voices that carried through the walls, the flatulent sound of shuffled cards, barked laughter from adults, from the center of town, from the cities way off in the distance, called to her. Always had.

Television no longer went off anymore, and the test pattern that used to signal to decent people that it was time for bed had gone the way of the dinosaurs. These days televisions from the neighbors' houses flickered all night long courtesy of the satellites like Derby-worthy fascinators stationed on their roofs. Ava liked to be outside in that relative silence when the air was warm enough for only a long-sleeved shirt or light sweater. The sounds of dogs barking in some distant yard the only voice she heard. Some of the girls she'd known in high school and college smoked to have something to do with their hands when they found themselves alone, anything was better than looking cheesy and vulnerable

Some nights, when she was young, Ava would sneak out and just drive through her ghost town, hers the only car on the streets. Back then, she'd park in front of Cynthia's, a boutique that catered to middle-aged white women, and imagine the women who exited the building the way they'd adjust their sunglasses and purses in casual clothes that the initiated knew to be expensive; held their shiny lavender Cynthia's shopping bags, with ownership on their faces. Ava and her family had gone to the five-and-ten store with the rows of discount socks and familiar woodworked crafts, its wild, wild west saloon doors that separated the customers from the employees, the squeak and give of the soft wood floor. Simmy's Homestyle was still right there, the sole survivor from all those years ago. The sign was a prominent one on their mostly signless landscape, though even Simmy's was dark by nine, earlier if the town was dead. If her mother ever knew that Ava wandered Pinewood in her car, she hadn't let on. But there was no real danger that Ava could see. She rarely got out to explore. And only once when she walked Main Street, did she see another person, a thrill that almost gave her a heart attack when she happened upon him humming to himself on the courthouse steps.

Ava did not drive in town in the middle of the night anymore. Those days were long in the past, but Ava found herself up anyway on the deck at Jay's house, waiting for something she knew was coming. She hadn't slept at all. It had been a long time since she'd had a true all-nighter. Ava half hoped she would interrupt Jay's quiet snoring with her restlessness and he would wake up so she would have company. She'd hoped that he might reach for her during some blurry haze of a dream. Jay had not moved.

SO MANY YEARS AGO, she and Jay had ridden to the spot where Devon was killed. "This is it," he'd said and tried to sound matter-of-fact and not scared out of his mind.

"It feels like a horror movie out here," Ava had said but she was immediately embarrassed. What they were seeing was worse than any horror movie. Dust swirled in the light, like in a dream, the light a living thing pushing back the dark, a losing battle anyone could predict.

"I don't want to be here," Ava had said.

"Let's just go. Come on, Ava."

Ava opened her car door and stepped out onto the dark road.

JJ followed her on the road, picked up a package that held a grocery store bouquet, dyed improbable colors, from the side of the road. "What's this?"

"Put those back," Ava'd said.

"Flowers," he said as he looked them over, like he'd just realized what they were.

Joy, the strange little girl Ava had found slumped in front

of Devon's bed one day, clunky military looking shoes, a parrot green and blue dress bunched up around her thighs, picking crud from under her fingernails. "I'm waiting for Devon's nap to be over," she'd said, like that explained everything. She must have left the flowers.

"Put them back," Ava said.

JJ placed the bouquet back where he found it. "Are you ready to go?"

"What a terrible place, JJ. It's worse than I thought."

JJ did not speak but took Ava's hand and led her back to the car.

"Not yet," Ava said as they watched the dust swirl in the headlights. Moths were coming already into the white beam. "We might feel him here. Do you think that's possible?" she'd whispered.

JJ had been afraid of that very idea. "No, Ava. That's the last thing that will happen."

"What are you doing, Ava?" Jay said. "How long have you been up?" Ava hadn't turned to see Jay approaching. "Come back to bed."

"I'm okay."

Jay stopped just behind her. The deck was a large one and looked like it went on forever, since the night was too dark to see where it truly ended. A body could get confused easily in the dark and take one too many steps thinking there was a solid surface underfoot.

"You want me to go back inside?"

"No, no, you can stay," she said.

Jay moved beside her but not close enough to touch her. He stretched his legs in front of him, but couldn't see his feet at the end of his body.

"You should put on a shirt. It's chilly out here."

"It's not cold. I'm okay," Jay said. The air actually felt punishing and good on his skin.

"I don't feel the baby anymore, Jay."

"It's too early, right? Too small? Even I know it's too soon, Ava."

"I just feel like me."

"You're tired. There's a lot going on."

"I feel like me. I was almost there. Close to seven weeks."

Jay put his arm around Ava, but she did not lean into him. He patted her shoulder, held her for an uncomfortable time as she sat still as a rock. He finally let his hand drop behind her back.

"Don't worry. That's not good for you or the baby. You don't know anything yet," Jay said.

Ava said nothing. She couldn't imagine what she could say that Jay might understand.

Jay listened with Ava to the wind skittering through the maple leaves. He imagined their red stems like the stems of jarred cherries holding on tightly to the branches. There were so many things that deserved to be really seen.

"Do you ever feel your mother, Jay?"

Jay shrugged. Talk about his mother made him nervous. He had tried to ignore his mother for years as she sat quietly in the corner of his mind. He clicked her away like an image from the Viewfinder toy he'd had long ago. He would not think about her on purpose. But she persisted and skittered along the edges of his brain, popped up when he least suspected she would. Though she was smaller than she'd been, she did not disappear. "I'm still here," his mother said to him every once in a while. "No, I don't really feel her anymore," Jay said.

"But you did, right? You did?"

"For years I did. At least I think so." Jay had met Ava soon after he'd been sent to town to live with Alice Graham. He'd been lucky, at least that's what the caseworker said. Alice was willing to take him right away and he wouldn't have to languish in limbo without a home. Jay knew the other kids whispered about him but he was too numb to care. That wasn't entirely true. He did care, but only in retrospect could he appreciate how deeply he was wounded, and only the onslaught of years would reveal to him how much he had truly lost. The pain would come to him by degrees and for years. But there at the beginning, Ava had come to him. She approached him in the way of beautiful girls, like she had nothing to lose, like she was unaccustomed to a man saying anything that sounded like no. He had never forgotten that moment after school as he waited for the bus. She said hello. She'd asked him where he was from. He had been drowning. He'd wanted to touch the downy sideburns on her face and melt into her *thank you, thank you, thank you.* Ava'd had no reason to be kind to him. He could have broken down at that moment in worship to her. Only the idea that she might run away stopped him. We are not ashamed to be saved.

"Come back to bed."

"Do you want to go for a ride?" Ava asked.

"No, baby."

Ava nodded but Jay didn't see.

"I don't want to drive, Ava. We're okay."

"Why not? Let's drive and keep going. We could drive to Alaska if we wanted to." For a quick exhilarating moment, Ava saw a way out. She could pack a bag of clothes in five minutes. They could make sandwiches, grab a jar of peanut butter and bread from any convenience store, get some fruit and soda for a cooler, she could drive until she collapsed from lack of sleep.

"Nothing's going to help, Ava. You can't outrun it," Jay said. "Whatever is going to happen, we can deal with it."

Ava yawned and thrust her arms above her head in a dramatic pose visible even in the faint light from the house. "You think you can deal with it?" Ava asked. "That's good, Jay, because I'm fucking exhausted."

32

Sylvia knocked on the door to Ava's room though she could see Ava with her eyes closed, head leaning against the headboard. She almost walked back down the stairs. She'd half expected Ava to have ransacked the room in anger at Henry and emptied out the drawers and closets like robbers had come. But that destruction was more her style. She would have made a mess, and then she would have to be the one to clean up later. The fact that little looked disturbed was somehow not surprising either.

"I thought I'd find you here. Are you going to the doctor's?"

"In a couple of hours," Ava said. She wondered how her mother knew, but maybe it was obvious. She hoped so.

"Why are you going by yourself? Don't I go with you every time?"

"They're just going to test my blood, Mama. Just a quick check.

I spend longer in the lobby than with the nurse. I don't want you to have to wait around."

Sylvia would not look at Ava's face. "Well, I'm ready now. I just need my pocketbook. You should have somebody with you."

The memory came back hard in her chest. More than forty years had passed, but her first time in Dr. Nathan Yount's office at the Carlisle Hotel remained. Dr. Yount delivered the black babies in the county. He was the only one. Too bad he was a mean man. So much so that the beautiful black women in town, even they, the ones unaccustomed to scorn at their naked bodies, found themselves both uncovered and ashamed in his presence. What was hard for the beautiful women was even worse for the ugly ones, worse still for the fat ones and Sylvia Ross was among the fattest, her homemade dresses as wide as the bedroom windows. Sylvia wished invisibility when the jokes turned to fat girls, when the song "Ain't Gonna Bump No More with No Big Fat Woman" came on at the nightclub, or when somebody announced something clever and original like "ain't that girl big as a house, a cow, an elephant?"

Sylvia had been pregnant once before, though it had not taken. That was probably the reason she ended up with Don in the first place, who was a good part of the reason she packed on pounds like insulation, like protection from the hurts of being someone who loved him. But that first baby didn't stay, and losing it left her raw and sensitive head to toe, inside and out. No baby would ever survive in her, that same Dr. Yount told her. But Sylvia saw an unmistakable pregnancy mask around her almond eyes. Though her stomach was prominent already, she knew that she felt what the other women called a flutter, what she thought felt like kernels of popping corn poking in her belly.

Sylvia Ross waited at the Carlisle Hotel in a washed-out gown that did not begin to close around her frame, seated herself on the examining table. The small room was dim and gray like old meat, though she could point to nothing that seemed soiled. In came Dr. Yount. Sylvia watched him look at her fat drool like maple syrup off the side of the narrow examining table. There was no chipper banter, no what seems to be the problem, not even hello, but Dr. Yount snapped the gown up, attempted to lift the massive dimpled belly that obstructed his view. "Goddammit," he said and walked out, leaving her legs exposed in the stirrups, embarrassment on the old nurse's face. Sylvia's brown ringlets like the flutes of a pie surrounded her broad, pretty face. She did not twist in pain. A crying fat woman she would not be. A crying fat woman blubbered in the retelling—she knew enough to know that. Dr. Yount and his nurse returned in ten minutes, fifteen, Sylvia stretched back out while the nurse held the red sea of her stomach away from the doctor. It is important to remember her name, she thought. She was Sylvia Ross, not anything outside of that. After the exam, with the doctor out of the room, the nurse whispered to her, "You okay, honey?" It was not until then that Sylvia began to cry.

"I'M GOING WITH YOU," Sylvia said.

"Okay, Mama. We have a few minutes. I'm going to rest."

Sylvia didn't move but sat at the edge of Ava's bed. Her daughter had not taken off her clothes from the day before. "Do you need a shower?" Ava smelled of new paint.

"You tell me." Ava laughed. "I showered at Jay's. I'm just here to change clothes. I don't need much time." Ava knew her mother had more questions than she knew how to answer, but she just wanted to close her eyes for a few minutes.

"When are you going to work?"

"I sent you a text."

"I know you did. I might not send them, but I can read. Don't mess around and lose your job." Sylvia went to the closet and moved the hangers one by one. Ava's pants and blouses hung on padded hangers like in a showroom. "Everything reminds me of something else. I can't help it. Seeing you there in bed not sleeping, reminded me of when you were a baby and not sleeping."

"I know, I know, I wasn't a good sleeper." Ava closed her eyes.

"I had to hold you on my chest, rub your back. Every night. For years. I think you were seven before you grew out of it."

"I wasn't seven, Mama." Ava smiled.

"Maybe not seven." Sylvia scooted her backside more comfortably on Ava's bed, rubbed her daughter's leg. "I'm leaving don't worry. Just a minute." The nurses told her to let her babies touch her skin to skin, it comforted them, they'd said. What did she know of comfort? Sylvia held her daughter's baby-smooth leg.

"Mama." Ava began speaking with her eyes closed. "Henry has a son, Mama. He has a child."

The blood rushed from Sylvia's head to her chest. For too many years she had expected to hear about Don's child, lived in fear of it. Someday, some pitiful woman would show up at her door. Or worse, some skinny, hard-mouthed child with a high forehead like Don's would come knocking, saying with Don's lips that he didn't want anything that she could give him, didn't need anything he had any access to, but had to meet his father. With all the dirt that Don had done, Sylvia knew it would catch up with him someday.

"What do you mean?"

Ava shrugged. "It means what it means."

Sylvia twisted the bedspread in her hands. "Are you sure?"

"I saw the boy."

"Did he tell you that, Ava? Did he say it?"

"Of course he didn't say it. Am I supposed to ask him? I saw his son."

"Who's the woman?"

"Some girl from high school." Ava didn't want to say white girl. White girl would have brought on her mother's pity. She would not understand that the woman being a slut trumped the fact that she was white. Her mother would never see the world in those terms.

"Do you know her?"

"Not really. She's not from here."

"Then how do you know for sure?"

"I. Saw. Him. Mama," Ava said slowly and too loudly.

"Then you don't know," Sylvia said and crossed her arms over her chest. She hoped that if she believed it enough maybe she could wish it away.

"You are hilarious. You know that. You don't even like Henry. Aren't you the one who said, 'I give it three years'?"

"How many times are you going to bring that up? Yes, I said that. I wish I'd been right. You have to know," Sylvia said and set her lips.

"Mama, what would *knowing* mean? Do I need a DNA test? All that would tell me is he could be the father. Isn't that enough? What will that tell me that I don't already know?"

"I can't believe it. Do you know her?"

"Mama, I said I don't. I knew it. I just didn't want to believe it."

"So you do know her? Is she from high school or not? Is it that Kim? You know I never trusted her."

"Mama, please just let me rest a minute. I don't know her. He does. It doesn't matter. What could it possibly matter?"

"I can't believe it."

"Stop saying that."

"Well, I can't. A man like Don you expect anything to happen, but Henry, he's the kind to run off. Now that wouldn't have surprised me one bit."

"He let me keep trying. You believe that? Knowing what he did."

"No, no, you wanted that baby. A baby and a husband are two different desires, Ava. Don't get that confused."

"Mama let's stop talking about this. Please. I'm not going to debate it with you."

"I've never liked him. Never. Not from the minute you brought him to this house. But you picked him. I told you."

"Why did I expect you to understand? Just let me rest here a minute, Mama."

"How did you find out? Did you see the woman? Did she come to tell you?"

"She didn't need to. It was obvious. I don't want to talk about this anymore, okay?"

"You can't just say something like that and then nothing."

"I need you to just understand what's going on here. That's all. Don't try to help. You can't help."

"Why did you tell me if you didn't want to hear what I have to say?" Sylvia yelled, her voice shriller than she meant.

"Be careful, Mama," Ava said.

"Be careful? Who are you talking to?"

"Mama, I remember James Martin."

"James Martin? What about him? What are you talking about?"

"You know what I'm talking about. James. The one that came around all the time back then when Daddy was gone. I saw the two of you."

"What are you talking about, Ava, because I truly have no earthly idea."

"Okay, Mama, okay. Let's just play it that way."

When Sylvia and her sister Lana were girls Sylvia told Lana to run inside the house and tell their mother that she had fallen in the well. In a minute their mother was running as fast as she could out the door, screaming Sylvia's name, terror, disbelief, and rabid unreasonable hope flashing on her face. Sylvia had watched her from her position behind the well and stepped out so her mother could see her. Their mother stopped, looked at them both. In seconds she was collapsed on the ground in front of the well, like to collect her thinking she had to stop as many life processes that she could to let the truth penetrate. She didn't move for a moment. That love we have for mothers has to be cut with vinegar and maybe even acid. Otherwise it will overwhelm us. She will overwhelm us. Great love invites pain, must have it or it becomes too big to contain.

"You're hurting and you want me to hurt. Okay, I understand that. I guess I have to take that. But you are not going to accuse me of something I didn't do."

"You don't have to tell me your business, Mama. I shouldn't have brought it up."

"James Martin was a friend of mine, my only friend. That's all." That wasn't all. Sylvia loved him, was in love with him, but even at the time she knew her love was mostly a matter of convenience. She loved him because he was there. "I spent some time with him, Ava, and talked to him." Sylvia paused, not sure what the conversation had become. "But nothing happened, except for a few laughs. Not like I have to explain myself to you."

"Your life. Your business."

"Oh, now it's my business."

"I saw him kiss you, Mama."

Sylvia stopped to think if she had ever kissed James Martin. She had wanted to and had imagined his body, his face. Some mornings she woke up almost choking with longing imagining his arm slung over her waist, his dry, scratchy foot pressed against her leg. She'd felt like a teenager dreaming about him wanting her, telling her how pretty she was and how every part of her was just what a man desired—her skin, her rounded hips. They had never kissed. He hadn't wanted to. James Martin would never desire her. Don traveled with a friend with a big rig on overnight trips when he could. Helping Buster out, he'd called it, but Sylvia suspected he was helping himself. That night she and James had stayed up late. They had waited until the kids were asleep before they started drinking but drank well into the morning. I've got a girl's mind, he'd told her. He'd wanted to sleep with her that night to please her, because he thought she needed it. But the sure knowledge that once again she was not desired kept her from saying yes. They never got so close to sex again.

"I never kissed him. That's not what you saw, Ava. That I know."

"I saw him kiss your head," Ava taunted.

"You think you know everything." Sylvia was suddenly too tired to stand. She felt her weight sink into the bed, into the mattress, into the black hole that followed her, always had, was sometimes just a step or two behind her and would swallow her one day, sure enough, that much she understood. "I need a rest." Sylvia stared at the ugly low shag carpet on the staircase, willing her legs to move. She turned to her child. "And let me tell you this, I wouldn't have taken my clothes off in front of anybody in those days for everything in the world."

Ava snorted like she'd heard something funny.

"Don't you laugh at me!" Sylvia felt her hands shake. "I was fat and I was miserable. I didn't have any friends. I had a fool for a husband. Just like you."

"I've got what I need."

"Do you? You don't know what the hell you're thinking. You can't go live with somebody like you know him. What's wrong with you? Don't be in a rush. That man's not going anywhere? Wait and see what happens."

"Don't even try that, Mama. You've made some bad decisions. Should I just be like you? Is that what you want? You do know that Don is no prize."

"He is not Don to you. He is your daddy. A sorry bastard, but the only one you've got."

"Let's just stop talking now. Can we do that?" Ava asked.

"Oh now you don't want to talk. All right. You think I don't know. I was by myself. Just like you. I didn't want that for you, but maybe we are just lonesome people, I don't know."

"I shouldn't have brought it up."

"I know what I did. It wasn't what you think. I know what this is about. You might fool yourself but you're not fooling me," Sylvia said.

"I don't care. I really don't. What difference does it make?"

"Yes, you do care, because you think you know something. You think you've had something on me all these years. I shouldn't have spent time with him. That was a mistake. But this is wrong."

Sylvia wagged her finger. "And, you don't get to treat me any way you want to."

"This is about me and Henry, Mama. This is just about me. Not you. I'm being a bitch."

"I can see that," Sylvia said. She felt her head go hot. She held her breath, tried to count, get her right thinking back.

Ava's face had screwed from angry to tortured. She wished she could cry, but she couldn't feel anything but the cracking apart, the hollow feeling of impotent despair.

Sylvia turned to the door. She couldn't watch her daughter's crumbling face. If she didn't get out of the room she might throw up.

"I am nothing, Mama."

"You better stop it. Just stop it."

"That's how I feel now."

"Well stop it! I don't care how you feel. You don't get to feel the way you want to. What's wrong with you? You've got a life people would kill for."

"I don't give a shit. I can't live for you or anybody else. That's not on me. Quit trying to make that about me."

"Okay." Sylvia sighed and started down the steps. "I'm glad you know everything and see everything. You're so smart, aren't you? So Henry has a child. Well, guess what? You don't want him any damn way," Sylvia yelled. "You probably never have and you know good and well that I'm right. If this is going to defeat you, I don't know what to tell you. Fight for your life, Ava! That's what it comes down to."

"Fight for your life. That is so funny coming from you. They might as well have buried you with Devon."

Sylvia turned her back on her daughter. She felt unsteady on her feet. "You don't get to say that to me. I hope your child never looks down on you or talks to you just to say how much better she is."

"Mama? Please, I'm sorry," Ava called after her. "I shouldn't have said that. Mama?"

How many times had Sylvia wished she'd been dead and buried too. If they had let her she would have crawled into the ground with him, the glad relief of the end of pain. Only people who have not felt the kind of pain she had would ever believe that death was the worst of life's outcomes. She climbed the rest of the way down the stairs to the kitchen though she couldn't have told you how she got there. What was there to do? Wash the sludge of juice from the bottoms of a few glasses? Sweep the faded linoleum on the floor that never looked clean anyway? She couldn't stand the thought of moving her limbs. When Devon was a boy his hamster had gotten stuck under the very same refrigerator still there in the kitchen. The poor little thing had died there before they could find him. Days later, the stink announced to them where the hamster had fled. There is an instinct to hide, and against our better thinking we find the darkest place to squeeze ourselves into. Someone has to be able to find you on those days. Somebody has to pull you out. Sylvia slowly got up from the kitchen chair and went up the stairs to her child, her breath ragged from the climb. Sylvia avoided her daughter's face and yanked the covers off of her, exposing Ava's naked legs.

"Mama, please mama," Ava cried into her hands like a child.

"Get up, Ava," Sylvia held out her hand to help Ava up from the bed. "We've got to go."

33

I'm not going to tell you everything. Sylvia washed the frying pan and stacked it in the drain with the three or four other dishes and a few utensils. *So much of it doesn't matter anyway.* Sylvia rearranged the dishes on the counter so they wouldn't collapse to the floor in the middle of the night. *I should say that Ava's pregnant again. We're hoping. I didn't want her to keep at it, but what can I say? When I was pregnant with you, I saw the doctor two times. That's it! And one of them was when you were born. I probably told you that old story a hundred times.* Sylvia dried the dishes and put them away in the cabinets, wiped down the stove and counters, and quickly ran over the floor with the lazy woman's spray mop her mother would have rolled her eyes to see. How many times had she done that set of motions, fired up the neurons in that groove of her brain? She could be twenty, forty, fifty-eight. Eternity lived in those well-worn grooves. *When I was coming up all your mama had to do was keep you alive. Keep a roof and keep you breathing until your eighteenth birthday. Life was harder then. People didn't have time like they do now. I thought I was so much better than them.*

After Ava's doctor's appointment, Sylvia had gone to her apartment, but there was no chance she could be comfortable there. She had come back to her home to eat and maybe get some sleep if she was lucky. Sylvia found the remote and sat on the sofa, slowly changed the channels. The closed captioning could be a source of entertainment, the misspellings, sometimes the captioning for one show got put on another one. Gilligan mouthing the words to *The Price Is Right.*

What's left? Sylvia wiped her hands and got as comfortable as she could on the couch. She watched first the KitchenAid mixer infomercial with the beautiful mixers in rainbow colors lined up like cars in a showroom, couples and families, happy people churning ice cream with one attachment and making zucchini spaghetti with another. Their smiling happiness contagious. *I always figured it would be you and me, Devon. What do we do now?*

Though she hadn't believed it possible, the combination of dinner and the lull of the television, the warmth and stressful day had all conspired against her. By the time the phone rang, she had been in a dead sleep for hours. She had dreamed of being alone in an empty white room the light in it yellow and warming on her skin. The readout on the phone said Burkson County Corrections. She almost didn't answer. "Marcus?"

"Hold please," a voice announced.

"Sylvia. Are you there?"

"I can't talk right now, Marcus. I've got too much going on."

"Sylvia, Sylvia, wait, wait, please don't hang up."

"Marcus," Sylvia said as she sat upright on the couch. "I have to go. You don't know what kind of mess I'm dealing with right now. I'm going to hang up, honey. I can't do it."

"Wait, wait, please. Get a message to my daughter."

"I'm not going to do that, Marcus." Sylvia sighed. "You're going to have to get somebody else."

"Tell Charlotte to come and bring Dena. You tell them, Sylvia. They'll listen to you." Marcus paused, searched for the right words. "Tell them it just seems like a long time, but it's only the days that are long, just over a year. That's nothing, Sylvia," Marcus said, his voice broken. "Sylvia? Sylvia? Are you listening?"

"Marcus. You don't know what's going on here. I'm tired."

"Please Sylvia, tell them I am a changed man. No don't say that. Tell them I've learned. Please Sylvia, please tell them not to forget me. I can make it if they don't forget me. Can you tell them? Will you?"

"Marcus," Sylvia began. She wouldn't tell him that she had tried to see Charlotte but couldn't make herself walk into that woman's life, like she had a right, any right to be there. She couldn't tell him that. She wanted to tell Marcus that his family could not keep waiting for him to come back. They have to get on with their lives. She should say. Think about what is best for them. Sylvia wanted to say that they can't get too close to him, white-hot when they could spend a minute with him, icy death hoping for him to return. She wanted to say that only an idiot would take the word of a man unlucky enough, miserable enough, to land himself in a cage. Wouldn't that man make any promise? But Sylvia heard the small voice of failure again whispering to her like it did, reminding her that she was the last person to be telling somebody else to get on with it, reminding her that she had never known a single true thing.

"I can't get involved in that, Marcus. I'm going to go now." Sylvia was at her house, alone at last, the life her mother had feared, the life she'd feared. She'd gone to the grocery store and bought real food to cook for herself. The moment of eating had felt sustaining, but never lasted, never helped for long. The cleaned-out shell of her sweet potato, vacant like an abandoned snakeskin. The Y-shaped bone from the pork chop was gray and left over on her plate like the remains of a dinosaur. She'd even chewed the gross spongy fat of the meat for punishment. She should never eat anything recognizable from an animal's body. All the time, with every bite, she contemplated the mistakes she'd made, the nasty ones she knew about, and the sad ones she hadn't understood at the time.

"Sylvia, Sylvia? You've been good to me. Please don't leave me now. Please. Sylvia?"

"I can't do it. I can't handle another thing. Everything has gone to hell, Marcus. I can't do anything."

Neither Sylvia nor Marcus spoke. When Sylvia was much younger if she remained quiet on the telephone line she could hear the sadnesses, the rantings, the soft love professions of other people in conversation on party lines. Most of the time she could make out just a few words, but the timbre of the voices, the cadences, made the intentions clear. She'd felt a secret thrill at being witness to all those feelings right along with those strange voices as unknown to her as ghosts.

Now the line was silent. Sylvia had not planned to say good-bye to Marcus, but that was exactly what she was doing. "I'm sorry, baby. I am."

"You said you helped me because of Devon. You know he'd want you to help me. He understands about being a black man. Please. I know you don't have to, but please."

"Devon is dead."

"I don't know what you mean? What are you talking about, Sylvia?

Sylvia thought that she had never said those words before. "I can't say it again, Marcus. I'm not going to. Devon doesn't want anything anymore. Just like me. Neither one of us wants a thing."

Sylvia could hear Marcus's breathing. For the first time since they began their relationship, their conversation would be over before the line went dead.

"I can't believe you," Marcus said. "I don't believe you."

Sylvia held the phone. She would not hang up, that felt cruel.

"Mrs. Sylvia, are you there."

Sylvia said nothing. She hoped her silence was less hurtful than hanging up the phone. If she hurt along with him, maybe he wouldn't judge her so harshly. Maybe one day he would understand. Nobody ever understands.

"Mrs. Sylvia? Sylvia?" Marcus held the phone and waited for Sylvia's reply. "I just need you to answer, Sylvia. Please."

Sylvia listened to his breathing on the line. She used to listen to Don this way when they loved each other. Both of them hanging on to the phone, content to know the other was alive. Not when they loved each other, that was wrong. When she believed that he loved her.

"Okay, Sylvia. I'm sorry about Devon. I'm really sorry. Sylvia?

Okay. I get it. I get it. I'll call you some other time. I can wait. I'll call you. Is that okay?"

Sylvia did not answer.

"Sylvia, please," Marcus said, but Sylvia could hear the resignation in his voice.

"You did good by me, Sylvia when nobody else did. I appreciate you. You'll never know how much. Okay? Okay? I mean that."

34

Ava had been sitting on the sand for too long, her behind and legs stiff with inaction. "Help me up, Jay," she said and reached her arm out to him. In all the books Ava had loved as a girl the plucky heroine and her friends had a special, secret place, known only to them. Ava had decided back then that theirs would be the fourth exit at the reservoir. Jay pulled Ava to him and tried to envelop her in his arms. She gently moved out of his grip.

It was unbelievably still the month of May, and the light though fading still shone too brightly on them. There were no other people on the man-made beach area yet in the middle of the week. But soon when the real heat arrived families would line the shore with sand toys and buckets of Kentucky Fried Chicken. Big and small boats would float or buzz through the muddy water creating the shallow waves that lapped up on the shore. The reservoir wasn't an ocean and didn't give you the feeling of the infinite, the miraculous sight of water that could rise up like a wall and swallow you up without compunction or remorse. But who needed the brine of the ocean, the constant reminder that whatever the end was you would never see it for yourself, when the bathwater of the reservoir was a few minutes from your door? Ava listened for the violent, recurrent snap of the flag she kept hearing but had not spotted to reset her thoughts.

"We used to think about having a house up here. Remember that? We were going to live on the water," Jay said.

"Yours is better than all the ones we picked. Isn't that amazing?"

"I never really liked it here," he said and looked around at the landscape as if he were confirming his original idea.

Ava stared at Jay, not sure what to think, "Why didn't you tell me that?"

"I knew you liked it. It's pretty, baby. I just never got it like you do. I want to take you to a desert. Have you been?" Jay had crossed into California for the first time years ago into the town of Needles and the Mojave Desert. He was not prepared for the rush of feeling he experienced seeing the starkness of the moonscape, the many shades of red and brown in the rocks and mountains. Generations of travelers looking for a new start or just a chance had passed through that town. That idea gave him hope. Years ago he'd gone there to get a message from his mother. He knew it couldn't be true, he was not insane, but he couldn't shake the idea that with the arrival of Hale-Bopp he would see her too. He did not know where to look in the sky for the comet to appear, but he waited for as long as he could. An idea can come to you with such force that it can stick, get stuck, get you stuck. That night standing outside his truck, he searched the sky, leaned against his truck, then behind the wheel, until he thought he would be too worn-out to drive to his rented room, if he didn't get going. A few times he thought he saw a smear of a star in his periphery, but he couldn't be sure. You can see in the natural movement of the universe a sign, a message, maybe even salvation. He did not see the comet that night, and months later when it was in its glory and millions of people watched for it nightly he looked along with them, but the message from his mother did not come.

Ava felt like laughing and crying at the same time. "Did I ever ask you if you wanted to be here? I probably didn't. I'm sorry. I thought this was our place."

"It is, Ava. It is." Jay spoke too quickly to try to reassure her, but he knew he did just the opposite.

"You were too nice for a teenage boy, Jay."

"I was just too stupid."

Ava had thought he was probably just too sad.

"Do you feel lucky?" Ava said.

Jay shook his head.

"Lana told me I was lucky. Do you feel it, Jay? I mean for the most part."

"No, Ava, I really don't." Jay shrugged his shoulders. "I don't know. Probably not. Luckier than some. I'm still here."

"You know why you feel that way?" Ava said as she stared at him. "Because you had too much hurt too early. That's the reason. I don't feel lucky either, but I should. I've had a lot go right." Ava pressed her toe into the spongy sand and watched the water rush to fill the hole.

"We should go, Ava. Let's get away from here."

"Not yet, Jay." Ava smiled and tipped her head up at him. The sight of her false cheer made Jay nervous. If he had not been sure that she was close to screaming he would have thought she was flirting with him.

"Ava, baby," Jay began. "I don't feel right here. We've got to get out of memory lane sometime."

"Do you even listen to yourself? Memory lane is all we've got. Isn't that why you're even here?"

"We can go anywhere we want to now," Jay said, wishing he believed that they were still talking about locations and places that grown people can go.

After Devon's death he and Ava had talked for days in the dorm, exhausted themselves with talk. Jay rested on the roommate's always empty bed, and tried to ignore the stucco nubs of the cinder block wall that dug into his back. Ava spread herself out on a blanket on the floor, her voice wafting up to him. Devon's death still pulsed in their chests like they'd been kicked. She had wanted him to say everything he could remember about his mother, Donna Ferguson. He told her about his mother driving one-handed while she held him on her shoulder. His mother's eyes were deep set and very dark but looked sunken and raccoonish in the light of cheap cameras. She had been the kind of woman pictures did not flatter. She'd pulled back her hair into a French knot, rarely wore it curled around her face, in the wavy, soft kinky halo that made him think of birds' nests. She cranked up soul music every morning to help her forget that she had to spend eight hours on a factory line. But Jay could not see the picture of her in its entirety. He would always be too close to her to recount anything but the nuances, the gestures, the small stinging details of her.

"Don't tell Mama yet. Not yet," Ava said.

After a few days together in the dorm room, Ava had told him that he couldn't stay. He had known all along that it couldn't last and shouldn't last, but for a few days they both had pretended it would. He had gotten them what food they needed, watched television with her. They had even managed to laugh together. If they could have lived in that room forever, they could have made it. But she would have to go back to her classes and march into her life. She would leave the stale little cinder block space and move into the unknown future. She would have to get on with it again.

"I went to his school. Henry's son. I drove up at the pickup time and waited." Ava stared at Jay and waited for shock to register on his face. Jay looked past her into the water. "When he came out to the bus, I left."

Jay sighed, it had been a mistake to come here, but how could he refuse her? She'd seemed so sure seeing their place would help. After the horror of the morning, the awful scream about the blood she'd felt before she saw. She'd settled down, calmed quickly, too quickly, Jay thought. But that calm had been seductive and had scared Jay into doing whatever she asked. He'd known better. "You know you can't do that. Don't torture yourself, Ava."

"I didn't scare him, Jay. I swear. I just wanted to see him again." The boy had run out of the school like he'd been spring-loaded and was herded by a teacher into a line to the bus. The boy dragged his oversize backpack on the black top as his group crossed the parking lot. Ava could not make out his voice or hear the song he sang as he rushed past her car. She willed him to look in her direction, and for a quick, foolish moment she'd wanted to step out of the car and touch him. Nothing else, just touch his face and look at him with concentrated attention. Thank god, he hadn't seemed to notice her at all.

"I wouldn't do it again. I felt crazy being there at all." Ava said.

"You know what, Jay? You're the only person in the world I can tell." Ava took off her shoes and socks and inched her toes into the water.

"Good lord, the water is chilly. The sun's been hot all day, you'd think it would be warm, wouldn't you?" Ava asked like she'd wanted a real response. "Take off your shoes. Get in."

"No. Ava, please. I want to go now. This is not the place for us."

"Why didn't you tell me you hated it so much here? All the time we came and you weren't even happy?"

"I wanted to be with you, Ava."

Ava waded ankle deep into water the color of weak tea.

Jay couldn't have told Ava exactly what bothered him about the reservoir, the brownish murky water, the drive through the woods that always felt menacing to him. The scene unfolded then as it had now. But then he was dying to fold into her and let her envelop him, cover him up, like a kidnapped boy, sightless, helpless, letting her lead him anywhere but where he started.

"If I'd gotten pregnant back in Raleigh our baby would be in college now or living in our basement." The luxury some people had of children who stumbled into their lives, Ava thought. "Is that incredible to you?"

"We loved each other. It was okay to do whatever we wanted."

Ava stopped her mincing steps in the water. "We were important to each other, Jay."

"Isn't that the same thing?"

Ava turned from Jay to look out at the water. Jay thought that there were turns of Ava's face when he could see the age flowering and he could catch a glimpse of the older woman she would be. He thought he could see the years developing on her face. She looked not quite like her mother in those moments, but a version of her, another artist's interpretation. He couldn't figure out a way to tell her what he saw that wouldn't insult her or remind her that she was aging, but he loved the feeling that their eternity, his and hers, was built in their faces.

"I used to park at the Ingrams' house and stand in the ditch outside your house. I'd wait to see the light go on up in your attic. You took me up there a few times. Not with Sylvia around." Jay laughed. "But we went up there."

"Can you believe that was us?" Ava had found one of her old diaries she'd kept back then. Most of what she'd written was teenage stuff, girl problem anxieties, but for a few pages she'd written about a girl who shepherded her mentally challenged brother on the bus. The girl couldn't have been more than a couple of years older than her brother, but she was patient and uncomplaining. So much duty in love, Ava had written. She remembered the moment like she'd just lived it, like she had stepped off of that bus only minutes before. "We are all so lonely, Jay."

"We're okay. You don't waste feelings loving somebody. I believe that, Ava."

Ava closed her eyes and imagined the water around her filling her up in an inhalation.

"Feelings go away, Jay. You know how I know it? Look at Mama and Don. Now they can't stand the sight of each other. I'm not nineteen, Jay. I'm not the girl in the dorm room."

"They don't go away, Ava," Jay said.

"Don't joke with me. How much has happened? God, Jay, we're old people now."

"And we're still here. Right? Here we are, Ava."

"I'm not stupid and you're not either, Jay. You can't just decide to erase everything, your whole past. You have to fill in the gaps."

"What for? Who cares about gaps? Do you? I don't give two fucks."

"You do some, don't you? I know you care some," Ava said.

"Probably," Jay said. "Probably one fuck."

"Don't joke around. This is your life. Why wouldn't you care about it?"

"Doesn't matter. Not to me."

"It does to me. Where have you been? Who have you been all these years, Jay? "

"Do you really want to know? I can tell you, if you do. I'll tell you year by year." Jay said.

"Have you been in jail?"

"One time."

"Don't you want to talk about it? I thought it didn't matter," Ava said.

"You can. I can tell you about it. What's to tell?"

Jay's posture stiffened. She had hurt him though she hadn't meant to. She was just making a point. A stupid point. Ava glanced at Jay's embarrassed face and bent to roll cuffs into her already wet jeans. She wouldn't ask about the particulars. Something terrible happened and he lived through it. How much more complicated was it than that?

"You remember that boy who killed himself up here? When we were in high school? I knew him. I had homeroom with him."

"Don't, Ava. No more, baby."

"How does that hurt you?"

"I don't want to talk about that kid. He's not here, Ava. We are."

Jay couldn't have been more wrong, Ava thought. The two of them were surrounded by ghosts they nudged out of the way just to get up in the morning. Ava waded deeper into the water.

She'd read that drowning happened so quickly and silently that most drowning victims died with no thrashing or screaming out for help like in the movies but were gone in minutes before people noticed they were missing. "It's pretty cold," she said as she marched up and down, mostly to keep from crying. The jagged rocks bit the soles of her feet as she walked through muddy swirls of water. In seconds she was underneath the water too full of sand and mud to see her hand in front of her, so she closed her eyes. She was ten or so in a hotel room in Raleigh. The room was a cheap one with a burgundy bedspread flung over the double bed like over a cadaver. She and Devon had looked out the window at the buildings much taller than the ones at home. They had loved the particleboard built-in desk and the swivel chair, the television perfectly positioned for viewing from the bed. They even loved sleeping on makeshift beds on the floor. It was years before Ava knew that Sylvia was seeing a specialist because of a cancer scare. Years before Ava understood that one of her fondest memories was one of the most trying days of her mother's life.

Debris swirled around Ava, the sloughed-off bodies of animals, dirt and twigs and now Ava, all part of the soup, the graveyard. She couldn't shake it that her own body was a graveyard too. Jay's faraway voice sounded into the water, curling into the folds of the water's ripples like the sound was coming from another time.

In her journals Ava had written about Kim, the friend she despised when she was young. Ava was sixteen and her friend Kim was seventeen. Though they spent a lot of time together, they both knew that their arrangement was not permanent. Still they spent hours and hours together, full of glances over their shoulders (is anyone else coming?), ticktock on their faces, sighs disguised. What enormous capacity for boredom people have had. Maybe it's not such a marvel. Every kid knows it is far better to be bored than lonely. Better to be anything but lonely. What a great flood of relief when Jay had come to town and became her new and much improved best friend.

Years after Ava had not spoken to Kim anymore she'd heard that her child had been attacked by a tiger. All it took was the trainer's lapsed attention as he strolled alongside the tiger, holding the puny leash in his dominant hand. The trainer seemed arrogant, waving and preening like he was the star attraction in the animal parade before the circus proper began. The tiger walked in slow motion, lifted up red dust clouds in front and behind him, the crowd hushing as he passed them like a king or god. People said the same things, the tiger came out of nowhere, one minute, dull-eyed and bored-looking, the next his paws on a tiny girl, a five-year-old, one he seemed to have memorized in the crowd, since his aim was so true on her fragile chest. How Kim's child survived was a miracle. The girl, now a teenager, said she remembered nothing but the humidity of the tiger's breath, not his sharp yellowed teeth, not the weight of his face-size paws, but the breath that seemed to suck up her own. If she didn't have the scars on her chest, she would be willing to believe the whole thing never happened at all. Ava hadn't heard this story from Kim, but through the grapevine. She hadn't contacted Kim when she found out. That sounds callous and maybe it is, but she didn't think it at the time. What would make a difference? When the miracle, the catastrophe, the unexpected event that ruptures our lives into meaning, foul or ecstatic and forever changed, flashes back to us, how comforting to catch glimpses of the faces of people who love us enough to say "I'm here."

"Oh my God. Oh God!" Ava screamed as she plunged back up, her head out and treading water. She swam as fast as she could toward the middle of the reservoir.

"Ava! Ava!" Jay yelled.

Ava turned around to Jay in time to see him kicking off his shoes, rolling up the legs of his jeans. He was ready to come in after her. He probably thought she was fighting for her life. "I'm coming. Stop, stop," she yelled. It was wrong to hurt him. Jay stopped undressing and watched her approach.

"Get out of the water. Let's go!" Jay yelled.

Ava turned back to the shore. She was farther out than she had imagined. People can't drown themselves on purpose. Your body won't let go of life even when your mind tells you it is the best thing to do.

Ava swam to the shore and dragged herself out of the water. "I'm sorry." Ava panted and held her hands on her knees to try to catch her breath.

Jay put his arm on her back, waited for her to stand upright and led her to the car. "Come on, Ava, come on." Ava sat in the passenger seat with her eyes closed while Jay started the engine. "Do you want heat? Are you cold?" Jay turned the heat on low.

"Look at me." Ava shook her head at her reflection in the passenger mirror.

"No, baby, no," Jay said. He grabbed her hard, kissed her face, her head, her neck. "No, no, no."

Ava closed her eyes. If they drove the car into the water, how long would it take to fill up to the roof, drop, and sink like a stone. A mother and her two children had disappeared into a pond when Ava was a child. Days had passed before anyone thought to look there or maybe it was the silver of the hood of the car, a glint of sparkle peeking above the surface of the green pond slime. Ava never passed that pond without remembering.

"I'm okay now," Ava said and fastened her seat belt, readied herself for the ride back to Jay's house. She would have to go to the doctor eventually and take off her clothes and lie back on deli-style paper, tilt back into the squeaking vinyl chair. As she stared at the ceiling she would hear the crab click of instruments, she would not witness it but the monitor of the ultrasound would flicker pale blue in a darkened room like she was in an eighties arcade, the screen graphic barely more complicated than Pong. There would be no movement, no pulse on the screen. The tech would purse her lips and would not say, but her silence would signal the need to start over, rev up, and try again. But not before the sadness, the terrible days that turned her inside out, her organs exposed and sensitive to the slightest hurt. But not today. No doctor today. No more. No more. No more. No more. She would go to Jay's house and she would recuperate there. She would stay with him as long as she could. So many black people stay somewhere. Where do you stay? They'd say. I stay with my friend; I stay with my mother. Don't you live anywhere?

Jay put the car into drive and they pulled away from the parking lot onto the road to the house. "Your baby is with me." Jay stared at Ava. "Your baby is with me."

"Stop it," Ava said. "Don't say that again. Don't ever say that again, Jay. I swear to God. Don't say it."

"I'm telling you what I believe. You get to decide, Ava. Don't you get that? You get to decide about your life. Maybe our mothers didn't, but we do."

Ava's clothes were wet but she knew for sure that blood trickled out of her, from the deepest part of her body, running in narrow rivulets down her legs, mixing with the dirty reservoir water on her skin. She could sleep for days, maybe a week. "You keep thinking you get a say, but you never really do," Ava said.

"All I know is I've carried a picture of you for years in here." Jay pointed to his chest. "I've been through so many things, but the picture is the same. You understand. I know you do, or we wouldn't be here together."

"We are confused," Ava said.

"Does it really matter? Let's just be confused."

"It matters to me," Ava said.

"I have felt you. You asked me if I felt my mother. She's there. She'll always be there, but so are you. In everything."

What Ava thought was that when they were young Jay had been a dying, sad boy, new to town, mother and fatherless, a swirling cloud of the irresistible rumor of tragedy hovering all around him. She had felt her own longing in his, his desperation on a frequency she could hear. When her brother died and her mother moved to another planet and she was abandoned to look over her own shoulder, waiting for Devon to march up the road sweaty and alive, JJ had been there. She would never forget that. They were bound together. What she wanted to say to him was, "I love you. I love you so much. Please be my friend. Please don't leave me." What she managed to say was "I can't do this." Ava felt a loosening, a washing over her.

"You just don't know it yet, Ava."

"I don't want to hurt you," Ava said.

"You just don't know, Ava."

"I won't hurt you, Jay."

Jay said, "You could try. Don't you think? Do you think you

could?" What Jay thought was that if Ava didn't want him he'd have an empty room of a life that he could not fill.

I am not going to have a baby. How everything can go from fine to gone, I will never understand. Before I even got up from bed this morning I started bleeding. I've read enough of your stories to know many of you have felt what I felt. I have never admitted that to anyone, not even to myself, but I believe now. In a way it's a relief to finally, really know. In all this time I always figured that some way I would have a child. Some way, somehow. I didn't consider being a woman without a baby. I've been too stubborn to admit that I was wrong after all. Some of you know what I mean. I am worn-out—no much more than that. I AM DONE. You can't imagine the relief just typing that. I am sorry that I wasn't more sympathetic to you who are in pain. To you who are in pain, I send out my feeling to you. I am transmitting to you. I want peace for you. I want peace too. If I've learned nothing else it is I haven't felt enough in my life or stopped to understand anyone enough.

I went to the reservoir and got soaked. When I got home I took off all my clothes, my shoes, even my underwear and put them all in the trash. I was numb, almost serene, if you can believe that. The last time this happened a nurse said to me, "Was this not a pregnancy that you wanted?" Can you believe that? "Was this not a pregnancy you wanted?" I didn't look at her, didn't even bother answering. But I want to tell all of you. I wanted my baby more than I've ever wanted anything.

I wanted to write to you all to thank you. I've taken such comfort in all your stories and the ways you celebrate the brief bright lights of your pregnancies, the ferocity of your love for the children that miraculously find their way to your lives. I am not one of you anymore. At least not after today.

Thank you, thank you for your help. I have loved reading your messages and your journeys. I hope you all live well. I really do. I thought my baby was on the road to me. I thought so many times that I could see her from a distance and she was waving saying "hang on." I believed it for years. I knew it to be true. SHE. IS. NEVER. COMING. If there is a god who is merciful she will be cared for and loved until I can see her face-to-face. AVA

35

The delicate little thing at the door had to be Charlotte. A pretty girl, tiny, all flat and straight like a grown girl, Sylvia thought. Behind her was a smaller version of herself, Marcus's daughter on the floor just in sight behind her mother.

"Hello, can I help you?" Charlotte asked, her face unmasked surprise.

"Hello, I'm sorry to bother you. I'm Sylvia Ross. You don't know me, honey, but I know Marcus." How foolish it was to come to this girl's house. She might have a man moved in here or already be moved on and finished with the Marcus chapters of her life. Anything! But she'd felt sick about the way she'd treated Marcus. He needed her, really needed her, and she couldn't help him. It wasn't enough but what would be?

Charlotte glanced back at her daughter, hesitated before she spoke again. It was clear she wasn't sure what to do next. "Do you want to come in?"

"Thank, you, thank you," Sylvia said as she stepped into the house. She smoothed her long shirt down over her skirt. She felt large and ungainly next to Charlotte, like she was taking up too much room the way she did around small women. "She must be your baby. I have a daughter too. Of course she'd old now, almost forty, but I remember those doll days. The number of baby dolls we had in the house back then." Sylvia chuckled politely, tried to fill up the dead air in the room.

The little girl avoided Sylvia's face and looked directly at her mother for cues. "Hello, honey. How are you?" Sylvia said to the child.

The girl was bewildered by small talk, as children are. "I brought this for your daughter," Sylvia said as she handed the bag to Charlotte. She was talking too much, but she couldn't stop herself. "It's not much. I just thought she might like crayons and I see that Dora everywhere I look."

Charlotte took the bag and glanced quickly inside, then handed the bag with crayons and a coloring book to her child. The girl had not been prompted to thank Sylvia. She felt her hand shake. Why she couldn't calm down, she had no idea. "Did I say that I'm Sylvia?"

"I'm Charlotte, but it seems like you know that. How do you know Marcus?" Charlotte had on a pair of the tiny shorts young girls wear now like panties in public, shorts they keep digging at to keep from bunching into uncomfortable places. Sylvia was hardly ever that undressed in her bedroom, she thought.

"He's been calling me from the jail," Sylvia whispered. Just in case the child had not been told about her daddy or was fortunate enough not to know anything about prison. She hoped she didn't look as ridiculous to Charlotte as she felt. What did she look like to this woman? A rival? Surely not. But certainly a meddler in another grown woman's business.

"Is she your daughter?"

"She's mine. With Marcus. Her name is Dena, but you probably already know that too."

"She looks like you."

"I used to look like her."

Sylvia looked closely at Charlotte again. She was all of twenty-five or -six at the oldest. The little girl would be lucky to wear her mother's face in a few years.

"Are you Marcus's aunt or something?"

"No. I don't know him, except over the phone."

"What are you doing here?"

"Marcus was hoping you were okay. Both of you," Sylvia said and glanced at the little girl.

"We're fine." Charlotte turned and spoke to her daughter. "Stay in here, baby, Mama's going outside to talk to this lady."

Dena looked up from her crayons for a second and seeing nothing interesting kept coloring. "Okay, Mama."

Sylvia followed Charlotte outside. Years ago she had wanted to come into some of these houses, just to look around. A few times Don convinced her to bring the children trick-or-treating in this neighborhood where the factory line bosses and supervisors gave out chocolate bars and not just peppermints from the Christmas before or homemade cookies or worst of all, apples. Charlotte flopped against her front door and sighed hard.

"You want water? That's all we've got other than juice boxes."

"No, thank you. I'm fine."

"So let me get this straight. You know Marcus from the telephone? Is that right? You're not even kin to him?"

"That's right. We've been talking a little while. He's a sweet boy."

"That is the craziest thing I ever heard. Don't you think so? You must be a nice lady," Charlotte said, but it was clear from her face that she was thinking Sylvia was at best a strange lady. "But let me go ahead and tell you. I'm done with Marcus. I warned him. I told him that anything that looks too easy is a trap. I told him that he was going to regret hanging around with those ignorant friends he loved so much. See where that got him."

"Charlotte, people can do better."

"I promised him when he started running drugs. Slinging. That's what they called it. Like he's in the wild west. I told him."

"I know this is not my business. But if I was locked up I'd want somebody to help me," Sylvia said with as much gentleness as she could.

"I did try to help him. More than anybody knows. A whole lot more than I should have. You don't know anything about me. I'm not mean. None of this is easy for me."

"Charlotte, you can't always have a choice to lose somebody. You understand what I mean? Think about that child in there. She will want her daddy."

"Oh she will, you think so?" Charlotte mocked. Sylvia was surprised at her defiance. How the conversation had gotten away from her she couldn't say.

"She'll always want him either way, Sylvia."

"I'll tell him you'll wait for him. I'll do that. It's not going to hurt anything."

"Tell him what you want. I can't stop you."

"You don't throw people away, Charlotte. You keep on trying."

"Who got thrown away? You don't know what the fuck you're talking about. I know he's got some good points. I know that better than anybody. But he's done with us. I'm done with him."

"He can go to court. He can see his child. You can't stop that."

"Who are you anyway? Don't come here threatening me."

"I didn't mean to threaten you, honey. I'm sorry. I'm not myself these days."

"You know what? Let him go to court. I'd love to see that. Because, that will be the most contact we'll ever have with him. And let me tell you another thing, he'll never get to that courthouse if he lives to be two hundred. He'll still be talking about it when our baby is grown and gone. I know him."

"I know you do."

Charlotte poked her finger into her own chest. "So don't tell me. I know. I live with all this."

"People can change, honey."

"Look, maybe you're a nice woman. I don't know. But I need you to stay away from here. Just please don't come back. This is not doing either one of us any good and I really don't feel like cussing you out. You probably don't mean any harm. I don't want to hurt your feelings, okay?"

"I've been talking to him. He knows what he did."

"I really don't want to hurt you, but I've got to tell you that if you come back I'm not going to be nice."

"You can be wrong. I've been wrong. Maybe you are this time. Could you go to see him one Sunday? Could you do that?"

"You might not believe this but I am hoping he gets out and has a wonderful life. I really am. There's not a thing in the world that I would want more, except for my child."

Sylvia saw in the young woman's face that she was decided. Sylvia was done too, failed and defeated and done. She wasn't sure if she had enough energy to even get back to her car. The fact that she had done more than could be expected was just beside the point.

The woman looked at Sylvia, shook her head in disbelief. "You don't get it. But you know what? You're not supposed to." Charlotte looked her up and down, took in her ugly outfit, the bulges of fat in her middle she tried valiantly to conceal. "Mind your business." Charlotte opened the door to her house and disappeared behind it. The soft click of the closing front door sadder than if she'd slammed it in Sylvia's face.

36

After the parking lot party at Simmy's that the grandparents (old but still walking under their own power) attended and sat like royalty in high-backed chairs; in the parking lot; after the editorials in the town paper, thank-you after thank-you from generations of customers; after 1952 week when the child's Simmy burger was fifty-two cents; Simmy's finally, and for all time, closed its doors. The parking lot was full to overflowing, some of us stood in the McDonald's lot across the street to get a glimpse of it all, full of nostalgic well-wishers, family and friends, as a man in a bucket crane unscrewed, unlatched, removed the big sign from the pole. A grandson had already claimed the sign to decorate his barn, to man-scape his place, he'd said in the booming microphone. We all laughed. As the strapped sign floated down to the awaiting flatbed truck, the crowd stood without speaking, hardly moving, their eyes locked on the sign's progress.

We cheered with real emotion as the sign reached the bed of the truck without a scratch. Something had worked out exactly how it was supposed to. We would have stories to tell. Even a few black faces dotted the crowd. We are all in this together after all. This is how an era ends, in one festive, happy moment. A cardboard CLOSED sign won't hang in the restaurant window long. In a few months, a group of women will open a consignment store and sell used (but still good) children's clothes and toys and start the ever revolving attempts to make a go of a business in the building. In a few years, brothers will even try a diner again, fifties style with giant hamburgers running over with homemade coleslaw. Carolina style, for sure, but it won't take. But all that is to come. Now the parking lot is cleared except for a broken-down Corolla no one has claimed. We drive through town, glance over at the empty building, look for the sign we think we remember seeing our whole lives. We are missing something, we think. We check our purses, our pockets, move the car seat forward then backward to look under the seat. Sometimes the lost can find the strangest places to hide (now where is it? we just had it); but try as we will we won't find it. We drive on with the sure-feeling there is something important that we have forgotten.

37

"**G**ood god, Sylvia," Henry said as he popped up from the couch, quick moving like a little boy with his hand in the cookie jar. "What are you doing here?"

"Don't ask me nothing, you hear me?"

"I didn't think nobody would be here," Henry began, not sure what else to say.

"That's right you didn't think. Like I'm surprised about that."

"You stay, Sylvia. Sorry, sorry." Henry moved toward the front door. "I'm leaving right now." Henry brushed off his clothes like he could brush away a week of sleeping on the floor with a few quick motions.

"Where have you been? You look terrible, just terrible."

"I probably do. I know."

"Where are you staying? With your girlfriend?"

Henry's eyes watered. He couldn't stand it if Sylvia berated him. He had not wanted to do or be what she expected from him. "No, ma'am. No. I stayed with daddy."

"And in the car from the looks of it." Sylvia turned off the television and stood in front of the screen. She would get his full attention one way or the other. "I can't even believe you, Henry."

Henry stretched his arms over his head, pretended to yawn so Sylvia would not notice his tears. "I've got to get out of here."

"Have you talked to Ava?"

"She won't talk to me, Sylvia."

"That boy is yours isn't he?"

Henry checked his pockets and lowered his head. He found nothing.

"What are you looking for? You're not going to find it there. Are you going to answer or not?"

"Did you see him? Did they come here?" Henry said. "I didn't mean for that to happen, Sylvia. I swear to god. I didn't want to hurt you or Ava."

"That's low-down. You know it. I don't have to tell you." Sylvia turned to leave the room. "Y'all children are going to kill me."

Henry heard the sloppy sound of the refrigerator closing and Sylvia banging around through the cabinets. He had to pass her to get out of the house. His instinct was to slink out the back door. Henry followed her to the kitchen.

"I knew I should have stopped at McDonald's," Sylvia said as she banged open cabinet doors.

"There's nothing in there, Sylvia. I checked. Ava's trying again," he said. Sylvia looked up at Henry too quickly, confirming his suspicions.

"Did she tell you that?" Sylvia asked.

"She didn't have to say, I can tell."

"Well that's her business, and if you think I'm going to talk to you like your pitiful self matters then you don't know me very well," Sylvia said. She searched through the cabinets like a drug addict for that sleeve of saltines she'd started. If she could find something maybe she wouldn't throw a heavy pot at Henry's head. The mess of her children's lives all originated with her. If she'd been a better example, if she'd had more respect for herself, if she'd done more, maybe Ava would think more of her life than to be tied to wounded Henry. Children can't see you vulnerable for too long or they tend to never believe anything you say. Sylvia had loved to tell her children stories about their lives in her body. She had meant to make them strong. Let them know that they had been wanted, even if the world declared its indifference or hostility to their presence. She insisted to them that they had been wanted. She shouldn't have stopped there. There was so much more she should have done. "Talk to her about what y'all are going to do. Be a man and do the right thing."

"She won't talk to me. She won't even let me text her."

"I never did like you, Henry. I knew from the minute I laid eyes on you that you were the wrong one for Ava. You have some weak in you. I can't stand weak."

"Is JJ the one?"

"Of course not. Oh dear god. Of course not." What a sad piece of man Henry turned out to be, all hangdog and dirty, a pleading beggar in front of her. She did feel sorry for him against her better judgment, but that's all she could feel. Her pity was almost the most accessible, most enduring emotion she could ever call up for Henry. She'd never liked him, never wanted to get to know him, and surely never understood him. He was a handsome man, a man with a job and few dollars, and nothing but his own warped mind holding him back. But always sad. If a man with most anything couldn't find happiness, who else had a chance?

"See what I'm talking about. I just said you are weak and all you can think about is what I think about JJ. You need to work on yourself. Get yourself together. I just hope you will do right by your child. That's the main thing. Children have to have somebody expecting them to do better. If you don't expect much you won't get much. Can you understand that?"

Sylvia was embarrassed, like she'd done something wrong. If she could have found a way to love weak-ass Henry, maybe she could have saved Ava some heartache. A sob almost escaped from her chest as she continued to search for food.

"I won't see you much from now on."

"Take care of your child. Nothing else matters now. You hear me?"

"You've never cared about me, Sylvia. I don't blame you. I didn't look like much. I still don't. I'm sorry you have to be in all this."

"You made your own bed, Henry. Just don't ruin your life."

"You are a good woman. You should know that. You made a good woman. I probably won't see you anymore. How long have you been waiting for me to say that?" Henry sighed. "I'll get my stuff some other day or maybe never. I don't care about it. I hope you make it all right," Henry said as he opened the front door to leave. "You take care."

The figure Henry cut in the world was of a confident man, so handsome, so sure in his body, a natural coolness that made him look like he belonged anywhere. A man like that you expected to be haughty, a player with a player's mind. That he was an insecure fool didn't make Sylvia like him better. It should have, but some-how his most significant failing was failing to be what he seemed.

Sylvia rushed to the doorway. "Don't ruin your life, Henry. You hear me?"

"I ruin everything, Sylvia. You know that."

38

For a few panicky seconds when she awoke that morning Ava was unsure where she was. Death is an empty house hollow and echoing. She quickly calmed herself and sat up from Jay's bed while the morning still crackled awake, the air cool like an exhalation on her skin. She heard the manic whir of a lathe in the back of her brain that meant Jay was already building something in his workshop. She'd fumbled for her jeans, slid her cool, bare feet into tennis shoes. She didn't want to talk to anyone. She considered never speaking another word. It was too early to be awake and stirring, but Ava walked outside to the front of Jay's house into the yard, bald except for the dandelions and wild onions that had already taken root. Before her was the kind of vista you might see in a romantic movie. A stately house surrounded by tall pines at the top of a mountain. In the movie, sheets would hang from a clothesline and billow like sails in the breeze. The white girl in the scene would walk between the sheets, her shift dress clinging to her thin frame with the blustery wind, her hair flapping behind her, like at any moment she might take flight. Ava stepped into the yard. In two steps her shoes were covered with a thick sole of red mud. She cried at the sight of her ruined shoes. Couldn't she have one moment safe from the threat of ruin? Ava then cried because the damn shoes made her cry in the first place. After her brief commune with nature she had planned to get back in the bed and stay there all day, but her mother called. Henry was on his way to her.

Henry had parked far away from the door and from their cars, like he hadn't wanted to intrude. He blew the car horn and turned off the engine. He'd considered driving to Pores Knob to the lookout, maybe walk one of the trails, maybe get lost somewhere in the woods. He'd been to the mountain only once before on a church trip, but the view, the highest in the Brushies had made him feel strangely powerful like he was in on something few other people knew. Henry took out a coin and let it roll on his knuckles, back into his palm and onto his knuckles, one to the other again and again. Though he had wanted to be a magician when he was a kid, even checked out books from the public library, this was the only trick he'd learned. The idea of being in front of an audience, begging for their approval, trying to make them forget that he was an ordinary man unable to harness even the most ordinary powers of the universe, made him self-conscious and ashamed. Nobody wanted to watch a shamed magician.

Henry's gauntness made him look shifty, like he could easily dart in and out of places. He was dirty and unkempt, like he had not seen himself for days, like he'd turned out to be a person nobody gave a damn about. Henry got out of his car and leaned against the passenger's side door. Ava stepped out of the house with Jay right behind her.

"Did your mama tell you I was coming?"

"You know she did, Henry. What are you doing here?" Ava said.

"I guess she figured," Henry said. "I didn't tell her I was coming here."

"What do you want from me? I don't want to see your face."

"I just wanted to talk to you, Ava. I need to talk to you a minute, one minute. That's all I ask."

"But I don't want to talk to you, Henry. Did you ever consider that? I get a say in this and I say no. Not right now and not ever."

"Will you get in the car with me? One minute. I swear to God and then I'll leave you alone."

"How I got stuck with you, I'll never know. I don't want to talk to you. You need to hear me, Henry. I know all you have to say. I'm tired and I'm tired of you. I'm tired of your depression and your problems. And then on top of all that you betray me. Do you think I owe you? Don't be a dick all your life. People get tired of that." Ava turned to go back into the house.

"I'm going through a slump, Ava. This is not me."

"You better get some help," Ava said.

"I should have told you about Zeke, Ava. Things got out of control."

"You killed me!" Ava screamed. "But what do you care? Everything is always about you."

"You've been in a doctor's office for the past eight years and everything is about me? Is that what you're saying, Ava?"

"Shut up, you fuck. I can't believe you won't even let me be mad at you. I hate your ass."

"I know. I know. I'm sorry. I'm a fuckup. I know it. You think I don't know it. But we had a good thing. I know you felt it. I know you did." Henry held on to the top of his head like he was being arrested.

"Why are you here? Nothing ties me to you. Nothing at all. I can't wait to never see you again."

"Please don't say that."

"I'm so glad, Henry," Ava said.

"Look, Ava," Henry said as he riffled through his pockets. "I brought my paycheck. I want you to have it. I'll move out. We can still keep talking. This doesn't have to be over. I know what I did." Henry took out his pay envelope full of bills and held it out for Ava to come get it. Ava rushed to Henry, greedily took the money out of the envelope, and threw it up into the air. The three of them watched the money, too little money, float onto the ground.

"You are so funny, Henry. You don't even realize how hilarious," Ava said. "You think I care about your pitiful little money?"

"Okay, this is enough, Henry. You need to leave," Jay said. "Let's go, man."

"I brought a gun," Henry said and did his best to ignore Jay. If he didn't acknowledge him then he and Ava could work it all out. "Do you believe that? I brought a gun with me," Henry said as he pulled out the gun from his pocket and held it on his pants.

"Oh my god! I never thought I would hate you Henry. What a shitass you are," Ava said as she turned around to walk back into the house.

"Ava! Ava! Come back." Henry wasn't sure what he expected from Ava or what the proper reaction should have been, but he never thought she'd be furious. It didn't occur to him that she might just walk away. He'd miscalculated everything. Again.

"Baby, baby, I'm not trying to scare you. I'd never hurt you. Never. I swear to God," Henry said. "I don't have any more choices."

Ava stopped and turned around to face Henry. "I am walking in that house and you are getting the hell out of my sight. Don't you think you've hurt me enough? "

"I do," Henry said and put the gun to his head.

"Henry! Stop it!" Ava stared at Henry like she wasn't entirely sure who he was. It only then occurred to her to be afraid. "Stop it," she said with more calmness than she thought possible. "Nobody gets what they want."

"Give me the gun, Henry." Jay walked toward Henry's.

Jay was too close, Henry could not ignore him any longer. He lowered the gun to his pants, thought better of it, and placed the gun on his temple and pulled the trigger.

"Henry!" Ava screamed

Jay's father, Frank Ferguson, threw plates to the floor, the crash of them loud enough to bring the children into the kitchen. Get back in your room, his father yelled. His sister fled, but Jay waited in the hall. He was not a child. He imagined that he knocked his father to the floor, that he took his father's beating while his mother ran. Or maybe, he whisked his mother out of the yard and out of the house and into a future. He and his mother in the car on the way anywhere else. But Jay had not moved from the hall. He did not see but he heard his father's booming voice, his mother's protests, their two voices strained and taut, coiled together like wires, both of them on the verge of tears. He had never heard a gunshot before. A country boy like him but he could not remember ever hearing the sound of a handgun. He flinched but he did not move. He knew without question what had transpired out in their poor people's yard. At what felt like the very same moment he heard the boom from the gun he heard his father's noisy sobbing, his screaming so loud everyone on the street came out to witness it. "Donna, please get up! Please baby, get up!"

Jay waited for the noise, the boom. There had been a click, but no other sound. Wasn't there supposed to be sound? The gun didn't go off.

"Henry? Henry?" Ava asked like she expected him to have an explanation.

Henry stood in place comically holding the gun to his head. He looked more surprised than anybody. Before he could gather his senses, Jay swatted the gun from Henry's hand and banged his head repeatedly against the hood of the car.

"Stop it JJ, stop it!" Ava screamed.

Jay didn't hear Ava screaming until her felt her hands on him pulling him away from Henry.

Jay backed away from the car. He had not meant to hurt him, but he'd grabbed him before he knew what he was doing. Ava put her hands on Henry's forehead to staunch the blood trickling through his hair and down his face. "Take off your shirt," she yelled to Henry who pulled the shirt over his head like an obedient child.

"What's wrong with you?" Ava screamed at Henry through her tears. "I hate your fucking guts."

"I didn't want to hurt you. Everything got away from me." Henry said.

"Don't," Ava said and grabbed his shoulders, squeezed until her fingers hurt. "Don't say one more word, Henry. I won't be able to take it if you say another word." Lines of blood slid down Henry's cheeks.

"Don't be cruel to me, Henry," she said. "Not another word. Get in the car." Ava pointed Henry to the passenger seat in Henry's car.

Jay checked the chamber of the gun. There were bullets there, but none of them had emerged. He tossed the gun into the woods. "Ava, please stay here," Jay said, his hands on the driver's door.

Ava hesitated for a moment. The resignation on Jay's face almost made her stop and return inside with him. "I'll be back. I'll take him and I'll be back."

"I'll go, Ava. You stay here." But Ava had already started the engine, a mournful sound.

Jay did not turn around as he walked the muddy steps to his beautiful empty house.

Ava and Henry drove the few miles down Brushy Mountain Road and to the house where they lived their lives together, where Sylvia waited at the kitchen table for them to arrive.

IN THE COMING DAYS when Ava considered what had happened to the three of them, she wondered why she left with Henry down the mountain. There were moments she thought that the feeling of total loss like she had felt at the end of her pregnancies would ultimately consume her. As much as she tried tamp it down, a part of her looked forward to the day the feeling would eat her alive. The more pain the better. They say same knows same and the fact of Henry's desperation drew her to him. Other times she recognized that she was likely looking for an opening in the fabric of the world she had carelessly slipped into with Jay. Henry had given her an easy escape. Mostly she knew that the scared shitless keep moving. To dwell is to die. Where do you stay Ava? Is there somewhere, anywhere, that you live?

There was no easy explanation. Maybe the same reason Ava stood with Henry in the driveway a couple days later when he carried his two duffle bags to the trunk of his car. The same reason she threw her hand up in a wave that looked like a blessing as he pulled out of the driveway and onto the main road. She'd told him she wished he'd find what he wanted and she meant it. For a few moments as she watched him leave, she felt like a sucker, a fool. Women forgave the shitasses in their lives anything, took it all on themselves, let them slide with any sad mess they brought to their unsuspecting doors.

But soon and in clearer moments she knew she had made her own choice not to lose him or at least not to lose all of her memories of him. She wanted the past where they lived and struggled and loved each other. A past that couldn't and shouldn't be erased. The possibility of the past, if it is a good one, or even if it has good moments, is that it can be alive, if you let it. All of it alive, not just the terror, but the beauty too. And the young encompassing and smothering love she'd felt for her lovely man—all that alive too. Otherwise all those years, her years, her life had not meant a thing.

39

In the backyard Ava and Devon run through the grass, they are children again. The game is tag or run or follow me all at the same time. Don never got around to putting up lattice on the back of the small trailer, so every ball they own has rolled under there in the dark. The children do not retrieve them from the place where anything could lie in wait. But they do not consider dark places today. Devon's feet are bare the way he likes, and when he runs they touch his behind; he is elastic. Ava follows him, mirrors him the best she can. Don has brought the large boom box outside, and the plastic click of his rummaging through home-made cassette tapes softly punctuates the day. He is looking for the right song to thread through the air, set the tone, be the music they feel smoking through their brains, the particulars of the day probably lost, but the feeling, the feeling, snatched back when the song plays.

Sylvia sits on the unstained deck watching, but in this dream she has gotten up and is making her way down the rickety deck steps. Her clothes are large and unflattering, a long-sleeve shirt over a long dress, even here in the heat of summer. She grabs onto the deck railing, and slowly makes her way down the stairs, balancing her bulk, the redistribution of her weight making her waddle. She is winded from the descent. Ava turns as her mother approaches. She is dreaming she knows for sure because she sees her mother, not just glances at her in her periphery but she feels her mother's struggle to reach them to play with them the nonsense game in the grass. Sylvia's face is twisted into embarrassment. How had Ava ever missed that struggle? In the way of dreams she cannot talk to her mother, cannot signal to her or touch her. But she can watch. Again and again and again her mother gets up from the lawn chair, holds on to the railing, takes the steps slowly, with the care of a large woman, always on her way to stand with her children in the sunshine.

40

"Where are they?" Henry asked and took the seat to Ava's side at the back of the dance studio. He had texted her to say he would be late, but the class had barely started. Ava pointed to the children.

"I was afraid you wouldn't make it." Ava moved her pocketbook from the chair for Henry to sit. A few other parents, cell phones in hand, stood or sat along the back wall. Ava put her hand over Henry's and looked at his face. He'd lost weight. It had been a hard year and he looked older maybe. Or probably he looked like he was supposed to. Not seeing him every day had made his face strange, unlike itself. Ava was most likely seeing Henry as the rest of the world had always seen him.

After a couple months of searching Henry had found a steady job (still mostly part-time, but that could change) at East Carolina University, helping admissions call and then put together and send out materials to prospective students. From Goldsboro Henry was a couple of hours from the white bubbles popping on the shore like living things. He couldn't smell the clean but slightly metallic fish smell of the sand, but he liked the change. What was most surprising to him was that he didn't miss the hilly landscape of the North Carolina piedmont, a place he thought was imprinted on his brain as home. On the drive there, almost to his nephew's house where he would be staying, turtles had dotted the road washed up by a heavy rain. Henry tried to drive but he couldn't stand the idea of popping them under his tires and stopped his car to watch them plod their way past. Henry didn't like turtles especially, but it made him hopeful to think that nature still interested him, moved him enough to make him stand still and look. Just maybe he wasn't as unreachable as he feared. He still lived with his nephew's family, and he felt like a pet, the unloved cocker spaniel, that tried not to beg at the table. But he could see the end of that. In a month or two he'd get a room of his own and really start over.

Zeke was still young enough to be excited to hear his voice and to hear his father's stories about the beach, his poverty that sounded like adventures to a child, the sights Henry would share with him when the time came. Zeke didn't know yet that his father fouled everything he touched. It could be he didn't have to know. Either way, Henry had to make sure his son loved him, so if he found out the truth, the real truth, he would consider his father with kindness and forgiveness and not pain. Henry had met Zeke three times at a McDonald's half the distance from Pinewood. Carrie drove their son to his father for them to eat and play together, but she would not stay. She smiled at Henry when she saw him and she even talked cordially to him in front of Zeke, but no part of her wanted any part of Henry Bailey. She would do better, and if she couldn't do better, she'd do without. Henry decided he would do better too. Just in time for his fortieth birthday.

Ava pointed to the little boy, a skinny little thing with big eyes and long lashes that girls would always covet, smaller than most of the girls in line at the ballet barre. Girls would admire him, giggle with excitement behind their hands when he passed. He would avoid the chunky stage so many boys struggled through and sail into his old boyhood and manhood as straight and lean as a dancer, though this class would be the closest he'd ever get to that profession. "See there, I keep telling him. He won't follow directions." As if on cue, the only boy in the line of ballerinas glanced up at her. Warned by the teacher against waving during practice, he held his hand in front of his chest and gave Ava a tiny peace sign with two fingers.

You need to mourn your pain or it will rot you. Don't let anybody tell you different. Ava spent months on her couch watching every game show and every real housewife that came on television, wishing for a different reality and then not wishing at all. After a few months her mother said, "It's time." And to Ava's surprise she realized that it was. She got up. On the North Carolina Adoption Services site pictures of her children popped up. *Free and open for adoption* the caption said. *The pair wants to stay together. They are bright, happy children. Wesley loves music and loves to play board games. May is a pretty, sweet girl who wants to be part of a family.* Ava called the agency the next day and they began visitations.

"Look at him trying to be slick," Ava said and tried giving him a stern look. "He's the only boy in the class. Free lessons."

"The only boy? He'll appreciate that in a few years," Henry said.

"Actually he's the only boy in the whole school," Ava said. The children were aged four and six, a sibling pair. How it happened that she couldn't remember her life before their arrival was a balm and a miracle to her. Some glorious trick of memory inserted their sweet faces into every circumstance and location of her life past, present, and future.

"Well, he's making the most of the lessons looks like." Henry laughed. The little boy counted on his fingers, marched in place while the little girls in line moved their feet from first to second position.

"Look at May." Ava pointed.

"She's getting good," Henry said, though he had only seen her dance on a video. Their time together now was the longest he'd spend with Ava in almost a year. "They look just alike." The little girl tried hard not to look in Ava's direction and concentrate on the precision of her feet, her tiny pointed toe.

Ava and Sylvia had cleaned out their house. They considered having a giant yard sale but instead stacked the junk in a pile and put a FREE sign in front of it. The room that used to belong to Devon was now a room for the kids, full of hard plastic toys in cheerful colors. Ava liked to think that Devon had been too good for this world and he must have been raptured, but with her children in his room she could not believe that he was fully gone. There had been no rapture, because the rest of them had not been left behind.

"Zeke is coming to Daddy's tomorrow. I told you Sean got out, didn't I?" Henry asked.

"He is? Home already? No, you didn't tell me. I want to see him. You don't tell me anything. Tell him to come by and see us."

Ava smiled but kept her attention on her May's serious face.

She would have to remember to tell her to have fun, to not worry about being perfect, that she is loved and can make mistake after mistake with the certainty that her mother, her grandmother, and a small but passionate group of people would open their arms, cluck their tongues, but keep their arms open to her every single time. "I told my May about perennials, you know the flowers? You know what she said?"

Henry shook his head no.

"She said, 'Mama, if I die, I'll come back, but maybe not in the same way.' Can you believe that?"

"Kids. They kill you, don't they?"

Ava and Henry watched the little dancers run through their jetés and frustrated leaps across the room. Miss Parsons's slicked-back brown hair was clasped into a neat bun at the base of her neck. She was very young and full of the zeal of the young. Marking time with claps to the music, pointing to errant feet and arms, her mouth in a grim set. Though the kids were babies, she did not smile. She would make dancers of these preschoolers and they would return to her in a few years, thank her for the hard lessons, the harsh instructions that had seemed angry at the time but now felt necessary. They would all name her as their inspiration. She clapped her hands, the signal for the kids to surround her.

"I've got an Atari for the kids," Ava said.

"Atari. Where did you find that, Goodwill?"

"No, they make new ones now. Everything comes back if you wait long enough," Ava said. Ava almost told Henry to bring Zeke to her house to play. She could feel the words forming in her mouth, but she couldn't yet say them. Maybe in time.

"How long have we been here, a week? Is it Sunday yet?" Henry whined.

Ava laughed. "It's almost over."

"You know, I didn't used to think that black people did this." Ava turned to look full-face at Henry.

"Did what?" Henry said.

"Spoke to each other after they hate each other." Ava half-smiled.

"Me neither, tell you the truth."

"I thought it was like if I wanted to talk to you, ever, I would have stayed married to you." Ava laughed.

"Well, we don't have to be what everybody else is," Henry said. "I think we've proved that enough times."

Henry had begun calling her every couple weeks and Ava looked forward to talking to him. She even let him talk to her children. He asked them stupid questions like did they drive, did they work? did they know how to plow a field? Ava wanted to talk to Henry. She couldn't remember when she'd wanted to talk to him while they lived together. For a couple of fleeting moments she had considered taking him back into her home and her life, but the simple truth was he had killed that part of her. She didn't want him. Lana was right. She'd been lucky or at least lucky enough. Maybe she would welcome another man into her life when the time came, but right now, too much had happened that could not be overcome. She felt peace. Her mother had asked her if her heart was healed with her babies in the house. "What is dead is dead, Mama, not gone. But I'm like you, the part that keeps on living, lives large."

"Did you hear Plant Four is closing this summer?"

"I hadn't heard," Henry said, but the news sucker punched him. Both his parents had spent years pacing that concrete floor imagining that life might be lived differently behind a desk or at a job with clean, unstained clothes. He had spent his young adulthood there himself. Good lord how he had hated it, and every single day he felt the fist clench of his shrinking soul contract a little tighter in his gut when he knew he had to punch that clock. What a disappointment that the place, even the death of it, could still move him. He was glad he wasn't in town to see it happen.

"You look sad. Are you sad about it?" Ava said, an incredulous look on her face.

Henry shrugged away the tears that threatened his face. "Hey, I was young there."

Ava squeezed his hand. The children stood in a line and waited for the teacher to adjust their posture. They were supposed to keep the bowl of their pelvis straight not tilted.

"Keep the milk in the bowl," Miss Parsons said.

"Stop fidgeting. It only seems like a long time. Wait until the recital," Ava said.

"I'm busy recital day," Henry said.

"You're coming," Ava said.

The house on Development Drive was full of sounds and movement and people, again. Devon's room made the perfect space for toys and two small beds. How could she have ever wanted otherwise? What will she do when they want separate rooms? They will have to cross that bridge later. Ava had insisted that her father come around. Children need old people, even trifling run-down old people like Don Ross. We all enter the story too late, and old people can tell us what they know about the past, at least some of it, at least the important stuff. Thank God the old tell it slant so the jagged edges don't kill the babies. That's what family does, sanitize the filthy or at least dust it off, give it to us in bite-size morsels. Sylvia didn't seem to mind him anymore. It occurred to Ava maybe for the first time that her mother loved her father. Not loved, loves. There had never been a past tense. Her good mama had loved wrong, but not for nothing. They say that life can give you another chance, but don't believe it. You choose to find another chance. Either way, don't strike out for the territory, there is no undiscovered country.

The children knew to walk, not run to collect their bags and shoes. Ava stood up to gather them, to say the warm things, to encourage and envelop.

"Was Simmy's already closed when you left?"

"Oh yeah, I was here."

"The time runs together, I can't remember anything," Ava said. She missed the sloppy king burger, but she was glad her children would not ever remember seeing it on the landscape of the town, would never even know the place existed. One day she would tell secondhand stories her mother had told her, and her children would listen to them with skepticism and wonder at the unbelievable bad old days. Or maybe if there was mercy, they would shrug off the terrible old news, shift their eyes to their own bright futures, the past as indecipherable and finally over.

"I thought Jay might be here," Henry said.

"We see him a good bit, but he travels. His house still hasn't sold. A house that big will sit for a while. Not many people are working around here."

"The Google people will buy it. They must have some money," Henry said.

"It's a hike to there, but maybe," Ava said, but she hoped not. She'd hoped a local person, a local black person, might live there after all.

"I know you love him," Henry whispered. "I know you do. You deserve it, baby."

The last time Ava went to Jay's house was to see the completed deck. "Somebody will buy this house just for the view," Ava had told Jay. And many would have if they could. Group after group came through the oversized doors, remarked on the fireplaces, the glorious view, the winding secluded road. Only one couple had been serious enough to put in an offer, but they'd been unable to get bank financing. Jay hadn't seemed to be crushed by it the way she thought he would be. He worked in his garage when he was at home, and slept in his bed. Houses come and go, he'd said. But both Ava and Jay had understood that what had lived between them, years ago and then for a few days in that house on Brushy Mountain Road, would not be revived.

And, though Ava would see Jay often and talk to him on the phone even more frequently, Jay was not a live presence in her mind. He was not insinuated into her memories or her dreams, and he lived only in the spaces where he had actually moved and existed with her. If Ava were being entirely honest, even some of those honest memories of him were now leaving her, sloughing off in her brain and becoming unstable, their half-lives not even as long as her trek into middle age. The tragedy of that was almost too much to bear. A whole swath of feeling, entire departments of her brain had gone to knowing, loving, and missing JJ Ferguson. He was a past with a name. This is what it all amounts to, all that feeling a footnote, a relic of a bygone time and mind. But gone too was the shame, the hurt and embarrassment of acting without knowing enough, acting without being sure enough. But there is mercy. Jay was one of the few friends she'd ever made. He loved her. She would love him as long as she lived. There is mercy.

Ava paused and watched May help her brother put on his jacket. She had to remember to tell her what a kind girl she was to help. She would remember to tell May that someone would be there to help her too. She'd asked herself how she felt about Jay many times. She'd even considered going back to him, letting him transform from the person of her youth, her best friend and witness to her pain. But her feelings for him had fossilized and though she didn't know if Jay could believe it now, his feelings for her were trapped in amber too. That didn't mean they didn't love each other. Love was too small a word for how she felt about him. But her feelings for Jay would not grow—not then and not now.

"I don't love him in the way he wants, Henry. I never did," Ava said. "But you know as well as I do." Ava paused and put her arm around Henry's back. She was close to him now, their faces almost touching. Kinky gray whiskers sprouted out from his chin that she didn't have to touch to know were stiff and would be hurtful if scrubbed against her own face. But his laugh lines, like large parenthesis surrounding his mouth! Black might not crack, but given time would fold. She almost ran her finger in the shallow gullies of Henry's face. She and Henry were the same age. What she felt next to him was exhilaration, a gratefulness that threatened to make her weepy. They had made it and despite everything she would always love Henry too. "You know, love isn't a cold, Henry. You don't just get over it."

41

The day Frank Ferguson showed up at her house, Sylvia was expecting him. Not really him, but a nasty wind, some bad luck. They say bad omens, bad signs, bad luck comes in threes. Don't believe that. But be sure if you are feeling okay, if the world is off your back, even for a minute, you have forgotten something. At least that was how it felt to Sylvia most days. Jay's father, Frank, showing up was just the very bad penny she'd missed.

A thin man stepped out of a car, with a head full of hair combed up in a stiff Afro, like he'd stepped off the set of bad seventies TV, looking more out of place than if he'd had no hair at all. He was clean-looking at least, but ragged, like life had taken a distinct dislike to him. His clothes were too big, probably borrowed or thrift store. His mouth was sunken in from the loss of many if not all of his teeth. Even with all those differences, Sylvia knew without question that this man was Jay's father.

Sylvia walked outside her house. She had moved the few boxes and suitcases of her belongings and dismal wardrobe back to her home and turned in the key to her apartment. She would never have to see the stark white of the anonymous walls again. She would stay in the house she had loved from the moment she saw it. There is a blessing in that.

Her neighbor's music was obnoxious and full of bass. He knows he's too old for all that mess, Sylvia thought. Forrest, the music man, was not a teenager who could be forgiven or at least assumed unknowing, but a fifty-eight-year-old doing some lazy man's gardening pulling weeds from his seated position in his lawn chair.

"Sylvia, how you living," Forrest called out.

"I'm okay, Forrest. Are you?"

"I can't complain. Doing a little yard work. Mostly sitting. You let me know if you need me," he said. Sylvia was sure Forrest's comment was more for the man walking up her driveway's benefit than hers.

Frank approached Sylvia with his arm outstretched to shake her hand, hurried to meet her in the middle of the driveway.

"How you doing, ma'am? You must be Mrs. Ross. I'm Frank Ferguson. They told me I could find JJ Ferguson here."

"You're his daddy?"

"Yes, ma'am." The man smiled, he might have four teeth still remaining.

"He left. I don't think he's even in town anymore."

"I went by his house. Any idea where he is?"

Sylvia knew that JJ had driven to the beach for a few days, but she didn't want to tell Frank that. "He's selling his house. That's about all I know."

"Never thought one of mine could do something like that." Frank rubbed his face. He needed a shave, which made him look down on his luck, poor.

"Do something like what?" Sylvia asked.

"Anything really." Frank laughed. "You always get told the apple don't fall far. You pray that's not true, you know it?"

Sylvia paused. She wasn't prepared to feel badly for Frank. She wasn't going to. "He's a good boy. You would be proud of him."

"I am proud."

"I can give him your phone number when he calls."

"Oh, no, ma'am. I don't have no phone, ma'am."

"Do you have an address?"

"Not really. Not a permanent one."

"Well, I'll get him a message if you tell me how." Sylvia said this but was not sure she was telling him the truth.

"Ma'am, I know you must know the worst things about me, but I'm not the same man JJ knew."

Sylvia looked at him, tried to keep the disgust off her face. "None of us is the same," she said. Frank looked like JJ, if JJ had been tossed in an industrial clothes dryer, set to burn. She would not feel sorry for him, but a pitiful sight provokes an involuntary response. She was trying her best to stop feeling. Some lives are built and some get made, she thought. You get what you deserve if you make a disaster of your life. But only a body that hasn't lived long enough to see anything would believe that. "He's selling the house. There's nothing for anyone to get."

Frank chuckled, rubbed the gray naps on his chin. "I am long past wanting anything. Nothing would be enough. You know what I mean, don't you?"

Sylvia did not want to be in league with Frank and she resented the association. "There's nothing to want. He even sold the refrigerator."

"I don't have anywhere to put a refrigerator anyway." Frank hesitated, like something was being decided. "Well, I'll be around here for a good long time until I get some more money to go back home. I'd appreciate you telling him I came by."

Sylvia nodded and turned to go back inside the house. Her neighbor had his side to them, concentrated on the same spot of ground, pretended not to eavesdrop.

"All right then, you take care of yourself, ma'am."

"You too."

Frank opened the door to his car. "You know just before I got out I heard James Brown on the oldies station. I didn't mean to sit in your driveway, but I couldn't turn off the car until I heard that song. Remember we used to listen to James Brown? He was something else."

Sylvia felt her face soften. She turned all the way around to look directly at Frank.

"Not you and me. I don't mean that. All of us back then. We loved that rusty Negro. Me and JJ's mother waited all day long to get tickets one time. Long time ago now."

"Yeah, we loved him. No doubt about that. We sure did."

"He used to sing that please, please, please." Frank shook his head, scraped the bowl of his memory.

"You can't forget that," Sylvia said.

"That was exactly right."

"What was right? What do you mean?"

"We all thought so at the time. Remember?"

"What was right? I don't know what you mean," Sylvia asked.

"What else can you say? If there's something else I don't know it. Is there anything else? There's nothing just please, please. That's all you can say."

"It doesn't make any difference does it?" Sylvia said.

Frank chuckled little snorting sounds that didn't sound like there had ever been a happy thought. "Oh, it makes a difference. No doubt about that."

"There's no please. There's no getting beyond some things."

"No difference?" Frank said, genuine surprise in his voice. "Oh shit. That can't be true."

"Why not?" Sylvia asked. "Because you don't want it to be true?"

"Of course it does." Frank had an incredulous look, his almost toothless face a Greek mask of exaggerated sadness. "Every word makes a difference. Please makes a difference. It does. All the difference in the world."

42

Sylvia had poured the buttermilk over the washed chicken early in the morning and left the meat in the refrigerator to marinate. In the late afternoon she prepared the egg wash and flour for dredging. Some people liked to shake the chicken in a cleaned out bread bag or later a Ziploc bag but Sylvia dredged hers through the flour like her mother had done, piece by piece, into the egg wash, into the flour, that was dusted with salt and pepper and a little red pepper. When it was time she put almost two inches of vegetable oil in the large cast-iron skillet, always cast-iron, to properly distribute the heat, and turned the stove on medium high. Vegetable oil not lard was her concession to modernity. When a few drops of water flicked from her fingers sizzled on contact with the oil, it was ready. Don't crowd your chicken. The temptation will be to put as many pieces as possible into the pan, get the cooking over with as quickly. But cook a few pieces at a time, stand and turn them, get them done on all sides. The oil will pop like a bee sting on your fingers, on your arms, even toward your face. The process will take time. It will take your attention. You fry chicken for the people you love.

Sylvia had the children set the table. Children needed chores and obligations. Otherwise they were never family, just pampered guests. The cloth place mats, not plastic, one fork on the left, one spoon at the right at each place. Four places set around the small kitchen table. Sylvia fried chicken and mashed potatoes, made cabbage and black-eyed peas, banana pudding for dessert. She never could make passable biscuits or anything baked for that matter so those were store bought, but the rest was all from her own hands.

JJ ate until he hurt a little and still considered eating more. They'd waited as long as they could for Ava, but this was her training night at the bank and she might not join them for an hour or two yet. The children had been sent upstairs to clean their rooms. "Clean your room and you can watch *SpongeBob,*" she'd said. Sylvia had never bribed her own children. She'd threatened them sure, but negotiating was for lax parents, parents who wanted friends not children to raise. But the story is different for each generation, reimagined every time, and new times require new rules. Who wanted the only people in the world you threaten to be the people you love the most?

Decades ago, some of their people, close relatives, had packed their few belongings, closed up their shacks or gave away what they couldn't carry, and set off for a northern state. They got as far as Washington, D.C., where the word was that jobs were plentiful there, even for a black body. The way they told it, a grown person could breathe, have a home, grow a family with a kind of independence and dignity only imagined in the South. Sylvia's Aunt Dee and Uncle Fred had gone with their children to find out what they'd all been hearing. At first they got no word from them, but as the weeks progressed, the months, word trickled down that the family was living like kings, walking on gold-paved streets, frequenting clubs, shows, and restaurants, like high society, right there along with the bourgeoisie black people in fur coats and high-buttoned shoes, haughty expressions on their own faces just like the Negroes they'd rubbed shoulders with. Sylvia had ached to be one of them and had listened with rapt attention when they came home to visit every year with their stories of affluence and triumph.

Years would pass before her cousins revealed to them the particulars of their real lives in the city and the scrum of too many people in too little space. Living in thin-walled slums with a backbeat of constant angry noise and on the streets of seeker after seeker, fresher and newer black immigrants hell-bent on conquering another hostile world. Aunt Dee had cleaned for rich women, Paul had bowed and scraped. And on good days, they watched the final drops of amber liquor slide out of one bottle then another bottle. They, with their fellow displaced southern friends that they had glommed onto like life rafts, sat together in somebody's too hot or too cold room and cried woeful tears about the vicious shithole of home they foolishly missed that they could not come back to without the permanent stain of defeat.

All of that came to Sylvia's mind as she watched JJ eat, as they finished the dishes, as they talked only enough to be polite and moved in and out of each other's orbits. She wanted him to know that he could come home, even if he was running. There was no shame in it. Twenty years ago JJ had been sprawled out on her couch, the sole object of the yellow light from the window streaming on his face, the dingy couch a canvas. He had not heard her enter the room that day or his feet would not have been up on her coffee table. Ava had been in the bathroom maybe, and Sylvia had time to look intently at JJ. In that light, she had thought she saw his face the way it was supposed to be, young, unknowing, relaxed, even the crease he wore between his eyes smoothed out. She had wanted to put her hand on the smoothness of the forehead, lie to him and declare that everything would be fine someday.

"One time some of us integrated the Liberty Theater in town. Did I ever tell you that?" Jay shook his head no, though he was sure he'd heard Sylvia's story before.

"I must have told you." Sylvia laughed. "I walked into that theater with a crowd. We were all supposed to get there while the lights were still on and we would walk in together. I was scared—more than I've ever been. But we did it. It was an Elvis movie and it was packed in there. The only seats left were on the very first row. You should have seen us. Scared rabbits. But we did it. Not one person got harmed." Sylvia laughed at herself. "Listen to me. Let me say this, not one person got hit. You think you can't make it, but you do."

"Maybe you do, Mrs. Sylvia."

Sylvia had not wanted to talk to JJ about her difficult past. She wanted to tell him that he was no longer a boy. She would tell him now that he was living in a sweet time of his life, the best time. He was a grown-up but not yet old. He was too young for the past to be most of his conversation, the condition of the elderly or the hopeless. She wanted to say that amidst the chaos of days, the great detritus of living was your actual life. She wanted to say stop looking for it, honey, this is it. What she did say was, "You've got a house here, JJ. Live in it."

But JJ was not going to live in the house for good. He would never buy furniture for it or plant a single tree or azalea bush. Plenty of people are interested, he'd said. It will sell, he'd said. He said he might go to the West Coast again or overseas. He said there were all kinds of opportunities for a youngish single man. Was he disappointed? To say he was disappointed is an understatement and also a lie. He was a gambler. He had known he was going to lose. Ava had asked him if he was lucky. Luck had nothing to do with it. Luck was beside the point when the outcome was determined.

"I still got some fight in me. I'll let you know when I'm coming back. Don't look at me like that. I will."

That day coming home from the reservoir, Jay made a note of the landscape, the closed business now that was a general store, the gas station the old man with the goiter on his neck owned, the acres and acres of ruined industry, parking lots as open as ball fields. He took in as much as he could as he and Ava passed by in his car. Pinewood was a town he would always think of as home, but he memorized the landscape like he was seeing it for the last time. In the retelling, whenever that might be, he would want to know what he saw. He would want to remember how things were to tell the story true. In minutes, he and Ava were in sight of his house, a miracle in a muddy field. What he would give if his mother could get a glimpse of it, even for a moment. He'd opened his car door to get out and go inside, thought better of it and sat with the car turned off. He and Ava waited together. The feeling washed over him again that if they could just stay inside the car's cocoon everything would turn out okay. They waited there for a sign or revelation that might change everything or at least point to everything. Jay's mother had not appeared with Hale-Bopp. He had known that she wouldn't, but the act of looking for her made him feel hopeful. The message his mother had for him had taken more than twenty years, but there it was. *Survive, Jaybird. Get on with it.*

"Listen to me. The kids will start screaming any minute, so let me say this quick. Don't just disappear, JJ. Not again. I know you think you can't stay here. But every person you see around here is walking around with a busted life story. Stay, honey."

"I won't leave for good. How about this, we'll go to Vegas together. How about that?" Jay laughed in a nervous false way that fooled neither of them. He couldn't stand it if Sylvia saw all over his face the fear that he felt.

"You teasing like that tells me you're not coming back. Is that right?"

"No, that's not what I meant."

"That's the kind of joke you make when you never plan to see somebody again. Don't do that to me or Ava either," Sylvia said.

"I'm not joking." Jay laughed. "I was joking a little bit, but I'm coming back."

"I'll help you see your sister. I know you need her. You must know that it is the rare family that doesn't suffer. You understand?"

"Sylvia, nothing will keep me away from here for too long. It won't be as long as it's been."

Sylvia got the dishcloth from the sink and wiped down the table for the second time. She poured herself coffee and sat down across from JJ.

"I was thinking about all this food we had here, JJ. When we was kids one night we had a blackberry pie for dinner. That's all there was. I was a child, a couple of years older than May, but I knew a blackberry pie wasn't dinner. But I could tell from how my mother was looking at us that I better not ask for more. I knew the pie was all there was. But more than that I knew asking would make Mama angry because she was poor and all in the world she could offer us was that small piece of blackberry pie and she knew it would never be enough. She was ashamed of that and worse of all ashamed in front of her children." Sylvia sipped her coffee. She glanced up at JJ and caught his gaze. "I'm ashamed." Sylvia felt her face and neck go hot.

JJ reached out for her hand. "Don't say that."

Sylvia squeezed JJ's hand back and stared intently at his face. "You don't either. You did everything you knew how. What else can you do?"

"I will see you next summer. I promise. I'm going to travel, but I'll be back."

Sylvia nodded. She'd never begged a man, even when her needs threatened to swallow her whole. She wasn't begging now just asking for what she needed. Of course that would feel strange. "You can make a life. I'm here. I know I don't know about what's out there in the rest of the world. I know there's a lot to find. Important things. Things I won't ever get to see."

"I need you to hear me, Mrs. Sylvia. I don't kill that easy. See." JJ pretended to open his shirt like Superman. "Stronger than a locomotive. I'm coming back."

"But you need to come back. Don't wait too long. Listen to me, if you wait too long, I won't be here or anywhere else."

"Sylvia, I'm not running," JJ started but he wasn't sure what else to say.

Sylvia held up his hand to stop him, though he'd said nothing else. "If you need your sister, go find her, baby. That's worth it, but come back. None of us have long."

43

The long corridor at the prison was cinder block like you might expect, but bright and open, more hospital than jail. Sylvia had announced herself to the woman behind the bullet-proof glass. She was a Perkins, no doubt but Sylvia wasn't sure if she'd known the woman once upon a time or if she knew some of her people. No flicker of true recognition had registered on the woman's face. Sylvia waited for the woman to check her computer screen, and shuffle some papers. Lana had sent a cake. *Don't eat it all before you get there, heifer,* Lana told her. The Perkins woman glanced up from her typing at Sylvia's silly cake wrapped in foil. "Honey, you have to leave that in your car," she said. Sylvia had seen so many shows about a file hidden for a prisoner she was surprised that this detail had turned out to be false.

The door to the visiting area buzzed open. The room was like the movies, small, windowless with metal chairs on either side of a transparent partition clear as glass.

A small, pretty man in a baggy orange jumpsuit appeared. A lovely face. He held his long fingers interlaced in front of him. He sat across from her without looking in her eyes. Sylvia's hands sweated. She fumbled in her pocketbook, looked for a mint, a tissue, anything to hold on to. He looked at her face with no emotion on his. He had the patchy start of a beard on his smooth cheeks.

"Hello, Mr. Marcus," Sylvia said and searched his face for his disapproval. "It's me, Sylvia. Don't fuss at me now, I can't take it. I'm not going to hear it." Sylvia arranged her purse on her lap. "I needed to see you. I'm sorry I didn't come before now. I'm sorry about a lot of things. Tell me how you are. It won't be long until you get to come home. Almost no time" Sylvia nervous laughed. She shouldn't have come. She shouldn't have come.

Marcus hesitated for what felt like an intolerable amount of time, twice Sylvia had to shush herself to keep from bridging the silence with some kind of sound in the room. Sylvia thought he might get up from the chair, motion to the guard, or turn completely away and refuse to talk to her. Marcus hid his face with his hands, the glint of the cuffs on his wrists slid down on his forearms. Sylvia caught her breath at the metallic sound.

"I hope you're getting along all right, Marcus. I have thought about you again and again." Marcus looked at her face, pursed his lips. His face shadowed like he was in pain.

"I meant to tell you the truth about my son. I didn't mean to deceive you. That was never my intention. I don't know if you will ever be able to understand this. I don't know if I do." Sylvia hesitated, shuffled the thoughts around in her mind, not sure what to say next. "Talking to you made me think of him. I got to think about who he might have been or even little things he might have done. I'm ashamed of what I did."

Marcus threw his head back and looked up at the ceiling. Sylvia couldn't tell if he was annoyed or in pain. "You don't have to talk about it," Marcus said.

"I brought you a cake, but they wouldn't let me bring it. My sister made it. She's the cake maker."

"You didn't have to do that," Marcus said.

"It wasn't all about Devon. I need you to know that. I wanted good things. Sometimes you fall in a hole and you keep yelling until someone comes to get you, except nobody comes. You start to wonder if anybody's coming. Sometimes they don't." Sylvia wasn't sure what else she could say. If he had not forgiven her then they would part. They were not family and they could walk in different directions and never again look back. Do people ever really do that?

"Mrs. Sylvia." His face clouded, his voice thick with unshed tears. He cleared his throat. Sylvia thought he was moments from rubbing his eyes like he was waking from a dream. "You're here," Marcus said, cupping his face. "I can't believe you're here."

44

Jay had the dream again.

Ava and Jay are at home. No one doubts that they are in love, even after all these years. The house is showing the wear and tear of decades of busy life, but the imperfections and scuffs and scratches on floors and walls don't disguise that theirs is still a nice house. All of their children are coming. They are empty nest-ers now, but a few times a year the riot returns and they all eat, talk, and play together. *Let me see you. Ah! Just like your mama. Keep those kids away from the pool, you know how they are.*

The house is a little run-down now, the sheen of new gone, so many goings-on rubbed up against the edges of it. Tastes have changed; people have yearned for different amenities and options— the house is far from in style. Ava loves pictures and they are everywhere. She poses in a few of them, self-consciousness on her face. She is too fat or too old or not dressed well; but she looks fine; she looks beautiful. Everyone says just that. The grandparents are gone, but how loved they'd been, especially the grandmothers. The youngest grandchildren will never remember them, but there are pictures to fill in the gaps and stories that comfort even as they confound.

There are so many more lights in their little town. And my how big the trees are on Development Drive. Once from this vantage point you could see some houses, churches, the curves of some roads. How it's all grown. Growing. But don't ask the locals about that. Nobody around here is too happy about all the outsiders. They like it the way it is, the way it was. Or at least the way they imagined it was. Just visible during the thick of the day are wisps of gray smoke from the furniture plants, or are those cirrus clouds? Probably smoke. There are new businesses in town, coffeehouses, bars, and restaurants where young people like to be. The older grandkids will make it down the mountain there before the day is over. You can't expect them to sit with a bunch of old people for too long.

Ava is in her element with the busy, the noise, the preparing, the great clamor of life in the house that she has looked forward to for weeks. Her children are celebrities or visiting dignitaries and they prepare for them like they'd never screamed them awake on a school day or wiped their behinds. For JJ the moment when the kids and grandkids are all gone, when the residual presence of them, the feeling of all they've done and seen together lingers in the air with a freshness like dew, the walls still humming with their sounds and movements, the house a tuning fork, when the kids have all left them again and the house is empty except for the comfortable movement of the two of them, is the moment he craves. He senses Ava even if she isn't in the room, a feeling he will carry with him all his life. He looks out the window to the deck. The past is finally behind him. Ava is closed off, content, lost in her own thoughts. He will let her be. She loves these hours to worry over the day, relive the moments by herself. In time she will tell him what she's made of it all and he will feel the sound and timbre of her voice, though he won't be listening to her words. That is all to come, but now they wait together. He feels finally collected and connected, this land really his land. Peace, peace, Jay Ferguson. Nothing can hurt you. Nothing at all.

And Jay will feel peace. Ain't no stopping us now, isn't that how the song goes. Nothing can hurt us here at all. We follow the path we can, the only one we can. Going home is easy if you can find it. JJ didn't find it there, but know this, there is more than one home for the seeker for the hustler, for the grown-up looking for refuge. Haven't we always done this trick? If you can't get what you want, want something else. See that the something else is good too.

But for now we dream. For a moment, a blink that can stretch over a lifetime, look out over the valley JJ, take it all in the points of light for miles and miles. God help me, God help me, the seeker says many times at the dead end, the crossroads, the fork in the journey. Help me bear it. God help me remember this. Help me take in the wide open forever, the endless yes. Help me love it as I live it. Help me see today what the richest man sees.

ACKNOWLEDGMENTS

I am grateful for the support of Ben Furnish and BkMk press. What a lucky life to have you in it. I am forever indebted to the Mrs. Giles S. Whiting Foundation, the Baton Rouge Foundation and Ernest J. Gaines Award, PEN/Hemingway Foundation, Chautauqua Institute, and the Bread Loaf Writers Conference. These foundations and organizations gave me a writer's greatest gifts: time and validation.

Lehigh University has given me an enormous amount of support to write and complete this novel. Many thanks to Donald Hall, Scott Gordon, and Dawn Keetley for their many kindnesses. Thanks too to my accomplished colleagues in the English Department, Zoellner Arts Center, Africana Studies, American Studies, and the Creative Writing Program.

The people that love you see something in you that you didn't know yourself. This book could not have been possible without the help, influence and love of the following people: Edward Jones, Sigrid Nunez, Roy Weaver, Ernest Gaines, Diane Gaines, Marjorie Hudson, Tina Wilson, Pat Towers, Lynn Mitchell, Joanie

Mackowski, Viv Steele, Sylvia Robinson, Susan Schurman, Stan Patten, Sandra Govan, Deborah Sacarakis, Ruth Marcon, Ruth Ingram, William Clark, Lynn Clark, Annette McCann, Julie Manzo, Joseph Manzo, Seth Moglen, Kim Schaffer, Lee Upton, Margaret Moffet, Monica Najar, Marly Swick, Aisha Ginwalla, Angela Scott Ferencin, Carol Laub, Ruth Ingram, Maryann DiEdwardo, Carol Ann Fitzgerald, Marc Smirnoff, Honoree Jeffers, John Pettegrew, Trudy Lewis, Candy Dula, Vera Fennell, Sarah Stanlick, Michael Collier, Holona Ochs, Mellie Katakalos, Carol Laub, Kristin Handler, Brooke Rollins, Tamara Meyers, Julia Maserjian, Patricia Hempl, Amey Senape, Anand Prahlad, Tahya Keenan, Betsy Fifer, Ken Fifer, Jan Fergus, Beth Dolan, Joyce Hinnefeld, Ruth Knafo Setton, Rod Santos, Lynne McMahon, Nancy Kincaid. My parents and siblings: Brenda Gilreath Wray, Billy Powell, Keya, Kelly, Aimee, Joel, Marc, Brent, Mitchell. The Watts family, especially the formidable women: Mary Watts, Terry, Gale, Bernadette, Mary S., Savannah and Molly. Many thanks to my agent Ellen Geiger. I am so thankful for what you've done and everything you do. Park Road Books gave me my first reading of my first book in my home of North Carolina. Thank you for taking the chance on a newcomer. Ecco! Many thanks to the wonderful team that helped make this book a reality: Ashley Garland, Emma Dries, Eleanor Kriseman, Meghan Deans, Andrea Molitor, and Sonya Cheuse. I marvel at the intelligence and moxie of my extraordinary editor Megan Lynch. I'm so proud to say I'm with her.

Bob Watts is my husband and the love of my life. Thank you for helping me lie about my age, thank you for being a wonderful father, thank you for showing me love in action. How lucky I am that your town was dry.

I am grateful to my grandmother Ruby Powell Dula. How

you survived the daily struggle and kept the hope and faith in the promise of a better world that you dreamed about but knew you probably wouldn't see. You passed to all of us the necessity of the passion to keep on loving. I miss you every day.

The horse jumped over the fence. Your sentence made it in the book! Forever and ever, my dearest love, my baby Auden.

ABOUT THE AUTHOR

Stephanie Powell Watts is an associate professor of English at Lehigh University, and has won numerous awards, including a Whiting Award, a Pushcart Prize, the Ernest J. Gaines Award for Literary Excellence, and the Southern Women's Writers Award for Emerging Writer of the Year. She was also a PEN/Hemingway finalist for her short-story collection *We Are Taking Only What We Need*.